Deceptive
Delivery

A JOURNAL

MARK GRAHAM

DEDICATION

To my family — Jackie, Kristin, Mackenzie and Parker. Thank you for your continued faith in me when it seemed the last page would never be written. Thank you Kettle One Vodka for always being there at precisely 5:00pm (It's 5:00 somewhere). My eternal gratitude for the creative boost you gave me.

ACKNOWLEDGMENTS

My heartfelt thanks go to Suzanne Sherman for titling this book, to my editor, Bobi Arnold for catching my errors and to my friends at B&C for their intelligent insight. I could not have done this without my team of professionals, my family and friends.

Thank you all!

PREFACE

Maskirovka One

Vitali Sokolov was eighteen years old when he lost his entire family — mother, father and two younger sisters, during the final days of the battle of Stalingrad. Because the city bore the name of the leader of the USSR, Joseph Stalin, Hitler took a masochistic interest in destroying it. Stalin knew of Hitler's plans and took every military precaution imaginable to prevent him from achieving his goal of leveling Stalingrad. Both army's obsession to be victorious transcended military strategy, causing one of the bloodiest battles in modern human history.

Most buildings had been pulverized, and the city was reduced to a pile of rubble — eighty percent of its citizens died or were severely wounded. Vitali was informed that his parents and two sisters had been killed, execution style, by an American soldier fighting side by side with the Nazis. He was deceived.

In 1951, Vitali immigrated to the United States of America, changed his name to Thomas Worthington, a name he took partially from the address where he would work for the rest of his life — 125 Worth Street, New York, NY — the Office of Vital Statistics for the state of New York. His job — to create birth certificates. His first directive — to create 563 for children who hadn't even been born yet.

On July 4th, 1987 Thomas committed suicide, jumping from the 62nd floor of the Hilton Hotel in Manhattan. He was to have retired the following day.

Thomas' code name was Maskirovka One.
Maskirovka: Deception.
One: The first soldier.

Maskirovka Two

John Smith. An unassuming name — and over 45,000 of them live in the United States — the first being Captain John Smith in 1596. But this John Smith's real name was Alexy Popov. He had legally immigrated to the United States in 1952, and began working at 1905 9th Street NE, in Washington DC — the U.S. Social Security Administration. His job was to generate and log Social Security numbers for children born in the United States.

On October 12th, 1962, John received a new directive. He

was to generate and log Social Security numbers for 563 children who weren't born in the United States. A system was devised whereupon each nine-digit number would contain four specific digits randomly scattered among the nine. That directive did not come from his boss in America, it came from his boss in Moscow, Nikita Khrushchev. John Smith continued to carry out his orders for the next thirty-four years. No one ever suspected him of falsifying those numbers and, in fact, was considered a model employee.

On November 7th, 1986, John died in a car crash on the George Washington Parkway, two days before his retirement. While his crash was officially noted as an accident, some believe it to have been suicide. There were no other cars involved.

John's code name was Maskirovka Two.

Maskirovka: Deception.

Two: The second soldier who coordinated with Maskirovka One in what would become the former Soviet Union's most consequential battle against the United States of America — D6

"One must always take personal responsibility for one's own actions."
- My father, Mark McHale -

There were two men in my life who had profound effects on who I am and who I became. The first was my father, Mark, who taught the meaning of Patriotism, love of country and of a God who he believed still blessed it. The second was Professor Julian Kilgore who unwittingly taught me the exact opposite.

I blame neither of them.

Confessions

* * *

Good Christians would chastise those who believe in reincarnation. The Bible offers no compromise, it's heaven or hell and nothing in between. That said, should it occur, I'd happily come back exactly as I was, to pick up precisely where I left off — unfinished business.

Dear Suzanne,

This all began seven years ago and, as I confess all I've accomplished, I wouldn't change a damn thing. To be honest, I'm not sure what to call this — journal, diary or just a plain old confession, the kind that's good for the soul. But when pure callousness renders one soulless, is it still effective? If the Bible is to be believed then, according to my father, it is. As a kid he prayed with me that the Good Lord had promised "my soul he'd keep." I miss my father, but God has let me down and this is why I am writing to you.

My father was obsessively proud of me. Unlike many young men whose dads never confirmed that or told them how much they loved their sons, mine never missed an opportunity to let me know. Like the Bible verses he'd constantly quote, his need to remind me of this was both sincere and heartfelt. I'm not sure he'd feel that way today. He was a God-fearing man and religiously adhered to those Ten Commandments he hung over the fireplace in our living room. My friend's had razor thin LED TVs hung over theirs. Knowing that, over these past seven years, I repeatedly ignored God's Sixth Commandment would devastate him. Death, in his mind, came either from natural causes or from the hand of God himself, never from those he created.

My birth name was Aiken McHale, but on August 16, 2020, the government placed me on its A.C.T. list along with millions of other Patriots. **A**merican **C**itizen **T**hreats who had done nothing wrong other than speak freely and hold to our God-given right to defend ourselves against a growing tyranny emanating from Sector 1, what was once Washington, D.C. Although your and my rights to speak freely and to defend ourselves predate the establishment of our government, many who cherished our First and Second Amendments surrendered those inalienable rights the moment the infiltrators abolished them. They were the first to be removed, and it was remarkably easy to accomplish that feat.

I now go by the name, Joshua Hunter. Joshua from the bible and Hunter from my lethal career path. I execute people — traitors, to be specific. I'm either headed towards the outskirts of Heaven's gate or Hell's flames. It's up to Him where I end up.

Your father,
Aiken McHale, a.k.a., Joshua Hunter

History Ignored
The Tip of the Spear

* * * *

"One if by land, two if by sea. The Russians are coming. The Russians are coming."

Every kid learned Paul Revere's warning, alerting us to the British invasion of 1775. We'd reenact it every year in some lame elementary school play complete with childish songs, each sung out of tune. Cringe-worthy performances, but pure American Patriotism, never-the-less. The set designs weren't much better, with rainbows of paint splattered everywhere, it was hard to distinguish a tree from a lamppost or a Patriot from a Brit.

I was perhaps the last kid in America to play the role of Paul Revere in such dramatic fashion. My parents were proud as hell. Mom stood up in ovation repose while Dad shouted, "That's my son," as I walked onto that stage with my lantern in hand screaming, "The British are coming, the British are coming," at the top of my lungs. For added measure, and to drive that point home, I improvised by injecting an expletive to one final refrain, "The God damn British are coming!" Half the parents laughed while the other half gasped. My father — he smiled and gave that sly wink of approval, the kind that only a kid could appreciate. Every generation before mine remembers the role they played and the costume they wore even if they were just a tree.

In 2016, that play was banned, having offended an entire

generation, even though most of them couldn't verbalize why. In reality, they could have rewritten The Midnight Rider by noting the old adage that, "Those who ignore history are bound to repeat it." But this time, unlike the informed Patriots from the eighteenth century, America was totally oblivious to what quickly became the enemy within.

Oh sure — Yuri Bezmenov made the lethal mistake of alerting us of the Soviet's Ideological Subversion plot with David Frost in 1986, but no one listened, and Yuri was summarily dispatched home — we think.

> History repeated itself, we ignored it and the
> end result was drastically different.

I learned of a silent invasion that my father had suggested, actually happened, but it was Professor Julian Kilgore who filled in the details — at least most of them.

"The old saying goes," my father began, "that revenge is a dish best served cold. If I were to enact it upon a frog, I'd resist the temptation to toss the little critter into a pot of boiling water, for it would assuredly leap to safety, sensing its instant demise. Place that same frog in cold water while slowly increasing the temperature to a brisk boil, and it is gradually lulled into submission and certain death."

The frogs in that pot of boiling water weren't critters at all, they were humans, American citizens, and the ones cranking up the heat were Herons, the infiltrators sent to our shores in 1962 by Nikita Khrushchev. He told me that analogy when I was eight years old, leaving out the identity of the master who had devised that sinister plan. He never spoke of the Russians.   Sixteen years later, as if on cue, Julian told a similar story, but added more details — dates, objectives, classified information, a historical perspective and eventually — twenty-six names, coded on a crumpled piece of paper which he always kept stashed in his right pocket. "The most destructive," he'd remind me.

Dad's clever analogy became Julian's unwritten history lesson which eventually put me where I am today.

Herons, The Invaders

* * * *

While all eyes remained focused on the coast of Cuba, the real weapons of mass destruction had been off-loaded 1,302 miles due north — right here in America.

Julian leaned in closely, as if to whisper a dirty little secret meant only for my ears, and then narrated his version of the story my father had told me sixteen years prior. But this time there were no frogs, only Herons. Sounding more like an English lit professor than one caught up in the study of mankind's past, he waxed poetically about the weather cooperating for an eventual doomsday plan, a mass funeral for an entire nation.

"The weather was perfect that night as a dense fog hovered above the ripples of the cold Atlantic offering suitable camouflage for the precious cargo carried aboard that ship. The first ship, Vsevolod, left Murmansk on October 3rd, 1962 and arrived nine days later under the cover of that fog at 41 degrees North, 72 degrees West — thirteen miles off the coast of Montauk, New York. Code-named Noah's Ark, it continued its crossings for the next three years, dropping anchor at precisely the same coordinates on the 14th of each month and then off-loading its cargo — orphaned children. Each shipment contained somewhere between 500-600 infants, none older than two-years old thus easily adjusting their language to English. Each of them had been pre-adopted by American citizens willing to partner with the Soviet Union as traitors to America. They were well compensated for raising the children under the terms of a most specific contract, complete with addendum noting the dispensing of violence to either the parents or their children for not following the contract to the letter."

"The Cuban Missile Crisis was all a masterful diversion, a lethal fraud. The Soviet ships we were tracking had only hollow tubes meant to mimic nuclear missiles. The real weapons of mass destruction were the children, and their lethality was far worse than anyone imagined. The mission, which was to have taken decades to accomplish, was code-named D6.

While the Soviet Union could not defeat us militarily, they could, however, defeat us from within. Stealthily infiltrating an entire nation, they continued their silent invasion of the American shores on the 14th of each month. The significance of that date should not be underestimated. Like your name, it's biblical as were the yellow X's they painted your rooftop with."

With each word Julian uttered, he revealed exactly how much he knew about me, my family and what had happened to each of us. Yet I knew so little of him.

"The weather cooperated," he repeated. Their battle plan, D6: Dumb us down, Delete our history, increase our Debt, Divide us, Disarm us and, for their Grand Finale, Destroy America — all from within. Sadly, political correctness, which became the Golden Rule for a new generation of millennial, coupled with massive illegal immigration of people uninterested in adopting American morality, turned my republic upside down and into something even I didn't recognize.

Suddenly, it all made sense. E pluribus unum, which had guided our peaceful, civil society since the birth of our nation, had morphed into E unum pluribus, and that's precisely when all hell broke loose. D6 was working — flawlessly. The trigger for that final piece of the puzzle was the planned collapse the U.S. dollar. The societal divisions and ignorance that had been so carefully manicured over decades would take care of the rest, thus creating mass anarchy from sea to shining sea.

Khrushchev died long before his brilliant plan had come to fruition and those fifty autonomous states became the 1,218 sectors you now live with. While we were all too willing to tear down the statues and plaques of most of America's founding heroes, Jefferson, Madison and others — a new breed of Americans was absolutely giddy when on August 25, 2021 they hoisted Nikita's statue in Lafayette Square — directly across the street from the White House.

Like the paper leaves on those trees, the Midnight Rider fell off the radar as the Herons first infiltrated our education system. Kids never recited it again and, over time, even our Constitution became mythical, something most refused to even speak of. To the Herons, that document and others, like our Bill of Rights, were roadblocks to their patient plan to destroy America from within. "The mind is a terrible thing to waste" took on a more sinister meaning as teaching became indoctrination and those minds willingly began to chip away at each of our Constitutional Rights, beginning with the elimination of the First and Second Amendments.

They tore down monuments, removed plaques, moved statues to dusty warehouses. The historical messages they contained vanished because its contents were deemed offensive. They had successfully deleted our history all the while convincing an entire generation that America was evil. It wasn't but, as I entered high school, the scales had tipped in the wrong direction and most of my generation believed it was, in fact, evil. Hatred of America became fashionable while hatred of each other became rampant.

America was officially gone. Mission Accomplished! But on July 4, 2020, the Herons made a critical mistake, one that ignited a silent army of Patriots, like me, whose battle cry wasn't "We want our country back," but instead, "We want them dead!" They didn't eliminate everyone's free speech — they eliminated only ours and that would never stand.

On December 7th, 1941, President Roosevelt declared that date "A day that will live in infamy," while twelve thousand miles away, Hirohito warned the Empire of Japan that he feared that they had awakened a sleeping giant. On July 4th, 2020, the Patriots declared the same as Roosevelt, but the Herons never followed Hirohito's prophetic warning. They kept coming. They kept taking our rights away. But taking away our free speech and deleting our websites and everything that contained the word Constitution was a bridge too far. That single act awakened many of us. I had no idea what they had just done, but knew I had to take up arms. And so — I did.

Presidential Directive

****

White House Briefing Room

J.B. was an odd, perplexed looking man — British, short cropped hair, rosy cheeks and eyes that bulged. It was difficult to both stare and not stare at him. One wondered if that look was purposeful and meant as humor or if he really looked insane and couldn't help it. Bad teeth too — British, you know.

OFFICIAL TRANSCRIPT

Presidential Decision Directive 63 (PDD-63)
Oval Office Transcripts:
Date: July 3, 2020
Time: 8:03am

POTUS: How does this work?

J.B.: Mr. President, the kill switch allows me to shut down the entire Internet. I and thirteen others each hold keys which unlock safety deposit boxes that hold a special smart card that creates a new master key which activates a machine that authenticates the DNS. It's a fail-safe system and, to be honest, is convoluted. A selective shutdown of certain sites would only require my killing each individual IP address. This will take time, depending on how many you want killed. But I can do this without alerting the others.

POTUS: Perfect. We don't want this to go beyond this room or this group. Start with the big ones and then isolate the outliers if needed.

J.B: The big ones? Can you be more specific? Can you give me their domains?

T.S.: Yes we can. Here's a list of the initial sites we want shut down.

POTUS: C.J. You have the story and the talking points? I mean, we want to get this right and leave no stones unturned.

C.J.: Yes, Mr. President. I've read through the points and am ready to go live as soon as I get approval.

A.V.: Mr President, Alexander is ready.

J.B.: To confirm, sir. The Washington Free Beacon, The

American Thinker, The National Review, The Blaze, PJ Media, Twitchy, Red State, Weekly Standard, The Federalist, Breitbart and Fox News?

POTUS: There's one more. She's got a loyal following, most of them preppers. Cerberus Radio. Shut that damn domain down too. As for Fox — shut off their TV feed as well.

J.B.: I can't do that, sir.

T.S.: Don't worry, we can!

Delete everything, domains, blogs, commentary, live feeds and history. America starts anew tomorrow and all remnants of her past must be expunged. How appropriate. It'll be July 4th.

Eliminate the First and Second Amendments

* * * *

It was often said, building a nation that mirrors your own ideology requires that you must first destroy all vestiges counter to your utopian vision. Key among those to be destroyed by the Herons were our First and Second Amendments. Ignorance and complacency were rampant, making that task easy to complete. For their grand finale, imprison all who opposed them. It was remarkably simple. Killing fields, concentration camps — we had them all.

The term Heron was a code word hatched deep in the secret halls within the Kremlin at the end of World War II. In nature the Heron is a bird — a frog's worst enemy, but to the Kremlin they'd become the foot soldiers embedded over decades within American society. Orphaned infiltrators whose sole purpose was to set the stage for America's eventual collapse. Patience was their secret weapon while stupidity was our Achilles heel.

Each orphan was assigned a nine-digit code into which four numbers identified the classification or career path of that child. For example: having the numerals 7997 scrambled within those digits, designated the child to become a teacher. Four random numbers — career path, the remaining five became the nine digits necessary to generate a Social Security number. Made me wonder what other departments or federal agencies they occupied. When asked, Julian's reply: "All of them — they're everywhere!"

As the new millennium began, there were over two-hundred thousand of these traitors living unassumingly within our society. Add in the children they spawned, who became just like them, or worse, and you can easily see the possibility that, by the turn of the century, we had millions of traitors imbedded amongst us, many of them in critical, high level government positions. The careers they held inside and outside of government allowed them to reshape public opinion, to rewrite our laws, thus changing forever the foundational principles upon which our Constitutional Republic had been born. The only identifying mark for the original boat children was a well-hidden tattoo on the left side of the fourth toe on their left foot. It noted those four career-identifying numbers. You'd need a magnifying glass to see it.

These are the Herons who landed on our shores as infants in 1962 and continued coming every month for the next fifty-seven years.

EGRET, 7997: The educators. Perhaps the most useful of the Herons, this group took the old saying, "A mind is a terrible thing to waste," then bastardized it into something sinister. Teaching our children and young adults that America was not a land of the free nor home of the brave, but instead one where unwelcome colonialism, racism, terrorism, war mongering and capitalistic greed played roles in our position as a global power.

From child care all the way through college, the Egrets molded our minds from the parental teachings of patriotism and love of country to pure hatred — hatred towards America and towards each other.

BITTERN, 8346: The media. Part and parcel to destroying any society is to embed the enemy into one's press and then ultimately control the media. Germany had Joseph Goebbels the propagandist, we had an entire sector hell-bent on lying through omission or outright fake news stories. The Egrets taught us to be stupid and, once accomplished, the Bitterns regurgitated that stupidity 24/7 through the propagandist media, which they controlled. Social media then shared the propaganda.

AGAMI, 2050: Judiciary and legislators: Once you've taken control of the education system and of the media, the next necessary step is infiltrating the courts and legislative branches. This allows for a subtle, stealth transition away from the Constitutional foundation of our nation to one which effectively obliterates the principles of small, limited governance noted in those founding documents. The end game — neutralize the Constitution and The Bill of Rights. The Bitterns and their control of the media will assure the enemy that nothing nefarious ever gets reported. Their first target — Our First and Second Amendments.

HERODIA, 5454: The enforcers, law enforcement, military. No battle plan would be complete without enough traitors embedded into those institutions meant to protect society from enemies foreign and domestic. While the vast majority of our military and law enforcement were Patriots, enough of them were Herons meant to sow doubt among the ranks and within society. When trust of law enforcement or of your military dissipates, it's remarkable how disruptive this can be to a peaceful, civil society.

BLUES, 6660: The most violent of the Herons, they had been predisposed to violence through their genetic lineage. Their sole purpose was to alter public opinion against our inalienable right to bear arms — what was known as our Second Amendment. Although a God given right, many incorrectly held to the belief that it was that Second Amendment that guaranteed us our right to bear arms and to protect ourselves from a tyrannical government. Therefore, by eliminating that Amendment, they could accomplish the total disarmament of American society which opened the doors to an even more tyrannical government, one where its citizens would forever be ruled by a lifetime dictator, Neville.

The Blues were the only Heron group that used brute force through mass shootings to accomplish their goals. A concert in Las Vegas, a Colorado movie theatre, an elementary school in Connecticut, a high school in Florida and many others. Each of those horrendous events were carried out by Blues who received their orders to commit mass murder and then to kill themselves to avoid interrogation that could lead back to the puppet master who gave them their criminal orders. These were each orchestrated events.

GOLIATH, 1111: As with all successful military operations, you must have dedicated, well trained foot soldiers, and the officers who lauded over them. The Goliath were the Generals of the D6 operation and had complete control over the other five Heron groups. No one knows who they are, but in 2025, I was so close to finding and executing one. So, close. But I was also careless, and he became my Waterloo.

Their first initiative was to eliminate our First and Second Amendments and this feat took all six of the Heron groups to pitch in. It went as follows:

"I have accepted a seat in the House of Representatives, and thereby have consented to my own ruin, to your ruin, and to the ruin of our children. I give you this warning that you may prepare your mind for your fate."
John Adams, 1770

Genesis 2.2

* * * *

"And on the seventh day God ended his work which he had made; and he rested."

My father was a difficult man to grow up with. At least that's what I thought before the Great Collapse. Beyond his constant need to tell analogous stories, he frequently recalled the genius of great philosophers and cultural leaders, but most important for me he'd quote our founding fathers' brilliance. History and the rule of law was important to him, so he'd recite those lessons repeatedly ad nauseam.

He told me; even great nations rise and fall but they all follow the same path to destruction. The people go from bondage to spiritual truth and then on to great courage. From courage they seek liberty, and then on to abundance. Abundance leads to selfishness, and then complacency. Complacency breeds apathy which always instills dependence. Finally, once you become dependent, you'll always return to bondage, often without a fight. That described the history of the United States of America as I grew up. Like the Ottoman, Persian and Roman Empire, nothing good lasts forever. It was the circle of life and what eventually happened to America, me and my family.

I loved him, even when he'd repeat those analogous stories, forgetting he had already told them many times before. His recitations from the world's greatest leaders were educational but again, he'd repeat them over and over. But it was those forced Bible studies that I hated the most. Although I've taken my identity from those books, I never read them, I didn't have to. My Dad had read every single passage to me at least three times by the time I was ready for college. Repetition was a habit of his — a bad one.

Beginning with the whole Genesis thing and how wonderful God's green earth was, we'd say a blessing before every meal. "Bless this food, our family and friends." We'd bless our Little League team before crushing the opponent and then thanked God for allowing us to win. I was convinced that God had his hand in everything we did and that common refrain - "God Bless

America" was not some lofty wish, but it was reality — the Good Lord blessed us and our nation. America was "land of the free, home of the brave," and we still had fifty autonomous states.

Approaching my high-school years, Dad's Bible verses changed from the good stuff to the scary shit. He became masochistic in those studies, obsessing over Revelation, the rapture, even Armageddon. From there it was Mystery Babylon. To him, America was just that place. But as I sit here now, like John Adams, he was prophetic. Everything he believed came true and I'm still in awe of how he knew. How did he know the Great Collapse was soon to be upon us?

The Great Collapse

* * * *

Knowing God took six days to create heaven and earth and then rested on the seventh must have been deliciously ironic for the Herons and their supporters, as they destroyed damn near everything he had created in the same time, six days! But unlike The Almighty who rested on the seventh — the Herons just kept going. They never rest!

I hated its name, the Great Collapse, as if its greatness was admirable, like the Great Houdini, Alexander the Great or the Great Wall of China. But to them, describing catastrophic, historical events that only government could fix always had the word "Great" attached to them. The Great Depression, The

Great Johnstown Flood, The Great Recession and so — the Great Collapse made perfect sense.

All I can tell you was that our world was upside down and, like Orwell's 1984 — "war was peace," "freedom was slavery," but most important to the Herons, "ignorance was strength."

August 2, 2018, twelve days before my birthday — I couldn't wait — it was my sixteenth. That rite of passage, a time when a guy stops being called a kid and enters the realm of manhood all because he can drive a car. I counted the days until it would arrive. Getting that driver's license and the freedoms it afforded me, was like waiting for Christmas morning. My anxious behavior was clear to everyone, not the least of whom were my parents. Little did they know, however, that my reasons for wanting that license so badly went beyond what's normally on a young man's mind — driving his friends around with no final destination or parking in some remote area for a long make-out session with his girlfriend. Nope, that license represented freedom, the freedom to escape a dysfunctional family whenever I needed to. Freedom to escape Dad's endless stories which had now turned conspiratorial. That's all I wanted for my birthday. A small laminated card with my goofy picture and a notation that, "YES" you can have my organs should I die in an accident.

I never made it past T-Minus-12 days. That's when our world came crashing down and Dad's bible versus became a reality. I was no longer hearing his annoying recitations of Armageddon, Revelation and end times, I was witnessing them right there in Leesburg, Virginia, Sector 7 or, as my father called it, "32 miles due west of Babylon." Within a one-week period, the dollar collapsed and inflation became the nuclear weapon that landed squarely on our shores. Like dominoes; currency collapses, inflation rises, gas becomes prohibitively expensive and everything that requires trucks for delivery to the stores just sits on the docks and rots. Food, prescription drugs, life's necessities — everything. It wasn't weeks before the shelves had cleared, it was days — three to be exact.

When food is scarce, people will resort to the vilest methods for satisfying their hunger, caring little about whom they sacrificed for that repugnant meal. All hell breaks loose and, before you know it, you're living in a war zone, something no one could have ever imagined would envelop Main Street USA, but it did.

No mushroom clouds, no radioactive fallout, but the devastation was equally abhorrent. After having experienced what followed that catastrophic event, I'm convinced that it's far better to melt instantly into puddles of goo from a firestorm rushing across the plains when a nuke is detonated than to wither away from starvation or end up slow-roasted in some back alley as a supper for someone else's family.

America met two new weapons of mass destruction that week. Their names were "Fear" and "Division," both guided by their masters, the Herons. Cowering in fear, we transformed into a divided nation of recluses on one side and vigilantes on the other. It was our second Civil War.

"Civil," a word that should never precede the word "War."

And on the seventh day, we emerged.

* * * *

Experiencing The Wizard of Oz in reverse, coming from the beautiful Emerald city and awaking in Kansas after tornadoes had destroyed everything in their path; we opened our front door and walked out. It was surreal. No munchkins, or good witches but plenty of scarecrows, lions and tin men; people with no brains, courage or hearts. It wasn't Kansas; it was Leesburg Virginia, a wealthy suburb of Washington, D.C., our nation's capital.

The wicked witch was our government, and like Dorothy and her little dog Toto, we were being listened to, watched and hunted, continually. Trust disintegrated, fear permeated the air like the smell of burning garbage in a county dump.

For the Patriots, pleasant smells emanated from the essence of guns and grenades as they fought to keep their properties from the anarchists. The occasional human sacrifice left smoldering in some back alley brought a sick balance to the essence of gunpowder as its stench reminded all of us that this was war. People fought, people died, and inhumanity had taken control over the peaceful human spirit. It made me gag.

Cannibalism was rampant but hidden. It was silly to imagine that under our skin we're all brothers and sisters, pretending to love America. The truth was more likely that some were traitors, assassins, liars and hypocrites, but many of them infiltrators — Herons. And when the walls come tumbling down, many of them will also become cannibals. And so, they did.

Like a good Christian secretly having an abortion, we hid our cannibalism. I'll never forget the expression on the face of that mother as she handed small pieces of burnt human flesh to her three young children who looked as though they hadn't eaten in weeks. Her eyes were dark and sunken, her expression was distant, numb and hollow. She stared over at me, frozen in time, then looked back at each child making sure they had finished what remained of that poor man.

Burning flesh, I've never smelled something so repulsive. Made me gag. I wondered who he was and whether she had killed him, or had he succumbed to the painful death of slow starvation like so many others in Sector 7? To her, he was sustenance. I couldn't blame her.

The United States of America was Mystery Babylon. Dad was prophetic in that prediction and the prophecies were correct. It didn't matter what they had professed would be the trigger leading to our fall from grace, it just happened, and the reasons were too many to list. But, at the top should be the stupidity and ignorance that blanketed our society, compliments of the Herons through their total infiltration of our educational system and of the media that reported their progress. We stopped teaching civics and our Constitution became nothing more than an annoying road block to D6. Calling it a living and breathing document became popular and was most effective at marginalizing the importance of its brilliance.

We missed the mark

* * * *

The thought of mass destruction, always of biblical proportions, caused TV preachers, famous as magnificent linguistic sociopaths, to use the occasion to increase their ranks and then grow their coffers. Social media was abuzz with their posts.

Divide and conquer. It's an old but most effective military tactic, one that Philip II of Macedonia, Julius Caesar and Napoleon each exploited to defeat their enemies. The Herons used that same strategy, but it was far easier for them. Using patience while employing a strategy of stealthily infiltrating our shores changed to one of open borders where all were welcome. Decent, hardworking people, ready to assimilate and become patriotic Americans, were the minority. Far too many of them weren't and that single-handedly altered our balance of power in the voting booths.

Not knowing your enemy is always problematic. Complimenting Sun Tzu's prevailing theory for the most effective art of warfare, "If you know your enemy and yourself, you need not fear the result of a hundred battles. If you know yourself but not the enemy, for every victory gained you will likewise suffer a defeat. If you know neither your enemy nor yourself, you will succumb in every battle." Their plan was ingenious, their execution near-flawless. An uncivil war for the Twenty-First century where the enemy's divide was neither North and South but instead rich and poor, black, white, brown, yellow, Christian, Jews and Muslim, capitalists, socialist, gay, straight and transgender. The perfect storm! They divided us across all segments.

Many of us thought radical Islam would engulf us and that we'd be bowing twice daily towards Mecca while our women wore a hijab and stopped driving cars. Sharia was a looming threat even though we completely misunderstood it. Although radical Islam played a small role in the societal divisions which blanked our nation, it wasn't the trigger that caused her collapse. It went much deeper than that and came over a period of decades, ending in a crescendo as you'd expect from a grand symphonic masterpiece where the volume gradually increases to a deafening level, causing the audience to shutter in total surprise.

Collapse the dollar thereby leveling the economic playing field and suddenly equality becomes dangerous. What were once historical battle sites in the heartlands of America shifted to our inner cities. Gettysburg became Philadelphia, Bunker Hill was Chicago, Fort Sumter, Atlanta, Hokes Run, Washington, D.C., and the Alamo was Dallas and damn near every major city west of the Mississippi. It was hard to keep track.

On August 2, 2020, under Article 1, Section 8, Clause 15, President Neville declared Martial Law and the Presidential election was cancelled. Our Constitution was symbolically burned as the National Defense Resources Preparedness Order was initiated. Neville was instilled as a dictator for life and The United States of America ceased to exist. As with the rest of our fellow citizens, we remained barricaded in our home for six days.

Fox News was blocked and the only source for information was Neville's favorite propaganda stations. The Patriots were now the enemy.

I questioned God and those four words printed on our currency, "In God We Trust." It no longer applied. Although we had no Paul Revere to alert us of the pending invasion which continued for decades, I began to take stock in my father's subtle warnings over those many years - most of which I thought were just rants of a man I believed to be at the doorsteps of conspiratorial insanity.

Warning Signs

* * * *

Looking back and wondering about all sorts of things I shouldn't care about, one question kept entering my mind. Warning signs, were there any? For the Great Collapse there were plenty, but for my change in moral capacity, I'm not sure there was.

"Aiken, it's difficult to predict the future, but in America it's just as difficult to predict the past," he said. I pondered that for a moment and then realized the wisdom of exactly what he meant. The Great Collapse was not a catastrophic event like a massive flood, or a devastating tsunami, something that God had a hand in and that mankind couldn't avoid. It was meticulously planned, not accidental like a house fire started by someone who negligently smokes in bed.

Mass shootings of innocent victims at schools and public venues occurred with increasing frequency even though the shooter had been on the radar of various law enforcement agencies before their killing sprees. The signs were there, but no one acted on them. We failed to identify our enemy and then, once presented with reality, we refused to admit it. That enemy truly was us.

I had already questioned God and the whole "In God We Trust" thing and wasn't completely convinced that He himself didn't have His hand in this. At what point does the Almighty say to himself, my greatest creation is beyond repair, perhaps it's time to clear the chess board and start all over again. Dad wasn't buying that one. He still had the highest trust and faith in the good Lord, something I didn't share.

"Shame on you for thinking that," he'd snap at me. "The Lord is your Shepard," Blah, blah, blah. "Mystery Babylon was not God's doing but instead, our own."

Unemployment, conspiratorial paranoia from Dad and a nagging, alcoholic mother is the most awful combination any kid should have to experience from parents he's about to leave. But I couldn't wait for college to begin. Cassie had already graduated and lived in Sector 79, formerly Columbia, South Carolina. She never visited us after the collapse, but she'd call once a week to make sure that I was alive, and Dad hadn't gone off the deep end. "I'm alive and well, but dad is questionable," I'd tell her.

With little in savings and a dollar that was worthless, things got dicey between the three of us. Cassie stopped calling, and I spent most of my time at my friend's house. What should have been a relaxing summer before heading off for those "four best years of my life," was a living hell.

Our backyard became one enormous survival pit, a huge vault where Dad had buried post-apocalyptic essentials like rice and pasta, water and even high-grade gasoline. He rotated them systematically by entering the vault from with inside the house where he had dug a long tunnel from the East wall of our basement all the way out to that vault. He took six months to dig it.

Stored in a massive metal container buried six feet below ground, he covered it with tomatoes. It pissed Mom off. Her beautiful roses and herbs were all replaced by gangly tomato plants. Although he hated the term, Dad was officially a "Prepper." We survived the after-effects of the Great Collapse and I'm thankful for his temporary insanity. After things settled down and we had gone through much of our supplies, he replenished them, convinced that we were not out of the woods yet. "There's more to come," he kept saying every time he'd head down to the basement, arms filled with more supplies.

For him, things happened for reasons other than what was reported in the news or in the annals of history gleaned from those revisionist textbooks they forced us to read as kids. Much of what we learned came from blogs, Twitter and the usual social networks, as legitimate journalism had died a decade before the collapse. The New York Times, LA Times, the Washington Post and others were offshoots of Novosti — their hallways were awash in traitors and became a virtual sedge of Herons — the

Egret type, propagandists.

Cronkite and Brinkley blessed my father, but for me, absorbing the rants of comedians masquerading as news sources mocking the Patriots for even suggesting that all was not well in Camelot, was my only source for the news. I'd scream at the TV knowing pure bullshit emanated through the liquid crystal displays. I felt more stupid with each hour I absorbed.

Dad's subject line in his daily emails to his closest friends and me was always the same, "MUST READ."

And mine was equally brief. "GOT IT!" I'd reply.

"Headline 26B, March 12, 2014, Port Angeles Washington: Army takes responsibility for two Blackhawk helicopters that terrorized a small town."

"Headline 32C: March 23, 2014, This one appeared precisely one week after the Blackhawk incident:

"The Department of Homeland Security buys 1.6 billion rounds of ammunition."

"You realize," he continued, "that DHS had only 100,000 peace officers in 93 agencies. Even the mathematically challenged can figure out that this amounts to a lot of shooting."

"Citizen's Protection Force," he'd close those emails with. Brown shirts. The anti-peace corp. that started during Neville's second term. Be careful!

While those stories were interesting, and even scary, what most concerned me were the rumors never found on page 26c of the local newspapers. Concentration camps, killing fields, detention and re-education facilities each within the United States but well hidden in the middle of nowhere. When mentioned in polite conversation, "conspiracy" was always the response and then the topic was changed. These places consumed my imagination, as I became determined to learn more about them. This was the forbidden fruit of the Garden of Eden we supposedly lived in. Utopia had its drawbacks, most notably, that inside every utopia was dystopia, and during my last summer before heading off to college, I learned exactly what dystopia was.

Rumors

****

Rumors were rampant — names like Vega 7, Kiowa and Rita Blanca kept popping up in social media and in quiet, secluded places where cameras and microphones weren't recording or eavesdropping on the whispers that echoed throughout those private chambers. They watched us; they recorded and followed us, but there were places we could always go that we knew to be void of their devices. Sometimes it was just as easy to take a road-trip. And so we did.

Folklore, fake news, they were all of them but somehow, my

father never commented or offered an opinion when the names of those encampments entered our discussions. He'd walk away, turn up the volume on the TV or change the topic. I became most curious to find the truth and to understand why my father avoided the subject.

There's an old saying, "Curiosity got the cat." It turned out to be true — and I was that cat.

Finding Vega 7

* * * *

Dad always promised that, together, we'd take the ultimate road trip: four days and 2,600 miles with the top down in his old, white Mercedes Benz, from sea to shining sea and a lot of nothing in between. I looked forward to it but didn't hold my breath it would ever happen. He was constantly "busy," even when unemployed, so most of his promises never panned out.

"Aiken, one day we'll drive across America, all the way to California," he promised me a dozen times, and each time he'd add something new that we'd discover on a journey that never happened: The Grand Ole Opry, the Mohave desert, the Grand Canyon, tumbleweeds and armadillos in New Mexico, classic old diners where only the locals ate, and — the grand finale — the sun setting over the Pacific Ocean. The seven or eight wonders of America, he'd call them. I forgot how many there were, but I saw none.

It wasn't until two years after the Great Collapse and those fifty states became 1,218 sectors that I took that trip, but I didn't go all the way to the Pacific Ocean, and I didn't go with him. I went with Queek, my best friend. We drove to Sector 773, formerly New Mexico and the grand finale — a classic old diner where only the locals ate.

His real name was Quinn. Every high school has their resident geek, and he was ours, but I felt obliged to rechristen him "Queek." That's what friends do, glorify those they care about by giving them cool, memorable names. It took a while, but it stuck, and everyone called him "Queek."

Unlike stereotypical geeks who are short, fat, and lack the hygiene regimens normal guys have, or tall and lanky with pale, zit-pocked, faces, Queek was athletic — not the bulked-up, contact-sports type, but the long-distance-runner kind with incredible speed and endurance. He could outrun any bully if needed and had done that plenty of times when he was a kid. We became best friends but couldn't be more different. I played Little League baseball and golfed; he played Xbox and not much else. I might have given him a simple nod once or twice while cutting our lawn as he sat on his front stoop fiddling with some tech gadget, but nothing more than that. For a decade, we were total strangers occupying the same half acre of God's green earth.

And then, one day in the middle of my last summer vacation before starting high school, he launched a drone right over my house. It took a sharp turn to the right and then across the street in a flight path destined to peer right into the bedroom window of the hottest girl in our neighborhood who had just moved in. Unlike the years I took to speak with Queek, I ran right over the day she moved in, introduced myself to her family and offered to show them around town. I was a fifteen-year-old quintessential young gentleman with ulterior motives.

Friendships can begin in the most bizarre ways, and mine with Queek began through two mutual interests: expensive, but banned drones and Cindy Bartow, that girl across the street. Best summer ever. There were fifty united states and the Great Collapse hadn't happened yet. I made a new friend, and I fell in love with another. Life wasn't perfect, but it was getting better. After the collapse, those fifty states became 1,218 Sectors. Loudoun County Virginia, my home, was Sector 7. The anarchists destroyed my neighborhood and most of the town of Leesburg. Cindy's family moved clear across the country to Sector 552 and I never saw or heard from her again. I hoped she survived the onslaught, as 552 was hit hard.

The following year and three weeks before heading off to college, Queek and I set out across the country to prove that Sector 773 didn't harbor a protected species of Vietnamese desert rats, as they told us, but instead detained thousands of human beings, Patriotic Americans who disagreed with our tyrannical government and the dictator sitting in the Oval Office, James Winston Neville.

Six days that forever changed our lives. And it all began in a diner where only the locals ate — The Golden Girls.

Alma, New Mexico was the nearest town to Kiowa, smack

damn in the middle of Sector 773. Three days in a Prius with no satellite radio made hours seem like days. Endless stretches of barren landscape and a friend who wasn't thrilled about going made the passage of time slow to a crawl. Traffic was sparse but Queek and I traded off driving responsibilities and, except for having a hard time finding gas stations that weren't still gouging the price of a gallon, it was uneventful, until we arrived in Alma.

Driving through Alma was a new experience for me since the smallest town I had ever visited still had a McDonald's, a Walmart, two banks and dozens of streets. Alma was tiny and, contrary to what my father had always told me about small towns, not very welcoming. But times had changed and in fly-over country, people harbored suspicion. Alma was the epicenter of flyover country.

Still, I suppose there's comfort in knowing everyone around you and that attitude of "we take care of our own" could cause eyebrows to raise when strangers appear. We were strangers, and I got that uneasy feeling that we weren't welcome. You could see it in their eyes and by the length of time they'd spend staring at you. "Who are you and why are you here?" was etched in their facial expressions.

Alma had no working traffic lights but had a four-way stop sign at the intersection of First, which was a dirt road, and a paved Main Street littered with cracks and potholes every couple of feet. Four-ways are for busy intersections, so having one there must have been an attempt at humor by the town council. There was no Second Street, nor any fast-food restaurants and the nearest Walmart was at least two-hundred miles away. The town's population sat at 143, less than a third what it was before the collapse. The cemetery on the outskirts stretched beyond its original boundaries. Like any town, people died but at a faster pace than they had planned for in Alma.

The night before making our way to the grasslands, we stayed at Alma's only motel, The White Water Inn, which offered cheap rooms with nasty, mold-infested bathrooms, pine-paneled walls, filthy red shag carpet covered with cigarette burns, and a suspicious front desk clerk. I felt his eyes boring into my back as he watched us through his tiny window all the way to our room.

"I'm thinking he doesn't like us," said Queek, who was more used to small towns than I was. He lived in one before moving to Sector 7, which at that point felt like a huge city. Loudoun County, Virginia was the fastest growing and wealthiest county in America. Damn government employees and contractors. It also took a huge hit from the anarchists after the collapse.

We ate breakfast the following morning at the Golden Girls Diner across the street. I got that uneasy feeling that this was a town that festered secrets and that the townies looked upon us as two strangers who might ask questions. Four middle-aged ladies sitting in a booth by the window eyed Queek and me up and down in slow motion while not bothering to hide their sneers the moment we walked in. Looking away, they clanged their coffee cups again and again on the table like a secret Morse-Code to each other and the rest of the diners. Who knows — maybe they telegraphed that we were okay. After all, we were teenagers.

One old man sitting alone in a ripped turquoise tufted vinyl booth, seemed more than suspicious about Queek and me. His intense focus bothered me, but he'd looked away every time I glared back at him. We played cat-and-mouse for a few minutes and then the cat turned his attention back to the scraps left on his plate — hash browns and crumbled bacon. He wore a newsboy hat and didn't appear that he belonged there either.

So, this was one of the seven wonders of the world my father promised we'd see on our cross-country adventure that never happened. I wasn't impressed. Classic, dirty and had seen better days, described this American diner. Dusty tables, sticky floors and countertops were not the most appetizing, but it was all we had. There were ketchup stains on the windows, and my trip to the men's room treated me to all sorts of cheeky stuff written above the cracked urinal which leaked urine all over the floor. Most of the random writings were anti-government with not one nice thing to say about President Neville, who the culprits called all sorts of unflattering names, mostly minor stuff like "Dictator" or "Hitler." Although the town folks made me feel uncomfortable, I felt at home in the men's room among the graffiti-covered walls and scrawled two choice words of my own: "Patriots Rule!"

When I returned from the bathroom, Queek trembled noticeably. "Let's get out here," he tried to whisper, but everyone could hear him loud and clear. His voice carried. I wasn't sure if he was just uncomfortable with the less-than-friendly treatment we were receiving or if getting the crap beat out of him by an old drunk sitting on the last stool at the counter was on his radar. Drunk, big and surly are a lethal combination against a gangly thin nerd like Queek. T-shirts with random ones and zeros are dead giveaways that you don't hunt for sport — or at all. It's a personal billboard advertising you're a nerd and Alma wasn't a nerdy town.

"What jew doing here, son?" he asked, slurring each word while swaying back and forth in an inelegant attempt at maintaining his balance. He was drunk, and it was only eight in the morning. Queek ignored him, but when that didn't work, "Just passing through, sir," seemed to do the trick. I was careful not to engage the locals and just observed. I'd always been a fervent people watcher, and that habit grew after the collapse, as people changed from being mostly kind and friendly to angry and suspicious. Flyover country was no friend of the government's, so the angry and suspicious types were prevalent in places like Alma. While observing them, I'd play a stupid mind-game with myself, wondering whether they were Neville supporters or Patriots like me. I kept score. The angry and suspicious ones were mostly Patriots, but I'd assume nothing. Dad's advice, "Things aren't always as they seem," was constantly on my mind. The objective was to determine the rough percentage of the destroyers in any setting. I wanted to know my odds should a riot break out. "Destroyers" were anarchists and had an unsettling habit of going ballistic on anyone that didn't kowtow to their victimization beliefs. Young and stupid was a common trait among them but that guy was at least sixty. I assured Queek that he wasn't a threat, just an asshole.

"Relax. Keep your voice down," I told Queek. Unlike him, my whispers didn't carry. "They're our kind of people. I can feel it," I added.

"Don't care, let's go."

We left after paying the check in cash. Alma seemed to have missed out on the technology boom and didn't accept credit, debit, or even EBT cards, which everyone had.

"Backward hillbillies," Queek uttered under his breath, shaking his head in amazement that they didn't have a chip reader, but I knew better. They preferred staying off the grid as I did. Queek was naïve about those things. I explained that to him as we headed to the car and he finally understood but still considered them backwards.

"To be honest, Queek, they're smart. Every card swipe becomes a government record and, based upon the reading material over the urinal, they wanted none of that."

"Good point. Again, let's get out of here," he repeated while hurrying towards the front door.

Driving through the middle of nowhere, especially in the desert, is like going back in time. Smartphones didn't work, and the radio offered only static. Although Queek wouldn't hesitate to add every option imaginable to his drone, he passed on getting Sirius satellite in his Prius, so we were at the mercy of whatever Clear Channel station came through, which weren't many. Most had been shut down. We'd catch a weak signal, every so often from God knows where, but it was either country music or some loathsome screaming preacher claiming to be the voice of God. Twenty-eight miles seemed like a hundred.

"Damn, Queek, you didn't think to bring any CDs?"

"We made it this far without you complaining. We're twenty

minutes away. Relax."

Static radio and a friend who was dreading the launch of his beloved drone in a restricted area under the most unfavorable weather conditions, made me long for the screaming preacher or country music. But the strong gusting winds made the Prius jostle on the road, so that added a small sense of adventure, at least for me.

"Are you sure about this?" he asked every damn mile. Twenty-eight times. "Are you sure about this?"

"Yeah, I'm sure!"

We took a back road to the top of Rabbit Ear Right, one of two mountains with narrow, tall peaks and a softly curved plateau in between them. Rabbit ear left was ground zero — Vega 7. Driving the back roads is a lonely proposition even with Queek in the car. Thirty minutes could pass between passing cars and, I'll admit, I kind of enjoyed that. We saw only domesticated cattle, and some abandoned old farms, but mostly desolation. Miles and miles of desolation.

Tall chain linked fences appeared about 5 miles out with "No Trespassing" and that "Radiation" icon warning printed on them. They were so rusted and riddled with bullet holes that you had to squint long and hard just to make out the threatening warnings. Regardless, we knew they weren't an invitation to "come on in" and had heard stories about those who did, never being seen again.

The road to Rabbit Ear Right wasn't blocked, giving us limited access from the top and parallel to the mountain that hid Vega 7, Rabbit Ear Left. Like Area 51, we could look into the distance but not directly at Vega 7.

Kiowa is one of those places where you'd expect an old western to be filmed. Cowboys and Indians gathering on the horizon, wild horses running free and some magnificent views from the jagged rock cliffs that rose 4,000 feet above the horizon. It was pure western and the perfect place to hide something nefarious. 7,500 acres of every imaginable terrain, I knew precisely where to go, and Google Maps wasn't what guided me, it was my father and the coordinates he had given years before we started our journey. Still, I worried that Queek's Prius was the worst choice of vehicles for this trip as the road to Rabbit Ear Right was unpaved and had short stretches of nothing where "the road" and the "off-road" were indistinguishable. Potholes left, right, dead center and just about everything else imaginable scattered across those narrow paths made our trip to 36.1667° N, 104.1672° W the road to hell, literally. What the hell were we thinking?

"Take the right fork," I told Queek.

"How do you know?" he asked

Queek once asked if my father was ok, and his inference wasn't about his physical well-being, it was his mental state of mind. Dad came across as a conspiratorial nutcase even to my friends. I'd cringe at what he'd say, even though he was right most of the time. No matter how unimaginable his theories seemed, history has proven him correct. My father was a modern-day Nostradamus, yet many thought him a raging lunatic. He convinced me that they'd eviscerate our Second Amendment, but not through traditional means. Congress would play no part and the Constitution wouldn't matter. By his theory, Homeland Security would take care of that and it wasn't by confiscating our weapons, it was by confiscating the ammunition. Sounded unbelievable at first, but ultimately proved to be true. The Patriots could have all the guns, rifles and AK47's they wanted, but finding ammunition would be damn near impossible. A massive ammunition-purchase would do the trick. America would be completely disarmed — shooting blanks, so to speak.

But it was also the gullibility of a nation incensed by the evil acts of the Blues, the most heinous of the Herons, who so completely swayed public opinion against man's right to bear arms, to protect themselves and their families. Those mass killings in Columbine, the elementary school in Connecticut, movie theaters, night clubs, Las Vegas and so many others were each initiated from within our own government and, although he never had proof, his contention was that the trigger was pulled from within the Oval Office. Figuratively speaking, of course.

Never-the-less, as the innocent bodies piled up, public opinion swayed far enough to allow for the stealth disarming of every American citizen, regardless of where they lived. Walmart no longer stocked ammunition. Their claim: Our supplier is back-ordered. This was their main intention, and they accomplished it without firing a shot. This was our Waterloo.

"I just do." I replied

"God, this is cool," he said leaving his temporary state of mutism behind while gazing down at the valley below. Due southwest and just over the horizon was the second peak where there were no roads, no hiking paths and no conceivable way to see what was beyond and below them. We were as close as we could get, yet I wondered how they had transported thousands of innocent civilians through the desolate landscape without the infrastructure to do so.

Poised on a rocky ledge, I looked out over the horizon. "This is where Jarvis will fly. That's Vega 7," I pointed to the second rabbit ear. We were both overwhelmed by the moment's beauty and what we were about to do as Queek stood still, pulled out his range finder to scan the horizon and the mountain in the distance.

"No problem, three miles," he said, "that's within our range."

"It's Christmas morning, Queek." He never looked up, just barked out orders in rapid succession while handing me his drone.

"Battery check?"

"Fully charged," I answered.

"Video feed working?"

"Coming through."

"Return to home coordinates locked in"

"Yep"

"Do exactly as I say." I prepped Queek.

"It's my drone, I know how to fly it," he shot back.

Queek was the pilot, but I needed to assert myself as the navigator, and so I did. It's that whole alpha male thing, I guess.

"Mission? I like that. Sounds paramilitary." Queek still had a lot of "kid" in him and sometimes I had to play along just to keep him focused.

The Phantom 4 had a range of 2 kilometers and a maximum capable altitude of 1000 meters. Top speed — 35 knots. We needed every bit of its range but nothing near its capability to fly over the Empire State Building. As for the speed — that was inconsequential — our goal was to capture video and then get the hell out of Alma. Radar would scan the skies surrounding Vega 7 but not directly over it, so we had to stay under two-hundred and fifty feet to avoid being detected.

I took out my notebook and drew a rough sketch of the terrain as I saw it from that point and then explained how Queek needed to pilot Jarvis towards and up Rabbit Ear Left.

"Radar will scan this area" I started, "so we have to remain below 250 feet all the way through that valley. Once you get to that peek I need you to hug the side of those rocks and then gradually take it up to the top. Got it?"

"How high is that peak? he asked

"5,062 at its highest. Why?"

"Maximum altitude is 3200 feet, but it uses Sonar, so that's based upon the ground directly below it."

"Plain English Queek!"

"I must fly sideways until I get to the top and then do the same as I'm coming down."

"Can you do it?"

"Yep, no problem, I can do this," he said unequivocally. His whole demeanor changed at that point and, for the first time since we left Sector 7, he smiled.

"Aye, aye, Captain," I added.

Although Queek would rather have been spying on girls

through their bedroom windows than on his own government, the challenge I had given him made it all worthwhile.

"Prepare to see how great a pilot I am," he threw down the gauntlet and flipped the power switch to "ON."

"Let her rip!" I shouted.

"One small step for two kids, one huge step for patriotism!" Jarvis whirled away, and it seemed a historically significant thing to say.

Queek understood the reference and gave a thumbs up while tightly holding the controller in the other hand. The wind picked up just as Jarvis lifted off. Like a cheap paper kite framed in balsa trying to dance with a strong ocean breeze, Jarvis lurched back and forth, left and right, up and down, displaying all the symptoms of someone afflicted with dystonia. But Queek remained calm while carefully guiding Jarvis down the side of the mountain.

Thus, began our undertaking to substantiate America's cruelest myth. Sasquatch, the Bermuda Triangle, or aliens in Roswell, there were plenty of still-unanswered questions about those myths, but cruelty to fellow innocent Americans never came into play. This one was unimaginable — death camps, killing fields, secret detention facilities, all of it run by our own government. All I could think was, "Not in America, not during my lifetime." I was second guessing this whole plan.

Flying an illegal drone over restricted airspace to film a top-secret government facility didn't bother me at all, even Queek was embracing the mission.

"Can't wait to see what's on the other side, Aiken."

This is where we differed. He was eager to see the truth while I was dreading it. I still loved America but wasn't prepared to see evil within the eyes of our own leaders.

Anticipation is an emotion filled with good or bad, life or death. I took one deep breath as Jarvis descended and prepared myself to answer my father's question when I returned home. Some people fear hearing the truth, I feared seeing it.

I remember my parent's promise, just as they remembered theirs,' that the life and country they'd leave their children would be more free and prosperous than what they grew up with. It was the adult version of Santa Claus or the Easter Bunny, something you wanted to believe but never quite knew if that affirmation would come true. It was as true for them as it was for prior generations, but that long winning streak, like all good things, ended. The Great Collapse screwed things up.

In the back of my mind, though, I knew there had to be something behind the increasing volume of chatter concerning Vega 7, but it was my father's insistence that it existed that made me plan the trip. "Where did all the Patriots disappear?" he asked, as if I'd have any clue. And then he gave me those exact coordinates.

Since we were standing on a cliff overlooking the valley, Queek needed to pilot Jarvis downwards while staying close to the edges of the rocks and then remain under 250 feet where it would skirt through the valley and towards Rabbit Left.

"Never flown one down before," he chuckled while guiding Jarvis close to the edge of the cliff, then gradually descending to the grasslands below. Queek wasn't a talkative guy, but when piloting a drone, he commentated like a sportscaster on its every move. He talked to it in an almost erotic manner, but in a more nuanced way.

"Easy, easy, at-a-boy, keep going down, down. What's our speed and altitude?"

"Eight hundred and thirty feet, 3 knots," I replied.

"Keep reading it off so I know when to go lateral."

"Five hundred, four-fifty, three-hundred. Ok, two-fifty. Better drop er down to two-hundred for good measure."

"Roger that."

Jarvis was performing magnificently and Queek was in his zone. He dropped it down well below 200 feet and skimmed the tips of some vegetation, mostly tall grass and thistle. He was a skilled pilot, but I wasn't happy with his showmanship.

"Watch this Aiken." He took it straight up, then did a barrel roll and flipped it over twice before dropping it down to just five feet from the ground and then sped forward. My concern was not what was below but what was ahead, a rock, a random tree, anything that it could crash into, which would abruptly end our mission.

"Whoa — Easy, Captain, stop messing around. If it crashes, we have no way to retrieve it." I reminded him. "And this will have been one huge waste of time."

"K." He erased that childish grin of excitement off his face and replaced it with the solemn seriousness fit for that moment.

It continued hovering at two hundred feet and then forward in a straight path towards Rabbit Ear left. Jarvis was now out of sight, but our video screen sent back everything Queek needed to monitor its flight path — visuals and data, altitude, speed and direction.

Grasslands are a polite way of saying expansive acreage of waste. What was once fertile ground for farming and grazing turned into one massive dust bowl because of over-farming and over-grazing. As the early settlers left and moved westward in search of more fertile soil, some vegetation returned, but mostly tall grass, thistle and not much else. The soil was not rich enough for crops. It was fascinating to watch and twice as we crossed the valley we saw skeletons of dead animals laying in a position suggesting that they had just collapsed and died. It was both beautiful and ugly at the same time.

"Houston, we have a problem, Queek said. I'm trying to go up and it's not responding. It's just hovering."

"What?"

"It's not responding, I mean — Damn, I have no control!"

Queek leaned back and screamed at the top of his lungs as if that precious drone was his lover, "He betrayed me!"

"Look at the screen, it's gone completely dark. Did it crash or are we not receiving the feed?" I shouted at Queek, like it was his fault. The on-screen data showed Jarvis' speed; 5 knots, altitude; three-hundred-fifty-two-feet and its direction was south-southwest, but it was still pitched black.

"Well — it hasn't crashed and whoever is controlling it is damn good at piloting in the dark. I'm impressed," he added, which surprised me. His tone was calm and mine was sheer panic.

I figured praying to God for help in regaining control of

Jarvis was as good an idea as any. Sunday school taught me that God was capable of some awesome miracles and that he always answered our prayers, so asking him to change the path of a drone wasn't a stretch for the Almighty.

"God, please send Jarvis back," was the extent of my prayer. No "Amen," "Dear God" or "oh blessed Lord," just a pathetic pleading to a deity I doubted, because of what he allowed the Herons to do to America. In God We Trust was a crock! It didn't work. Queek relinquished the controller and dropped it on the ground, then paced in small circles like a dog looking for a spot to pee. All that stuff they taught me in Sunday school ranked right up there with the rest of the stories we grew up believing — Santa Claus, the Easter Bunny, and the biggest whopper of all, that America was the land of the free and the home of the brave. In God we trusted.

For five minutes we anxiously stared as Jarvis moved forward in a slow straight path and at a steady speed of 5 knots. Noting nothing but a pitch-black screen added to my apprehension while making me more determined to finish what we came here for, to find Vega 7. Perhaps it was God himself who piloted that drone. I gave him a pass and pulled the religion card out to calm Queek down. Queek was an atheist, so it didn't work.

"God wants us to find this place. I can feel it."
"God. Gimme a break."

"What's that ahead? I see light."

"Looks like we're in a tunnel," I said, "and that looks like railroad tracks."

47

A long dark tunnel with a small glimmer of light in the distance and a shimmering of two metal tracks converging on the horizon caught the reflection off the light. It was one those "of course!" moments. Railroad tracks. After all, how were thousands of Patriots transported to Vega 7? There's no greater feeling than to see light at the end of the tunnel but that's for people overwhelmed by stress, or a life filled with tragedy. What I felt at that moment was not dissimilar. My idyllic world had crashed around me after the Great Collapse. What could be more stressful and tragic than that? Jarvis was not going over Rabbit Left but, instead, through it. The tiny bit of the stress I had been feeling while staring at a blank screen disappeared, but only partially. What was at the end of that light kept my heart beating at marathon pace. What was at the end of that tunnel?

"Screw that Queek, you gotta see this," I said, tapping my finger hard into the screen.

"My drone is rogue Aiken. Damn, I knew this would happen."

"Isn't sorting this out worth one drone?"

"You gonna replace it?"

Just as I was about to commit to replacing something I couldn't afford, that light at the end of the tunnel became — just light and the horizon was covered with grass and tall mountains, blue sky and something indistinguishable in the distance.

"Look, it's coming out of the tunnel."

Jarvis' camera was gimble-mounted and capable of filming in a 270-degree rotation but remained focused straight ahead.

The images looked like dots moving across the screen. My first thoughts were that they were cattle. But as Jarvis drew closer, we realized it was something else. People meandering like zombies in the grasslands below and dressed in camouflaged uniforms that blended with the landscape. Circling again and skimming the tips of the blades of tall grass like a crop duster, Jarvis pulled back and upwards.

"Are you seeing this?" I asked. Queek jammed his face right up to the screen, then grabbed his chest firmly, "Holy shit, are those people?" I thought he would pull his head off. "Holy shit Aiken, we found it!"

"Appears so," I said cautiously since we couldn't be sure that what we were viewing wasn't just a herd of cattle. Queek walked in circles repeating to himself, "This can't be, this can't be."

"It's moving faster and getting closer to whatever that is," I said, as Jarvis sped up and increased its altitude to five hundred feet.

"They're people, looks like thousands."

Most people are unfocused during moments of paranoia, but that's when my mind was its sharpest. It took five or six-seconds for me to realize that, yes, what we were looking at was one massive stretch of men, women, and children walking aimlessly through those grasslands, each wearing the same uniforms — camouflage. I don't remember responding. I took a moment to digest what we were seeing. As you might appreciate, the implication emblazoned on that screen was of such profound consequences as to provoke a certain disgust within me. I was sick to my stomach. Queek — he stopped pacing, stopped grabbing his head and just looked numb. Paranoia had the opposite effect on him.

It was a bitter sweet moment. Sanity confirmed — sweet. Government detention camps — bitter. But my father had also told me of killing fields and mass graves to bury those who had perished. They executed those who disrupted their reeducation process. We saw only a prison, a secret one, but still — just a prison. I had hoped to be wrong. I would have preferred a diagnosis of an early onset of paranoid psychosis instead, but what I had long suspected about that sector was true.

Most guys would never admit to crying unless someone close to them had died, but I teared up while trying to maintain composure in front of my best friend who showed emotion only when one of his gadgets failed to perform as expected. Even then, he'd never cry. He'd just throw stuff at the nearest wall and then pace in circles. Queek sat quietly staring at the screen with his mouth half-open, unable to speak. or blink his eyes. He was in shock. Not once since the moment we lost control of Jarvis did either of us consider who or what piloted that drone.

"Queek," I asked, "care to explain how Jarvis is flying. I mean, does it have autopilot?"

"Yes, but I didn't set in any GPS coordinates and I turned it off, so that's not it."

God works in mysterious ways, I thought to myself. The shock of what we saw, completely overshadowed the fact that Queek's drone was being controlled by someone else, someone who knew the area, and maybe knew that Vega 7 existed and how to get there.

I learned in high school history class of mass burial sites scattered around the world, sites that were always uprooted in areas previously held hostage by the world's worst dictators, their images burned in effigy by the citizens they ruled over: Phnom Penh and the Khmer Rouge in Cambodia; Hitler's death camps scattered around Germany, Poland, and Austria. It seemed implausible that, in our lifetime, modern society would ever witness such horrific treatment of fellow human beings again, and surely not in America. What we were watching, though, looked more like a detention facility or secret federal prison, there weren't any signs yet of mass graves.

Jarvis circled back for another pass, but this time dropped to near ground level and hovered, motionless, while transmitting an image that baffled us: moss-green color, textured but with no ripples or imperfections as anything naturally grown would have had. It was flat, fake-looking. Painted wood? Cloth? I couldn't tell.

"What the hell is that?" I asked, forgetting that he'd be as clueless as I and was more concerned with Jarvis' condition.

"Did we crash?" he replied.

At that moment, like a skilled film director, Jarvis pulled back and then upward, farther from the image, gradually revealing a wide-angle shot that exposed a detailed perspective of what had just confounded us. Long, narrow, camouflaged rectangles, each precisely the same size. One, then two, four, six, — they filled the screen. There were hundreds, side by side, equally spaced with only a foot or so separating each rectangle.

As Jarvis continued pulling back and away, exposing more

acreage, it became clearer that the entire landscape was not grasslands at all, but one massive canvas of painted images meant to mimic those grasses. Had there been headstones or brass markers, it would have resembled an enormous cemetery, and no one would have questioned it. Lacking those elements of honor and civility for those who had perished, though, made what we had fixated on a modern-day killing field — acre upon acre of camouflaged graves and thousands of prisoners similarly camouflaged milling around, presumably to dig them.

"What the fuck?" Queek said as Jarvis made a most unusual maneuver. It flipped completely over, exposing not the clear blue sky above, but a canopy of netting. With a last pass through the netted area, Jarvis sent back one final image before leaping the bounds of its rogue mission and vanishing into a black hole. That last image was of a single deep hole with three black body bags placed next to it. What at first, we thought was a burial site for thousands of bodies stretched over hundreds of acres, was actually a burial site for three times that many, hundreds of thousands. They piled three on top of each other. That light at the end of the tunnel went dark again, and Jarvis stopped transmitting data back to us. No speed, altitude or direction — nothing. It went dark, the signal stopped, and then it disappeared.

"Fuck this, Aiken," Queek said. "We need to get more video. This is seriously sick, and we need to expose this shit." Queek never swore, but on that occasion, he swore like a pro. What we had witnessed that morning exposed our government's most horrific secret. But unlike the classified secrets I had always believed were meant to protect the rights and safety of American citizens, this one did the opposite, to imprison and ultimately extinguish all who opposed Neville and his tyrannical government. What the Nazis, Soviets and the Khmer Rouge had done decades before was now being committed by our own government and on American soil.

"It's not coming back is it?" Queek accepted that Jarvis was gone but understood the enormity of what we had witnessed -- proof that Vega 7 existed.

"What do we do now?"

"I don't know Queek, I don't know."

Before heading home to Sector 7, we returned to Alma to fill up our tank and to the Golden Girls to fill up our stomachs. It was late, but we had committed to drive for the next eighteen hours and there wasn't much in the way of decent food along the I-40 corridor. It was desolate. Oklahoma City was still unsafe and basically a pile of rubble. Even midwestern cites couldn't escape the carnage brought upon America by the Great Collapse. We pulled into the Golden Girls at around 5:15 and parked near the back. A huge black dumpster took up four parking spaces.

There's a huge difference between the breakfast and dinner crowds at a local diner, even in a small town like Alma. You're either heading to work in the morning and in a bad mood or returning home in the evening, happier but exhausted. Breakfast greeted the early risers, blue-collar workers who sucked down tons of black coffee and a 5-second pour of sugar. Eggs, sausage patties, and hash browns were all we saw on the trays that morning, hoisted by Grace, the only waitress who seemed to know every customer by name. To that breakfast crowd we were infiltrators and again, they greeted us with suspicious sneers and that less than friendly service we expected. Grace never said more than two words. "Your order?" No smiles either.

Dinner had a completely different aura and, while the breakfast guests were split among men and women, dinner was mostly men. Just as they did at breakfast, they watched us closely from the moment we walked in till we paid the check and left. You could still feel their stares, like a cold breeze brushing against your back. More interesting was that the dinner crowd ate the same damn stuff — eggs, sausage and hash browns. It was breakfast for dinner and, based upon the frowns on those faces, those folks were heading to work — night shift.

But where? Alma had no factories, no large companies, just a few ranches, some small farms, and that was about it. It was one of those towns where you'd question where everyone worked and how they earned money. I'm not sure why, but we never saw one child or young kid anywhere in that town, just middle-age adults. Grace, who was still there, greeted them by their first name and "the usual?" was all she had to ask. There was routine written all over everyone's faces until she came to our table and actually struck up a conversation while handing us a menu.

"How's the just-passing-through going?" she asked.

"It was fine," I offered, "But the area's so beautiful, we explored a little."

"Good for you boys. See anything interesting? Leaving tomorrow?"

"Actually, as soon as we finish, we're heading back home. And, not really — just some dead animals and cool cliffs."

"Where's that?" she asked. I wasn't sure if she was inquiring about the cliffs or where home was, but decided it was the latter and told her a lie.

"Sector 24 — Pittsburg area." I was familiar with the area so had she asked questions or tried to trick me up, I was sure I could answer them. As for Queek, he'd say nothing. He's shy and was still in a state of shock.

Grace was more attentive than she was that morning. Bringing our order, striking up a conversation, albeit nosey, and offering a free slice of cherry pie. I got that uneasy feeling that she wasn't offering pleasantries, but instead was on a verbal recon mission. She was most curious about our exploits and where we hailed from. The heads were turning every couple of minutes staring closely at us with that look of wonderment on their faces as if to broadcast, "Who the hell are these kids and why are they here?" Never felt more unwelcome. In fact — it was as if we were behind enemy lines — like a black man at a Klan rally.

The food was greasy, but the cherry pie was good. It was time to take a leak, get the check and then head home. Couldn't wait to get out of there. Standing in the front of that leaking urinal, I noticed my patriotic graffiti had been erased and replaced with something else. "Dumpster Drone" — In all capital letters and in bright red ink, it stood out among a sea of thought provoking pee poetry written in black. That people are standing in a public place doing the most private things could easily skew a person's personality once they uncap that Sharpie. Neither those words nor that post was in any way poetic or even thought provoking, but I stood still for a moment trying to decipher what it meant. The other graffiti just made me laugh.

I finished my business, grabbed a paper towel then did precisely as the mystery artist had done to my words — erased it.

"Queek, let's go. I think I've got good news." My interpretation of that message was that Jarvis had been tossed in the black dumpster out back and that whoever put it there was our mysterious pilot that morning, an actual friend and ally in Alma.

"What could possibly be good news?"

"Just come. I think I know where Jarvis is."

The dumpster was halfway full and smelled like hell, not something I was eager to rummage through. Of all the desirable traits to inherit from my father — it was a weak stomach that his gene pool had tossed my way. There was days' worth of rotting food and the hot summer's air intensified the putrid stench even through the large black trash bags that contained the food. Still, I grabbed the top ledge and leaned over, expecting to spot something that didn't fit with the rest of the garbage, like a drone. Not that easy. Our mystery man had taken precautions to hide it among the garbage even if he had been less than subtle in the Men's room. Black trash bags were everywhere but underneath one of them was a green bag, dark green and much smaller than the rest of the bags. I ripped open a small section and sure enough — Jarvis was in it along with a sealed envelope with the letters "AM" written on the front. Aiken McHale?

As I was getting into Queek's car, I overheard two men talking in the parking lot. Not one to eavesdrop on other people's conversations, I couldn't help but focus on that one. Five words. "See you on the train," some old guy said to the other. "Ah ha" moments are when light bulbs go off and you stare into space. Those lightbulbs went off and the conspiracy side of my brain ignited with all sorts of unfounded but reasonable conclusions as to the destination of that train. I closed the bag, opened the Prius' back hatch and tossed it in. "Hit it, let's get out of here, I'll explain later."

Queek was thrilled that Jarvis was back in his possession and, although he wanted to stop and check it out, I convinced him that we needed to drive as fast as possible and to put as much distance between us and Alma as possible. It was at least ten miles before I felt safe enough to crawl in the back and check his precious drone, which was unharmed as best I could determine. I opened the envelope containing my initials and read what was in it — two handwritten pages in flawless cursive, something my generation was never taught. It was a history lesson, the kind I had never wanted to learn.

Within the short-grass prairie of the southern Great Plains lie the Kiowa and Rita Blanca National Grasslands. What was once thought to be protected federal lands abundant with endangered critters, devolved into something sinister as those threatened varmints quickly became another endangered species, armed but patriotic Americans.

Encompassing 230,000 acres in six sectors within New Mexico, Texas, and Oklahoma, those beautiful grasslands hid hundreds of thousands of deep graves — each containing three bodies, stacked one on top of the other — that had been transformed and covered over during President Neville's first term. There are no Vietnamese desert rats, no spotted owls, no weird little fish — just humans. It was as secretive and well-guarded as Area 51. No one could get near it. Vega 7 is the Supermax.

Caskets were unnecessary as the government had secretly stockpiled a special biodegradable burial bag that contained hydrofluoric acid within its fibers that would gradually but completely decompose any remaining bone fragments. Even twenty-first-century tyrants still considered themselves caretakers of the environment if not guardians of freedom. It wouldn't take long for the occupants of those plots to become one with nature and completely disappear, never to be discovered by future generations who might unwittingly unearth the atrocity. Ashes to ashes, dust to dust, there's nothing to see here.

Our revisionist historians will never acknowledge what they did to us and will, most likely, add those detention facilities to a long list of common myths still flooding our folklore: Roswell, UFOs, the grassy knoll, Area 51 and 52, weapons of mass destruction, Benghazi, and now Rita Blanca and Vega 7. George Washington once said that, Truth will ultimately prevail where there are pains taken to bring it to light.

Three days of driving back to Sector 7 and, while the trip out to the grasslands was boring but filled with anticipation, the return home was neither. Queek talked more than usual and seemed a changed man, and by that, I mean he became involved in something other than geeky stuff. Queek never swore - but he did that time for the next two thousand miles. We had agreed to never post the video, but two days later it went viral. Queek swore that it wasn't him. It forever changed my life and ultimately forced me to change my identity.

On August 3, 2020, I was upgraded to ACT status, American Citizen Threat, becoming a hero among fellow Patriots but marking my family and me for an unwanted visit.

My crime — exposing the truth.

Unplanned Sabbatical

* * * *

If only they hadn't screwed up my plans to start a new chapter on a positive note. College — something my parents had insisted I do. Two years had passed since The Great Collapse, but Sector 7 was still a disaster. The affluent towns and neighborhoods took the brunt of the rioting and we lived in an affluent town, albeit a blue-collar neighborhood. They were also last to be cleaned up. It was a subtle message meant to show the wealthy what it was like to live in abject squalor. It didn't work - it just pissed us off.

Just getting away was reason enough to be joyous, but I was still leery about leaving my parents. Compatibility and love had long since left their relationship. They existed — living together like roommates.

Billed as the four best years of your life, it was also a point in time where tolerance for free speech had disappeared.

Thought and speech police were everywhere, listening devices and cameras too. Speaking the truth was blasphemous and could land you in serious trouble. If your professor didn't agree with you, failing that course was a suitable punishment for your refusal to tow-the-line.

A new language had taken hold on most campuses lest someone offend a fellow student. Punishment for using politically incorrect language reached far and wide. Fat people were "people of size," gender was no longer a binary choice because some idiots had crafted twenty-six, allowing individuals to move among them based upon how they were feeling on any particular day. Even the term "Americans" was problematic as it excluded those coming from Central or South America. "Americons" entered the lingo because it considered the south, central and northern continent. Beyond the poor grade you'd receive for blasphemy or respecting brevity when addressing others, they'd shun you on campus, some doing so to remain in good favor with the elitist professors who watched the students like hawks searching for prey. Not everyone accepted our new system, but a good majority of them did, many only to avoid punishment. They were ass-kissers.

The Heron's infiltration of America's universities, like their occupation of K-12, was a huge success and those "four best years" were about to become "four dreaded years" for me. Their death meld to our First Amendment had taken hold on every campus and I wasn't one to shy away from verbally abusing the other side of the ideological spectrum. I knew I'd be in constant trouble. I was sensing daily lashings at a fictitious campus whipping post or being verbally berated through the university radio station or newspaper. Speech detention was on my horizon. I'd have few friends to lean on when the pressure to conform got unbearable. Conforming was good. Individuality was bad.

Packing my last few boxes of clothes and geek gear for my official send-off as a freshman at Mason University, formerly George Mason — I never finished that job. My collegiate experience began with an unplanned sabbatical, forcing me to hide from my own government. They targeted me. Vega 7 was never meant to be exposed, but it was and in doing so, it completely screwed up the next milestone in my life — college.

The Roundup

* * * *

Armed with Glocks, assault rifles, flash grenades and outfitted in a liquid body armor, Herodia were the most lethal — the Government enforcers and legalized assassins. We feared them the most. Oddly, they feared us too, many not sure which side they were on. Know thy enemy went both ways.

"Aiken, downstairs under the stairwell. Not a peep until they've left." Did my father know more than he led me to believe and was that visit no surprise to him? "No matter what happens, don't try to find us." I can't get those words out my head. What did he know?

"Ok, ok — they're equipped Dad." Armed was for those who carried rifles or small guns. "Equipped" meant a virtual arsenal was about to enter our world. They were equipped.

"Downstairs, downstairs" he whispered, motioning me to the basement. I moved swiftly, knowing precisely where to go. Most families trained for evacuations should an unforeseen act of God -- tornadoes, floods or fire, take place. We trained for our own capture by hiding within the walls of that poorly crafted bunker — dad's backup plan should time not be on our side. It wasn't.

"Open up! Homeland Security," the fortified agent shouted, his voice imposing a lethal sense of urgency. The protectors of our homeland and our porous borders had morphed into our own version of the Stasis, a national police force with a wide berth for what they considered to be criminal and grounds for detention.

I was armed, blasphemous to the core and an exposer of the truth - Vega 7. Having stockpiled food and water didn't help either, although I'm not sure how they knew. I suppose the Drone could pick that shit up. In their minds I had misfired on all cylinders.

Before Mom could reach the front door, a forceful battering ram smashed through our back door, shattering the wood frame and every pane of glass in the adjoining windows. Breaking the glass and reaching through would have been easier to gain entry, but these were thugs; optics and sounds were important when hunting Patriots. Fear — it what's they dispensed.

They breached the front door, tossing flash grenades which exploded just as they entered our living room. The sound that emanated from smashing that door echoed throughout the neighborhood. Having reinforced it with metal crossbeams after the collapse and the initial rioting made entry into our home a task requiring more than just turning the knob. It hadn't crossed our minds to remove them once our street had cleared, and the violence had subsided. Two years had passed since the initial onslaught, but the neighborhood was still virtually deserted. Anarchy knows no boundaries nor is it accountable to any timetable. Like unwelcome visitors, it shows up at the most inopportune times. Most neighbors had abandoned their homes decimated by the anarchists and, instead, settled elsewhere. Ours was a nice neighborhood, so it took the brunt of destruction.

Herodia did as they pleased; no one held them accountable. Armed to the hilt, they were masochistic, cruel and dispassionate in their neighborhood sweeps. Their targets, American citizens, most of whom had done nothing wrong other than arm themselves which was, in their minds, still a Constitutional right, even though it no longer was. As for my family, it was our God given right to protect ourselves and our loved ones. But a government that eschews the very existence of God cared less about our using that as the justification to ignore their weapons ban. They considered us criminals.

Embracing a Fabian strategy of slowly wearing us down, we were one family in millions, many of them innocent, who had experienced those visits. Keeping us wondering when they'd pull our ticket, most who they had targeted were never seen again. This wasn't good. I feared for my parents but remained silent while they combed the house looking for what I had assumed was me. Dad couldn't have been clearer. Stay quiet and don't move a muscle until they had left.

Sector 7, a wealthy suburb northwest of New Columbia and our home town, having been demolished during the first wave, was a virtual ghost town with no one to hear or see them this time, yet they stuck with intensified optics and deafening sounds in case others were watching. It kept the bats at bay and fear among loitering civilians who might just find their tactics worthy of videotaping and then posting. Don't do that!

While still maintaining town and county names, for utilities — electric, water and gas, we were to use our sector names should an emergency occur. Those sector designations took one week to devise, quite possibly the most efficient government program ever. One-thousand-two-hundred-and-eighteen. The theory being that small sectors lorded over by Sector Governors could keep a closer eye on all its citizens and then report back to Sector One - formerly Washington DC., now New Columbia. Sector One, was still our nation's capital. A family's roundup by Herodias was never deemed an "emergency." Expecting help was futile. We were on our own!

Encompassing the enclaves of Leesburg, Purcellville and Waterford, it was the ideal place to grow up. Gently rolling hills, horse farms and small family-owned wineries dotted its landscape. Huge drooping elm trees shading the narrow streets of the downtown area and dozens of antique shops made for weekend crowds, traffic jams and long waits to be seated at the local pubs or restaurants. It was straight from a Norman Rockwell painting, quaint, beautiful and represented everything that was good about America.

Refusing to abandon ship following the collapse, we were the last ones left on Brookmere Drive, although the Miller house still looked occupied with the lights always on. Huge mistake - it draws unwanted attention. A loner, widower and G17 career bureaucrat with no kids but the nastiest little dog who always pissed on our shrubs, Bernie was no friend of ours. An odd little man with a penchant for butting into our personal business, he wasn't a Patriot. Dad never cared for him either and avoided him like the plague, even when Bernie would ask him to lunch. He was probing, someone to avoid when your home contains a small arsenal of defensive weapons, several months' worth of non-perishable food buried in the backyard and you know him as one of them. I'd avoid eye contact whenever possible but on those rare occasions when I couldn't escape his view, I'd wave and beat a path to our front door or the car, whichever was closest.   I never trusted him. There were rewards for ratting us out and he was the kind of guy who would do exactly that.

Breaking down our door was deafening. The sound of stun grenades echoed for a few seconds but continued to resonate through my ears for several minutes causing a dizzying effect even though I was not in its immediate vicinity. My parents must have dropped to the floor from the disorienting combination of intense light, loud sounds and strong vibrations. They weren't young. Dad wasn't healthy, and mom had just finished a bottle of cheap wine. She was drunk.

I counted two agents entering through our sunroom, crushing broken glass beneath their bulky military boots. I assumed an equal number arrived through the front but wasn't sure. Four of them were now upon us. The odds were not in our favor, but they never were. Dad stayed silent while recovering from the sensory impact that they had tossed in his direction. Mom screamed, some unchristian profanities, never a good thing to do. Mom was antagonistic by nature, Dad was more pacifist, always avoiding confrontation when victory seemed a long shot or, in that case, when laser guided weapons were most likely aimed straight at his forehead.

"Don't move!" One shouted.

"This is crazy," my mom insisted.

"Not another word, kneel, hands behind your head."

"Start here then upstairs. Check everywhere, closets, under the beds, in the damn ceilings! There's another one here."

My father, still choking from the smoke, finally chimed in. "We've done nothing wrong. Why are we on your list?" The existence of that list was well known among the Patriots. Who was on it and why, wasn't. Dad played the "clueless" part with aplomb, even though he clearly knew why they were there.

"You too! On your knees! Hands behind your head!"

"Where do you keep your weapons?"

"In the safe, just a handgun, 32." My father was quick to give that up. Cooperating by handing them the weapon, he might have assumed they'd take it and leave, knowing the real assault weapons had been stashed with me and in the pit. He didn't care about a 32. Small caliber revolvers were for women's purses and close range, not for fighting Herodia draped in liquid armor. It was mom's anyway.

"Punch in the code then move away," The agent shouted.

"Beep, beep, beep, beep." Four digits, a long solid tone, the handle cranking downward and the suction sound of our safe door opening, he had relinquished his only weapon. It was astonishing how paper thin our walls were. I could hear everything. But could they hear me? The sound of a cylinder spinning and then six bullets dropping to the ground, Dad was completely unarmed.

"This all you have?"

"Yea, that's all."

"Tag it!" the agent said to another. I was surprised at how quickly they believed my dad's response and didn't seem interested in finding our other weapons, the ones jamming my kidneys, the AK47s. A small revolver wouldn't justify wearing liquid armor. It made little sense, but upon further reflection, it did. They weren't concerned about my parents, nor our weapons —collateral damage. They wanted me!

I was, as my father had insisted, safely under the stairwell, wedged far enough back that no one could see. The space was tiny. If by off chance they opened its door the normal reaction would have been to close it, noting that only a small cat could have squeezed into such a tiny space. No metal doors or thick concrete walls, no sophisticated electronics or video surveillance, just wood framing, dry wall and fiberglass insulation. The world's cheapest safe room, a worthy little bunker.

"Clear, Clear," the agents secured each room. Scurrying in unison, using their rifle butts to access each room. Closets, pantries, bathrooms, they checked everywhere, even the ceilings, smashing each door as they systematically covered each area.

They were masters of their own optics on the outside, but loud imposing sounds were their preferred psychological weapon once inside the homes of those they targeted.

Training me well in using firearms, I recited his golden rules for armed confrontation. At the top of his list, avoid whenever possible, analyze the odds, how many were there and how well armed was your enemy. Noting our own government as "the enemy" in my recitation about his rules of engagement gave me pause. This wasn't supposed to happen in America.

I waited patiently as they covered the house and focused on the unique sounds resonating from their boots pacing across a variety of floor coverings. Hardwoods and slate became remarkable sounding boards allowing me to track their movements throughout the house. First floor, broken glass on a slate floor, upstairs to our bedrooms, dense wooden echoes. "Clear! Clear! Clear!" Three bedrooms, two bathrooms and several closets, they'd be down here soon. My heart was pounding, my skin perspiring profusely, my breathing quickening, I experienced the full gamut of emotional and physical traits one would expect when being hunted. I can assure you — they are not pleasant.

The only part of the house that was carpeted, I strained to hear them as they headed down the stairs, listening as they whispered their next move. "Check the closets, under the bed and anywhere else he might hide," a deep, growling voice ordered the others. He was a smoker; the gurgling phlegm deep within his lungs exacerbated his attempts at carrying on a whispered conversation; most likely the leader. Why they whispered was a mystery. They were the hunters, and I was the hunted. No options for my escape, they had covered all possible exits.

They'd tag entire families as "subverts" even if only one member was the instigator. Social postings critical of the government were their first source for membership to that expanding group. Scanning those networks, while uploading our postings to their cloud, they isolated the most virulent bloggers for further watch. They upgraded the unrepentant and the vilest to A.C.T. status, although the process was slow. It could take a year. By detaining the entire family, they assured themselves of having at least one to leave behind as collateral for bad behavior should the other family members be released on good behavior and sent to infrastructure training. Mutually assured destruction on a small scale worked well.

Still, they watched us more closely as subverts than normal citizens with many upgraded by default to A.C.T. status. An unfortunate upgrade for some, a revered honor and rite of passage for many, but an eventual death sentence for all who failed to repent their beliefs and surrender their weapons. Many ignored their demands on principle alone, causing membership to grow exponentially.

Momentarily imagining that this was all just a nightmare and that I'd soon awaken safely in my bed, that thought vanished as I continued holding my breath in silence, fearing I'd pass out and never wake up at all. It was sweltering in that bunker and, dripping in sweat, I panicked as I watched the pooling puddles beneath me, rolling towards the door's edge.

"Move it, move it, move it!" The agent kept shouting at my

parents like a drill sergeant abusing his newest recruits.

Silence from Dad concerned me at first but, having no weapon and hearing no shots fired, I figured he went pacifist, politely following their orders like a cooperative prisoner hoping for a reprieve on good behavior. Silencers weren't standard issue. Their goal, should force be necessary, was always to instill maximum fear with the deafening noise from discharging their Glocks or Berettas. Effective at quelling crowds, even armed riotous ones, they were always at their sides. A reprieve wasn't what Dad was looking for. He wanted them to leave as soon as possible. His silent cooperation protected me. I was certain of that.

Left over insulation muffled my labored breathing, but my perspiration continued to pool beneath me and towards the door's edge. Staring at the shadow of a pair of boots propped against that door, I hyperventilated, fearing my cover would be blown and they'd soon be busting into my bunker.

The boots remained stationary at first, and then walked away, I took a shallow breath sensing that escape was not improbable.

"Looks like we missed him, I'm not picking up any signal," she whispered.

"You sure?" the leader demanded.

"Yes sir, picking up nothing, I've double checked," she insisted.

"What's this kid's name again?"

"Aiken, Aiken McHale."

"You know him?"

"Yes, a long time ago, knew his sister, not him."

The young, peaceful Citizen's Protection Force, one of Neville's pet projects, had been deputized as the brown shirts we always mocked them to be. It's that Nazi thing again. Somehow, having the word "force" after the word "protection" and a reworked peace symbol in your logo can cause considerable confusion as to your group's true intention as noted in the agency's mission statement.

"Peace, Honor, Duty." Billed as a 21st century Peace Corps, the collapse had caused mission creep, a term always reserved for the military and "peace" was removed from their objectives. She was one of them and I recognized her voice, a childhood friend of Cassi. She'd been to our house before.

"Sure this Aiken kid still lives here?" he repeated in a stern tone. Someone clearly wasn't happy with missing me.

And then she covered my pooled perspiration crossing the door with the soles of her red boots while her superior continued to grill her on her knowledge of my family and me.

"Don't know sir, we weren't close."

The whispering ceased, my perspiring slowed when they finally headed upstairs and out the front door, the smoker led the way. "Paint it!" he gurgled.

Painting roofs was their death notice, a marking visible to all that we were the enemy. A biblical reminder of sorts, but instead of blood on the door frame they used florescent yellow paint on our roofs, visible to returning drones tasked with completing their unfinished business. Their mark - a bright yellow "X."

Never sure if it was a Tagger for painting other roofs or a

Global Hawk for search and destroy, I remained motionless and silent for hours after they left, breathing at the slowest pace, drifting in and out of cognizance. It must have been one-hundred degrees in that hole, rendering heat detectors useless.

My sense of hearing, acute as it was, allowed me to hear the blood rushing through the veins in my ears, the rapid beat of my heart racing at marathon speed and my rhythmic breathing. "Calm down, calm down" I kept repeating to myself, hoping my organs would respond to that simple request not to go into overdrive.

Having left the back of our house exposed, I could hardly hear a low, steady humming sound similar to those toy planes we got as kids for Christmas or birthdays. Drifting back and forth, never up and down, I cringed, bearing down to detect what was flying above me. The spritzing sound like what you'd hear when passing a line-painter along an interstate highway, I was certain it was a Tagger. The sound continued for another minute and then stopped, giving precedence to a low humming sound of its engines, this time moving away, upward and out of earshot. They had tagged our home.

As sun set approached, I could hear the bats gathering. Not the flying type; displaced humans roaming in colonies searching for food, water, clothing or shelter; some to loot, hoping to find items to barter should their essentials run dry. They moved only at night. It was safer for them.

As time passed, they became increasingly more violent. You could sense their desperation as they'd meander through the neighborhoods. Starvation was wickedly destructive not only to the body but also the mind. The meek transformed in a matter of days. It was not a pretty sight.

A smashed door and a painted roof was a welcome-mat for the bats, knowing the residents and their weapons had already been removed and the Herodias were gone. Hordes of them roamed the streets hoping for a big score once the coast was clear. Keeping careful watch for roundups, knowing the houses were clean for picking and safe to occupy, they became nocturnal squatters. What they didn't know was that I was still a target or that my father had buried our food in the backyard, safe from marauders. Dad's "Armed and Dangerous" signs posted in our windows would no longer deter them.

This was my chance to join the colony and get some much-needed hydration before they moved on to more fertile pastures. There was nothing in plain view, my father made sure of that.

Waiting patiently for their arrival I remembered that there would be a price on my head and that starving bats would think nothing of turning me in for a reward. Not knowing how many there were or if they were armed I stayed put, keep quiet and let them ransack my home. There was nothing of value left to steal short of some TV's, artwork, clothing and furniture — nothing I needed.

My survival gear and food were safely buried in our backyard. Once I was sure they had left, I headed upstairs to quench my thirst. Any surveillance still in the area would consider me a bat breaking loose from the colony to squat for the night—nothing they'd care about. They hadn't shut the water off yet, another thing to be thankful for -- the inefficiencies of our new socialist system.

"You can discover what your enemy fears most by observing the means he uses to frighten you. They tagged our home to expose us to the rest of the world. Perhaps exposing them was what they feared most."

They say your entire life passes before your eyes as you approach death; a rapid summation of the good, bad and the ugly. Knowing I was too strong to be on the verge of dying, I was exhausted, hungry and thirsty but feared my capture even though the Herodia had left and the bats were just kids, starving and looking for the same sustenance I was. I thought only of my family.

It was the warnings my father fixated on, constantly repeating them like a demented lunatic that gave me pause, wondering how he was so prophetic in what he had predicted and why he had prepared well in advance for that moment. Sending me to that bunker with an arsenal of weapons at my side while insisting I never rescue them was not a momentary thought, but well planned. What did he know?

Time to Emerge from Bunker 7

* * * *

Even though it had been two years since the first onslaught of anarchy following the Great Collapse, hungry people, like living zombies, still combed every street searching for scraps of food, water or just a cool shelter to tame the oppressive heat that

August. Others derived pleasure from destroying stuff as if it was the last great accomplishment in their dismal lives; anarchy for the sake of anarchy. They were once called ANTIFA — Anti-Fascists! An odd bunch of losers.

Like locusts, once they had demolished all that was still standing and had cleared the place of every crumb and sense of civility, they'd move in packs to the next house or nearest neighborhood in search of another fertile field to destroy and annihilate. Some drove until their tanks ran dry, others walked until they collapsed from heat exhaustion, thirst or starvation. It was apocalyptic and, again, this was two years after the collapse.

Things hadn't gotten much better, but they'd still propagandize Neville's accomplishments 24/7 on the state-owned media. A nation at war with ourselves — it was "us" versus "them."

Our house, unlike most, wasn't vandalized; My father insisting we plaster our windows with warnings immediately following the collapse; "Warning, We Are ARMED" and my personal favorite "We Shoot First, Ask Questions Later," made sure of that.

In hindsight, not the smartest move when government thugs were roaming the neighborhood in search of armed Patriots or unrepentant subverts, but effective at keeping the zombies at bay. The gaping hole from the battering ram where our back door was once attached was the only damage we had suffered. We were unscathed after the first riots, but this time we were marked. No different from having one's house blown up — it was no longer habitable.

They had shut off my cell phone, effectively cutting me off from what little was left of my world. I removed the chip and battery, making sure I couldn't be tracked, but kept it for parts in case I needed some later.

Another advantage to our system -- agencies filled with workers who were not the most intelligent. Shutting my cell phone off was just plain dumb. They could have used it to track me.

I was perfectly diversified with Dad's doomsday fund buried six feet beneath mom's prized roses which had been replaced with gangly tomatoes. But, having only seeds to plant, boxes of pasta, dehydrated MRE's, a small sampling of canned food, but a decent supply of gas in our vault was not a long-term survivalist's dream. Having food and gas could be bartered for things I was short on. Dad's cash-stash was worth less than half of its original value.

We heeded most of Dad's advice, even during those paranoid times when his constant links to video clips headlined with "FEMA Banned," "The Beginning of the End" or some other catchy title would fill my morning email. I always assumed those videos were nothing more than a common internet marketing ploy whose only intentions were to enrich those that posted them rather than educate those who purchased them. Click-bait by conspiracy nut-cases looking to make a buck over some future event that might never happen accosted every generation. Clearly, I was wrong.

Unlike many who bought into those ploys, we didn't invest in the Chinese Yuan, gold or oil futures as was promoted; we bought seeds for planting the foods necessary for survival and kept that storage tank filled with precious high-grade gasoline. My mother canned fruits, vegetables and soups that could withstand a long shelf life. Dad left twenty-thousand dollars in the safe, but its value was less than ten grand two years later.

We kept two of our cars always with at least a half tank of gas and never parked together. Mine was left empty, a neighborhood away, license plates and VIN plaque removed fearing that a roundup would not only include our weapons but also our cars. A full tank of gas was easy prey for siphoning or outright theft and would do us no good once satellite-tracking boots were attached to the wheels of each vehicle. They were, but my Jeep was untouched.

All of this was accomplished without our neighbors' knowledge. When anarchy strikes, and the shelves are cleared from every food store in the nation and gas is no longer available, advertising your smart disaster planning isn't the most prudent strategy for warding off the hungry, the anarchists and bats.

A new cell phone, identity and somewhere to live topped my "must-do" list. I needed them quickly. I was worried about Cassi but would contact her later.

Achieving A.C.T. status forced me to become exceptionally cautious, almost paranoid in every move I made. Tagging our house magnified that paranoia. Finding friends would have to wait. Trust went out the window as substantial rewards were reason enough for anyone to turn on me. I became a recluse until I could sort things out and find a new place to call my home.

My primary objective was to mentally white-board then prioritize my next steps; where to live, how to access the Internet, obtain a new identity and when to use it. Name, date and place of birth, social security number, credit history and a P.O. Box as an address, all the basic building blocks for becoming a new citizen.

Although burner phones were still scarce, I knew where to get one quickly. Popular among Patriots, as most were forced off-the-grid, some entrepreneurial Patriots set up a secret supply house where bartering goods and services was the preferred currency in exchange for a phone. They were close by and I could easily walk there.

Foreclosures were common, so my confidence level was high that the pool of viable properties was reasonably deep. As much as I longed to stake a claim to one of the many abandoned mansions dotting the landscape of our sector, I knew it was best to take residence in a secluded little dump that had been vacated long before all hell broke loose. You never knew when the prior occupants of those enormous estates on the outskirts of Loudoun County would return to rebuild their lives or whose side they were on.

With no Internet access to scour foreclosures, I relied on memories to find the most suitable place to live - childhood memories. I remember a small house on the outskirts of Sector 79 that had caught my eye as a young boy, not because of the house, but because of a little girl who lived there - my first real crush. We had driven by it a hundred times on our way to Nutter's Creamery in Purcellville. I headed there.

House Hunting

* * * *

Tossing dad's old generator in the back of my Jeep, I headed due west along a narrow, winding country road running parallel to the busier Route 7. Expecting any home suitable for habitation might not have electricity, the generator would come in handy.

With gas rationed and prices still in the stratosphere, traffic was light on most roads, but groups of people walking aimlessly in varying states of confusion along the highways made it dangerous to stop or even slow down. Yep, two years after the collapse and this shit was still going on. Catastrophic zombies quickly learned that those who could afford to drive could also afford food, clothes and pretty much anything that had been looted from them during the riots. They weren't afraid to step right out into traffic to make you stop. Some saw it as a suicidal option to end their miserable existence. Keeping a steady foot on the pedal, I avoided eye contact with them and kept driving at blood splattering speed in case one of them decided to end their life.

Those Trips to the Ice cream Store

* * * *

Every Saturday evening during summer vacations, Dad would drive us for our weekly ice cream treat to Nutter's in the village of Purcellville, just a few miles away from home. Preferring the more scenic route, we'd pass an interesting old home set far enough back from the road and surrounded by enormous elm trees. You'd miss it if you didn't know where to look. I did and looked every time we passed it. I was obsessed with her.

Two stories with a clay-tile roof, mature moss draping down its sides and dark green European shutters that were always closed, keeping the house cool during the hot summer days even though it was shaded. Each window was adorned with planters filled with flowers. A huge lawn with a rope tire attached to a large elm tree and a small area towards the front with bocce balls scattered around was surrounded by tomato vines and a large vegetable garden. A red Alpha Romeo convertible was parked in the driveway. Mom adored that car.

It seemed out of place for Virginia, as if it had been transported from Italy and dropped into the middle of Loudoun County. Clay tile roofs weren't the norm, in fact, no one had them and I was surprised it had passed our strict zoning laws.

As closely as I paid attention to its architectural details, it was the girl, always swinging on the tire, smiling and waving enthusiastically at me that caught my maturing imagination. I convinced dad that Nutters was worth more frequent trips, so Tuesdays, Thursdays and Saturday became routine. The ice cream was nothing special but gosh, I finally understood what infatuation meant. Her long, auburn hair, engaging smile and searing sky-blue eyes became the focus of my daily day-dreaming when I was just starting to pay attention to girls. The last time we passed that house in the summer of 2015 the windows were shuttered including the lower level. The Alfa was gone as was she from the front yard.

Over time, the long gravel driveway became overrun by weeds and piles of trash were strewn everywhere. Bushes and trees were no longer pruned, the grass was knee high and the rope hanging from the elm tree was missing the tire that she swung on. The flowers that adorned the window boxes were mere stubs and the wood planks had rotted and were tangling from the window sills. It was abandoned.

Imagining the old house haunted with a history no one would speak of; I couldn't stop wondering about the owners and that girl. What were they like? Were they a happy family? What was her name? And, most important, what happened to them? While it would have been nice to know the answers to those questions, I desperately needed a place to call home and that house fit the bill. I headed up the long driveway, glancing in my rearview mirror making sure that no one had followed me. I always kept a careful eye on where I was going and where I had just been.

The trees and shrubs had grown beyond their suitable size, suggesting that the property hadn't been tended in years. The gravel driveway was now a pothole-laden strip of packed dirt and showed no visible signs of having been driven on recently — no tire tracks, no trash either, which suggested that strangers weren't wondering through that area — a good sign. I parked my Jeep outside the detached garage because the doors were locked. I was skittish about having my car visible by drones above, but there was nothing I could do. At least the tress were full enough to make it difficult to see from the air and I was far enough off of the main road that no one would see it when driving by. My plates were fake.

The smell upon entering, was musty but not offensive, and it was still furnished. The furniture was draped with simple white sheets that were themselves covered in several inches of dust, dead spiders and flies. If only humans could remain so remarkably intact after death, I'd reconsider my wishes to be cremated once I depart this world. The walls were barren and there were no pictures on the end tables at either side of the sofa. Beautifully inlaid Italian pieces were strategically placed around the room. Distressed wooden beams crossing a vaulted ceiling gave a church-like atmosphere to the interior, like a mini cathedral. A brass cricket lay on the fireplace mantle and a small gold cross necklace draped over it were signs of faith and good luck. Apparently God had let them down too. A roll-top desk to the right of the front door held family papers, several stacks of old mail and a leather-bound bible. Mail that was 15 years old could prove useful for reactivating the utilities, but the Bible was of no use. I was still pissed at God.

After taking it all in, I sat down in an overstuffed chair in front of the stone fireplace. Dust rose like a puff of smoke but I didn't care. It felt right, like home. I hadn't even gone upstairs or checked for power and water before closing my eyes and passing out.

Unwelcome Guest

* * * *

I awoke several hours later, pissed that I had nodded off in the middle of the afternoon without checking the entire property for signs of occupants or other things that might have caused concern for my safety. Yes, it was careless, but who could blame me. Spending two days in a hell hole with temperatures over one-hundred degrees, having never closed my eyes was both physically and mentally exhausting! I was officially a "Wanted Man" and constantly reminded myself of that wherever I went. I avoided the Post Office and kept my head down when walking in public.

Abandoned properties, while offering seclusion, also lacked in the amenities I took for granted. Hot water to bathe in, cold to drink, electricity and Internet with the flip of a switch — these were all missing. Darkness would soon be upon me and my only survival tool was a box full of candles. Time to start the generator which would bring normalcy to a place I was about to squat in. As I walked out the side-door towards my Jeep, I heard running water, a strong trickling, like rain striking pebbles. Someone was back there. Friend or foe?

Glancing back through the overgrown shrubs and towards the dry river bed I discerned the silhouette of what appeared to be a woman arching her back, washing her hair. It was auburn. An outdoor shower and an unwelcome guest, two things I hadn't expected. At eighteen, the thought of a young woman showering within eyeshot might have lowered my guard and heightened my visual senses but on that day, it raised both. I watched, feeling perverted while doing so. Was she armed, on the run, a Patriot or one of them? How did she get here and know of the shower?

As she turned off the water, I tossed a small stone in her direction hoping it might startle my unwanted guest, forcing her to show a weapon if she had one. It didn't, but she heard it.

"Who's there?" she asked and then gathered her clothes while slowly turning full circle, showing no concern that I was watching her. I had no answer.

"Turn around while I get dressed." She added.

There was a familiarity in her stride as she walked towards me, stepping over the broken stones and around the rising brush while never glancing down. As she emerged from the sun-drenched shadows of the backyard foliage, all I could think of was Patriot or enemy.

Auburn hair, searing blue eyes — she was that girl, just as I remembered twelve years ago swinging on the rope tire — my childhood infatuation, all grown up. Extending her hands towards mine, she introduced herself. "Tania and you?"

There are thousands of love stories, many ignited by a single phrase, or some pithy line meant to catch the attention of the one being pursued. "You had me at hello," "You complete me," or "Love means never having to say you're sorry." For me it was three words she said that day, just thirty-seconds into our meeting and I hadn't even mentioned my name yet.

"Can you cook?"

She had "guarded-trust" written all over her face and that went both ways — I did too. Unsure of her motives, I had a good sense that she was one of us.

"I'm not comfortable with my Jeep being visible to those damn drones. Be nice if we could get those garage doors open."

"I have a better solution." With that, she walked to the north side of the garage and pulled a huge canvas tarp towards my car, exposing and enormous wood chipper. Not exactly what I was hoping for, but at least my trust meter moved closer towards confirming her as a Patriot. Agreeing with my concern over surveillance drones was music to my ears.

"You hiding?" she asked.

"You hiding?" I replied.

"Yes," I said. "Yes," she answered but then followed with, "I'm trying to survive the mess we're all in but I'm damn glad to know you're ok."

I had so many questions to ask her as did she of me. For the rest of that afternoon we told each other stories from our past, our fears and our plans, but we got to know each other. And, yes, I fessed up to my childhood crush on her. She had the same on me.

My questions were the basic stuff. Do you live here? Why shower outside? Do you have a car? And, what do you do for a job? For her it was more probing, but I was all too willing to open up, including admitting that I was the guy who posted the Vega 7 video to YouTube. She seemed unfazed. My infatuation had returned and I couldn't help but remember the last time I saw her crying by the edge of the driveway. Why was she crying? But more important — why was that garage door locked and she unwilling to open it?

The Albertini Family

* * * *

Her real name was Mary Teresa Albertini, a good Catholic girl's name but, like me, the Great Collapse and our being hunted forced her to change it. Tania Pinazza became her post-apocalyptic identity. Still Italian but not as biblical as her birth name. She had a twin sister — an identical one, making me wonder — if I was infatuated with the right one. It didn't matter. Her sister, Odessa, was dead. Odessa, an odd name for a strict Italian Catholic family prone to naming their children with Biblical implications. It was Russian.

She had been living there for the past two years after returning from Italy where her parents still lived. The electricity worked and water still flowed through the faucets, but she'd shut them off each day before leaving for work, not wanting squatters to enter and take up residents or just destroy the place. She'd turn them back on once she returned home from New Columbia.

Hers was a family very much like mine. A Patriotic but conspiratorial father, a sister who pushed the boundaries of their

strict Catholic upbringing and a mother who drank excessively —
whiskey, an entire bottle throughout the day and Prosecco at
night, which Tania called her "happy intoxicant," perfect for
putting her to sleep. "She was a mean drunk."

"So was mine," I added.

I was twenty-four and still harbored that infatuation with
her. I'm not a very emotional guy but will admit that her
stunning beauty reignited those immature feelings because, to be
honest, I knew nothing about her. It was completely physical. All
I knew was that I preferred damaged goods — making her a
perfect partner. Love and infatuation, are different. Time was the
missing ingredient that made me fall in love with her that first
day, but not before we had spent hours discussing our families,
what had happened to us and, most important, where our
alliances were.

For the next two days, we talked, we drank, she cried and
my shoulder became her favorite place to shed those tears. She
slept upstairs in her bedroom while I dusted off that couch and
used it as my bed. "Chivalry was not dead," I told her, even
though I had little desire to be chivalrous. Infatuation turned to
lust, and that couch felt like a bed of nails. It was tortuous.

As the days past, those shared experiences, fearing for our
safety in a world turned upside down, I fell in love or I thought I
had. Love takes time, something I hadn't much of, so I
convinced myself that this was it. There weren't those butterflies
in your stomach feelings as most bear witness to, but instead a
total respect for what she had gone through, her strength and
determination to survive, her faith and yes, her stunning beauty.

On the third night she asked that I move upstairs and abandoned the couch. As they say — the rest is history — yours.

Her parents owned a small Italian restaurant on 15th Street, one block from the White House. Il Portico was popular among government bureaucrats, especially Herons who could afford its lofty prices. Authentic, Northern Italian cuisine, with her mother, Carla, as the chef, her father, Massimo, the maître d' and the two daughters doing everything else. Mary waited tables, Odessa bussed and helped wash the dishes. Like all good Catholic families, they closed every Sunday. Great food, friendly service and — your mother, the hot, underage, auburn waitress that every customer wanted to date, but couldn't. The best little Italian restaurant in all of DC.

Being underage would force older men with thoughts of lust in their hearts a moment of pause but, with Herons, that critical detail never crossed their minds. Morals were lacking to such a great degree that any father with an ounce of intelligence would never allow their daughters to work for one. She told humorous stories of attempted conquests by the lecherous Herons, most of whom were old enough to be her father.

Her father kept a careful eye on his girls and his guests, making sure that the two never mingled beyond taking their orders, clearing the table or whispering the family's not-so-secret Bolognese sauce recipe. She'd leave out the most important ingredient, a touch of goat's cheese folded in just before finishing. The male patrons convinced themselves that Tania had given that secret recipe only to them. She used that ploy frequently, which resulted in increased tips. She was a crafty little liar and proud of it, but also one hell of a story teller. In her own words, she bragged that she was masterful at physically teasing those who should have known better with her searing blue eyes while mesmerizing them with her quick, biting whit.

Odessa's Death

* * * *

That tearful moment at the edge of her driveway, that I had witnessed nine years prior, was the turning point in that family's lives, especially hers. At fourteen-years-old, her twin sister, Odessa, drowned in a shallow river behind the house one warm summer night when the parents were out for the evening. A freak accident, the investigators proclaimed, yet Tania knew otherwise. Odessa was an excellent swimmer, making her drowning in waters just two feet deep seem improbable. Her father, convinced that "It was God's will," never pursued the truth. It wasn't. God doesn't "will" those sorts of things and Tania knew better.

A young man was with her that evening but Tania never mentioned it, trying to keep her sister's year-long crush a secret from old world parents who didn't understand that kids did that stuff; holding hands, kissing and, in Odessa's case, skinny dipping in the shallow river behind the house with a man fifteen years older than her. One thing led to the next, and it wasn't mutual consent. Cause of death: slipping on the rocks, hitting her head knocking her unconscious face down in the shallow water — drowning. Tania held that secret, scared that her parents would never forgive her for not telling them the truth. She dressed her sister while she lay dead in the river, not wanting to give her father any reason to be suspicious. She hated that young man and vowed revenge but never followed through. His name was Barry Levin, a former Congressman disgraced for sexual improprieties just before the collapse and soon to be out of prison.

They returned Odessa's body to her birthplace in Valdobbiadene, Italy and buried her next to their Grandmother.

"Can you cook?" She asked again.

"Of course," I replied, stunned at what she had just told me and how she crafted every detail of her story with little emotion attached to her sister's death which was, in fact, murder.

I exaggerated my culinary skills and offered a verbal resume that allowed me to start as sous chef the following day. She needed help, and I needed the money. I was a great cook. Alcoholic mothers never cook meals — they drink them, so I did what mom couldn't, and I did it well.

As nice as it was to learn of Tania's family, her heartbreaking past, and to be able to hone my cooking skills at her family restaurant, I remained focused on those garage doors which she had yet to open in my presence.

And then, without my asking, she grabbed my hand and led me outside to the garage doors. "Come. I want to show you something."

The Great Reveal - The Garage

* * * *

Pulling a key from her purse, she unlocked each door. On the right was her black van and beyond the left door was something similar to what my father had done in our backyard — an enormous pit. The garage differed from what you'd expect in that part of northern Virginia. Its floor wasn't paved concrete, it was hard-packed dirt. I was in awe at how meticulously he had laid it out, straight lines with stakes at each end tied together by twine which were still tight, even after nine years. The walls in the pit were straight and smooth like drywall. Much care and precision went into its construction.

The pit was ten feet deep, eight feet wide, fifteen feet long and resembled a service bay for oil changes at Jiffy Lube. Splintered plywood with dirt glued to its surface covered it. The wood had rotted, so she walked around it instead of on top. I slid the plywood back and shoved it beneath her van. The old man was preparing for a catastrophic disaster. He had filled his pit with many of the post-apocalyptic stuff that my father stored in ours. Kindred spirits — they were both preppers. He began planning for his family's survival, years before the Great Collapse and had covered the four basic principles of post apocalyptic preparedness — stocking months worth of food, and water, creating suitable shelter for hiding and having an arsenal of weaponry available.

The impressive arsenal he had accumulated showed his

understanding of the variety of weapons that one needed to quell any armed resistance. Several shot guns, an array of semi-automatics, three Glocks, Benellis, a 308 and a 22-rifle with a long scope had been hung on racks on the far wall. Close-range, distant, maximum automatic fire power and, the silent killers. Cases of ammunition stacked on top of each other, lined an entire wall to the left. Thousands upon thousands of rounds were boxed and labeled. Like my father, he had stashed several gallons of gasoline, oil and some extra tires for his cars. Hanging conspicuously on the wall next to the gun racks were four military grade gas masks. Now that's something my father hadn't considered.

The front wall was lined with whisky bottles and Prosecco, apparently for mom — tons of arborio rice, pasta, canned tomatoes and vegetables on a baker's rack lined the right wall. MRE's, powdered eggs and milk were shoved under the booze. While the well in the back of the property was a constant source for fresh water, he had also carefully bottled that water in case it ran dry. Pictures of Jesus, crosses and statues of the Virgin Mary were everywhere. I could imagine my father with his whole "bless this" routine. "Bless this garage," he would have said, even though Tania's dad had already done so.

God intervening again? I'll never know for sure, but taking up residence in that house with its hidden treasures, family secrets and the beginnings of what eventually became my most important space made me reconsider my skepticism towards those four words, In God We Trust. It wasn't the food or booze that attracted my attention — it was the arsenal in that big ole beautiful hole in the ground with a small tunnel leading up and out to the back of the garage. Most important in God's intervention, though, was meeting your mother, Tania.

She returned to Italy two months later. Her father, at death's doorstep, was reason enough to leave Sector 7 in a hurry. Her confidence in my ability to run Il Portico must have given her some solace that her father's dream was in good hands. Vowing to never return to Sector 7, she continued making the lease payments on Il Portico for as long as she could. They owned the house free and clear, I paid only the utilities. Ours was perhaps the briefest love affair in history - at least it was in mine.

Before returning to Italy, she grabbed my hand and led me back to the garage as if we were heading to a secluded area for one final sexual encounter before leaving. I couldn't imagine what other secrets she had hidden within that garage or beneath the plywood covered flooring. She reached into a small hole in the wall covered by a picture of Jesus, grabbed a bible and then handed it to me. You can imagine my initial disappointment when being presented with a book I had little interest in. She saw the disappointment on my face and seemed to understand. Book-marked with my father's favorite section, a passage about Joshua and God's mission for him, gave me pause. "The Lord works in mysterious ways," my father was fond of saying. Now that one - I believed.

"Keep this with you." she said.

"I will." And then I recited the passage, verse and chapter number to her which wasn't noted in that Bible. "Joshua 8:1-35"

"So they are now told to take all the fighting men and to go forth at God's command trusting in the fact it was God who would give them victory." She was impressed and smiled back at me with a look that, to this day, I'm convinced was her tacit approval for the mission I had yet to embark on. She knew I wanted vengeance for my family and that her house would serve me well.

"You need to change your name," she reminded me.

"I will," I replied as the thought of Joshua entered my mind.

The following week, she left.

Identity Crisis

* * * *

It surprised me how common and easy it was to change one's name. People changed them for many reasons. Either they didn't like the name their parents gave them, it was hard to pronounce or spell, or it sounded stupid like, Summer Day. But the biggest reason was to escape the perils of being listed on the government's A.C.T. list. Those who changed them also altered their appearance as did I. Having your picture posted on a Post Office wall with an award offered for your capture was a constant temptation for being ratted out by old enemies or penniless friends. Refusing to turn over your guns or worse, speaking out against the tyrannical institutions that governed us were sure tickets to being "posted." Thank God I never made the wall.

Video cameras and hidden microphones were an accepted part of life, necessary to keep a careful eye and ear on Patriots or criminals — one-in-the-same to them. But when securing data through many government systems, they were as screwed up and inefficient as we always knew them to be. Social Security, Medicaid, Medicare, even voter registration and driver's licenses were a crap shoot if you were expecting to get accurate results. There was no sharing across the different departments because their systems didn't connect. Hacking was a growth industry and, before the collapse, someone targeted their most critical systems. I had friends who regarded it as a career. Weird, but they were heroes.

Breached systems, lost data, the whole network was a colossal mess. But the FBI's facial recognition network worked pretty well and there were forty-million innocent citizen's images on those systems, including everyone who owned a gun. I'm sure my fathers was on there, but not mine.

I was fortunate to have been digitally savvy most of my life, knowing that social media was the enemy of those who had posted pictures or videos of themselves doing idiotic stuff. Being a photography buff put me behind the lens for all of our family pictures. I never posted selfies on Facebook and was pretty much non-existent on social media except in private groups approved by my father. Sure — I posted shit; cartoons, memes with someone's stupid comments dropped in, but never my picture, I preferred avatars. I closed my eyes, grew a beard and slicked my hair back like a greaseball from the sixties for my driver's license. Bad hair didn't bother them but closing your eyes would piss them off. After the third try, the old hag at the DMV screamed at me "Fine, we've got people waiting." The picture wasn't flattering and looked nothing like me, just as I had intended.

All one had to do was to drop into the DMV, tell them someone stole or destroyed your license and birth certificates and Voila, they'd give you a new one with whatever creative name you came up with. It was a "Get Out of Jail Free" card for those of us who took that route to being reborn. As for an address, which they required, I made one up — it didn't exist. For once, the unintended consequences we'd rail against when debating stupid government policy, played to our advantage. The original intent for allowing this ease of changing identity was to give illegal aliens the documents necessary to access government benefits and, more important, to vote — for them. For the Patriots — it allowed us to be reborn in a secular manner in a country that despised our former identity. Having an employer I slept with and who had also changed her identity made the entire process a breeze.

While searching through my tattered wallet for cash to pay the DMV, I pulled out that Bible verse that your mother had given me and knew at that moment what my new name would be, Joshua Hunter. Just as after the death of Moses, God intended for Joshua to carry the battle forward, I was convinced that his intentions were the same for me. I was still dealing with lost love and an identity crisis, but the DMV accepted my story and handed me my new license. Joshua Hunter.

The Perils of Being Reborn

* * * *

Changing my identity came with its own perils because having to find new friends while avoiding old ones was time consuming. Altering my appearance was the next logical step in my identity make-over. By dying my hair dark brown, and then cutting it much shorter than I preferred, adding thick eyebrows, which God failed to bless me with, and then muscling through a daily regimen of hypertrophic routines, I gained a small sense of security when being out among society's criminals, traitors and old friends. It also gave me incredible strength and a level of confidence that I could thwart any physical threat should one come my way. I was buff!

As I became more confident that I could mingle within society, I learned to be alert and to avoid potential predatory strangers who, like vampires, came out in droves once the sun had set. I had honed my skills at recognizing pending dangers and could alter my gait from a casual saunter to a quickened pace without drawing attention to myself. But, most important, I had mastered the art of altering direction should an old friend be heading my way, which only happened once. Most had left the area after the collapse or had died in the riots. I was a loner and having to start over with a new social circle. Social media became my new playground and the perfect place to expand my network. I joined a private group of like-minded Patriots whom I enjoyed bantering with every single day. A cast of characters spread out across the country, so smart, yet so virulently anti-Neville that, had they known what I was about to do, I think they would have joined my private Army. They were my best friends, yet we had never met — at least not in the beginning.

Monday through Saturday, I ran Il Portico. It kept my body and spirit busy, but having to deal every day with customers, most of whom were my enemy, ignited my thoughts with delusions of grandeur as Joshua Hunter — Patriot Soldier fighting the resistance. My colleagues at the restaurant were themselves Patriots and knew exactly why I had altered my appearance. No one questioned it — a few said I looked better and then followed the comment with sly wink.

Il Portico

* * * *

Human contact, free food and a way to distract myself from the daily hell I was going through made working there a pleasure. Although those human contacts, most of our customers, were people I despised. Being able to hone my culinary skills by learning from Maurizio gave me more than I had bargained for and eventually led to my becoming head chef and running the place. Maurizio returned to Italy — family related stuff. Socializing daily with the Herons I would later call my subjects, made working as a chef also a reconnaissance mission for which I was paid. Funny how things work out.

Restaurant critics called it quaint, but all that meant was

small and old in a modern city still reeling from the riots. Upon walking in through the inlaid wood doors, it transported me to some tiny little joint in the smallest town in all of Italy. At least that's how I envisioned one to be — rustic wood beams, stuccoed walls and round tables covered in what everyone thinks Italian joints should cover their tables with — red and white checkered tablecloths. Fresh garlic hung from the rafters emitting an enticing scent that evoked a sense that good food was being prepared — and it was. Plates hung from the wall with glazed images of pasta, fruits and vegetables. Open to the dining room was its small kitchen exposing a back wall covered with old copper pans, utensils and, a picture of Jesus. An ornate silver cross positioned just above the door leading into Massimo's old office at the back added another layer of grace and faith to the place. The good Lord's image offended some clients — they'd point at it and sneer. I had fully expected some of them to begin writhing in pain from Jesus' picture and that cross that held him. Isn't that what spawns of Satin do when confronted with Christianity?

My father would have loved Il Portico — great food and blessings at every turn. Seating was limited, enough for thirty. I paid myself a small salary — always in cash. Il Portico was a favorite among high ranking Herons on unlimited government expense accounts even though they weren't doing the nation's business while dining there. It was a haven for mid-day rendezvous with mistresses and like-minded traitors from abroad. Massimo knew that and, although conflicting with his Catholic faith, he covered the front windows with a heavy blood-red drape trimmed in ornate gold, to prevent gawkers from peering in and snapping pictures of the slimy tyrants as they dined while slipping their hands up the skirts with whoever they shouldn't be with. He protected his customers.

Perfect combination — romantic, great food, discreet and, for me, profitable and the easiest place for reconnaissance of my enemies. I worried that Tania's departure would cause some to find other outlets for their Italian addiction, which Il Portico served with her as a side dish for their more lurid fascinations.

Bad habits are hard to change, even harder to expose when you control all segments of the Government and of the media that failed to report on those digressions. It didn't take long for past bad behavior to resurface after the purge of 2018 when it appeared as though every one of our Congressional leaders, media personalities and professors were guilty of some sexual misbehavior, the vast majority of whom were from the other side of the aisle. Corruption and sexual misdeeds had risen to new heights after the collapse and, through that job, I became privy to some of the most bizarre conversations. I'd frequently walk into the dining area to shoot the breeze with the customers, but my real reason for socializing with those I hated was to build a Rolodex of their behaviors, friends, enemies, mistresses — you name it. Like they had done to us, I placed tiny recording devices under the tables which activated by my cell phone. One must be proactive in life and business, and that decision yielded pay dirt on many occasions.

It was remarkably easy to steer their conversations towards sordid topics, and then eaves drop on them later in the privacy of my living room. They were proud of their conquests. In some small sense, I was very much like them, but instead of getting my jollies from watching, mine came from listening closely and taking notes on everything they said. Bribery was always on my mind should funds get low or business slump. Those recordings helped build the foundation for their final events. Payback's a bitch.

Herons loved to talk. Unlike Patriots, who feared being captured on video or picked up by random microphones saying unflattering things about our leaders, they had no worries, or at least they thought they didn't. Joshua was listening. They'd debate ideology, trash their enemies and praise their comrades, over a bowl of pasta and then move on to the perverse as they stuffed their faces with desert. They'd discuss mistresses over Tiramisu, but occasionally would comment on how well their movement was going and that the end-game of instilling communism as our form of government was close to being fulfilled. These were the soldiers and Generals of D6 and it wasn't the next battle plan they discussed, it was their terms of our surrender

I tried hard to obey God's commandments, but it didn't take long for that moral obedience to wain. Although I had fantasized about poisoning my first subject by crushing up some slow acting, undetectable atophan and then placing it into his pork chop, his lack of moral character wasn't what made him my initiation into the criminal world of murder. It was a single sentence he shouted through a bull horn in Sector 79 where my sister Cassie lived that lit that match. Those words — "Find the mothers of future rebels. Find the rebel chicks." They found her.

They killed her. It's ironic that a Man-of-God was the match that allowed me to burn that sixth commandment from his dubious list.

Caterpillars become beautiful butterflies, tadpoles turn into frogs. It was upon hearing the devastating news of my sister's death that Aiken McHale became Joshua Hunter, a name with biblical and now, occupational undertones.

The Trigger

* * * *

Homer once said: "The difficulty is not so great to die for a friend, as to find a friend worth dying for." I found that friend, and she was my sister, Cassie.

I can't overemphasize my belief that everyone's capable of committing murder but, most ignore the urge and find more suitable outlets to deal with those they despise. Shooting ranges or boxing rings work well at reducing the stress associated with having hatred in one's heart. Bad marriages end in divorce, the bully who taunted you as a kid meets karma and those jerks who cut you off in a fit of road rage get caught by the state police and lose their license. Karma — Justice served! When murder at the hands of some well choreographed riot pitched as a peaceful protest ginned up by a fraudulent man of the cloth visits one's family, all bets are off. It's that seminal moment when one faces the preverbal fork in the road having to choose to turn left, right or going straight ahead. I became obsessed with the Reverend and imagined him dead — at my hands. Looking back now, I can confirm that this single event changed my personality, setting my path in a direction I would have never imagined. It's what made my last name so appropriate - Hunter!

Her full name was Cassiopeia, a difficult name for a little kid to pronounce when I was still learning to count on my fingers. I shortened it to Cassie, and it stuck.

I headed to Columbia, South Carolina to retrieve her body. Six-hundred eighty-two miles south along I-81 and then a straight shot down I-77. It was hot as hell that day, triple digits, with humidity in the sauna range. Cruising at seventy miles-per-hour with the windows down because the air conditioning system was on the fritz, made the trip seem longer than normal. But, with little traffic to impede my excessive speeding, it was bearable. Sweltering heat and oppressive humidity are a horrible combination when one is not in a normal state of mind. Add to that a high school gymnasium with intermittent cooling as a morgue and you could appreciate if I had decided to randomly shoot anyone who looked cross-eyed at me. I made two mental notes that day, stalk the Reverend and get Freon.

Ten hours of windshield time to reflect on my relationship with Cassie wasn't easy since much of it had been shrouded in sibling rivalry. As I entered high school, we reached a state of peaceful coexistence — detente. She became my closest ally and best friend and was always willing to interject relationship advice even though hers were usually disasters. I'd have done anything for her as would she for me. I loved my sister.

As I merged onto 81-South my thoughts switched from what Cassie had gone though to the emotional stress of planning her funeral. Casket or cremation? Sector 79 or somewhere else? — Inviting friends or private? Questions I had given little thought to but knew needed my immediate attention.

Hilton Head Island

* * * *

Everyone has that favorite place on earth, a retreat for relaxation, or just to escape life's abuses. Mine was three hours southeast of Columbia, an island where old grudges faded away and I grew up, It was Cassie's too. I chose cremation, no guests, and I'd scatter her ashes into the sea. I knew exactly where I'd do it. We had walked that stretch of beautiful white sand many times before. The thought of a send-off into the cool blue Atlantic ocean with only me to witness brought tears to my eyes. I cried for at least twenty-miles.

Hilton Head — our island escape from whatever needed escaping from. She, from some idiotic boyfriend or the stress of college life and me from parents who were getting more difficult to live with.   Two miserable kids, each finding solace on a tiny stretch of beach off the coast of South Carolina.

As a kid, anticipating arrival on the island while dad meandered down I-95 at exactly the posted speed was insufferable. I'd count every damn South-of-the-Border billboard with Pedro telling me how many miles until we hit South Carolina. It was four hours further. Cassie would blast her annoying rap music, mom buried her face deep into some novel and dad seldom spoke. I loved those trips because happiness was always on that island and my parents, ever so briefly, tiptoed into a state of normalcy.

Wide, snow white expanses dotted with enormous homes but never high-rises, each spread far enough apart to claim their own private beaches. It was paradise and one of those enormous houses was to be my future crib. "Keep dreaming," Dad would say.

With staircases descending both sides of a pristine white deck that stretched from one end to the other, teenagers sporting binoculars peering at the hot life guard tending Station 16 always packed it. Two widow's peaks and six skylights dotted the pitched cedar shake roof. Straight palmetto palms on each side framed an infinity pool positioned dead center of the house atop a rock wall with gently cascading water falls. Randomly placed across the deck were massive, square, black umbrellas and plenty of chairs and chaises to relax in. I imagined huge parties with a guest list of celebrities swilling champagne and martinis, waiters passing finger food and a band playing smooth jazz in the background. A perfect compliment to my Master's victory. Dad was right, "keep dreaming, son." We were big dreamers back then and, for me, reality hadn't set in. America was great.

It was during that last trip that Cassie had convinced me to lay off of the Xbox, certain that I was joining the ranks of the basement-dwelling geeks she despised. She wasn't a big fan of Queek. Shaming me into dropping the controllers and reacquainting me with my golf clubs, I can say that she turned my life around during that final trip to Hilton Head. Three days was all it took. Cassie's uncanny knack for turning life's adversities into hope, always seeing the glass half-full was her most endearing trait.

Downing our last bowl of shrimp grits at the Quarter Deck in Sea Pines, she made that clear, posing a clever life analogy that stuck with me. My bucket list littered with materialistic garbage like Ferraris, huge yachts and cribs on that island wouldn't come easily to those at the bottom of their graduating class. My parents frequently lectured me on that, but Cassi's approach made more sense. Shrimp grits for each, two beers for her and a coke for me, life's simple pleasures seemed even more enjoyable in her company while sitting on the back bay.

That last quest to our island ended with the sun rising in my rearview mirror peaking above the Atlantic as we made our way up the Cross Island Expressway and over a bridge with no name. We looked at each other, silently acknowledging that our sibling rivalry had ended as we headed back to reality on the mainland — she, back to college to break up with her loser boyfriend and me home to County High and a more focused approach to life and my education.

"You'll be fine Aiken and, who knows — maybe one day we'll both live there." Those were her last words as we crossed over to the mainland. She believed in me.

One Final Act of love

* * * *

Emily Dickinson once said, "I would want more sisters, that the taking out of one might not leave such a stillness."

Funerals — I had attended two and both were depressing, although my grandfather's less so. I was seven when he died and, best I can remember, he was an ass. His death was a mere blip on my juvenile screen of emotions. I dealt with it well, my mother told me. My father assumed that I didn't care. He was right.

The second was more devastating. Cancer, a twelve-year-old boy. Why does God do that? Now I'd be handling Cassie's and, although her friends would have wanted to pay their last respects, I passed on having a formal funeral and opted for cremation instead. The thought of rotting in some wooden box, six feet under, especially on a cold, moon-lit night when the ground freezes solid like a block of granite, frightened her. She'd remind me every time we'd pass a cemetery on bitter cold nights where a dusting of snow caused the reflecting moon to light up the tombstones. "Damn, never do that to me Aiken."

Obsessed with death, she wanted to share her remains like children tossed between parents from a divorce. I had a lock on Christmas. Families were mobile and, by her logic, burial in Sector 7 would inconvenience those who wanted to visit her if they had moved away. The thought of having no flowers or worse, wilting ones, bothered her.

Ashes in an urn were mobile, like a valuable work of art being moved from one museum to the next. She was a work of art. But now, I had no one to share her with. The ocean was all I could offer. She would have wanted the whole urn and ashes thing but notifying her friends was too risky.

Having no one there for your final send-off is worse than dying alone or getting fired from a job and then escorted out of the building before you can say "goodbye, pleasure working with you" to your colleagues. There's no dignity in either. I couldn't do that to Cassie. What exactly is the proper number of mourners, anyway?

Finding Cassie

* * * *

Three hundred sixty-two people died in Sector 79 that week and The Rev was the match that lit the fire. They set up a series of public facilities to store the bodies because the county morgues were over-capacity. Having air conditioning was a perquisite for being approved to handle the overflow. Apparently the word "working" was missing from that memo. I found Cassie at her sector's temporary morgue with basketball hoops at each end, bleachers tucked away to maximize limited space and victory banners surrounding the perimeter. Go Wolverines! Eight straight rows crossing the gymnasium, with bodies, some covered in blue plastic sheets, made for the bad optics of death competing with school pride. It was surreal.

Shocked and in tears, most walked with a determined purpose down each row dazed but respectfully lifting sheets searching for their loved ones. A small sense of relief would capture their expression when discovering that theirs was not the victim they had just exposed. Moments later, that expression changed as they found what they had come for. Parents, children, brothers, sisters and loved ones, the look was the same, shock and devastation. Those were expressions I had seen before and hoped to never see again. I saw it up close and personal that day.

In the back corner was a young woman, sobbing uncontrollably while sitting on the floor by two young children, probably hers. They had turned a most horrible shade of ashen gray, like characters in a black and white movie, there was no color, not even a hint. Hands to her head, she screamed over and over, rocking back and forth with each outburst "Why, why, why?" I bowed my head to her and she did the same back at me.

Unlike TV crime dramas where family members break down in tears and uncontrollable anguish after identifying a loved one's body at the city morgue, I did neither. Laying center court, bruised, eyes still wide open and fluids oozing from everywhere, I froze and stared like a kid who had just seen his first dead body. Rage, sorrow, vengeance, the mind can conjure up a wealth of emotions but vengeance stayed with me for weeks afterwards. It was most potent. That was my sister.

After the collapse everyone knew the smell of death, but after three days of lying on a gymnasium floor where the air conditioning was erratic and the outside temperatures in the high nineties, that smell morphed into an unbearable, gag inducing stench. I struggled but conjured a mental whiff of her favorite perfume while shoving a wad of gum into my mouth to start the flow of saliva. Chanel, her favorite perfume, something I'd tease her about because of its popularity among elderly grandmothers. I asked the skinny old man hovering over her body how long she had been there.

"Read the tag, two days ago. We clear them after four. You're lucky you found her," he added, lacking any emotion one might expect from someone in that position. They carted off the unclaimed like Monday morning's trash, ending their final journey in some potter's field on the outskirts of the city. It was inhumane but so was everything else around that sector. Leaning forward I grabbed the tiny white tag attached to her right big toe. On one side were four numbers and several words, scribbled illegibly, most likely by a physician. 6835. I couldn't decipher the words, but snapped a picture of that tag with my phone in case someone else could. Morbid, but knowing the cause of death and what those numbers meant was important. On the other side, as the old man had said, was a date; August 23rd. Cassie died on her birthday. It's sad when people die on Christmas day or even New Years Day, but their birthday — that's coincidence of the worst kind and therefore even more depressing!

Morbid curiosity overcame me as I began to systematically examine tags from the others who were nothing more than strangers. Tomorrow's pick up would be a big one. Each body on either side, across and behind me were at their four-day expiration date. No one came for them. Humans being carted away like milk or meat that had met their expiration date in a grocery store. Inhuman was all I could think about. Ligature marks around Cassie's throat and bruises all over her face and body suggested a severe beating and strangulation. She suffered as some asshole pummeled her, slowly strangling the life out of her. Gun shots would have been more humane if that's even possible. Even though I had walked through the valley of the shadow of death, I feared no evil. A biblical reference, but a small turning point in my life.

I made the call to Shives Funeral Home and waited two hours after being promised that it would take 45 minutes. An old black van with no windows, a large Shives' decal on both sides in gilded gold, dents and scratches on the bumpers and front hood rolled up to the school; the driver motioning me to help carry her. He had no help. Cassie despised vans, especially black ones, but having no windows was her telltale sign that what was going on inside was never good! She was right and it bothered me that her last ride was in something that so terrified her, she'd look the other way when one would pass.

I quivered while helping slide her rigid body into the back of a van which was covered with tattered padding that had seen better days. I never understood the term "dead weight," but now know it to mean heavier than expected when a one-hundred-ten pound girl seemed like so much more. There were no body bags to mask that odor or to capture leakage but Ben covered her with a plain white sheet he had folded haphazardly on the passenger's seat. Ben was the driver, his name embroidered on his wrinkled, black shirt. He smelled as though he hadn't showered in days.

That scent differed completely from the odor of death, but was just as nauseating.

"I'm sorry about this," he offered. "Friend or family?"

"Sister." He looked down then shook his head and offered me a lift to the home. I agreed and went with him.

"Rough week, huh?" I inquired, thinking it might elicit some flavor of what triggered the riots. It didn't,

"Yep. That gymnasium was one night's work and that's not the only place I've been picking them up."

"Why no body-bags?"

"Stolen. Not sure why anyone would want em." I could, so I asked about them.

"What's the best bag to use?"

"Body-Seal, why?"

"Curious, that's all."

Ben explained, in greater detail than needed, how dead bodies expel fluids, and he wasn't talking about just blood. Urine, feces, pretty much everything. Impossible to rip open with an air-tight seal, I became interested in these marvels of human storage. I was already planning my next move. Another seminal moment, slow suffocation and no need to transfer the body. Killing two birds with one stone, so to speak.

"Tell me something, how were most victims killed? Guns, knives, beaten?"

"Everything, but a lot of beatings. I'll gurney her from here. Speak with Jake, he's the owner and can take care of you."

Cassie's final sendoff

* * * *

Cremation was quick, no heavenly mood music piped through a sound system or dim lighting to hide your tears. Like an assembly line, there were fourteen others waiting in cue for that short trip down the purple conveyor belt which was braided in gold, and then into the oven. It took an hour, so I waited in the chapel and planned revenge. I chose a simple, cheap brass urn because that's all they had, then returned to the school with Ben and her ashes to pick up my car. Gently laying her remains beside me on the passenger seat, it was on to Hilton Head and her final farewell. The urn was bubble wrapped to prevent spillage. Nice touch! I cried the entire way to the island.

The smell of sunscreen, yesterday's greasy fries and that briny salt air as the morning waves slowly sucked to eternity accosted my senses, bringing back fond memories of a better time with her. Our peaceful coexistence was brief but I am a better person for having known her but a more evil one for having seen her in that state of physical abuse and then having to scatter her ashes alone into the sea.

Walking over the cool white sand dunes and turning right, I headed up the beach towards that enormous home with the expansive white deck. The infinity pool was empty and several spindles were missing from the railings which had rotted, but the Palmetto Palms were taller than when we had last seen them. An old woman peeked over the broken rails, staring with her head pointed upward to the heavens. The house was a wreck and she hadn't aged well, looking more like a homeless person than the dignified woman I remembered from a few years before.

An entire life reduced to three pounds of ashes. Such a tragedy: Ashes to ashes, dust to dust, I hated those words but whispered them as I poured hers into the gentle breeze I had hoped would carry her soul across the waves and onward to eternity. Cremated remains are bone fragments that have been mechanically reduced, rendering an ash to the consistency of dust, similar to what you'd find in your fireplace, but denser. Hers dropped onto the beach like sand slipping through my fingers, there was no upward lift. Disappointing, but it was my first attempt.

Most people have difficulty dealing with death. I don't, it's the mourning that I struggle with. When forced to mourn a loved one and to celebrate that life alone, this is God's cruelest punishment for the survivors. Kneeling in the sand I prayed to the good Lord to protect her soul but never asked forgiveness for me. The point was moot as I was already planning to eliminate his foundational commandment, the sixth.

I did not understand how high up the food chain I'd be going or how far adrift from morality I'd venture. I never intended to lead my life that way, but circumstances had altered my moral compass and Julian Kilgore, who I had yet to meet, quickened that pace. God will judge me when the time is right.

Looking back at the house and noting the old lady had disappeared, I knew she had seen enough and wished to leave me alone in peace. I headed home to Sector 79, ten more hours of windshield time to plan my life and the mission I was about to take. Joshua Hunter.   I repeated it again and again. Joshua Hunter, Joshua Hunter, a name with biblical and occupational undertones.

Disappointed Parents

* * * *

My parents looked forward to all the special milestones in Cassie's and my life; our first steps, first words, graduation, weddings, grandchildren — accomplishments celebrated on Facebook as proud parents. But murder? My mother would have sobbed legitimate tears. "Aiken what happened to you, my sweet son?" As for my father — the jury is still out, but I'm leaning towards tacit approval.   He despised the Reverend even more than I.

Consider this. Committing the perfect murder is like baking a wonderfully moist cake and, for me, doing so without having ever baked before. I'm a chef, not a baker, so — the analogies between my day and night jobs come easily. Having the proper ingredients, tools and timing are important to the successful outcome of both. But, unlike baking, committing murder, perfect or not, requires balls of steel and a stomach capable of ingesting pure acid without experiencing debilitating reflux. Never mind that murder is illegal and, if caught, will earn you a life sentence in some decrepit institution or death by public hanging or the firing squad. I was forced to convince myself that what I was about to commit was not murder at all but, instead, an act of patriotism. We call that justification. That mental exercise went on for days and each time I thought I had properly atoned for what would be my future actions, another cog in the wheel would pop up, always revolving around getting caught. Convincing myself that I was a soldier in a justifiable war to recapture all that we had lost settled the immense conflict that tortured my mind. Justifying what I was planning as honorable and patriotic removed the criminality, but in no way lessened the chills that went up my spine while planning my first execution. Having justification from God and country seems to minimize the angst at having committed what would be a heinous crime under any other circumstance. Again — I was a soldier in a private war and it was at that point that I rebuilt my relationship with God. Our agreement was simple — I'd trust him if he'd trust me.

Subject 1: The Reverend

* * * *

They called him "The Rev." A fraudulent man, not at all what one would think of as a man of the cloth. He was my first and I did that one alone. My motive, driven by a questionable tinge of revenge and raw emotions surrounding Cassie's death, wasn't exactly worthy of justifiable homicide.

The Rev was a media personality who had annoyed damn near every Patriot I knew. But to me, he was trash and those six-degrees of separation we're told exists between any two people was just one — Cassie. His faithful followers gave him a hall-pass because men of the cloth with unquestioned faith always received one as long as they held God on their left side instead of the right. To the less naïve, he was a racist, traitor — a false profit and, in my mind, the perfect fit for our undefined code. Only the act of treason would initiate a death sentence and those convicted of that crime were all noted on a secret list held by Professor Julian Kilgore. Here-say wasn't enough. Confirmed lineage was. It was pure coincidence, or perhaps an act of God himself, that the Rev's name was at the top of that list, even though I had yet to meet the Professor. The Rev, as most knew him, was Subject #1 but to Julian, Atticus Phelps was target practice. His high ranking had nothing to do with perceived danger to the future of our country. Difficulty in completing his execution, as gauged by Julian, was a "two" on his dubious scale of one to ten. "One" being reserved for ourselves should we find it necessary to commit suicide. Again — I hadn't even met the Professor yet.

His full name was Atticus T. Phelps. Black, Baptist and hated whites, Jews and just about anyone who didn't kowtow to his aberrant rantings. A "shyster," my father would call him, often yelling at the TV, inquiring where he had received his divinity degree. The TV never answered back. I'm sure it was from the back of a matchbook cover.

Among his varied talents, and he had many, was his ability

to stoke the flames of racism where racism didn't exist. The Reverend's daily political sermons and journalistic rants always involved perceived racism, with Patriots on the rendering side of the equation. No single word strikes fear and disgust more than the word, "racist," and he'd spout it fifty times during his allotted one-hour broadcast. Racist! Five nights a week, fifty times each evening, that's a lot of bearing false witness from a so-called Reverend. Taking the high road was always our first play. The Patriots were ineffective at quelling the allegation of racism among a long list of other attacks against us — we never fought back. Bringing knives to a gun fight was our Achilles heel.

I can't recall ever hearing him saying the name "Jesus" on any of his broadcasts and "God" was always followed by a derogatory remark about Patriots, as in "God, how I hate them." I found that odd for someone titled as a man of God. That hint at holiness was meaningless and meant only to increase his followers. It worked.

After Cassi's murder I became most interested in him, bordering on obsessed. Having spoken in Sector 79 at a rally that fateful week made it easy to pin him as an accomplice to her death. A bigoted ambulance chaser of the highest order, and an unrepentant instigator of a fraudulent racism, his hands had stirred the violent pot that resulted in her death. I needed to blame someone. Guilty as charged — Death Penalty I proclaimed in a fit of understandable insanity. Yes, at twenty-four years old, I became a judge, jury and, soon to be, executioner — impressive.

While the thought of executing the good Reverend came

easily, how I'd accomplish that task caused a fair amount of confusion and soul searching. Having never taken a life before, not even an animal, I had frequently fantasized about the Rev as a suitable training ground should I ever go off the deep end and venture into human brutality.

Regrets? I'd have none, but at first glance, no well thought-out plan to accomplish it either. Recalling my favorite TV crime dramas and how some of the most heinous criminals had committed their murders, I built a short list of plausible methods for Atticus, always careful to not over complicate the process. This was my baptism into a dark world that I was prepared to live in, yet had zero experience at achieving what was necessary for membership. I couldn't afford to screw it up. "Keep it Simple" was my mantra.

When it came time to pull the trigger, slice his throat or beat the life out of him, each of which was a plausible method for his execution, I knew there'd be no hesitation. Therefore — I did what any rational person would do — I made a list with three columns, method of execution, pros and cons.

Gun shot to the head—guaranteed success, but loud without a silencer — I had one. Knife; risky, too much close physical contact resulting in my death. Beating; cathartic but also ending with a good chance of his surviving and identifying me. Knives were also wrought with DNA - mine! Rat poisoning — nope, a coward's way, depriving me of the opportunity to see him gasp his last breath, not to mention the negative Yelp reviews I'd receive should it occur at Il Portico. There were others, including the use of fire, suitable only for those who were the devil incarnate. Although Cassis' was a violent death, I chose to not douse him in gasoline and ignite his holiness on Mass Avenue for all to see, but instead opted for a less complicated, less painful solution with a high probability of success - bang, you're dead!

It's settled, I thought; gun shot to the head. My Ruger Mark II and its silencer was the perfect weapon to make this event quiet, efficient and successful — something where I could coolly walk away from with no one knowing what had just happened. I'd seen it done many times in the movies. It looked simple, something I could pull off, even as a neophyte. My referencing Atticus' execution as an "event" followed me for the next seven years. "Patriotic Events," he called them — something that Julian thought humorous, but took me a while to say with a callous heart and a straight face. With practice, I eventually managed to eek out a wry little smile when speaking of those occasions. I'm smiling now as I recall them for you.

While I didn't spend an inordinate amount of time or energy researching the ideal spot on the Rev's body to fire my bullet, consideration of when and where it would happen consumed my planning. There's a reason they call it "dead center" — enough said.

He was a public figure, and most likely well guarded. Three words kept banging around my head — "The Perfect Crime." This must be one. Perfection, however, takes practice and I had neither opportunity nor desire to rehearse, so simplicity was paramount. Building a list of obstacles and potential pitfalls started an annoying process but became a habit for the next several years. In business they call it a SWOT analysis. In murder — it's just detailed planning and good ole common sense, beginning with knowing thy enemy, stalking for as long as it takes to confirm a routine, and finally putting it all together into a fool-proof plan that ends in their death.

The Stalk

* * * *

As a local, broadcasting daily from his New Columbia studio, travel wasn't an issue; his schedule was. Did he have body guards? Knowing where he lived, ate and drank, what time he left in the morning and returned home at night were at the top of my stalking checklist. What was his ritual, his routine, or did he even have one? Routines are helpful, it takes the guess-work out of the formula.

Planning always begins with questions and for the Reverend I had many. Three weeks of stalking a man who so disgusted me tried my patience. I couldn't wait to finish him off, but was careful to be that needle in a haystack — blending in and hanging far enough back that no one would have guessed he'd soon be in my crosshairs. I mimicked the sycophants who surrounded him, but never got close enough to ask for his autograph or to show up in some random picture taken by a paparazzi, although I wish I had. A nice touch, don't you think? A parting gift from my subjects, memorabilia to replace that picture of Jesus hanging in the pit.

Body guards? Yep. But big guys packing bad-ass weapons who only flanked him during the day while he was jaunting from one public appearance to another were no threat to my plan. They'd disappear after hours to a popular, but seedy strip-joint on the corner of 15th and New York Avenue. Weapons, muscles and brute force never accompanied him for dinner or back to his home. In fact — he usually ate alone and did so at a snail's pace. Dinners took over an hour.

Like most Herons, he dined at Il Portico, but on a less frequent basis — he wasn't a regular. Our three-inch thick veal chop was all he ever ordered — never pasta, no appetizers, no deserts and never alcohol, not even an espresso to finish the evening. He was a meat and, whatever carb was on the menu, kind of guy. We spoke on one or two occasions but, on what I had considered being his last visit, I inquired as to his favorite eateries. Standoffish at first, he shared his Top-5. We weren't one, which was odd because he had dined with us several times and, to my knowledge, never complained about the food or service. Add that to his character traits — Asshole.

No surprise that his favorite eatery was the Art & Soul, a rib joint on Massachusetts Avenue, just four blocks from his townhouse. Proximity wasn't the reason for his frequenting it though — gooey, dry-rubbed pork BBQ ribs was, and he was a glutton for them. Known among its regulars as the A&S, it was popular among Black Caucus members, most of whom were hardened disciples of the Reverend. Atticus was a regular on Friday evenings after his last broadcast for the week, arriving at exactly 7:45 and seated at his reserved table in the back. He dined alone. Stalking yields such important intelligence and, after three weeks, I was able to place a check-mark in the "routine" column. It was a crude "to-do" list but it worked. I kept imagining that place and those messy ribs as the biblical equivalent of his "The Last Supper." Like Jesus, he had millions of followers, but also ten times more enemies. The list of suspects for what I was planning could fill a phone book. Who killed Hitler, came to mind.

A fan of soul food myself, especially ribs; I paid a visit one Friday evening to catch a closer glimpse of the Reverend. Observing his dining routine seemed important at the time although, in hindsight, it wasn't. Still, being too thorough when planning a murder hadn't crossed my psyche yet. I was still learning, and he was my first. Let's call it my baptism, since he was Southern Baptist.

I waited at the bar until a table in his section was available, bringing me as close as possible to my future "target." If he noticed me, I'd thank him for suggesting the Art & Soul and would then ask for a suggested entrée. And yes, I had those remarks at-the-ready should he strike up a conversation. I was appreciating the importance of being well prepared for every possible scenario. Thorough, thoughtful planning quickly became my mantra.

He was prompt, arriving at precisely 7:45 and ushered to his table, which sat six feet from mine. I could eavesdrop on his phone conversations, note what he ate and how much he drank. Drinking — you'd think that an intoxicated target is a wonderful thing, but staggering down the street complicates the difficult aim of hitting them dead center of their forehead, as I had planned. He drank only water — no alcohol, just sparkling water — Perrier, I believe. He'd feel every excruciating second of pain as my bullet entered his forehead and then exited through the back of his skull and into one of the tall oak trees that lined that street. I had visualized that — a through-and-through with very little dense brain matter to impede the velocity of the exiting bullet. How many seconds of painful suffering was debatable, but I had assumed only three, if that.

He ate at a snail's pace, carefully examining each bone and then licking them so clean that the bones shined as if a jeweler using a Dremel had polished them. He was sloppy. A pile of used napkins were all waded up and stacked to his right drenched with the sauce dripping from the corner of his mouth. Horrible table manners, I might add.

Dining alone, as usual, yielded nothing of substance on the conversation side but, watching him text frantically on his iPhone, slamming each key, suggested that something was amiss. The thought had crossed my mind to walk over, say hello and then glance at those texts, but I had committed to a no-contact reconnaissance. I extinguished the urge and remained seated, trying to ignore his disturbed demeanor.

He texted slowly, pecking at each key with one fat finger like a child unskilled at the QUERTY keyboard or not realizing that he could have used Siri to dictate. BBQ sauce covered the keys and, yes, he took his fingers, swiped each of them and then licked them clean. Who does that? What I focused most on was his trip home after the meal with a sprinkle of virtual target practice thrown in for good measure. I needed to find my mark on the street outside where I'd be able to say, in my mind - bang - you're dead! It was the theater for me and having that mark was important.

Practice Makes Perfect

* * * *

Murder — it's never shades of gray, always irretrievable once you set the plan in motion. There's no turning back or hitting a reset button if things don't go exactly as planned. I acutely knew of that and, to be honest, it scared the shit out of me, especially since my planning for his execution was minimal.

Practicing my golf swing came naturally, but practicing for a flawless execution was foreign and, honestly, impossible. Other than mentally rehearsing each step in the process up to the point of no return, pulling the trigger, I struggled to devise a system for perfecting my new career. Repetition was all I could rely on, hoping that my first "event" rendered him dead with no visible evidence left behind and no unseen witnesses in the area. What if he survives, or if I miss my target and he runs back into the restaurant, alerting others to my plan? These thoughts weighed on my mind, but most disturbing was the thought of killing someone. Murder, for God's sakes! It forever follows and haunts you. It places you at the top of the A.C.T. list - setting you up for execution for that crime. Aiken was already on that list but

Joshua wasn't and I preferred to keep it that way. Justice was non-existent but at least it was swift. I suppose what I most wanted out of the successful completion of this mission was to feel good about committing my first justified execution and to not go crazy afterwards with an onslaught of guilt.

Most serial killers harbored unhealthy relationships with someone important in their lives. They either hated their mother or prostitutes or were just freaks who got an initial sick thrill out of torturing defenseless animals and then ramped it up by adding humans to their conquests. It portends a mindset towards enjoying the act of killing, something I never felt nor wanted. I never harmed a fly, I loved my mother, had no experience with prostitutes and knew there would be no joy in carrying out the Rev's final sentence, no matter how much he deserved it. Justification, careful planning and a backup plan was all I had at that moment. Dealing with the after-effects was something I hadn't yet considered, but should have.

I thought about the animal kingdom and how the smartest had honed their skills at stalking their prey. Tigers — now there's a patient breed. Watching, waiting, hidden in the brush sensing the perfect moment to pounce. They knew exactly where and when their prey would gather. The most patient raised their odds of returning to their den to feed their clowder. They'd kill for survival and then rest well at night knowing that they had, as Darwin theorized, confirmed that the structure of the animal kingdom, including humans, assured survival of the fittest. How appropriate that my final justification for the Reverend's execution, beyond revenge, would draw upon the theory proposed by a man good Christians despised — Charles Darwin. The Rev was a Gazelle therefore, I had to think like a tiger.

I counted three entire racks of ribs sliding down the Reverend's gullet, forcing me to stay longer than I had intended — but again, patience was the order of that evening. Assuming he ran a tab and could walk out quickly, I asked for my check, paid in cash and left before he did. Never leave a record of your travels, always use cash.

There was a nice bench one block down under a light post. The inefficient system still hadn't replaced the broken light. Good for me. Darkness was my friend that night, so I sat like a tiger patiently waiting for the Reverend, hoping he'd take that route to head home. Glancing straight up the street awaiting my prey, I raised my hand like a kid pretending to shoot his friend with a CAP gun. Effective at picking the proper spot to pull the trigger, should I choose that bench as my position for firing the fatal shot. I went through the entire motion several times. Grabbing the gun from my pocket, aiming, pulling the trigger and then shoving it back into the coat pocket where no one would see it. I counted the number of pavers from the last step out of the Art & Soul to the point of no return — four. It felt right. He'd be close enough to assure that I not miss my target but far enough away to realize that a gun was being pointed at him. That was to be my mark.

The street was quiet and traffic nonexistent — there was no one watching my preparatory antics. I sat for twenty minutes, worried that he had taken a different route by going through the kitchen to socialize with the staff and then out the back door like a self-aggrandized rock star. Then, out of the shadow of the first light post, which was well lit, Atticus appeared, walking towards me. Four pavers from my position, and darkness began, the perfect spot for me to pull the trigger. While it was close range, like hitting the broad side of a barn, the darkness was a minor complicating obstacle in that "dead center" did not have a wide range of variance. Still, I prayed the inefficient system responsible for infrastructure repairs would not find it necessary to fix that lightbulb before my dedicated date with the devil. It was to be the following Friday. There was a confidence boost that evening and the act of doing a dry-run seemed to be the reason for that boost.

Although the air was warm that evening, I'd swear that a chilled draft wafted over me as he passed by. An omen, perhaps, for the next time I knew he'd be dead. Maybe he was the devil incarnate.

ßI returned home eager to transcribe my findings into an old tape recorder I used to keep track of my notes. A dictation machine passed down by my grandfather, was an ancient technology, but safe and effective when modern tools were so frequently hacked by the Herons. I hid the tapes under the floorboards and the recorder in the ceiling — separation of powers! Like President Nixon, I'm sure I'll regret ever having made those tapes — most revealing, but so too is this journal.

It's Show Time

* * * *

I had stalked the Rev for three weeks, wondering if I had the guts to carry out his final sentence. Was I being too thorough, too weak or was I just delaying the inevitable fearing that I'd get caught? I had done my planning, secured the proper tools, a Glock and silencer, and was ninety-nine percent certain that I could pull this off. But, one well-placed shot, walk away like a bad-ass and look at no one should a stranger appear out of nowhere does not constitute detailed planning — especially for a neophyte to the business of murder. A dead body sprawled out on Massachusetts Avenue bleeding like a fire hydrant onto the public sidewalk, spent bullets, unseen witnesses, DNA and cameras I might have missed — what could go wrong? The short answer — that one percent.

You've doubtless experienced the pleasant anxiety that overcomes you when trying to fall asleep awaiting Santa's arrival to deliver your presents under a decorated tree. On the opposite end of the spectrum is a different anxiety, the kind one experiences the night before a critical test or a painful medical procedure — sheer, incapacitating fright.

The anxiety I experienced the night before carrying out my first execution was beyond frightening, it was downright debilitating, causing me to shake in bed, eyes wide open, staring at a blank ceiling wondering if I'd get caught or worse, killed. I questioned my planning. Was it detailed enough and had I considered all possibilities, good, bad and, most important, the unintended consequences that my father always drilled into my head? I questioned my commitment to carry this out and to avoid post execution feelings of guilt. I was having serious second thoughts, or was it third?

"Now I lay me down to sleep," became "Dear God, bless and guide me through this mission." My testy relationship with Him caused me to question the effectiveness of praying to a deity that, after the collapse, I had stopped believing in, but I prayed never-the-less. Still, there was a small sense of glee within me knowing I was about to eliminate a man my fellow Patriots despised and whom I blamed for my sister's death. I'd be an anonymous hero to millions of Patriots and to Cassie, if heaven exists — just the way I had wanted it. Aiken McHale, the polite kid or Batman, Joshua Hunter, the Dark Knight? Talk about conflicted.

It had to be clean. It had to be perfect — leave no evidence pointing back at me and make certain there were no witnesses. I had rehearsed that to the point of mental exhaustion. "It's show time," I convinced myself, then headed to the A&S to sit on that bench twenty-six paces from Mass Avenue and four pavers from the light post. I parked ten blocks away on a darkened street where no one walked at night.

It was Friday around 8:45pm and a steady drizzle was falling upon the Capital. The cooling air caused a faint fog to hover over the area, testing visibility from afar but at my intended range, didn't seem as if it would affect my ability to hit my target dead center. Rain reduced the likelihood of random witnesses out for a casual evening stroll. All I could hope for was that the Rev continued with his Friday dinner ritual and that a sudden hankering for pork chops at Il Portico didn't dissuade him from showing up.

Was I forgetting something? Did I want to do this? My breathing was more strained and loud, my hands mimicked someone afflicted with Parkinson's disease. Dead center or even hitting his obese body seemed doubtful. I took one final deep breath, then waited patiently for the perfect moment. Time and location now invaded my already scrambled thought process. I was a total, shivering mess.

While shaking on that bench, awaiting my prey and questioning my commitment to pull the trigger, I had an ah ha moment. I was the hunter and no longer the hunted. I was a tiger. Cassie was dead, and the Rev played a role in her brutal attack — one degree of separation. My doubts disappeared. I had mental clarity and a deep desire to finish him off. Ah ha moment — sure. Opioid moment — without a doubt.

At 9:22pm his routine would have him leaving the A&S shortly. The point of no return was set. One last glance around the area and, thank God, no one was there. Three minutes later — he walked out. I took one last deep breath and steadied my hands. The shaking stopped. I was ready, and he was five pavers from entering darkness, figuratively and literally.

Just as he approached the fourth paver, he turned away and shouts "It doesn't get any better Calvin, you bastard." The entire neighborhood could have heard him, which bothered me. Most adults drink — it's a given, right up there with death and taxes, but the Reverend never drank. Not at Il Portico and not once during the three weeks I had shadowed him at late night events. Quenching his thirst from the salty ribs at the A&S came from water - Perrier, every single time. Was that night different? He stuttered and walked in a drunken, uncoordinated fashion.

"Yo Rev" came a reply from inside the door, loud but sober. He stopped again, looked back and paused, turning as if to return to the A&S.

God, no! Please don't go back inside, I thought to myself. Don't give me a chance to chicken out or him to escape through the back door. He screamed at the top of his lungs. "You're the best Cal, see you next week!" "No, you won't," I whispered as he headed my way. Sitting on that rusted, wrought-iron bench, twenty-six paces from the corner of M Street and Massachusetts Avenue beneath the street light that wasn't lit, I hesitated and hadn't even pulled the trigger. I heard a muffled popping sound and then he fell like a tree, straight forward with a hard thump, opposite the direction I had expected since I had trained my gun dead center on his forehead. Was he drunk? I hadn't pulled the trigger yet!

Then, out of the shadows and behind my intended target a short, stocky man wearing a long, brown overcoat strewn with pockets up both sides and a newsboy hat hurried towards me, stepping over the body without so much as a casual glance down to see if he was still alive. In that moment of moral conflict, I wasn't alone on my first mission. My well-planned event with the Rev as my only guest and myself as the host, took an unexpected turn — I had an accomplice. There was no backup plan for that.

As if on cue, we both shoved our weapons back into our pockets. Synchronized to perfection, in a blink of an eye, no one would never have suspected we were both armed and that one of us had just attempted murder, me, while the other had committed it. That execution had no witnesses and, no clear perpetrator. He used a silencer, and I still hadn't fired yet.

I remained motionless on that bench as the stranger approached, clutching a rolled-up newspaper under his right arm. He had an odd limp to his stride with a slight dragging of his right foot which appeared longer than his left. My first thought after assessing his identity and why he had just shot my subject was; am I his next target?

Like a showdown on some dusty street in the Wild West, waiting for "the reach," I kept a careful eye on his hands, making sure he made no movement towards that inside pocket. As the distance between us narrowed, I readied myself to counter any aggressive change. Three pavers away, my heart pounded, two, my breathing sped up again. One, who the hell was he? Then, he walked past me at a brisker pace, tossing the paper into my lap. Glancing down, I looked back up and he was gone. Just like that!

He had folded The Washington Times at the upper right corner, earmarking a page meant for my attention. That section noting an ad for Mason University with the header in bold Times Roman and circled in bright red ink stating "Finish It," meant something. Many college students were forced to withdraw after the collapse — some for financial reasons, others to attend to their changed family dynamics or dead parents. I was one of those, but for different reasons, and hadn't started college yet. I gazed up the street towards my target writhing in pain while trying to drag himself back towards the A&S. His blood pooled beneath him and down the pavers towards me. I pondered those words which he had circled in red, then took it as a sign to finish the job he had started and not as an invitation to enter that university.

Standing up from the bench, I mimicked the stranger and walked just as casually towards my target. Breathing heavier as I approached, I pulled my silenced 22 Ruger out just as I was vertical to his body. Hesitation again, maybe three-seconds, it seemed like an eternity. An agonizing flashback to the last time I held Cassie's severely beaten and bloodied head while sliding her lifeless body into the back of a hearse — aha — I knew what I had to do. Finish it! Execute the Reverend Atticus Phelps. Justice served.

Two shots, dead center to the back of his head, he quivered with each hit and then all movement stopped. The body contorts when a blunt force hits the brain. A jolt which initiates an involuntary response causes arching of the spinal cord and rapid contortions in the neck mimicking electrocution. I'd seen it in frogs during biology class. Yep - live ones and it was my lab partner who doled out that cruelty!

His blood pool expanded, covering the entire paver then creeped towards the grass edge. No visible breathing, no movements at all, there was no way he could have survived. So much blood, it wasn't red but instead a deep brown color. Darkness reduces our ability to see red. Coagulation was quick with him — having, at first, the thick consistency of pancake batter and then thinned like water as the intensity of the rain picked up. It splattered onto my pant leg. Some small sense of remorse overcame me as I stood over his body but, like the sweet essence of the cherry blossoms dotting that street, sweet revenge joined my emotional parade and then took over. Remorse became everlasting joy. I had done it! My first kill! Hard to imagine and yes, I'm almost ashamed to admit that it was exhilarating in a Patriotic sort of way. Bombs bursting in air, rockets red glare, justice for Cassie — that kind of exhilarating feeling. I sensed a wry smirk of satisfaction altering the muscles on my face. You can feel it — like an annoying twitch. I had expected to freeze up in a state of shock and that I would cry at what I had just done. I didn't freeze, I didn't cry. I walked away.

Continuing at a brisk pace, like a bad-ass assassin, towards the next corner, I turned left, passing a young couple out on an evening stroll with their dog. I looked straight at them and, sure enough, they looked away. They continued down M Street, never turning the corner onto Massachusetts Avenue and towards our crime scene. Breath in, breath out, I continued that pace for the next several blocks and then headed to my car parked ten blocks away. Avoid the streets, stick to the backyards or alleys — fewer cameras or street lights, and always park far from the crime scene in an area where most don't venture.

A dead celebrity body sprawled out on a public street will quickly alert the authorities to review every available video in the vicinity while also combing the streets in search of armed or suspicious suspects. Weapons were illegal for all but Herons and they could stop anyone for a pat-down — even without cause.

One final emotion struck me as I sat in my car, too afraid to drive back home — FEAR! Hesitation, remorse, closure, exhilaration, revenge, satisfaction and fear. Who would have thought the act of murder was both physically and emotionally complicated?

It's official, I thought; I'm not a psychopath. Having experienced the full range of emotions, closing the loop of sanity which starts with remorse and ends with fear, I felt relieved and slept well that night knowing what I was doing was best for our country. "Justification" became my battle cry. I felt reborn, but not religiously.

Humorous Facebook memes posted before the Rev's death changed to what most would have considered being politically incorrect. "May you rest in Hell BASTARD," or his smug picture embedded into a Queen music video with "Another One Bites the Dust" playing in the background. Oh - the beauty of that group - we could say the vilest things but knew that we were amongst friends and that no one would call each other out. It was the first time I had considered outing myself among my private Facebook friends as the guy who had taken out Atticus Phelps. A simple post bragging about my exploit seemed like an appropriate way to build group stature. Fleeting thought but, never acted upon.

Bird Watching

* * * *

The Patriots were a resourceful bunch of heroes, creative too. In a city that rivaled London in the sheer number of cameras spying on us, we took it upon ourselves to destroy as many of them as possible and, while doing so, turning it into a game. A simple check of a most imaginative Facebook group, "Bird Watchers," was all one needed to do to get the most up-to-date information on camera destruction. Joining required an extensive social media background check, but everyone still operated under assumed names, just like me.

The administrator of the group's page would note the destruction of CCTV surveillance cameras, not as acts of resistance or anarchy, but instead as bird sightings. For example, "Bobby saw a beautiful female goldfinch on the corner of K Street and 21st NW." Translation: Someone named Bobby just destroyed the camera on the corner of K and 21st. Noting it as a female was a signal that the person who destroyed that camera was also one. Paintball guns, even a child's squirt gun loaded with paint did the trick, but the more permanent solution was to cut the fiber optic cables. Splicing fiberoptic is impossible, causing those cameras to be replaced, and that could take weeks. Government efficiency at its best once again working to our advantage.

I scrolled through the page for recent bird sightings to make certain my image wasn't on any I might have missed. A most interesting post from someone who posed as "Guardian Angel" popped up. "Saw two beautiful American Eagles along Mass and M Street." Dated three days ago, it had to be meant for me. God works in mysterious ways. Who was the Guardian Angel?

The Days After

* * * *

Panic. It's a common, often acute human emotion but one I had hoped to avoid. I don't deal with it well. I'd panic the night before a big test and then fail it, before a few of my high school golf matches and come up short and once while imagining my father's reaction after totaling his new car even though it wasn't my fault. He grounded me though. Panic wraps itself in dozens of questions, most of which have no good answers. You can't understand the panic that greeted me once I had returned home after executing the Reverend. I had just committed murder, my first!

What followed my initiation into the worst of criminality, taking of one's life, was downright debilitating. It lasted for months and, to be honest, I'm not sure I ever shook that emotion. Planning a perfect crime requires patience but the after-party invokes mental analysis, a revisiting of every sorted detail, all to calm one's nerves by dreaming up convincing evidence that all went well and that not one shred of evidence or witnessing occurred during those fatal moments. As if the two bullets lodged in his head had vanished, no one had noticed my stalking, and not one person saw me escaping through the back alleys to my car parked ten blocks away. Repeat often enough and, unlike fake news, it's still not convincing. Did I eat at the Art & Soul too often? Did I sit too close to him? What bothered me most was — who the hell was my unintended accomplice and why was he there at the exact moment I had planned to execute Atticus Phelps?

Hearing: It's odd how our third sense can be so acute when focusing on it. One can hear the rush of blood through your veins and the wisp of air when there is no movement. Sleep is necessary for human survival. It eluded me for three nights following my first execution — I kept hearing things, real and imagined. I was a basket case. As expected, cable news was wall-to-wall coverage on every available station, but ours was no longer broadcasting — the new world order was less than accepting of alternative views. State-owned media had taken hold, and this story had legs, it fit their narrative if they could only paint me as some right-wing racist -- which I wasn't.

For the next several days I remained glued to the TV, obsessively absorbing every nugget of news regarding the Reverend's death. Now that's a rite of passage no one should experience. Watching the news about a crime that shook the nation, knowing you're the person who committed it. Hit the pause button then rewind and play it over and over. Racism was the common theme, and nothing could have been further from the truth. No witnesses, no evidence or suspects was all I cared about, and, on the second day, they actually stated that.

As expected, the wall-to-wall coverage was interspersed with fraudulent biographies about his past and what an upstanding citizen he was — always fighting for civil rights like his mentor Dr. Martin Luther King. Laughable on face value but hearing the quivering voice of the commentator as she read her script was the final straw for me. My father was right. Journalism died years before and had reincarnated itself as propaganda.

The ticker on the bottom of the screen repeatedly scrolled the same message. "Reverend Atticus Phelps found dead from a gunshot wound outside a restaurant on Capitol Hill." "No suspects yet in this tragic event." Later that day it changed to "The Reverend Atticus Phelps shot execution style." I was most intrigued that the media referred to his death as a "tragic event." I thought about it and then kept repeating that word — event, event. It struck a chord with me and, helped to further relieve the need to admit that I had committed murder. I changed that word to "event," but instead of it being tragic, from that point forward it became "Patriotic." The words "no suspect yet in this tragic event," continued to scroll across the screen but I knew the word "yet" meant that they were hunting for someone, and that someone was me.

Three days of coverage with nothing new to report so the narrative changed to a rehashing of the Reverend's background, his lifetime achievements and, his notable enemies, all of whom were Patriots, each labeled as racists.

It was early in the investigative process — the Reverend hadn't been dead for seventy-two hours. As time went by, more information or leads would follow. Keeping up with the continuing coverage to know whether success at getting away with murder was in the cards, became an hourly obsession of mine.

Later that evening the update was brief, noting no additional information to impart to the viewers beyond two slugs from a Ruger being recovered at the scene. More important, no prints or video recordings which could lead them to a suspect. Shots to the back of the head meant "execution style" and they repeated that phrase on every update. I thanked God for my father's insistence that I use his old Ruger, passed down to him by his father, long before the new weapon's regulations took hold. Had I purchased a new gun just before the nationwide banning, the required micro-stamping would have led them to me. All guns manufactured after 2016 had their firing pins engraved with make, model, and serial number, which stamps the primer on the bullet as the firing pin impacts it. It's like mailing an anonymous threatening letter, with a return address on it — defeats the purpose of being anonymous.

On the eighth day, the commentator signed off with, "We may never know who committed this heinous crime or for what reason." Good — I hadn't planned on getting caught.

Over-thinking — it's an unproductive habit that rarely yields better results. I had left four things behind that evening. The newspaper dropped in my lap by an uninvited accomplice, the Reverend's dead body, the bullets that killed him and my sanity. My accomplice wore gloves, so no prints even though he never touched anything. It took a week for my paranoia to disappear and, on the twelfth day after hearing an update noting no suspects, I added murder to Mom's long list of proud accomplishments from my twenty-four short years of life. In chronological order — first spoken words, my first steps, asking a girl out on a date, parallel parking dad's Suburban, graduating from high school and, the grand finale, my first murder. A flawless record of accomplishments, only one to be left off Facebook. I had committed the perfect crime, but eight days of investigation does not a perfect crime make.

Morbid Curiosity

* * * *

Looking back now, clearly I had left both my sanity and common sense outside the Art & Soul that evening, not so much for killing the bastard but instead for thinking it a good idea to attend his funeral.

Perhaps it was to revel in the sadness of his friends and family as they walked by his casket, weeping as tears welled up in their eyes, while kissing his bullet-pocked forehead. Or, maybe I needed closure.

Although I had fired two shots into the back of his skull, those shots came at close range. Both were "through-and-through" but ricocheted back into his brain once hitting the hard concrete pavement. The deterioration of a human body and the remarkable work that a skilled mortician can do to make one seem almost alive, as if they were just sleeping, was an art — the kind I knew I'd appreciate. Death interested me. As an admirer of exceptionally good work of any kind, design, art, photography, I became curious to see the handy work of the mortician tasked with plugging those holes. Yes, I was an admirer of the morbid art of making dead bodies beautiful.

It's interesting — the things I thought about back then. His execution was my official baptism into a dark world I had never imagined living in, but there was no celebration for a job well done or any high-fives followed by "welcome to the club." Morbid curiosity got the better of me. Like a photographer having captured the perfect human interaction or well timed shot of a tragedy in progress and then never having seen the final picture, I needed to confirm a job well done, my personal acknowledgement that I could continue down that path. Thankfully, his service was an open-casket.

A Moving Memorial Service

✳ ✳ ✳ ✳

I remember thinking how remarkable that they even allowed me into his service. But it wasn't the quality of mourners they considered, it was the diversity and, since the service was to be nationally televised, diversity played a role in who entered those doors. They bussed many in from other sectors but most watched on an enormous video screen they had set that up outside the church. This was as worthy a send-off for the Reverend Atticus T. Phelps as the one I had given him ten days before. But, unlike the foggy night which ended with blood thinning rain showers that splattered him as he gasped his last breath, it was a beautiful, bright, sunny day, with not a cloud in sight. I took that as a sign of approval from above and winked upwards to the almighty as I approached his house of worship.

The armed body guards who had left the Revered's side to spend the rest of that fateful evening shoving dollar bills into the G-String of some poor young girl swinging from a pole were now in charge of choosing which of the mourners waiting outside could enter the church. The famous and well-connected were already inside having entered through a side door. It was well guarded. Like entering a nightclub where only the coolest, best dressed would get a nod from the bouncer, this event had a purple carpet and a gold rope line. I was twenty mourners from that bouncer so I prayed again that the Good Lord would see fit for me to pay my last respects up close and personal.

Data points were normal for most anything you did, but having one at a funeral raised my ire. They were taking names and asking for the REAL ID which, as you know, is chipped and would have added my name into their database of attendees. I couldn't allow that to happen. Thinking of a suitable excuse was easy, but I wasn't sure he'd accept it.

"ID," the heavy set, armed bouncer in full black attire flipped his hand out ready for me to place it in his palm.

"I live in Sector 4 and took the metro here. I didn't know."

Sector 4 was ten miles away. He'd never ask that I go home to get it or maybe he would.

He scanned me up and down and then stared into my eyes as if he recognized me, paused and then looked down at my feet. Blue-gray suit, white shirt, navy tie, silver cufflinks and expensive brown leather Italian monk-strap shoes — I showed respect for his former boss. Without saying another word he ran the metal detector front, back and up both sides making sure that I wasn't armed. "You're cleared," and then waved me through and into the church. I passed the entrance exam.

The church was enormous and, although it was a typically rowdy Southern Baptist service — celebrating inside of God's house, the life of a man that I had killed moved me in a weird way. Its washed gray stone facade surrounded by eight stained glass windows, each depicting a different biblical scene, large bright red double-doors, an enormous pipe organ and yards of ornately carved wood fixtures and moldings suggested that it was once Episcopalian. I felt religious just sitting there. Glancing around admiring all that went into its construction, it was beautiful. Again — I'm an admirer of exceptionally good work.

My father grew up Episcopalian, and he'd revel in the beauty of their churches because, to him, Baptists were too focused on the volume of theater-type seating and Rock inspired gospel music played on electric guitars. Attending church in the South was like going to a concert, and that bothered him. He wanted the pomp, subdued revelry and pews to kneel on. Stand up, sit down, kneel was the extent of his Sunday exercise ritual. But for African Americans it was all about the choir. The Rev had a chorus line of girls on the right, maybe twenty, robed in deep purple with gold collars while on the left stood just as many, but all men, robed in the opposite, gold robes with purple collars.

The service was beautiful and attended by a veritable "Who's Who" of Herons, although I didn't understand what a human Heron was at that moment. They all sat up front. The term "behind enemy lines" came to mind and in, of all places, God's house where the enemy never visited unless someone died. The media was everywhere as was law enforcement. The FBI and just about every three-letter agency in New Columbia was in the area, some attending inside while others watched from the rooftops of the buildings surrounding the church. Armed snipers looking as though they were expecting trouble were everywhere.

"Nice to see you Joshua," he leaned into the pew I had occupied which was filling up, forcing me to move towards the middle. I hate middle seats — at the movies, on airplanes and now in the house of a deity whose Commandments I had just trashed. I had no escape route should a bolt of lightening come towards me.

"You too. The Rev was a good customer and such a nice guy." I lied. I was shocked that the Rev's colleague, Chris Jenkins, remembered me since we had only spoken twice, once about mushrooms and another time about women. He was a misogynist pig. Still, having him see me at the Rev's funeral was the perfect opportunity to endear myself with the same people I despised. The doors closed, the organ played and six black pallbearers entered through the rear vestibule carrying the casket which was exactly as I had imagined it to be — white. As they arrived at the alter one of them opened the head portion of the casket and, again, as I had imagined, his was with a rainbow against a sky blue pattern. Why did black people chose white caskets and white hearses while Caucasians chose dark caskets and black hearses?

I can't imagine attending a friend's funeral if you had been responsible for that friend's death. An innocent car accident, a freak of nature, it didn't matter what the circumstances were, you'd sense that everyone was staring at you and that some wished that it was you inside that wooden box instead of their friend. They say the blind have heightened hearing and the deaf have heightened sight. I can confirm that the guilty have heightened remorse. Watching those who attended that day, his ex-wife and kids, who had their own issues with the law, and hundreds of followers all crying as they passed by that open white casket with a rainbow reflecting on the heavy glossy makeup, saddened me. Some kissed his forehead, others just touched his hands. For me, I stood there quietly admiring the work of the mortician who had so thoughtfully filled the holes in his forehead. Sadly, the woman behind me approached and then kissed his forehead with such extreme pressure, that she completely messed up that exceptional work. Just as I had imagined those bullets were "through-and-through," and the rest of the mourners behind us were treated to, not only the Rev's body with his hands neatly folded onto his chest, but brain matter oozing out all over his forehead and down his cheeks.

Like Cassie, he was now a mess. My temporary remorseful moment was now nullified. Karma on a level I had never expected.

I had underestimated the Good Lord's ability to forgive those who ignored his commandments, notably the sixth. Perhaps there were small disclaimers to each and I had found the only one that allowed me to take the Reverend's life, escape without being seen and to attend his final farewell without having my required ID.

As I exited the church at the conclusion of the service, I noticed a man across the street leaning up against the brick wall of an apartment building with his arms crossed, staring directly at me. The street was narrow and one-way. He was, at most, thirty-feet away. Long brown overcoat with pockets strewn up both sides wearing a newsboy hat, I stared back at him as he remained motionless and unfazed by my counter-stare. Déjà vu, it happens. That was one of those moments.

Finish it. Mason University. Unfinished business.

Off to College - Late

* * * *

College was free, worthless but free, challenging the adage that the best things in life are.

College was a bureaucrat's breeding ground. The list of majors would have sent my father into a seething rage, wondering what the hell had happened to his beloved country. Most weren't considered marketable for a graduate's career, but that was by design. The intended purpose of a college education was pure anti-American indoctrination sprinkled with enough shaming to sissify the male species while also pounding the final nail into the coffin of human intelligence. Most college grads were unemployable in what was left of the private sector, so serving as a fresh new crop of bureaucrat's hell bent on making other people's lives miserable was the preferred route to earning a living. The only subject remotely holding my interest was history. You could learn it, ignore and repeat it but, most appealing to me — you could also make it, as I had done six months before entering my first college lecture hall.

My father would have been none too pleased with that decision, reminding me as a young kid that there were few well-paying career opportunities available to those majoring in subjects concentrated on reliving the past or any that had the word "English" in their title such as English Literature. Spanish wasn't any better. Like gender identification, our new America had dozens of acceptable languages and English was no longer the language of the majority.

Approaching completion of the worthless elective courses required to earn my equally worthless degree, I opted to take a history class, American History 101, or as my more astute classmates would whisper, Revisionism 101. We whispered a lot — video cameras and recording device were all over the place, notably on campuses. Getting caught mocking a professor or the whole "safe-space" phenomenon was a quick ticket to a permanent banishment from campus. The Herons had so completely infiltrated our education system and constantly drilled into our heads how evil America was that they sold a majority of students into believing them. Colonialism, selfish with our abundant resources, polluters of the planet, war mongers, even terrorists — we were the driving force behind most of the world's troubles. The whole education system was upside down with the smartest among us having never attended college. They dodged the institutional propaganda that rendered us incapable of thinking on our own.

Some gangly, sick looking teacher's assistant taught the first semester with a warped perspective that was totally foreign to me. "What country are you talking about?" I interrupted his opening dialogue to our first class.

"America. This is American History, or did you miss the memo when you registered for this class?" Asshole!

Such a misguided, arrogant fool whose hatred towards America seethed from his pores made me wonder how he had ever become a teaching assistant. I'd always blow at him whenever we'd pass in the hallway, to see if he'd fall over. Small amusements in an otherwise boring collegian life helped to pass the time of day.

Julian Kilgore was my professor for the next semester. The classes he taught were less revisionist, "Just teaching the truth and nothing but the truth," he'd say. His style didn't fit well into the safe environment the school mandated for students. No arguing, name calling or bullying, it was all very sterile. He encouraged open debate, even shouting at each other if your point was well taken. Several students walked out when the discussions became too heated to handle. Snowflakes!

He was the quintessential history scholar, a PHD from Yale with thinning black hair parted to the right, a hint of aging, the salt and pepper peeking out from his bushy sideburns. His clothing repertoire, limited by what his meager teaching salary afforded him, was always a cheap blue polyester blazer, wrinkled khaki pants, and a white button-down oxford with ragged collars. He was a disheveled mess upon entering his lecture hall, but also a breath of fresh air, sharing many of the political leanings I had siphoned from my father. Having been reprimanded several times for breaking with the strict University teaching code, tenure, or something else, saved his ass from being fired. He remained the most popular among the student body. Everyone loved Kilgore. He was the nutty professor of history, but his popularity didn't translate to promotion. Loyalty to Neville did and he was no lackey for the current dictator. Julian was an outcast, a closeted Patriot working among an army of proud Herons who had completely infiltrated academia.

His Churchill cigar was always in hand. Since smoking was banned inside a lecture hall, or pretty much anywhere, he'd chomp on it while pacing back and forth across the stage — an adult pacifier, I'm guessing. His gate when walking was memorable with long deliberate strides back and forth, babbling aloud as he crisscrossed the platform. He favored the left foot with a slight dragging of the right — similar to my accomplice. Smiles were rare, making it appear that Kilgore was constantly unhappy or just pissed off at the world. He marched to a different beat, one that put him at odds with his colleagues and squarely in the crosshairs of the department head, Walter Saslow. I could feel his disdain when he was in the presence of Saslow, like a mongoose cornered by a cobra.

Saslow was your typical tenured department head, approaching sixty but appearing well north of ninety. His hands shook in the most odd manner, circular. Balding from the center and bespectacled by round, rimless glasses with buffalo horn inlays, he spent most of his time in a small, wood paneled office smoking his idol of professorial distinctiveness, a full bent billiard pipe. There were two sets of rules and department heads lived by the second one which allowed them to smoke wherever they wanted outside of the classroom. When he wasn't cleaning his glasses, he tended that pipe. Julian lived by the first set of rules which meant they only allowed his cigars outdoors.

There was no mutual respect or admiration between either of them. They were polar opposites occupying the same academic sanctuary. Kilgore had a limp — Saslow had the shakes. Odd, huh? I knew why Julian chose cigars over pipes as his personal prop. The mongoose was careful not to imitate the cobra.

He always reminded our class, quoting Edmund Burke, "Those who ignore history are bound to repeat it." That single quote touched me in a manner I suppose others might feel moved by a biblical quote from one of Jesus' followers or a catchy phrase barked out on some late-night infomercial by a huckster whose only goal was to make you believe in yourself and your ability to overcome life's unfairness. Fairness and equality were popular terms back then. The bookends for the utopian society they sought to achieve. They were anything but fair to the opposition.

Based upon what I had learned from Kilgore's lectures, there wasn't a lot in mankind's past that I was eager to repeat; I figured ignoring it was unwise and that perhaps history held some secret as to the reasons our nation had gone so far off track. My interest to continue with that degree peaked late sophomore year when forced with declaring my major. One's choice of majors was limited by "The State" and based solely on our future needs as projected in their dubious Five-Year-Plans. We couldn't predict the weather from one day to the next and global warming proved to be a complete fraud, yet those infamous Five-Year-Plans were the lifeblood of our feckless society and they drove most government decisions; poorly I might add. In their world I was to move on to teach revisionist history to the next generation. Too bad, I didn't take that path and instead made history.

Visuals of Kilgore's animated lecture hall antics, his

constantly disheveled appearance and quick, biting wit inundated my vulnerable sensibilities. His abundance of passion for a subject most showed little interest in, attending only to fulfill a core requirement before advancing to their more therapeutic, hyphenated courses, sold me on appreciating his perspective on the subject. His eternal fascination with the Cold War era, KGB, Pravda and anything having to do with the former Soviet Union and his fabulously graphic descriptions of Soviet life, made it easy to imagine him crossing Mokhovaya Street as a young man. We became close friends during the second semester of my sophomore year, best friends the following year.

I was elated when approved by the state to continue with my degree although pissed that I needed their approval. Julian was most helpful in securing that blessing. School seemed the perfect sanctuary for my misguided, indecisive soul and forging towards a graduate degree in history seemed the ideal solution.

Each afternoon at 2:05, I'd find Julian walking the academic loop surrounding the quad, secluded in profound thought, puffing on his accomplice of urbanity, that Churchill cigar. The sweetness of its oaken essence conjuring images of my father, neutered the smells of the exotic, magnolia blossoms positioned around campus. It's funny how certain odors can conjure up memories. Cigars did that, and they were always happy ones. Magnolias reminded me of mom.

I joined him on those walks senior year, not every day, just Tuesdays and Thursdays and learned more about our unwritten history on those strolls than in three years of sitting in crowded lecture halls. He was a good professor, but my classmates were distracting, and the undergrad curriculum was highly monitored and drawn from a system known as CATS, Common Applied Teachings Systems. CATS was nothing more than a cute acronym for a revisionist curriculum. Julian attempted to skirt those lessons and teach the truth, something his peers never rewarded him with.

Our early discussions maintained the perfectly balanced mix of little-known historical facts and current events, but mostly ended with recaps of his mundane, boring social life. He wasn't the type of man one would peg for having a social life outside the boundaries of the institution, let alone an active one. I was like most young men, approaching that important crossroad of life. Frat parties, girlfriends, bar hopping, the usual stuff. They told me that college would be the four best years of my life. I was determined to make it so. Julian would update me on his latest literary fix or research and I'd usually recap my weekend exploits, most of which he found to be a waste of time and brain cells. He'd interrogated me like a defense attorney who was far too interested in my life outside the confines of MU. I felt sorry for the man, but never questioned his loner lifestyle.

He was polite, always asking if I was OK with his cigar habit. I assured him that I also enjoyed a good cigar. I smoked my first when I was sixteen, a Rolling Thunder 50 Caliber. It pissed Mom off. That thing was huge, had a smell of leather and honey if you can imagine such a combination coming from burning tobacco. I got high from the experience — most enjoyable though. For two years Dad and I hid that secret from her. I was underage, and she was convinced that smoking anything would lead to an early death by cancer or, by her irrational leap-of-logic, to the less acceptable but perfectly legal, marijuana. Completely ignoring my story, Julian kept walking faster and faster and stared into oblivion. People do that when something isn't right, and on that day something wasn't right.

Julian, Meet Aiken

* * * *

The following day Julian and I returned to the quad, each with a cigar in hand, and began our usual walking route. It was the first time I had ever smoked with him and, to be honest, I wondered when someone would come running up and demand that we extinguish our restricted addictions. What started out as my best attempt at getting some advice on how to approach a paper for Saslow's class ended with so much more. Like the previous day, his pace had quickened but distraction was written all over his face. Our usual routine of four times around the quad ended at two.

"Aiken McHale?" he blurted. Nothing else, just my old name. You know that feeling you get when you've just been caught in a lie? You stutter while trying to explain it away by adding another lie and then another. I had that feeling but my lie was about my true identity.

"Relax" he said, while pulling a newsboy cap from his back pocket, then placing it on his head. Professor Julian Kilgore had an interesting and active social life outside academia. He was my accomplice, and I was about to become his new protégée.

"Bring it all down! The battle-cry of the children of the 60s, those damn hippies," — an opening salvo unlike our normal relaxed walking discussions. He tossed his cigar in the bushes and then stopped dead in his tracks. In some bizarre manner, we had formerly introduced our true identities to each other that day. Although he completely knew of mine, beyond his being my favorite professor, Julian Kilgore was, at that point, still a total stranger to me.

Dr. Watson meet Sherlock Holmes.

Saslow was approaching from the opposite direction. He was a man on a mission with lots of stamina for an old guy and was gunning for Julian. It was written all over his face. The clock tower rang three bells noting the next block of classes. Discussion over and we hadn't even broached the subject of stolen identity. He left me hanging.

Forgetting he had no cigar, he reached towards his lips for that usual flick of the nub into the hedges but found nothing to toss. Those daily breaks from the miscreants who occupied his lecture halls were always accompanied by that surly symbol of manliness. It was effective at compensating for his meager build. I once told him that a pipe would seem more professorial, but he countered that he hadn't the patience to attend to their propensity to extinguish themselves. I believed that it was Saslow's affection for them that turned him to cigars.

"Gotta run, another class at three. Let's meet at The Drip on Thursday, say around four-thirty? Great macchiato and the best scones." We had met there once before yet he still felt compelled to tempt me with his culinary opinion on the quality of their scones and richness of their espresso. I wondered why the emphasis on the 60's, the hippies and the protests that marked that generation. I wondered why he was so angry and how the hell he knew who I was.

Meeting at The Drip

* * * *

We picked up our discussion two days later at The Drip. It was MU's most popular coffee shop, which became my secondary classroom — a place where only the truth was told but cameras always watched and bugs listened. We devised methods to avert them. Julian knew where the cameras focused and where every bug had been hidden. Some he had deactivated. The man was a wealth of knowledge when it came to all things espionage.

Popular among students and professors, its strikingly dark interior awash in a rich espresso color and accented by a collage of matted black and white landscapes was a welcome departure from the sterile mint green walls of our lecture halls. Insane asylums, hospital rooms, college lecture halls and dormitories each shared the same drab, depressing color pallet — very institutional.

But landscapes of the great outdoors were not the only pictures dotting the walls. Che Guevara, Castro, Stalin, Mao, and other notable mass murderers also held prominent positions throughout The Drip. I felt a sense of kinship among those tyrants, but for the opposite reason.

Big, squashy chairs meant for one, but large enough for two were randomly positioned throughout. We always grabbed the most secluded ones in the back of the shop, far from prying eyes and inquisitive ears and perfectly angled away from the nearest camera. Turning our heads to the left made it impossible to read our lips and there were no working listening devices in that section. Julian had made sure of that. Bereft of the propaganda Julian was forced to spew in his monitored classroom, it was our safe-house, the Pentagon where all of our planning would ultimately take place. One still had to be careful about discussions that wavered from what they considered socially or academically acceptable, lest the cameras glimpse our lips berating the system or worse, the President. Everyone whispered as they sipped, some not realizing that trained lip readers were on the other end of those fiber optics.

The place was a study in contrast with the essence of bitter espresso and sweet cranberry scones wafting through the entire room. It was the most perfect atmosphere to discuss history's conflicts and to do so among the enemy within. We were Patriots behind enemy lines.

The conversation that afternoon focused on each other, but didn't delve too deeply into details other than Julian reminding me that he had once substituted for a history class at Loudoun

County High School and that I was in that class.

"You came in late, sat in the back and then stared out the window for the rest of the class." I didn't recall that ever happening since arriving late and staring out the window with my zombie expression was typical for me in high school.

"And you're ok that I lied and changed my name?"

"Of course. You had no choice," he whispered, turning his head to the left and winking at me. I had to know what and how much he knew, so I asked, "What do you mean?"

"Vega 7."

My makeover hadn't fooled him. He knew of my video and that I was more than just a kid who was habitually late to history class. I was the kid that everyone was looking for, yet he still befriended me and kept my secret to himself.

Just as our previous discussion had been interrupted by Saslow, that afternoon's session suffered the same fate. While I was debating whether Julian had been stalking me since high school, I was certain that Saslow was watching him and that our close relationship was cause for concern. I got up went to the bathroom to avoid seeing Saslow and returned five minutes later to find that Julian had left. Class dismissed.

"Dinner my place, tomorrow," he texted me.

Dinner at Julians

* * * *

Tuesday night was my only night off from Il Portico and Julian knew that. It was eery that he had my schedule. I assumed that I'd be cooking and sure enough I did — paella. For a professor, he lived well, not what you'd expect from a guy draped in cheap polyester clothes and smoking a drugstore brand cigar. His house was brick on all sides, not just the facade like most in Sector 12. Large trees, trimmed shrubs, sod lawn and fresh mulch that looked and smelled as though someone had spread it that morning — in-ground sprinklers too.

The inside was staged for Architectural Digest but themed for the Smithsonian Museum of Natural History. Old African art, weapons from what appeared to be the Genghis Khan era all the way through Vietnam, Egyptian artifacts, and assorted tchotchke interspersed with modern art and fine crystal. He placed large picture books of the world's capitals and wars on coffee tables. The cheap cigar smell permeated every room, but was most noticeable in the weapons room. Like The Drip, it too was a study in conflict.

Although Julian never touched alcohol, he knew I would, but offered only warm beer and screw cap wine instead of the vodka I would have preferred. The man was socially clumsy, telling me where his "stash of booze" was and to help myself. I opted for a cheap Cabernet instead of warm beer. Before delving too deeply into what Julian had wanted to talk about, he treated me to a brief tour of his home including detailed explanations of the history behind each artifact. How he had acquired them was a source of great pride — bartering and sometimes stealing. That social engagement turned into a history lesson.

African art, which included an ornately carved wooden shield, several spears and a shrunken head, came from a trip to Mogadishu as a graduate student at Yale. The Genghis Khan stuff was nothing more than old Chinese weapons acquired from barters he had made while traveling through Vietnam. On a shelf inside of a glass etagere was an old roulette wheel that he had stolen from a casino in Macau that had burned down. His Egyptian artifacts would have been worth a considerable sum of money on the open market. Antiquities such as those would have been illegal to smuggle out of Egypt. I never asked, but imagined Julian working with the most bizarre characters to build his requiem to the Egyptian Gods. It fascinated him. The overall theme of the first floor of his home was weaponry.

Downstairs in the basement there was so much more but its focus was the former Soviet Union. Marx, Stalin, the Revolution, KGB interrogation and torture tools. There were several old wire tape recorders, cameras, Cold War and spy stuff. I was most impressed.

It was over dinner that Julian broached what was to be the intended purpose of that meeting, a coming-out party of sorts where each of us would reveal our true identity, even though he already knew far too much about me. The lesson began and Julian weaved a story as if we were in a lecture hall. Untold, unwritten history.

The Herons

* * * *

Planning for the Great Collapse began at the conclusion of WWII, but the Soviets started the plot to defeat us from within in 1962 at the height of the Cuban Missile Crisis. My video exposing Vega 7 should never have happened, but Queek was more interested in garnering "likes" and "shares," than in protecting his only friend. Two events connected by a well-planned invasion of America's shores, known as D6, which resulted in my parent's detention in the same facility I had taped and that Queek exposed. The story of my life — short, wrought with unintended consequences, but lethally consequential.

D6 took decades to complete. After World War II the Soviets, and many of America's enemies rightfully determined that they could never defeat us militarily. Dropping two atomic bombs on Japan, vaporizing over one-hundred-thousand civilians and bringing an end to "The war to end all wars," set us up as the world's sole superpower and one that should never be messed with.

The period following World War II was more than just an ending to the atrocities of war, it started a tense period that affected society at all levels. Fundamentally different ideologies, Communism, Socialism, Fascism and Democracy collided with advances in science. The nuclear bomb was the catalyst to those ideological collisions. A dangerous environment ensued that created an atmosphere of paranoia throughout the world and, most notably, within America. They maintained peace through the philosophy of mutually assured destruction. You nuke us, we'll nuke you. There are no winners in that scenario and I thought it a damn good strategy.

Hitler's final solution was to exterminate an entire group of people, Jews. The Soviets and their cohorts to D6 would be involved in our complete societal destruction from within and that began as a massive invasion plan that would take place over decades, fifty-seven years, to be exact. The underlying premise — we'd destroy ourselves. While we were the most powerful nation on earth, we were also the most paranoid, a combination that helped set in motion the D6 battle plan. Dumb-down, divide, debt, delete history, disarm and destroy. Patience was their weapon — stupidity was our Achilles heel, and that began with their takeover of our entire education system. It all began with our minds.

To successfully pull off this societal alteration, the Soviets would need the help of other countries, each of whom were also our enemies. There's safety in numbers and the opportunities afforded by partnering with these diverse nations made the plan more lethal. A multicultural invasion force the likes of which America had never experienced was about to hit our shores. China, Nicaragua, Iran and Zimbabwe were all involved. Exporting infants who were white, black, Asian, Hispanic and of Middle Eastern descent made for a diversified battle plan where each group would be pitted against each other when the final trigger was pulled — collapsing the U.S. dollar. That collapse set the stage for mass anarchy from sea to shining sea, something they had choreographed from within the Soviet Union. And to think — it all began with the launch of one ship in 1962, mockingly code-named Noah's Ark.

The Ark's Captain, Anatoly Sorokin, having been successful at guiding his ship month after month to that precise location off the coast of Long Island, had a pencil factory named after him and, to this day, all Russian children learn to write with a Sorokin. Julian never offered details of the other country's shipments, only reminding me that this was a global effort involving five countries, collectively known as "The Trust." Their leaders were each called Goliaths, the king of the species of Herons and they were never to be trusted.

"Egrets, Agami, Bitterns, Herodias, Blues and others awakened from the gentle monotonous swaying of the ocean waves that evening. Their lives completely planned out for them. Their adoptive American parents awaiting their arrival were totally prepared to contract with the devil as enemies of their own country — the United States of America. Finding suitable guardians was easy; keeping them in line with their stated objective was not."

When I was a kid, they printed pictures of missing children on the back of milk cartons. Every week they displayed a different missing child, a new location and fraudulent circumstances for their disappearance. The dairy section of the local grocery store became ground zero for conveying their sick message. That evening I learned where most of them came from and why their identities had been printed on the back of those cartons.

"Those who ignored the contract found their child's image ensconced on the back of a milk carton, MISSING, a constant reminder to the others that the Goliaths meant business and were not to be screwed with," Julian added. "They could be most cruel to those who didn't meet expectations but generous to those who exceeded them. Money, cars, boats, new houses were all dangled in front of those parents as incentives to do their job for the Motherland or whatever country their child came from."

"The Trust." A peculiar name to call themselves because they are not to be trusted — ever!

Predestined to fill the ranks as future day-care workers, teachers, college professors, lawyers, journalists, military commanders, journalists and our own elected leaders, I grasped the destruction they could reap upon an unsuspecting society. Hundreds of thousands of Trojan Horses born overseas, unceremoniously dropped upon our shores then raised among us with a singular goal, destroy America from within. Herons, in nature a frog's mortal enemy, but in 2018 the Patriot's worst nightmare. They avoided Ellis Island. An ingenious plan! Targeting our minds, our patriotism, and our sense of unity, we willingly welcomed the Herons into our lives while allowing them to denigrate our morals and the foundations of a once free society. They were infiltrators, and it all began with education or, as Julian termed it, indoctrination, beginning as early as the Day Care level. Devious little bastards. Imagine that. Taxpayer funded propaganda camps - daycare for our precious children!

Beginning early in childhood development and continuing all the way through college, they owned our malleable minds.

"The mind is a terrible thing to waste," "never let a crisis go to waste." Repeat that message often enough through the media you control, and it becomes downright sinister. They openly telegraphed their battle plans and mocked us while doing so.

The children were each categorized based upon their lineage, background and the inherent skills of their biological parents and the parents who adopted them. They made a match with the host American parent who showed the greatest ability for successfully raising those children according to the terms of each contract. The deep state has been active for longer than we had thought, and it went much deeper than we thought.

Teachers were matched with children marked to be Egrets. Future Herodias were adopted by parents in the military, and they normally placed law enforcement and Blues with families living in poverty or in the worst sections of the inner cities, but not always. Surprisingly, those who had committed the most heinous of gun crimes were upper middle class. They miscalculated those, but it made no difference to their objective. Blues were the violent ones. They regarded their biological parents as criminally insane and their singular goal — to alter public opinion against our right to bear arms which, I must note, had nothing to do with the Second Amendment. But, in their world, it did. Their method? — to commit heinous acts of mass murder and then commit suicide, leaving no one to interrogate and no tracks to lead back to their masters. There was no limit to their targets, and they had no boundaries. Young school children, innocent folks in a movie theatre or fans watching their favorite group perform in an outdoor venue were gunned down, all at the behest of the master who remains a mystery. I can't overemphasis the degree to which the Herons would go in their effort to disarm America. They triggered those mass murders from inside the Oval Office.

It was easy for their handlers to track and follow the Heron's progress, communicate with them through a secret government network known as SQUAWK, named after the sound herons, the bird, made. Tracing their adoptive lineage was easy should punishment be necessary. That punishment was usually doled out to the child, but sometimes the parents.

Captain Anatoly died a tragic death after shipment #34, apparently taking a capitalistic stand by demanding more money as compensation for his heroic adventures on behalf of the Motherland. Khrushchev despised the eager ones, preferring to silence them instead of coughing up one more rubble for exceptional efforts. They say he accidentally fell into the milling machine one evening while visiting that pencil factory, making his DNA a permanent part of a few thousand bright red pencils. While carried out on Soviet soil that execution order emanated from inside the United States, probably from the Oval Office. The true master was none other than President Neville.

The Cold War was upon us and, as Julian confirmed, several KGB agents had secured low-level positions within our own State Department and a few ended up in the Social Security offices, responsible for generating those numbers we all have. It was somewhere within State that they messaged their superiors with a kill recommendation for Anatoly. "Take him out, he's served his purpose," read one cable. "They're researching his background, his bank accounts, looking for friends." Read another. "CIA moving in." Lord knows they're scattered throughout C Street today, occupying small gray cubicles, churning out reams of worthless paper while reporting back valuable intelligence to the Goliath in Moscow. It was the twenty-first century Detente. Translation: SURRENDER. What a web we weave when trying to deceive.

There still stands a small statue to Sorokin at the Severnaya shipyard; it's plaque noting only his contribution to the communist state and cause of death. "Missing at Sea." What's most astonishing, though, is that they erected a duplicate statue across from our Capital dome in 1984 noting the good Captain as a nautical hero, having saved the lives of a few hundred Russian immigrants to America one cold day in March 1963. No one questions it. Revisionist history on a completely different level, I suppose. That statue mocked us and, unlike the other historical statues they took down during an intense period of citizens being offended by a hundred-year-old history, Sorkin's remained standing.

"Isn't history interesting? The weather cooperated," Julian repeated, knowing the irony of what he had just told me.

"Mutually assured destruction had been taken completely off the table, Joshua. Why risk that when you can destroy your enemy within? Herons and frogs — you understand the analogy now?" I did.

I was three glasses of cheap cabernet into the evening and Julian had barely touched his iced tea. We hadn't eaten yet, so I moved to his kitchen and prepared the paella. His story stunned me. Like during his lectures or our campus strolls, Julian was a tease and always left the best for last. Anxiety and hunger, a bad combination when cooking -- I under-cooked the rice. True to form, he promised to finish the evening by showing me something he kept locked in a safe. We walked downstairs and into an unfinished room which was dark and held all sorts of dubious treasures. On its wall, hung a dart board. Jamming darts into 20, 18 and 7 on the outermost ring opened a hidden door into another room, exposing his "War Room." Weapons, ammunition, news clippings and, a small, tungsten steel Sentry safe. Meek, mild professor Kilgore was a bit of a spy enthusiast having built that secret passageway himself. I felt like James Bond entering Q branch for a quick review of the latest gadgets I'd be using on my next mission. He rotated the cylinder left, right and back to the left again making sure I turned away and couldn't see his code, even though he was fine with my knowing the dart board sequence. Items stored behind lock and key or, in that case, six inches of tungsten steel, are either mystifying, highly valuable or illegal. What he pulled from that safe was none of those, it was lethal, a piece of paper that would become the foundation for our battle plan and the silent war we waged for the next several years.

The paper contained a list of twenty-six names, addresses, and four-digit identifier codes of the original Herons who had played active roles in our nation's downfall, the accomplices to the Great Collapse. He had deep background information on each of them, bragged about it and then handed me the list and said nothing. The first name on it was the Reverend Atticus

Phelps. Next to it was a bright red check mark. I looked over the list which contained a virtual "Who's Who" of the rich and powerful in America — the thought leaders, scholars, military, journalists, judges, cabinet officials, even Congressmen and Senators — each of them men, not one woman on the list.

The pieces of a puzzle that had confounded me since Queek and I had flown Jarvis over Vega 7 and continued up till the night I had killed Atticus Phelps began to fall into place. It was Professor Julian Kilgore who had taken control of Jarvis and returned it to us in the dumpster and it was Professor Kilgore who was my uninvited accomplice that foggy night outside the Art & Soul. He told me that as I looked over his list.

If you listen to what people say and don't say, sometimes the unspoken words are the most important as they hold hidden secrets or real truths. Before leaving Julian's that evening he left me with one final thought and it has perplexed me ever since.

"We will kill everyone on this list," he said without hesitation while jabbing his fingers at the paper. Unlike the manner in which he'd dole out homework assignments, Julian was dead serious and my killing the Reverend Phelps was the reason he knew I'd join his army.

"Before we were just family but now, we're partners."

Building a Code

* * * *

For the next several weeks we continued our ritual, meeting at The Drip on Tuesdays and Thursdays and once more at Julian's house. He explained the rationale behind the ordering on his list which was meant to avoid patterns which could alert the authorities to a serial killer. That would start a behavioral analysis by the FBI and other 3-letter agencies, clearly something we needed to avoid. Next, we began the process of building an executioner's code. We were very business like — Murder Incorporated. That code became our mental constitution and my subconscious for justifying every execution I have committed. With each successful mission it grew less refined and I gained more confidence as I grasped the destruction they had done to our nation. It was a simple code, and we followed it to the letter.

Most important to our code was the need for unquestioned "justification" for killing a subject and that came largely from Julian's deep knowledge of their past and the secrets they held. My input was usually, "Hate him, asshole, commie!" No females or young adults, no one who was not a verified traitor and willingly involved in our downfall. Methodical cunningness trumped stupidity. There was no mercy, no reprieve once my subconscious and Julian had mutually agreed on the target. Revenge for personal reasons was never allowed although personal vindication occasionally played a role. The list contained only the names of men, although there were several women who, in all honesty, deserved the same punishment. Julian had a soft heart, so cruel and unusual punishment was never permitted. "Quick and painless," he'd say, but cruel and unusual was a debatable point. What defines "cruel," and isn't the act of murder "unusual" on its surface? Julian's list contained twenty-six names, but not all were considered initial targets for execution.

Justification was always first on the list of considerations and that came about as a result of a thorough understanding of the subject's background and how successful they were at turning the tide of victory towards the Herons. We focused on the worst of the worst, the most despicable while remaining careful to never execute on ideological whim alone. Hating someone was never justification for execution although, at some points, I wished that it was. Our focus was on genuine traitors, all who hated America and had willingly worked towards its downfall. Those who sanctioned detentions and the killings of innocent civilians topped the list which grew well beyond the original twenty-six. This would take time to finish and, early on, I realized that it would also take others to compliment my lethal skills. I was an Army of one.

Julian remained cautiously obsessed with the prospect of getting caught while I stayed morally conflicted about my role in this war we were about to wage. Still, we remained a remarkably effective partnership like Holmes and Watson or The Justice League. We sought not to solve murders though, but instead to commit them all in the name of patriotism, not revenge. Hunter and Kilgore — had a nice ring to it, didn't it?

Code Words

* * * *

It's essential you understand our thought process and realize how pathological, yet also cunningly methodical we were in every execution we planned. Code words were necessary in our highly monitored society. Using words that could be overheard and ignored on campus or in a classroom allowed us to speak freely without fear of being eavesdropped on and ratted out. "Suspicion always fell upon those who looked suspicious," Julian would remind me. He insisted we be open in our discussions as long as we coded them. "Executions" were "events," our "targets" were "subjects," and each was followed by a number, which was essentially the order in which they were executed. The Reverend Atticus Phelps was Subject #1. Our entire vocabulary, including our weapons, was very collegian. Missions were called "exams," reconnaissance was "studying." When needing to meet Julian outside of the confines of campus, I'd text; "Need help studying for my next exam." A clean execution without any problems was "Aced my exam!" One with problems — "Not sure I did well on that exam."

As for our weapons, a knife was a "pen," which was loosely based upon the phrase, "The pen is mightier than the sword." "Prescott prefers that you write in pen instead of typing." A gun was "paint" like a paintball gun. "Paint a nice picture of the Senator." Strangulation was coded "the prom" and the weapon was a "tie." I'll be wearing a tux and tie to the prom.

As an aside, this was Julian's least favored method of execution because it posed serious risks and, to him, was also cruel and unusual punishment. By his calculation it took twenty-two-seconds to render a person unconscious once the act was initiated and seventeen-seconds more for them to die. Thirty-nine-seconds of agonizing pain was too much for him to handle, even though he'd never be present for the execution. I figured Julian had probably used that method successfully once before, thus his incredibly accurate numbers on how long it took to take effect. A lot can happen in thirty-nine-seconds. I understood his concern, but couldn't care less about the subject's feelings — Lord knows that they didn't care one whit about ours.

In Julian's mind, the most humane method of execution was lethal injection, similar to how criminals were executed in state prisons before the collapse. Potassium chloride, the death cocktail, was code-named "beer." What college kid doesn't drink it? "I hear that he loves to drink beer." Or, "Be sure to bring a six pack with you," should the subject be large and require a huge dose. Among the many weapons Julian had stored in his vault of lethality was adequate amounts of Potassium chloride and other pharmaceuticals.

Lethal injection smacked of being state sanctioned, so there was a bit of irony in choosing to use the death cocktail on any of our subjects. To me, it was all very anticlimactic though. After all, in a round-about way, our subjects were themselves serial killers. I could have cared less about being humane. They deserved all the inhumanity we could heap upon them. Hell, in earlier days, they would have been hung in the galleys, electrocuted, gassed or tied to a wooden post and shot. Humanity towards Herons was never on my radar, but Julian played that card frequently.

We carefully assessed the viability and risks associated with each method of execution, performed a SWOT analysis, and then assigned a number for each weapon. Julian would rattle off questions and scenarios in rapid succession all in an effort to get me to think fast, analyze the situation and then make a logical decision. "Think about every possible scenario that might happen when using a Glock against a Senator on a dark deserted street," he'd ask. "Now add into that scenario, rainy weather." "Quickly Joshua, what about the long rifle from a rooftop in broad daylight?" "It's windy, how do you adjust?"

Rankings were not just based upon my ability to carry out the task successfully, but also considered any possible evidence left behind after the act was committed. Spent shells, footprints, blood spatter from close confrontation, hair, DNA, etc. His formula was complicated but made sense.

Our logic went as follows: Shooting a subject with a rifle was a relatively low risk proposition and could be accomplished from a safe distance. But, the possibility that someone might see you afterwards raised its risk level considerably. Just wounding the target added more risk, so shooting rated a 4 on our scale of 1 to 10, with 10 being the most risky. Knives received a higher risk profile due to the proximity needed to fatally stab someone coupled with the same potential witness issues from using a rifle. That method rated a 7. The death cocktail also required proximity to the subject and had to be administered through a vein. Essentially, I'd have to walk up to a subject, put a stranglehold on him and then play a well-trained nurse for a few minutes. In an uncontrolled environment, lethal injection fared poorly, rating a solid 8. Too many unknowns and a knowledge of human anatomy that I simply didn't have. The drug takes some time to take effect so there was a whole host of issues with that one. It's not as though they immediately die.

No matter the method; blood spatter, DNA, hair fiber, footprints, a subject's ability to fight back, missing the target and the worst of all scenarios — witnesses, each became problematic if we were to be able to repeat our crime over and over again without getting caught. We weren't planning the perfect murder, we were planning perfect murders — serial executions. As we ticked off each option while white-boarding risks and remnant evidence, it became apparent that our first batch of executions must not occur in public, but instead, somewhere remote where no one could witness the crime — a death chamber. No body, no crime. There's a big difference between walking away from a dead body and having to take one with you. This necessitated transporting our subjects to another location, and that meant incapacitating them. Another cog in the wheel, I thought. It was at that point that Julian nonchalantly added, "And of course, that means we must destroy the body."

"I'll do it at my place," I quickly volunteered without thinking things through to their logical conclusion. I had no clue as to how one goes about destroying a body other than burying it in my backyard — but that wasn't destroying, that was hiding and Julian was emphatic that they be completely destroyed. I wasn't about to turn my vegetable garden into a killing field.

He was teaching me to think like a master, to analyze and consider all risks and options. He was indoctrinating me in how best to pull off the perfect crime. Eventually, I'd become a full-fledged assassin with some intense training in the proper usage of each weapon and we'd eliminate body destruction from our code. Julian wanted me to become completely comfortable with the act of committing murder. Destruction of the body, he informed me, would desensitize me to any misgivings I might have about inflicting destructive, lethal, messy acts upon a human body. His logic — one must be fearless and completely comfortable before taking the act of murder onto an open stage. He spoke with authority and it seemed from prior experience. It was at that point that I knew he'd be passing the torch on to me and that I was now his protégé. Julian was my uninvited guest that night when the dearly departed Atticus Phelps hit the pavement. He informed me that he was officially retiring from committing murders. The Teacher student relationship had just left campus and was now completely within my brain.

"A death-chamber. I like that," he said while glancing upward as he always did when pondering things. I informed Julian that I had already prepared one in my detached garage. He was pleased yet mildly disturbed, wondering what in God's name would have provoked me to take that initiative before learning all that he had taught me.

My reply; "TV, of course!"

The Pit

* * * *

I can assure you that we weren't just two hotheaded lunatics killing for the sake of killing. Justification was paramount to each lethal decision we made. The process, while clumsy at first, was not overly complicated but, as with anything new, there was a learning curve.

Our well planned missions didn't always go as planned. But on those occasions where screw-ups occurred, I fudged the reports Julian required, keeping him in the dark as to my weaknesses with killing and disposing of the subject's body. Cleaning up a crime scene was no easy task, and what we had settled on as our method for eliminating the body made me gag — something that took getting used to. It also added another layer of complication to what should have been a simple murder — transportation of an unconscious subject to the pit.

We'd begin by minimizing risks which required devising a foolproof plan, then routinely do test runs from extraction site to my home, which was where all executions were to take place. Remote, hidden from view, it was the perfect setting for bidding a final farewell to our nation's worst traitors. It felt right and Julian was in full accordance, but took time to agree with my terms. He thought about it for three days.

History is replete with serial killers who had successfully used their homes to hide heinous crimes. Jeffrey Dahmer's refrigerator, John Wayne Gacy's back yard and Fred and

Rosemary West who scattered bodies everywhere. These were not geniuses; they were sick, criminally insane individuals who evaded the authorities for years by bringing their work home. I was much smarter and obsessively cautious. In no way did I consider myself to be anything like them. Patriotic warrior versus insane criminal; there's a huge difference. I was tasked with eliminating the enemy within while they killed innocent victims who were loners or drifters for the sick thrill. We carefully chose subjects who were famous, but destructive to the foundation of the United States of America, their victims were random.   Still, getting caught was constantly on my mind as our subjects were public figures. The Herons noted their disappearance as all methods of investigation through various law enforcement and government agencies took effect hours after I had executed them, even though there were no bodies to alert them. Our events became headline news, 24/7 for a few days and then dropped off their radar.   Although we hadn't earned a spot on the Post Office wall, we knew that all of our best laid plans only delayed the inevitable. They would pursue us until caught.

I knew my home was the best place to further our objective, and to do so with no one noticing.   Remote and far off the beaten path had its benefits. They scattered herons throughout every sector, so at some point Julian would redeploy me to another sector. He called it a job transfer. Conquer one territory and then, similar to cicadas, move to the next. We hadn't even started yet, but had planned to replicate the Schlieffen strategy from World War I which later became known as a blitzkrieg. In the meantime, home sweet home became a house of horrors, or at least my garage and that pit on the left side did. I could have just as easily torched the place and had an enormous bonfire, but instead felt that the garage might someday become a historic landmark, similar to Gettysburg, or Bull Run — places where the enemy went to die.

What began as my best efforts to finish Massimo's underground vault for storing food, water, fuel and weapons evolved into a death chamber shortly after Cassi's murder. The project took six months to complete.

Proper insulation and removable coverings along the walls of the pit allowed for complete containment of evidence, mostly blood splatter, within a small manageable area. Professional painters used drop cloths, smart executioners covered floors and walls with plastic tarps which could be burned in the outdoor fireplace after each event. Dig a hole, brace it with some two-by-fours add screening, place plywood on the floor and a hinged door on top is fine for storing food and weapons. But, when complete secrecy was required, as was necessary while constructing a death chamber with full disposal capabilities, I needed a different set of materials — soundproofing, ventilation and PVC piping. My hidden door was nothing more than three-quarter inch plywood hinged three feet from the edge. Glue dirt to the surface to mimic the rest of the flooring and you've got the consummate secret passageway to hell. To a stranger who entered the garage, they'd never suspect the chamber below.

Yes, I've since filled the pit in and paved it over with cement, but it's important to know what used to lie beneath. I had thought of everything, right down to the soundproofing and ventilation flow piping. The final touches came once we had agreed upon the disposal method and all that took was a simple winch to lower the equipment into the chamber and a shovel to vent the output up and into my garden.

Unlike in state prisons just before they'd yank the switch or push a button to start the drip, I never asked if they had any last words. Didn't care. I damn sure didn't give them a final meal either. Still, many were frequent customers at Il Portico, they ate well anyway. They gave that sort of humanity in the face of death to those incarcerated in government penitentiaries, but not Vega 7, so why bother.

As my final act of Patriotism, I'd always salute the American flag and play our glorious national anthem through Dad's boom box before carrying out the final sentence. That was my underhanded version of cruel and unusual punishment. I never told Julian that I did it. In my mind, it was justified and avoiding cruelty wasn't my concern. This was war and I believed in forcing each subject to hear the words that so many patriotic Americans stood up and sang in proud salute to this once great nation. Bombs bursting in air, rockets red glare — I cherished each refrain. Great song but in 2019 they banned it, something about offending this group or that group, it was hard to keep track. Cue the music, raise the flag, proceed with the execution. It was downright theatrical and it amazed me at how loud that boom box played. Damn near deafening down there in the pit, the walls were extremely close. Point being, I had a routine.

Eventually we refined the declarations within our code but not until becoming more comfortable with what we were doing and had notched a few successes on our executioner's belt. Our first revision came after subject #4, a minor one not worth noting, but the method of disposal remained the same, organic but still messy. Chemistry and agronomy, it's a wonderful combination. Coded debates at The Drip, and a simple thumbs-up were all we needed. This college junior and an aging history professor became calculating and viscously efficient executioners.

Incapacitate Them

* * * *

Our final consideration was devising a foolproof method for incapacitating our subjects long enough to transport them to their final destination, my pit. The simplest solution was to taser, then drug them. Etomidate, a drug used for anesthesia during surgery was quick acting and for some unknown reason, Julian had plenty of that as well. The only downside to that drug was that it wore off quickly, so I had to use large doses. We coded that, "playing darts."

I was reevaluating my mentor. Was he a history professor, or a cold-blooded killer masquerading as one? He confessed to hating the sight of blood, though, and I found that to be odd for someone who had done this before. His stock of pharmaceuticals was concerning as well. Where did he acquire that stuff?

Julian was a fan of Potassium Chloride but, since I was to

be the executioner, the method was my choice and that depended on how I felt about each subject. Executions in a confined and protected environment negated our need for a risk ranking. Death by a firing squad of one, stabbing into the heart, strangulation or potassium chloride, it was my choice. My mood drove those decisions. Julian was never in attendance so the whole blood thing was a moot issue. I felt empowered.

We had settled on a four-step final solution. Taser, inject, transport, execute. To avoid checkpoints, which were random in and around the capital, I'd use the back roads even unpaved ones that ran through the woods and between farms but eventually connected to Route 7. Although railroads were the preferred method for moving troops during the Civil War, the Confederate Army sometimes used these farm roads knowing that the Union would attack the trains instead. As an added security measure, I modified Tania's van by adding a false bottom with a sliding drawer similar to what you'd find in the county morgue. Over top of that drawer, which would hold and hide the incapacitated subject, I'd stack fruits and vegetables that I drove daily to Il Portico. I kept business cards in the glove compartment. Joshua Hunter, Head Chef, Il Portico. We had thought of everything.

Egrets

* * * *

"Education is a weapon, whose effect depends on who holds it in his hands and at whom it is aimed." — Communist dictator, Joseph Stalin (1934).

"My object in life is to dethrone God and destroy capitalism." Karl Marx

It all began with the mind, our minds. Julian contends that the Soviet plot to take over our education system started in 1962 when the first Egrets, who were only children, landed on our shores. But just as they were being offloaded and shipped to their secret orphanages, a landmark decision from the Supreme Court took the first small step in banning the Bible and God from our schools. Karl Marx was alive and well in America, hidden deep within the documentation that became know as D6. Enough of our Supreme Court Justices were unwittingly doing the bidding of our enemy across the Atlantic Ocean through our Judiciary. Eliminating prayer or any form of religious expression in the schools was their first success as it explicitly targeted morality. Nine men in black robes were more powerful and destructive than 535 in Brooks Brothers suits.

Beyond banishing God, any God, there were four driving principles that would set the foundation for the dumbing-down of several generations beginning with their takeover of our education system. First — Discredit the American Constitution by calling it old-fashioned, out of step with modern needs, a living and breathing document and, on a global scale, a hindrance to cooperation between nations. Second — Discredit the American Founding Fathers. They were to be presented through our books and lessons as selfish aristocrats who supported slavery and had no authentic concern for the common citizen. Third — Belittle all forms of American culture and eliminate the teaching of American history. Give more emphasis to Russian history and, in doing so, paint them as the heroes of peaceful, modern-day coexistence. The Cold War was to be painted as America's silent aggression towards the Soviet people. And finally — Teach the students that violence and insurrection are legitimate aspects of the American tradition. Teach them to rise up as a united force to solve the economic inequities and social problems which blanketed America, compliments of their demoralization of our society. The individual was to be replaced by the community and group-think was heralded as a better way to solve problems. It was a circle-fest, but it worked.

Julian's first target had run the gamut through our education system, doing more damage than you can imagine. Beginning at the elementary school level, where a young mind was a terrible thing to waste and then moving through several Universities throughout America, our first joint execution was to be of the grand daddy of our entire system, the Czar of the Department of Education. He oversaw the writing of our text books, state mandated lesson plans, testing, you name it. He controlled it all but he was also a criminal himself. Justification was a no-brainer. I was doing double duty — killing a traitor while also ridding society of a vicious criminal. His name was written in all caps.

Subject #2: Our First Joint Kill

* * * *

Emotions complicate our most basic instincts but, with murder — it must never play a role. Julian reminded me that killing the Reverend was entirely emotional and from that point forward would never be tolerated. I'd call it revenge, but what's the difference? The end result was the same — one less Heron to deal with.

Killing for justice was the only logic we applied, and that, along with Julian's insistence that the body be destroyed, became the foundation for all who found their way into my pit. Thus began the first bullet point in our evolving executioner's code. In a nutshell — a patriot's justification and no body, no crime. It grew from there.

Although we hated those who called our Constitution a "living and breathing document," over the next several years, something forced us to edit that code. It too became "living and breathing." Let's call it extenuating circumstances. It lived and breathed daily and, depending on who our subject was, it either breathed easily or with some difficulty.

For our second subject Julian was emphatic we target a Cabinet Official, a Czar. "Less risky than a Senator or Sector General and easier to carry out," he assured me. I wasn't buying it — convinced that it was his clever way of saying, "Son, you need practice and this guy is a perfect subject to hone your skills."

I was less than excited about his questionable confidence in me, but Subject #2 was also an archenemy of Julian's, so I couldn't completely discount him being a revenge killing. I had mine, he should have his. From the very beginnings of our criminal partnership, our code was being challenged. He wanted this one badly.

Although our code prohibited revenge killings, there's a fine line between murdering for revenge and executing a subject who had committed treason against our homeland. Julian's list contained the names of those who had committed the most despicable acts against the United States of America and we both sought revenge for what they had done. I considered that fine line to have been officially crossed. Secretary of Education, Lawrence DeSoto, was about to become Julian's revenge killing. The Czar of Education was the perfect choice. Egrets were absolutely the most dangerous of the Herons and cutting the snake's head off seemed logical. I was ready to begin the planning and stalking phase. It felt good to have a partner.

Subject #2 was a purist, an Egret whose specialty was economics and history, the revisionist kind. Capitalism was bad, Socialism was good, Communism was even better. Thirty-two years of dumbing-down our children at the elementary school level and then it was on to the collegian crowd where he implanted the final kernels of anti-capitalism to a naïve, but willing generation. From there he spawned a new crop of Egrets who, like him, began their mission teaching young children. Teacher, pupil, traitor, teacher, pupil, traitor. It was the circle of life in academia.

Having arrived in 1966 aboard shipment #52 from Minsk, his entire life, including time spent in the government, was filled with anti-American rhetoric, yet he still became the Czar of Education. Mind-boggling — had it occurred before the collapse, but afterwards, this appointment was standard fair. Confirmations for the most virulent anti-Americans came quickly, while those with a hint of patriotism in their writings rarely made it past the initial background check.

Like Julian, Lawrence was once a college professor; Yale: Trade and Industrial History. His thesis considered the effects a country's governing structure had on a litany of social and economic variables. He discussed racial unity, income equality, economic equality, health care, incarceration statistics by race — a laundry list of socialist causes. His conclusion: Capitalism caused the world's troubles and America was its worst offender. He applauded Socialism and Communism for its fairness and civility, even suggesting that America would have been great had Karl Marx replaced Jefferson as our ideological father. That was a common reply among them when reminded that Socialism and Communism have failed everywhere it had been tried. "If only America would follow those ideologies, the rest of the world could learn from us." They hated federalism and applauded nationalism. Lawrence adored Cuba and the Soviet Union. No surprise, but Sweden was always their poster-country representing a prime example of the success of Socialism while Cuba was a Communist utopia — healthcare for all! Venezuela didn't even exist in their curriculum.

He made no bones about his hatred of that "pesky little

Constitution the less educated citizens so loved." No one cared. They had already shredded our Constitution, so bitching about it made no sense other than to further browbeat those of us who still revered it. We were "out of touch," "less educated," "stuck in the past."

His occasional vile media ramblings caused even the most left-leaning viewers to scratch their heads wondering if he was on drugs, rendering him temporally insane.

Lawrence had a secret past though, and Julian knew every sorted detail. Secretary Lawrence DeSoto was himself a murderer, twice in fact, and that helped earn him the coveted spot at the top of our list. Subject #2; combined justification brought on by an urge for revenge and our sense of patriotism. I nicknamed him "The Chipper."

Lawrence DeSoto

* * * *

I found it curious that, as a child, he was plain old Larry instead of the more sophisticated Lawrence. As he aged and rose through the Heron ranks, becoming the more elegant version of that name played to his advantage. It sounded smarter, more refined. Larry was a cable guy, but Lawrence was a leader, an educated elitist. That was important to them. They were, in their minds, smarter than us common folk.

Learning of his violent past gave me a small sense of comfort knowing I'd be following biblical teachings — an eye for an eye. The more I learned about him, the more at ease I became with the thought of executing the bastard. Julian's rationale for choosing him as my first was working. God himself would have approved of his sentence so my comfort level rose even though God was still on my shit-list for allowing America to fall and my parents detention at Vega 7. Making lists with plusses and minuses, pros and cons became the bedrock for our justification formula. My stream of logic was simpler and always followed the same path. First, imagine the subject as worse than a serial killer or rapist. Then, I'd ask myself; "Would the world be better without him?" The answer was always the same — YES! From there, I'd draw great comfort knowing I was not committing a crime but instead a patriotic act sanctioned by my own state of mind. Once the execution was complete, a red check-marks removed and replaced those pluses and minuses on Julian's guarded list. I liked those. Completing tasks was a source of great joy back then and these were critically important tasks in our master plan.

Amanda

* * * *

Her name was Amanda, and she followed Lawrence all the way from the farmlands of Barnhill, Ohio to Boston where he attended college. Although she was his girlfriend, Amanda was also suspicious of him, leading her to rummage through his personal effects whenever the opportunity arose. He kept a diary.

She discovered that diary and, upon reading some of his writings, learned that he had raped and then strangled to death a young girl from his hometown. She was only thirteen, and he noted in the diary that he wrote that as a short story for a creative writing class, leaving him some wiggle room should anyone discover that diary. A confession masked as a short story — clever, but Amanda wasn't buying it. Murderer, rapist, a traitor — the justification trifecta!

They never found Chelsea Wadsworth's body. According to Julian, he had wood-chipped her into gooey shreds and mixed those remains with cow manure then spread her like fertilizer in his father's tomato field. The braggadocios bastard noted, "Dad's tomatoes that summer were sweet, a bumper crop." I can attest to that fact and, suppose I owe a debt of gratitude to Lawrence for giving me that agrarian tip.

Curious about his story, she researched the library's microfiche for missing persons in Barnhill during that time period. Sure enough, it was true and, authorities had never found her body. Amanda realized that she was in love with a rapist and murderer. His communist beliefs were inconsequential as she was one too.

Being a stranger on campus, with no friends, she confided her discovery to his roommate while also confronting Lawrence before their regular session of excessive drinking, smoking pot and having endless sex in his dorm room. Voila, she too went missing the next day. Amanda Mueller disappeared and no one ever noticed. Poof! Drunk, stoned and mad as hell, what could go wrong?

DeSoto's family was wealthy and capable of affording the finest defense lawyers in town should he get convicted, but he wasn't — no body, no crime.

Not satisfied with having a cloud of suspicion hanging over him, which would have dampened his chances of rising to the Cabinet-level position he held, Lawrence took matters into his own hand by turning suspicion away from him and towards his roommate. A bogus letter from his girlfriend accusing the roommate of having raped her one evening while she was drunk, stoned and incoherent did the trick. Not the most creative ploy but it worked. She warned in that letter she'd go public with the indiscretion thus ruining his reputation as the upstanding young gentleman he was. That roommate was none other than Julian Kilgore, crediting Lawrence with concocting the first fake news story, which eventually became sacrosanct to the success of D6.

"Are you serious?" I asked Julian after hearing his story.

"Yep."

"How'd he copy her handwriting? Surely they checked."

"You're forgetting. We didn't have computers, but we had typewriters and he typed those accusations on hers."

Lawrence had no intentions of setting Julian up for her murder but instead kept that bogus letter as an insurance policy. There was bad blood between the two and Lawrence still possessed that letter. At some point Julian realized it, but that was long after both had graduated.

DeSoto had guardian angels, and they were most effective at keeping him out of trouble by erasing records of his criminal past. Not only did they occupy the Social Security office and

Offices of Vital Statistics, they were also deeply embedded within the F.B.I. and our other three-letter, unconstitutional agencies. They had all bases covered — birth, work, and for those who strayed, criminal absolution. What better position to place him in than as the Czar of Education to further their plans to instill a stealth communist agenda into every school across America. It started with a publicly funded, free pre-school system that began about the time I had entered high school. It wasn't my father's kindergarten. Columbus Day was no longer a holiday, Christmas became Winter Break. Our most vulnerable were being indoctrinated at an early age, as early as Day Care. Young minds are a terrible thing to waste.

"And her body?"

"Never found."

"What about you? How d'you escape suspicion?"

"A few guardian angels of my own."

Convinced that DeSoto had returned to his murderous roots, Julian continued his story, reminding me that a murderer will always return to the scene of his crime. But for Lawrence, he returned to the tried-and-true method that allowed him to get away with that act in the first place. Wood chippers. No body, no crime.

In Dalton Massachusetts resides the paper manufacturer that supplies the US Government with the paper onto which our currency is printed, Crane and Company. It was open to the public from July through October. She disappeared in November. Up stream from that paper factory were numerous lumberyards. Small gasoline-powered sawmills run by local entrepreneurs, served many communities in the early twentieth century including supplying wood pulp to Crane and other paper manufacturers scattered throughout the state. Abandoned but still operational wood chippers were all over the place if one knew where to look. Convinced that his roommate had driven Amanda early one Saturday morning to an isolated area outside of Dalton, killed her then wood chipped the body, Julian contends that he hauled her remains to a nearby river and, along with the wood chipper, floated her down the river. He returned to campus before most students had awakened. No Body, no crime!

"Amanda confided in me after discovering his confessional paper, she'd be going to Dalton later that evening with Lawrence to see a friend." Julian knew that Dalton was littered with old wood chippers and that Lawrence would have found one and used it. He was returning to his roots.

Justification confirmed.

I accepted Julian's history lesson on Lawrence DeSoto as a fact but Google'd missing persons from Barnhill Ohio, specifically Chelsea Wadsworth and Amanda Hague, later that night. Trusting Julian was not the issue. My father's insistence that I always follow his favorite President's commandment of, "Trust but verify" was. I was merely verifying, and by doing so, proved the Professor to be honest. But honesty goes only so far when that honest person is also evasive.

The Plan

* * * *

We returned to The Drip the following Monday afternoon to discuss the process for carrying out a flawless execution of a member of President Neville's cabinet. No easy task, in my mind, but Julian continued to assure me otherwise. Code words were flying as quickly as the espresso being drawn by the barista. Julian focused on strategy, the "where," "when" and "how," while my attention fixated on the disposal of his body. Live by the sword, die by the sword, or in DeSoto's case, the wood chipper came to mind.

"I have a wood chipper — really helps clear the dead limbs and branches around the yard." An odd thing to say when Julian had just finished discussing strategy, but it needed to be said.

While not amused at first, Julian saw the brilliance of that idea, especially when reminded of his insistence that complete annihilation of the body be Code Declaration #3. He'd swish his espresso, glance upwards and close his eyes before swallowing when pondering something. We both had weak stomachs and felt that such vile treatment of a human body, even a dead one, bordered on the psychotic. But how else does one fully eliminate a body other than to cremate it?

He leaned in and whispered, "What the hell Josh. This is not who we are. We're Patriots."

"It solves our problem, and I know I can do it." I whispered back. Seriously, I had no idea how difficult that would be but figured what the hell — I was pumped!

My adrenaline kicked in. Fear, revulsion, maybe a hint of excitement, I'm not sure what made me quiver, but it was noticeable to everyone around us. People looked away. Our normal meetings were brief and entailed downing two macchiato before ending with, "class dismissed," but for this one we consumed four, maybe five, I lost count. The caffeine was like speed, the subject lethally serious. Caffeine, fear, disgust, criminality; bad combination.

We spoke at a quicker pace always conscious of the cameras mounted in each corner. I kept my U.S. History book opened on my lap as a prop, bookmarked at The Cuban Missile Crisis. It was a rambling, but coded session and we occasionally spoke over each other. Confusion would have ensued should anyone pick up pieces of that conversation. To be honest, I got confused myself. It's like learning a new language but "Rosetta Stone for Murderers" hadn't caught on yet. You'd have to pay close attention and then decipher our words back into understandable sentences. At one point we laughed, noting the absurdity of our paranoia and the lengths to which we went to avoid being overheard.

Being so callously ambivalent about what we were planning made me sick to my stomach. Not a good start even though I had already pumped two shots into the back of the Rev's skull. We're talking about murder, the taking of a human life and then shredding it like dead tree limbs in the forest or rotted food through a garbage disposal. But when the word "innocent" is missing from that equation — "the taking of a human life and then disposing of the body" becomes less heinous. It becomes justified! It was a turning point for me. I became callous and uncaring. I stopped caring.

I had to imagine how best to shove a guy's body into a wood-chipper. Does he go in whole or do I slice him into small pieces similar to what I would do when making potato soup or dicing vegetables — manageable cubes? Not sure I could carve a man up, in fact I was certain I couldn't. Kill him, yes — carve him up like a deer, nope. I was having serious doubts about a process that I had suggested we use. It didn't take long to assign the term "pencil sharpener" to the chipper and Tania's father had a huge one in the backyard which is what solidified my suggesting it in the first place. Don't bother looking for it. I dismantled it and dumped its rusted, DNA riddled components into the same area I scattered Cassie's ashes — the Atlantic Ocean.

Still, the wood chipper was not a weapon of execution, but instead an efficient tool for completely eliminating and disposing of the body. She was powerful, rendering its contents into little more than a pile of saw dust in a matter of seconds. But, with a human body, it was less dust and more mush as our bodies are ninety percent water. I'd have to do some test-runs or risk splattering DeSoto's DNA all over the place.

Just as ships are named after women, so too was the Barka Biomass CH885. I called her Chelsea. If there is a heaven, I hoped that she'd look down upon what I did to him and appreciate the small irony in his final solution. My tomatoes needed a boost. The Barka's spec sheet noted that it gobbled large quantities of limbs and tops quickly. If only they knew the limbs and tops I'd be feeding her.

We coded the disposal of our subject's bodies as a "date." Spreading the remains over my garden to serve as fertilizer for my vegetables seemed an efficient agrarian solution, something the tree-huggers would appreciate. Lawrence was about to have a date with Chelsea. I'd be feeding those who would be future subjects, the foods fertilized by the essence of their fellow traitors. There's something poetic in that. The culinary circle of life.

Time for bed. 10:00, the same time every night. I'm a creature of habit, although sometimes it's not by choice.

Code of Execution: Declaration #2:
Method of execution shall not be cruel or unusual.

We were to afford the highest degree of respect for our subjects before following through with their final sentence. The words "cruel" and "unusual" were subject to interpretation and left me a fair amount of wiggle room. Still, we tried our best to be honorable in our methods. Although Cassi's death was cruel and her memory continued to haunt me, I assured Julian that I'd follow his orders.

All that was left was arriving at a consensus on "where, when and how" to incapacitate DeSoto without being noticed. A Czar, while not of the stature of a Senator or Congressman, had a small security detail assigned to them but only during working hours. DeSoto was unguarded once he arrived at his home in Potomac. Julian had already verified that. His routine after work and before arriving home became our next focus. I remember thinking to myself "Good Lord, I hope the bastard even has a routine." Boy did he!

The Czar's Secrets

* * * *

Everyone has secrets and Lawrence was no exception. Sure, his were criminal but decades later he hatched a whole new cache of hidden gems — deep, dark and psychological. Like an archeologist digging in the rich soil of the Calakmul Mayan ruins, Julian was relentless in his pursuit for information on each of our subjects but with Lawrence, digital digging wasn't necessary. Beyond his honorary membership in The Perfect Crime Club, Lawrence was also a huge fan of massage parlors, not the fancy spa type and not the ones that promised a happy ending for a few extra bucks. His addiction was pain, and he fed that as a frequent customer at the Masochists Master's Massage, or the 3M as it was known among its loyalists.   An underground BDSM sex parlor for some of society's most demented individuals, featuring a menu that served up nails, strangulation and, of all things, oxygen depravation. Not fingernails, real nails, the type a carpenter would use to secure two wooden boards or the ones the Romans used to hang Jesus upon that cross. Hardcore stuff and DeSoto was a Platinum member.

Still, I wondered if these revelations were new or had Julian known of Lawrence's sick proclivities long ago. They kept in contact for years. Blackmail? It goes both ways.

Intelligence of this degree wasn't found through Google searches or cursory background checks, especially of a Czar. The Herons were careful to scrub all databases containing incriminating evidence of their soldier's backgrounds. Julian had gathered this information over years through his network of associates, many of whom were, by his admission, not normal. Normal — what the hell was that? Nothing was back then.

The boring professor and now my closest friend, while reclusive outside of his lecture hall, remained deeply embedded in secret societies that sprang up after the Great Collapse. This was most helpful to our cause since many of our targets swam in those same swamps.

Families torn apart by the collapse and forced into an odd array of social networks to reestablish some small sense of normalcy created Facebook groups to fill that void. Odd as it sounds, people sought abnormal behavior. Mature men and women started all over again and that unleashed an army of depraved individuals willing to do anything to feed their obsessions. Many found family members, former Facebook friends and Tinder hookups either serving time in Vega 7, off the grid or dead. Social networking took on a new aura, and it wasn't a good one. Many had been so desensitized watching, taking part by force or desperation in the mass anarchy, murder and cannibalism, that morality had taken a back seat to kinky, demented, immoral behavior. God had been removed from the public square decades before, so this shift was to be expected .

Sounds strange, my moralizing while recapping the vile things I did to God's creatures, but it's part of our code of "Justification."

The 3M was in SW New Columbia, near Capital Hill in an area dotted by old warehouses, a gay nightclub and torn up railroad tracks, coincidently on M Street. Although that area had gone through a revival before the collapse, afterwards it became a makeshift tent city due to its proximity to the Potomac River and its water supply. Fresh water was scarce, due in large part to people being unable to pay their water bills. Shut off was automatic for those who were ten-days Past-Due and there was no mercy given, even to those who could muster a tearful story. Walking buckets a block from the river became the only way of parching thirst for many city dwellers who had lost everything. That river was a cesspool of microbial garbage and I'd rather drink my urine than swill from it, but most people understood the need to boil it before drinking. God blessed me with a well deep enough for a constant supply of fresh, clean water. For that, I am eternally thankful.

"I'm guessing you want me to visit the 3M?" I asked Julian.

"Yep," he replied with that wry smile, knowing how uncomfortable that made me feel.

Julian took odd pleasure in the discomfort of others, especially me. Made me wonder if he was also a 3M member. He wasn't.

It's late. More tomorrow.

The 3M

* * * *

Three days had passed since Julian sprang his 3M-reconnaissance request on me; three days of wondering why the hell I needed to visit a temple of pain and pleasure which are diabolically opposed. But Thursday was around the corner and he'd be expecting my report. I had no clue as to the objective but went, anyway.

Restaurants in the that part of town were closed on Mondays by order of the Sector Captain, but bars could remain open, which was odd since they served food too. The control they had over how you operated your business was relentless and, from an economic standpoint, made no sense. But, what began with bakeries being forced to ignore their religious covenants, expanded into a legal entanglement that allowed anyone to enter and tour facilities they didn't belong to. The 3M was a private club and I'd use that ruling to my advantage. It looked busy, or as busy as a club catering to a niche market in a dank part of town could be. The parking lot was filled.

They had removed the tents which housed displaced people after the collapse, but the area surrounding the 3M was still seedy with trash strewn everywhere and the air wafted with the essence of urine. Homeless people along with assorted drug dealers congregated in back alleys, so walking alone after dark was a terrible idea. Dilapidated buildings with plywood covering their windows as protection from squatters was all you could see.

Even though six years had passed since the first riots, there was still much to do in the public works sector. Materials were scarce and labor slow, so any changes came at a snail's pace and, when finished, were always over budget. Street lights were a hit or miss and the ones that worked exuded an orange hue you'd associate with warehouse districts or high-crime areas. Burned out lights took months to replace and, on that night, the orange hue was less noticeable as many had flickered out — it was dark. It wasn't Georgetown or Foggy Bottom, so the 3M was an oasis among an otherwise blighted area. The perfect spot for an extraction and, based upon my initial scan, there'd be no witnesses to worry about.

I parked several blocks away then placed a different set of license plates on the van to avoid any connection with the target being followed. That night it was New Hampshire — Live Free or Die, most appropriate. Dad had collected ones from every state and, although states were now Sectors, their plates were still acceptable. While that might seem extreme, one never knew when cameras were capturing license plates to locate potential suspects, or other assorted criminals. It could happen anywhere. We lived in a police state and guilt by association was also guilt by location.

My father drilled into my head the importance of observing your surroundings. As I approached the brick building that housed the 3M, I took careful note of the cars parked around it and any cameras that might be perched in the trees or lamp posts. European models Mercedes, Porsche, even a shiny red Ferrari tucked away in the back alley showed wealth, but that clientele were not fans of our surveillance society since I saw no CCTV cameras on the building or anywhere near it.

The front entrance was welcoming, well lit with doors painted in a deep purple and black-faux marble pattern and the white 3M logo decal had been glued askew, to its center panel. The back door was a rust color but, unlike the front, a total mess. The southern exposure had blistered the paint and rotted the wood. There were no lights in the back. I understood the purpose for the contrast between front and back. Dark and unwelcoming make for perfect entry and exit points for clients whose privacy was more important than whatever sick jollies they experienced from visiting the 3M. Larry was a backdoor customer. Could I enter? And through the front or back?

The fear I felt at the thought of entering that establishment filled me with angst and distress, not knowing what to expect behind those doors. Breaching its entrance looking like a lost child would draw attention so I opted for surveillance around the immediate vicinity to bide some time in the most useful manner until I could calm down, compose myself and enter like an experienced deviant. I took a walk and recalled my father's advice on walking with a purpose and without drawing attention to yourself.

"When needing to appear inconspicuous." he'd lecture me, "it's best to walk at a normal pace, always gazing straight ahead as if the surroundings are familiar. Constantly looking around is an instant marker for a stranger — someone who doesn't belong.

Blend in, walk casually and with a purpose. Keep reminding yourself that your destination is just ahead and around the corner. When strangers approach, stare directly at them. They'll look away every time. In an elevator, they'll look down at the floor or up at the ceiling." People weren't friendly any more. Dad's advice stuck with me but fortunately I saw no one that night.

I strolled three blocks in each direction, looking ahead for cameras, but saw none. In the trees, on the lampposts, the tops of abandoned buildings, anywhere one might place one; the area was clean. The moon was full but sat low enough in the sky allowing the tall oak trees dotting the street to mask its glow — perfect for forcing Lawrence into a peaceful nap before shoving his listless body into the back of my van. Clouds are always preferable.

I was so methodical in my search for cameras and of the surrounding area that thirty minutes had passed since I arrived at the 3M and I hadn't even entered yet. Traffic was nonexistent, and no one walked the streets. Another good sign. Julian's request that I visit was making sense. It was time to enter.

Since the 3M was a Members-Only club, I rehearsed a variety of answers to the most likely questions they'd ask me. "How can I help you?" was likely. Would I say whips and chains or some dark torture chamber where the mistress ties you up and humiliates you into a state of submission? I was a virgin in a world I cared little about becoming a member, so I thought, "I'm just looking," like shopping in a store that is above your financial means yet still enjoyable to see how the other half lives. In my case it would be to see how the other half abuses themselves or others. My intentions were to secure a tour — not to indulge in their offerings.

The 3M flourished on the anonymity of its clients, so giving my real name wasn't an issue — I'd lie, anyway. Just beyond that door were more fetishes and hedonism than sensible folks like me could handle. Deep breath, hard swallow, suck it in, I opened the front door and entered. Dark, but in a weird almost psychedelic way, with black walls illuminated by fluorescent up-lighting which highlighted phosphorescent nude Roman paintings. The floors were down-lit by small LED lights which changed colors and intensity in perfect unison with the tempo of the loud, heavy-metal music blaring through a premium sound system. Someone paid a lot of attention to detail and the 3M was decked-out for the more affluent sexual deviant. Drinks were $20 a pop. Their revenue came from services rendered, and sober sexual deviants spend more than drunk ones. I would have thought the opposite as a drunk gambler is a profitable gambler. On the wall was a menu noting services offered and upcoming events, the most humorous being a Sadist Hawkins Day. It was two weeks away. I knew Larry wouldn't be attending. They offered each service in sixty, ninety or two-hour blocks. No quickies or thirty-minute sessions and the cheapest was still $300 per hour.

A young lady with long, jet-black hair and covered with fire-breathing dragon tattoos along her left side, greeted me as I walked in. She was pleasant enough but seemed suspicious, never having seen me before. She presented me with that haughty, private club attitude where the maître d' looks you over, up and down deciding on whether to welcome you in or dismiss you as unworthy of their fine establishment. This was a BDSM sex club, not a country club. Her cautious attitude was meant to protect the privacy of those who had entered before me through the back door. She was the gate-keeper and was both sexy and annoying at the same time. Not someone you'd be proud to take home to meet the parents, but could envision yourself hooking up with — once.

"Happy to show you around Mr ...?" She paused.

The brass tag on her blouse noted her name as "Silly." What parent would name their child Silly?

"Graham," I said.

Hushed screams emanated from the back hallway. Not the "help, someone is trying to kill me" kind but the sadistic happy ones, if that makes sense. There's a subtle difference. I couldn't imagine working eight-hours a day in that environment because this was not a bright and cheery place. The short time I was there was painful enough and I was merely touring.

As we entered the main hall, shrouded behind an etched glass wall with purple water cascading down it, the smell changed from the splash of woody cologne scent to an odd mixture of burning incense and human sweat, or something else I didn't want to imagine. They positioned a large open area with round, marble tables each surrounded by three deep upholstered chairs around the floor space. Either a lady dressed in business attire but tilting more towards the high-end hooker-look or a young man looking as though he had jumped off of the cover of GQ magazine, occupied one chair. Both men and women frequented the establishment. After the collapse the boundaries between men and women, moral and immoral had disintegrated. Even public restrooms were gendered-neutral and, as I had expected, their bathrooms were open with no doors or dividers to hide the urinals or toilets. "Pee and be seen" was painted above its entrance.

As I watched the interactions between the men and women, I realized that the three chairs at each table encouraged threesomes because their menu of services noted that option as the most expensive they offered, $500 per hour. As luck would have it, or as God had planned, Silly's cell phone rang just as we were readying a dungeon tour. Her headset's red pulsating LED signaled that a call was coming in. She turned away but remained within earshot.

"Yes Mr. DeSoto, it's quiet tonight and Bambi's available, Calvin's coming in at nine. Will you be joining us?"

So much for keeping their client's privacy from prying eyes or, in that case, attentive ears. I glanced away pretending to be oblivious of her conversation while staring at a young Asian girl who looked most uncomfortable with her career choice. She looked all of sixteen. The collapse forced many into dangerous, immoral professions to provide food for their families. I felt sorry for her but her sales approach was amusing. She wore a cowboy hat and had sharp spurs on her boots, tools of the trade for clients with foot fetishes.

It was past 8:30, and I knew that Lawrence would soon walk through the door for his rendezvous with Bambi and Calvin, whoever the hell they were. A threesome? I thanked Silly for the tour even though we had yet to breach beyond the social area which was nothing more than a launching pad into the bizarre world of something I wasn't interested in witnessing. Going down a long hallway with narrow purple doors on either side and hearing screams of orgasmic pain was all I needed to hear. That's where the essence of incense and that other smell was coming from.

"If it's ok, I'd like to grab a drink at the bar," I asked.

"Enjoy yourself. If you need anything, just ask. You should consider more than a tour," she added with a wink and smile.

I walked over to the bar, sat down, ordered a martini, stared at my burner phone while pretending to text someone. Blending in as a fish out of toxic water wasn't easy. But, since I had twenty-minutes to kill, I sat, drank, fake texted and then drank some more. Inebriation hadn't visited me when Lawrence entered the establishment. I wish it had though. The guy grossed me out.

Like clockwork, he walked in at 9:00 pm and Calvin, I assumed, was right behind him. A warm, long hug and that "I've missed you" look appeared on both men's faces. Entering through the backdoor confirmed that this was routine for DeSoto. He was a regular. State-owned media chose its stories carefully and the ones that involved DeSoto's work at the DOE were edited and always positive. The fool was a two-time murderer. His masochist addiction made no difference in the broad scheme of things but were clearly interconnected with murder. I wondered if Lawrence was the recipient of the pain they doled out behind those purple doors or if he imparted it on others, perhaps Bambi and Calvin. Based upon his history, I guessed the latter.

People Watching

* * * *

I'm an avid people watcher. Observing interactions among friends or strangers on the street, in Julian's lecture hall, even The Drip, it didn't matter, I enjoyed doing it. Maybe I was looking for that glimmer of happiness between a man and a woman or parents and their kids. Those were rare after the collapse. Human interactions changed. People were paranoid of others and suspicious of their surroundings but couldn't tell you whom or what they were leery of. They watched and listened to us constantly, even when you'd least expect it. Glancing around while talking to a friend wasn't rude, it was common sense. Everyone did it. Trust no one.

Sitting at the bar watching Lawrence and Calvin in what appeared to be a heated discussion or a lover's quarrel, that "happy to see you" feeling disappeared. How rich, I thought. A catfight between two bisexual men fighting for the affections of a woman and captured by a small group of people would have been spectacular for fueling all the insinuations about potential motive surrounding a murder or a disappearance. It was Clue worthy, like Professor Plum murdering Lord Grey in the study with a candlestick.

Code Declaration #5: Never frame
someone else for our crimes.

People watching had its boundaries, and I'd never watch to the point of seeming rude or, God forbid, looking like some psychotic stalker, even though I was. I'd seen enough, so finished my watered-down martini and left through the front door. Never draw attention to yourself when on reconnaissance or places you don't belong. Blend in. Emulate the crowd. Look natural. There was a group of men leaving, so I joined their exit. The managers would have noticed had I left through the back.

Pain must be administered slowly to have its most potent affect for those who enjoy it. To Julian, slow and painful was torture, but in DeSoto's world it was a bizarre form of orgasm. If ever there was a candidate for such treatment, he was its poster child. Five minutes of staring up at the night sky with its full moon rising, then looking down at my burner and Lawrence comes out. What the hell could they have done in five-minutes? I wondered what or who had cut his session short. Calvin, Bambi or both?

Visions of that 13-year-old girl and what he had done to her was building as justification for torturing him that night. Patience, I kept telling myself. Emotions were rising, and that wasn't good. Check them and remain ambivalent about the subject lest my guard drop and mistakes made. It was difficult while stalking him. It was getting personal, and I believe that was by design.

We were the only people in the back lot, so I turned towards the warehouse backing up to the 3M and walked away. The full moon helped me keep a visual on him, but also illuminated me, so I followed at a safe distance, far enough back to avoid drawing suspicion but close enough to not lose him down some random dark alley or backyard. Dilapidated row houses lined the street, all of them deserted. He had parked several blocks away on a darkened street where no one would see him, no lights were functional. I had parked on the same block, just across the street. We shared two things — a propensity to kill and an abundance of caution. How far did his caution go? Mine was endless.

Like most of the 3M's clientele, DeSoto drove an expensive car - but he was a Heron, so no surprise. Black Mercedes S class, dark tinted windows, decked out like he was a celebrity. They paid Czars handsomely for doing nothing while ruling over their departments like dictators. Becoming prime targets for blackmail from the people who protected them was not uncommon. I crossed over to his side of the street and walked towards him, looking for any unusual reaction he might exhibit from a stranger approaching. No reaction, he got in, closed the door and drove away. He was oblivious to his surroundings, and me. Julian was right, he'd be easy prey. But, perhaps his mind was elsewhere. What cut that session so short?

What caught my attention, though, was that missing double-chirp sound that all Mercedes Benz's made when unlocking the doors with the remote key. Chirp chirp, the lights would illuminate, the doors would unlock. Lawrence didn't lock his doors and had disengaged the interior lighting system or it was burnt out. Either way, it didn't work. Good to know. He's wasn't attentive of his surroundings and the failed lighting in his unlocked car opened the possibilities for me to attack from his back seat.

Reconnaissance Recap

* * * *

Thursday came quickly; Economics, History and Psychology tests, which never received grades, all on the same day. Not sure why we bothered with tests since taking them had no effect on your final grade. Schools were nothing more than indoctrination facilities and boy were they successful at dumbing us down. Just attend, take in whatever garbage was being spewed by the professor, write glowing reviews of communism and then move on, you're now a college graduate. Add to that, working at Il Portico every night that week, and time flew by.

Our usual seats in the back of The Drip were empty — the big cushy ones. The place was busy, as usual, but no one ever sat there. Lots of naïve chatter from the misguided masses discussing global affairs, the climate, utopian dreams or their sycophant love for our sitting dictator. It ruined an otherwise pleasant atmosphere.

I briefed Julian on my recon mission and my good fortune with having seen Lawrence there. There was more to that mission than introducing me to the seedier side of humanity and the lengths to which people would go to inflict pain upon themselves and then pay for it. He knew I'd see Lawrence and that I'd consider the surroundings to be a suitable place for the extract. It was a teaching moment.

It didn't take long for Julian to admit that his 3M ploy also exposed me to our subject's penchant for pain. He was hoping the experience would trigger some clever ideas allowing us to close the loop on how I'd finish him off. It did.   Strangulation and oxygen deprivation — Prom night! What Julian considered cruel and unusual, was orgasmic to Lawrence. Slow and painful, but in his case, not cruel or unusual at all. It would be his last hurrah and he'd probably enjoy it. Julian was ecstatic that I had come to that conclusion. The teacher had completed his lesson and the student passed the test.

"How?"

"Play darts in Mercedes' backyard. Have a few beers, then drive to DC for the prom. Wear a tie."

Translation: Plant myself in the back seat of his car, wait for him, Taser him, dose him with etomidate, load him in the van then drive him to my place and strangle him. The maximum range for Tazers was thirty-five feet and you get one shot before having to reload. Successful second shots if you missed were rare, so hitting your target on the first was essential.

It was August, and we were in the throws of another heat wave so Lawrence would wear light, breathable clothes. The Tazer's dart could easily breach the fibers and render him spastic and then motionless.

"You'll want to park close, so get there early and…" He never finished that sentence. He was about to breach our code.

"Shh." I put one finger over my lips. I understood what Julian was trying to tell me. He didn't need to finish.

"So, a formal event huh?" he asked.

"Yes."

My First Formal

* * * *

Strangulation. I'd seen it done many times but only in the movies or on TV. Carlo, from The Godfather strangled in the front seat of a car for ratting out Sonny to the Barzini family and then Luca Brasi just for being in the wrong place at the wrong time. Boy did his eyes bulge out. Julian was right; it takes a while to die from strangulation. Carlo could kick out the front window of the car before he croaked and it seemed like forever before Lucca dropped dead. Gruesome stuff. Not sure it took 39 seconds though.

"Wonder why I sent you to the 3M?" he asked.

"To learn."

"And what did you learn?"

"He loves pain."

That familiar glance upwards, the swishing of his espresso while closing his eyes and, "Yep. Class dismissed."

As we walked towards the front door Julian reached around my neck as if wanting to choke me, then whispered in my ear, "Do it slowly. Let this be his last meal." There was a reason for telling that story of Lawrence's past and it wasn't just to make me comfortable at the thought of executing him. It was a lesson about the real meaning of justification.

"Live by the sword, die by the sword." Those were his final words. It didn't take long for that to sink in. The wood chipper, of course!

I worked the day shift at Il Portico on Mondays, Wednesdays and Fridays for the next two weeks, allowing me to stalk Lawrence in the evenings. I parked my van on that same block, just before 9, but never again breached beyond those purple doors and waited for him to finish his masochistic sessions. He was habitual and, like clockwork, always rounded the corner returning to his car at 10:30 alone and with a quickness to his walk as though he was late for another appointment. He never locked his car and he had disabled the interior lights. That would be the perfect extraction site. It was too good to be true.

From Sous Chef to Head Chef and finally — Butcher.

* * * *

Beyond his carnal fantasies, Lawrence had a more refined side — Italian food, expensive wine and dining out at Il Portico. He was a semi-regular on Tuesday nights. As sous-chef, it was normal to aspire to becoming head chef, and I did. Better hours, better pay, and a bit of celebrity status allowing me an opportunity to get closer to my subjects. Herons loved Il Portico. People in power enjoyed being able to say, "I know the head chef, we're friends." It was a culinary power-trip for them and a recon bonus for me as it allowed me to work two jobs at the same time. Sadly, he'd never have an opportunity to brag about my talents or our short-lived friendship.

There was a consistent theme among the Herons; they ate like kings, spent like millionaires and drank like drunken sailors. I was their enabler. They say you are what you eat, but in Lawrence's case, a ragu of baked eggplant, Cocozelle zucchini and some ground pork tossed in and then drizzled with tomato sauce, could not have been more ironic. His last meal may have been the tipping point in my otherwise sane approach to this whole execution process. It got me thinking. Recycling, organic; never thought about it before but was fast becoming a convert. Human fertilizer.

His favored wine was Stags Leap. Expensive stuff and he'd always down a full bottle even when dining alone, which was often. Lawrence wasn't social outside of the confines of that club and wasn't all that popular within his Department. A weird character for sure and the more I learned of his odd habits, the more convinced I became that he was a worthy subject. Lousy tipper too.

My Birthday - Lawrence's Death Day

* * * *

It was Wednesday, my birthday and Lawrence's last day. Smack damn in the middle of the week so I took the day off. Il Portico on Tuesday — Lawrence's last meal. 3M on Wednesday, his last hurrah. Seemed appropriate.

They say the human body's natural reaction to a heightened sense of impending disaster is fear. It arises from an expected event that diverts from both social and moral norms. Sometimes it's labeled irrational but in my case I knew it to be normal. I was committing murder, albeit justified. Still, it shut me down. That day was a blur leading up to the actual event. I went completely numb.

I'll begin by telling you precisely how that day began. I awoke at 6am dripping in sweat, confused over my nightmare, which might have been about the Reverend, or it might have been about Lawrence — ghosts of the past or of the future, I wasn't sure which. All I remember was that dark, scary images filled the scene and I was running from someone. A recurring theme in my dream repertoire was never having the muscle strength to get away. Like being tethered to a huge ball and chain, my legs simply couldn't escape. I'd commit to a psychiatry session to seek the answer someday. As of this journal entry, I still don't have one.

A cappuccino and some dark fruits, picked from my garden was the extent of usual breakfast. Blueberries and raspberries, easy to grow, easy to freeze, and they thrived on my fertilizer. I had neither that day. By mid morning I was clinching my forehead — migraine, lack of caffeine and food, most likely, or the thought of my pending mission that evening? Possibly both. I threw up twice. The rest of the day was nerve-wracking. Sitting at home checking my Tazer, charging its batteries, filling my syringe and then calculating the best time to leave for the 3M, and in what position I'd park the van. Lawrence was pudgy so dragging him a block wouldn't work. Parking across the street was best, but I needed to be closer, for accuracy when I fired the Tazer. I settled on parking behind him with the back of my van facing the back of his car, maybe even touching bumpers. Perfect for a clean handoff.

Knowing his schedule and usual 10:20 departure from the 3M, I left early, grabbed a bite close by and then headed over to 1st and M before 9:00. "Never work on an empty stomach," my father would say. Mom would push the importance of protein. My plan was to be there before he arrived and then position my car once he left for his session. A "session" was something you'd have with a psychiatrist, but for Lawrence it involved an hour of inflicting pain on someone else or having it exacted upon himself. The depths of depravity society had sunk still astounds me.

Stopping for a bite in the vicinity seemed like a logical plan — protein. I'm convinced that, while children have visions of Sugar Plum Fairies dancing through their heads, my visions were of BBQ ribs, compliments of my first subject — the Reverend. I needed protein, but also to settle down and avoid novice mistakes. It's true. Criminals always return to the scene of their crime and I was that kind of criminal. I dropped into The Art & Soul. Sitting in the back precisely where Atticus Phelps sat was Saslow and his dinner partner was none other than Lawrence DeSoto.

It's a small place, maybe twenty seats, where everyone sees you enter and knows when you leave. Slim Joe, the owner, was fat as hell, and always shouted "Welcome to The Soul" with a long trailing extension on the word "soul" when entering his establishment. He'd bid you farewell with a robust "Come again Mr. Smith." Most never glanced up, but some did and that meant witnesses to dining there. Saslow and DeSoto looked at me as I entered and I looked back at them. DeSoto wore a thin, short-sleeved shirt, perfect for tazing him.

I took a seat up front as far away as possible although still within earshot. Saslow caught my glance and acknowledged that he had noticed me, with an uncomfortable smile crossing his face. I hadn't yet to make the social rounds with my customers as the newly appointed head chef at Il Portico, so DeSoto and I were complete strangers. It was 8:00pm. I remember thinking to myself why anyone would want to have a full stomach when pain and torture was just an hour away. Downing a full rack of ribs, and two beers was painful enough, but literally gut wrenching when torture was to be the desert. Then again, it didn't differ from a condemned prisoner gorging on his last meal before they lit him up in some 3000-volt electric chair, hung him like a side of beef or gassed him. Maybe it was intentional. Their last hurrah and that included vomiting in the gas chamber, or on the gurney leaving a mess for the executioner to clean up afterwards. I wondered what he'd toss up as I strangled the bastard later that evening. The thought bothered me — weak stomach.

Good Bye Mr. DeSoto

* * * *

Finality. It's why we hug longer when the time span seems like an eternity before we'll see our loved ones again. Whether as a goodbye before heading off to war or on our deathbeds before that trip to heaven, it's perhaps the most chilling experience anyone can have. I understand that perspective, and the irony of it too.

Service was slow at the Art & Soul that evening, even though it was half empty. I kept wondering who should leave first, them or me. If it were they, the chance was high that Saslow would stop by my table and strike up a conversation about some flaws in my paper. He spoke slowly and could go on endlessly about mundane theories. Having Lawrence slip out while conversing with him couldn't happen. I got up, left a twenty on the table and then headed out. Always use cash and avoid paper trails, but in that case, it avoided my name being shouted upon leaving the A&S.

It was dark but with dense clouds and no working street lights made it pitch black where Lawrence's car and my van would meet. God works in mysterious ways and I believe his dimming nature's lights that evening was the Lord's way of telling me to be careful. My stress had washed away, and I felt confident that things would come off without a hitch.

Like clockwork, he turned the corner of M and First Street at 9th and parked in his usual space. A creature of habit — I liked that. I parked down the street, then waited till he headed to his 3M rendezvous and repositioned my car directly behind his. Rear bumper to rear bumper, leaving just enough space to open my back doors without dinging his Benz.

T-90 minutes

* * * *

I hate waiting. It makes my mind wander to places it shouldn't go and that whole BDSM thing was a place I didn't want to revisit, even if just mentally. Most people wonder what goes through the mind of a killer as they await their prey. Do they meditate, read a magazine or stream Spotify then close their eyes wondering if they'll get caught or just screw up? I didn't read and didn't stream music. I sat there staring at my van's ceiling, shaking like a child awaiting punishment from a pissed-off father. Beethoven puts me in the zone — classic 107.9. My violent shaking became nothing more than a nervous shiver. My friends used to listen to rock while jogging. I became a fan of Beethoven that evening while waiting to kill. 9th Symphony, I believe.

It never gets easy, but with each mission, time spent

planning events became more relaxed and Beethoven filled the cabin of that van every time. It became routine — my theme song; I guess. Knowing that the world would be better off with the target dead and my garden more nutrient rich with their essence scattered across the soil was helpful as well. There was a sense of pride and accomplishment. Like walking on stage for opening night, I was both an actor and director in my own play. I practiced my lines, made sure I stood on the correct mark, then visualized every possible angle, every scenario before readying myself for the curtain to open. I'd take a deep breath. But, unlike Broadway, I played to an empty house, exactly as I wanted it. The house lights dimmed, and the antagonist entered stage right. Lawrence turned the corner five-minutes earlier than usual, but I was ready. "Showtime." I focused only on him.

People telegraph their feelings while walking down a street. Uneasiness causes most to slow down, maybe even stop for a moment as they look around and then proceed. I watched his gaze and pace of walking. We were the only cars on the street, so parking behind him was like having some stranger at a bar sit right next to you even though every other seat is empty. I hadn't thought that through and recalled Julian teaching me to always think like the target. How will they access the area as they approach? Have you left suspicious markers or drawn attention to yourself? Yes, and yes.

He continued walking with one hand in his pocket, jingling car keys and the other scratching his neck. He seemed oblivious to my proximity to his car. As he approached his unlocked door, I opened mine, took careful aim and fired the Taser. What surprised me was that he never looked over when I opened my door. He was the epitome of unaware and appeared as though he was on drugs! Direct hit, just below his left shoulder. He shivered like someone entering sub-zero temperatures heightened by a gusty wind and then dropped to his knees while trying to remove the dart. Screaming like a child who had scraped his knees, I rushed towards him, stuffed his mouth with a cloth to shut him up and then injected the drug into his carotid artery. His neck was bruised and what appeared to be rope marks encircled it — strangulation and oxygen deprivation was that night's ecstasy.

Julian always said count to ten before trying to subdue a subject that had been tased because it took ten-seconds to take effect. Screw that. Lawrence was still screaming. The dart continued jolting him with a steady stream of electricity. It looked painful, but for him was just another pleasurable event to wrap up his evening.

I pinched his lips hard to make sure that he was unconscious and that I could safely drag him the four feet separating us from the back of my van. Sounds like a small distance to drag someone, but when that person is overweight and unconscious, it adds a few pounds — thus the term "dead weight." Thank God for adrenaline. While pulling the dart out I felt for a pulse, making sure he wasn't dead, although that was the end-game, having him flat-line in the street from a lethal dose of electricity and potent pharmaceuticals wasn't on that night's menu.

I had retrofitted my van with a hidden sliding compartment, perfect for stowing a body. It was a most ingenious little drawer, deep enough to hold obesity with a good three inches vertical to spare. Once closed, it was indiscernible to anyone rummaging through the van provided its contents remained unconscious. I covered the flooring above with wood planter boxes each holding small trays for the fruits and vegetables I'd bring to Il Portico every day. It was tomatoes and zucchini that night. Food was expensive, especially the fresh stuff. If needed, I could bribe my way out of anything with a few boxes of veggies. My own personal morgue on wheels, except its passenger was still alive. I wanted them to experience death's entire morbid equation should they awaken while still in transit. Buried alive would scare the shit out of anyone. I can't imagine a more horrible way to die.

The trip home was uneventful, thank God, and I did. Sticking to the back roads to avoid random security barriers was necessary so traffic was non-existent. You'd think that those would be the first roads they'd set up checkpoints at instead of the main thoroughfares. Idiots.

As I turned up my dirt driveway, I remember thinking how quiet it was in the back of the van, not a peep from my subject. That is either good or bad. Lawrence was a crafty guy capable of committing the most heinous crimes and getting away with them. I'm not the paranoid type, but it concerned me.

It was a warm night, so I put both windows down. A cross-wind pushed by a nice breeze from the west, loud chirps from the frog pond to the right, an eerie sound of cicadas hanging from the trees above and a crystal-clear sky with stars covering its landscape stretching down to the horizon. Add in the strong scent of honeysuckle which is most potent at night, and you have a creepy sensory combination compliments of God. Silence from the back of a van carting an unconscious killer while being driven by a neophyte killer made it more surreal. I absorbed all that God had created while rehearsing what would soon be the execution and pulverization of one of his most magnificent creations, man. This was the official christening of the pit and my first attempt at concocting human fertilizer. Praise the Lord!

I backed into the garage, closed the doors, leaving just enough space to slide the drawer out. Lawrence was still unconscious. As my first attempt at drugging to incapacitate someone, I might have overdosed him a wee bit, just as a precaution. It had been 35 minutes since he first fell victim to the cocktail. His pulse was strong, his breathing normal. At least I hadn't killed the bastard. You never know exactly how things work out in the complicated recipe of committing a perfect crime. One learns as one does and the learning curve is steep and dangerous. Adjustments are necessary.

Do You Have Any Last Words?

* * * *

My execution chair was a simple piece of furniture with no leather armrests or cushion seats. I had bolted it to the concrete floor. The chair which was an old school desk and was made of solid oak, was uncomfortable but that was the point. "Pay attention Aiken" a harsher way of saying "don't fall asleep."

Teachers were fond of saying that. They seemed to be perfect for dozing off. Arm rests and a nice little top to rest your head, it was nap-worthy.

A loose chair is a potential weapon, so I'd ask my subjects to lower the desktop and then strap themselves into lap restraints I had fashioned from some leather left by Tania's Dad. It resembled an electric chair without the electrical leads but was scary as shit. Pointing a gun directly at their heads was incentive enough to follow that order, but Lawrence seemed unconscious. As I leaned in to remove him from the drawer, his eyes opened, pupils dilated, a wicked grin crossed his face as he thrust upwards and forward, knocking me square in the middle of my forehead. Hurt like hell. Temporary setback for my ego, but just as painful for him. His head snapped back, hitting the bottom of the drawer with a solid thump. He let out a long sigh. Bound hands left him no chance to overpowering me. It was a desperate attempt at freeing himself or maybe just the effects of shock.

"Out!" I shouted while pointing my laser sighted Beretta at his forehead. It's amazing how effective that tiny red dot is at quelling any delusions of grandeur by the subjects. Calmed them right down as the splash of red light bleeds downward towards the eyes which always close when that focused dot hits their forehead.

"Ok, ok." He shot back.

I motioned to the ladder and told him to go down, sit in the chair and strap himself in. While saying that, it occurred to me that one might consider this to be their final walk to some sick, painful torture chamber and that it might be better trying to escape or just take a bullet to the head and be done with it. I'd gain none of the intelligence that Julian had asked for. The Barko chipper, hidden behind a black plastic tarp, kept him in the dark as to what was about to happen. Torture, and wood chippers were his thing, but with my face exposed, clearly, I had no plans of releasing my prisoner. Everyone knows that. Mistake #1

Had it been me, I would have done anything to avoid going down that ladder and would have fought like hell to escape, even if it meant dying while trying to do so. I'm not the surrendering type, especially to someone who had taken great pains to build a scary looking pit and to anchor a chair with leather restraints to its cement floor. I hate pain.

"Relax, I would have killed you back in Sector 1 had I wanted to." I'm a great liar, but he wasn't buying it. Exposing my face ruined my chances of interrogating him.

At the bottom of the ladder, I had secured a serrated knife within the wall. Its blade was short but meant to allow my subjects to cut their own binds, freeing their hands while I stayed safely above. I had positioned it waist high and embedded its handle in cement. It was secure as hell and wasn't going anywhere. I made sure of that.

When a man is confronted with a roulette gamble where the slots are not black and red but life or death, one chooses wisely even though the house always wins. When a man walks to the galleys, he goes up the stairs. This time he went down. With that, Lawrence walked towards the ladder and, with hands tied behind his back, shimmied his way down each step and into the pit. He turned around, raising his hands to cut the ropes as instructed then sat down in the chair, fumbled with the desktop, but secured the straps as asked. Most cooperative chap. He had nothing to lose. He'd be dead either way but cooperated, anyway.

"Good job, Mr. DeSoto." He stared up at me waiting for my next move. I walked down the ladder, face forward positioning myself directly in front of him, stood there staring for a full minute observing his eyes, and his facial expression. Fear, you can see it. I wanted him to feel like Amanda and Chelsey did just before he strangled them to death. He looked concerned, panicked and perspired profusely. His body shivered even though the pit was hot as hell and his face went ashen. The same sensations washed over me. I shook, perspired and, although I couldn't see it, my face had probably turned pale white. I was nervous at what I was about to do.

The beautiful thing about carrying out an execution in the privacy of one's own death chamber and under one's own house rules is that time doesn't come into play. There are no anxious witnesses, no edicts brought down by the state requiring that the execution must occur at 12:00 noon and there is no medical examiner waiting to pronounce death upon the victim. For me, there were no neighbors either, so he could scream as loud as he wanted and only the birds and cicadas would hear him. But in case someone was to wander on my property, the pit was sound-proofed as best I could. Time is on your side and I could have waited forever to carry out the sentence. Knowing that, I felt like delaying the inevitable until my nerves had settled down and the shaking stopped. Although our code kept Julian away from the actual execution, I wanted Julian to be present since this one was personal to him. This was his revenge killing and it was justly deserved. I texted him.

"It's prom time, care to join me?"

"Nope but enjoy yourself and don't rush home." Translation: Make it slow and painful, which was odd coming from the man who avoided cruelty. Defining cruelty is in the eye of the initiator of that act. There's both physical and mental cruelty. Julian was against the former but had no issues with the latter. I'd fuck with Lawrence for a while, prolonging his mental suffering. Letting him know that I knew of his murderous past and then lifting back the curtain which hid the Barka wood chipper seemed like a damn good idea, but that urge disappeared. I verbally engaged him with two objectives in mind. First, mental abuse but, more important to our mission, to extract information about his marching orders and gain some clarification on what appeared to be a chummy relationship with Saslow. Something seemed too comfortable between those two.

"Amanda and Chelsea. Mean anything to you?" His head was down, and he never looked up as I shoved their pictures into his face.

"I guess so since you're doing this," he replied.

"Chelsea. Thirteen years old. Why?" He looked up, tilted his head as if to relieve a kink in his neck.

"Not talking about them."

"Fair enough," I shot back.

"Let's try this," I added, and with that pulled back the black tarp hiding the Barko. His look of fearful astonishment was priceless. Seeing that machine in all its powerful, pulverizing glory drained the last menial shade of color from his skin — ashen gray became ghost white. I thought he'd throw up but finally his glow returned, and he looked normal. A glow of peaceful submission.

"Suppose you tell me how you're feeling now!" Not sure why I didn't just say, "Asshole, how you feeling now?" and then follow up with a brief description of the Barko's features and benefits, teasing him with horsepower statistics and how quickly it could pulverize a human body.

"They were already dead," he shot back. Guilty. Bingo! Justification and we hadn't touched upon the politics behind his death sentence. I was ready to finish him off at that point but needed to know more about Saslow even though Julian had never asked. This was off-script.

"You and Professor Saslow," I continued. "How d'you know him?"

"Who are you and why the hell are you doing this?" Logical question, so I answered as best I could without exposing too much.

"I am a Patriot and I'm doing this for my country. We have sentenced you to death as a traitor to our nation."

It was early in the game and, although I trusted Julian and his recounting the story of the Herons and their arrival on cargo ships, I wanted to hear it from an actual Heron. Did they know of their adoptions? Did they have a handler or boss to report to? Where did they get their orders from or did they even get any? How deep were they embedded in our government — the Deep State that we had always heard of? I glossed over the details but noted that I knew of his adoption as a child and that it wasn't his parents who planned his life, it was the Soviets. He listened but never corrected my assumptions. Did they all grow up thinking they were normal American kids led astray by misguided parents? So, I asked the obvious.

"Why do you hate America?" A long pause followed by an even longer dissertation on America's ills. But it all started with, "What makes you think I hate America?" His answer proved my assumption correct. Sounded all too familiar. I'd heard it since I was old enough to understand what cable news was preaching. Dad was a political junkie, watching and listening to talking heads, flipping from one network to the next for what he called "balance." Sirius satellite allowed him to continue with that obsession the minute he'd get in his car. I grew wary of the constant barrage which recycled the same message over and over, 24/7. "Balance," he'd tell me. Mom hated it. Starting each morning with "that incessant screaming" set her off, thus those coffee clutches, and heavy drinking as her escape mechanism.

"Happy to answer but first Saslow?" Lawrence obliged and described the history behind their relationship which was both academic and social but, also boring. I was half tempted to inquire about Julian, but I already knew the depths of their relationship and trusted it was true. He was another professor, just higher up the food chain. Saslow was the department head. I had missed an incredible opportunity to better understand the Herons, their leadership and how they received their orders and then carried them out. It didn't matter though. Lawrence would have never told me.

There comes a time in everyone's life when they're faced with decisions that are life altering, a fork in the road. Everyone's been there, and you will too. But, when you're in such a precarious position where, no matter which direction you choose, death awaits you at the end of the street, I'm convinced that the mind does some remarkable things and at a rapid pace. Do you spill the beans and fuck everyone over or do you take one for the team, clam up and keep those secrets guarded and your allies safe from exposure? All of this occurs in milliseconds as time is never on your side. Those expecting such moments clam up while the surprised ones spill the beans, hoping for a reprieve. Lawrence wasn't surprised at all and, in fact, he told me so.

It's not uncommon for prisoners facing the death penalty to clam up on the day of their execution. Either they're hoping for a last-minute reprieve from the Governor or they don't want to show any sense of remorse for their crime, thus showing that they're scared shitless at the thought of dying on the gurney. No, that would ruin their narrative and the reputation they had built while serving time in the big house. The tough guy, the guy who's bound and determined to go out in a blaze of glory must become their legacy. So, Lawrence's sudden bout of muteness was expected. By not wearing a mask to disguise my face he knew there'd be no reprieve. He wasn't dumb — he went silent.

Moment of truth for me. Proceed with the execution. Oddly, I felt nothing as I began the process. No emotions at all. I had expected otherwise and worried that I was suffering from some psychopathic psychosis.

"Rope or cord? I asked."

"Rope." I ignored him and chose a thin wire cord. It would concentrate the pressure over less surface area, making it agonizingly painful for him. I owed it to Chelsea and Amanda. Why I accommodated that sick bastard by strangling him to death still perplexes me. His last hurrah, if you will, in the demented world of masochistic BDSM. Live by the sword, die by the sword. I wished I had shot or stabbed him.

The Stars and stripes dropped from the wall facing him and then my boombox played. "Oh, say can you see by the dawn's early light."

How much can I journal about strangling someone other than to note the stages of oxygen deprivation and the changes in facial expression and skin color? A healthy glow followed by choking, gasping and redness from the neck up occurs rapidly. The eyes bulged in proportion to the depth at which the cord was squeezing his neck. Asphyxia sets in. Red changes to blue, healthy glow changes to ashen pale, almost grey, choking changes to gagging and then to gurgling. Wet at first and then a dry gurgle as saliva's pathway is shut off. Oh, and the feet kick incessantly. I didn't time it, but Julian's thirty-nine seconds was about right. It was at the halfway mark that Lawrence's expression changed from solemn to a wry smile and it was at that point that I realized he had finally achieved the BDSM equivalent of chakra. It was all downhill from there.

Things were clumsy in the beginning; perfecting a new craft takes time. It was messier than I had expected but still a momentous day. Although exhausting, strangulation is a neat way of executing someone, and by that, I mean no messy cleanup afterwards. No blood, no fluids short of a small amount of saliva which drizzled down his neck as the noose tightened. He slumped so no need to feel for a pulse and his face was now a royal purple color, dark and blotchy with spots of blue and a few red ones. Cold covered his entire body. Oh, and that fluid part. I had forgotten that after a body expires, all kinds of fluids expel. It happened again. That was a mess.

The Chipper

* * * *

The Barka had a feed tube which faced the wall directly in front of Lawrence's dead body. Its tube was adjustable, and I had positioned it at floor level, so shoving the body in was easy, no heavy lifting required. From there the contents would flow through the blade chamber out of the shoot and into a capture bin above ground and outside of the garage. I knew that the bin could handle much more than the contents of a single human body since Chelsea was a commercial grade model meant for large trees or, in that case, fat humans. I pushed the ignition switch and the engine chugged a few times and then, viola, she purred like a kitten or a lion, I suppose. It had a lethal sounding roar, like a lawn mower on rocket fuel. Turning it on before strangling the bastard — just to see if its sound and fury could initiate another color to his skin tone — ashen gray and white would be boring.

I tested its capabilities with a few large pieces of fire wood just to be sure that my adjustments to the feed tube would catapult his chipped contents into the bin instead of spewing it all over the back yard. I tossed in four huge logs, walked up the ladder and outside to view their final landing spot. Sawdust in the wind, but a direct hit into the bin which was large. Mission accomplished. It rendered four enormous logs, which were comparable to the weight of Lawrence, into little more than a small pile of sawdust which had jettisoned perfectly into the outside bin. There was plenty of room to spare. Test runs successful.

I was unprepared for the next set of emotions that overcame me. The strangulation process was easy, it was justified retribution for what Lawrence had done to two innocent girls, one of them 13 — not that age matters. But this was an execution, not so much as revenge for his past crimes, but more so as a patriotic act meant to send a message to the enemy within. "You're next." Pulverizing his body accomplished nothing more than removing him from his position as a Czar and then placing a final check-mark on Julian's hit list. He'd be replaced, and life would go on for the Herons. From there we'd move on to the next subject and then the next one and all for what? We were pulling gangly weeds that would eventually grow back? Relocating them into their utopian paradise would send a message. I wanted his body intact, so texted Julian to discuss this before Chelsea made my concerns moot.

"Exam finished."

"Great."

"Thin tie, not feeling good about the date."

"Why?"

"Just wanna leave him somewhere."

"Aww. No way. It's rude to back out after you've committed. Coffee tomorrow?"

Asked and answered. Sending a message was not on Julian's radar just yet. I should have known since Lawrence was our first. I had to feed the tube which I had wisely placed low to the ground to avoid heavy lifting of those who might be obese. Dragging was all I needed to do — and then shoving.

I shut her down, opened the access bin and slide Lawrence into it — closed the chamber door then latched it tight. Even though continuous feeding was its feature, I couldn't risk having bits and pieces of Lawrence spewed backwards and into the pit. That would have been unbearable. Weak gag reflex. I'd have puked all over the place. That door served two purposes — containment and muffling. I can't recall how long I hesitated before finally pulling the switch, but it was at least 20 inhale-exhale seconds before I got up the nerve to do it. Deep breaths, each successively shorter than the previous until there were no breaths left to take. I was hyperventilating.

That might sound strange since there was almost no hesitation in killing the bastard but the mental image of pulverizing a human body into gooey fertilizer was a bit much to handle at that moment. The thought disgusted me. One last short, deep breath and I cringed like a kid who was worried what would happen after reaching into a bucket filled with spiders or worms. I flipped the ignition switch to the "on" position. First sound — sucking, like an enormous industrial vacuum cleaner followed immediately by the sound of Lawrence coming in direct contact with the whirling tungsten steel blades and being shredded into tiny pieces — a marriage made for hell. It echoed throughout my enclosed chamber. I cringed even harder, clenching my teeth tightly while closing my eyes as if that would somehow lower the decibels of the gut wrenching sound of human flesh and bones becoming one and very quickly ground up to nothing more than wet, gooey slime. A minute into the process and that unbearable grinding sound changed to a quieter sloshing, similar to when shoving large pieces of watermelon into a garbage disposal. I'm not sure which was worse, but it wasn't pleasant. Unlike the fibrous, dry wood that Chelsea pulverized, the human body, even dead ones, are mostly water and so the end result is not dust but goo. It's messy. It was horrible. I puked my brains out. More wood was necessary to firm things up.

Not a spectacular first day on the job but, as with most things, the human spirit will adjust and, with practice I felt certain that I'd do better the next time. Our list was long, so opportunity abounds for critical adjustments, each leading to eventual perfection — the perfect crime.

My Down Time

* * * *

If you're wondering what life was like between executions, it was quite normal. Oh sure, I had brief moments of panic when the news would focus on the disappearance of one of those bastards, but those lasted only a few days, just as the stories surrounding them did. The Bitterns built fantastical lies about their missing fellow-traitors who, unknown to them, had become fertilizer for my garden. Their propaganda arm noted them as either retired, moved to another country, or passed away unexpectedly. Their ceremonies were always private. Except for the Reverend, the word "murder" was never uttered on public broadcasts or printed in their papers. Their rationale was to avoid having to admit that things weren't so rosy in the Camelot of their dreams. They disarmed society and the propagandist media always painted a picture of peaceful societal bliss, especially in Sector 1 were the dearly departed lived or worked. Thanks to me that Sector was fast resembling Chicago before the collapse.

Still, the underground, which was our resistance, was well armed and, like the locusts that spawned their invasion, they couldn't afford to have Patriots suddenly feel empowered with a sense of hope that their cause was still being carried on. They were fearful of copycat executioners even though no bodies were ever found. I had touched them in a manner never intended by me, but I was eternally grateful that I had done so. Between school, work and stalking, my schedule was quite busy. There was no love in my life, I had no time for that and doing so would make my days miserable as I'd have to worry, not only about my next subject but also my next date night. I wasn't ready for house guests quite yet, at least not living ones.

Subject 3 - The Bittern Writer

* * * *

You win wars one battle at a time but Julian and I had just begun ours. We knew we had a long way to go. Military experts taught the importance of cutting off your enemy's communication and supply channels early on, so that's exactly where our intentions turned — communication, specifically fake news, and the vast supply of it being shared around social media. Subject #3 was, therefore, a strategic choice. The rest were luck of the draw, or spin of the wheel, as it were. Like DeSoto, Julian, once again, pulled the "He's an easy target," card from his shallow repertoire of comments regarding each subject. Easy or not, I questioned his age — he was a few years older than me, in his early thirties, and not an original Heron as Julian assured me the list contained. "Offspring," he told me, and his execution must happen soon, lest a pending bill in Congress go down to defeat. I questioned our not putting his father first, but it was the mother who was the Heron and our code forbid taking a woman's life. The father was a traitor, but only by marriage. The son, was a modern-day version of the Nazi's Joseph Goebbels and far more dangerous to our republic than either of his parents.

Leading up to the collapse, we labeled news outlets as shills for the Herons, guilty by omission of stories that didn't fit their narrative, or fake in what they reported. That continued long afterwards, forcing many Patriots to set up private social media groups to countenance the false charges made by the mainstream media. In doing so, they offered their own version of the truth — sometimes taking on the same fake persona they were so incensed with in the first place. "The truth is out there" became "The truth is hard to find."

Alexander Vay, 32 years old, was the son of Sector Representative Anita Vay who graced our shores in 1963 aboard shipment #14 from Minsk. They coded her 7962, and she was a staple on the Sunday morning cable news circuits, always espousing policy initiatives that were unconstitutional. On one occasion she stated her disdain for that document even though swearing to uphold it upon taking public office was a requirement. Not surprising, videos of that statement disappeared from the internet within hours of our trying to make it go viral. Speeches to her caucus were filled with comments that made one wonder if, like DeSoto, she was insane. Suggesting that we had landed a man on Mars when the Moon was as far as we had gone gives you some sense of the lack of intelligence we were dealing with. Each week she'd find a new target for her bombastic accusations and those segments always went viral, not because of her stated position but, instead, because of the utter stupidity that would exit her mouth. As usual, they scrubbed them. Still, she had loyal followers and was never challenged for reelection. Gerrymandering had blessed her district, Sector 783, with equally stupid constituents. She was serving her 8th term.

When you insult someone, your goal is to shame, hurt, or humiliate. Hers was to destroy with lies so unbelievable that they often came full-circle back into the realm of believability. It's a shame that our code prohibited executing a woman. I despised her and the stupidity that swirled around her head, but it was her son who was to be our next target and he, unlike his mother, was brilliant.

Alexander lived alone in Sector 2, just outside of the capital. Julian's bio on him noted no girlfriends and that he was a loner which made matters much simpler for me. This was part of the reason Julian picked him in the first place. I was still training, even after two successful kills. What made Alexander a suitable target, however, was that he was also a professor at Mason University, teaching, of all things, Communication and Journalism. I questioned the logic behind this choice of subject as I had just completed the successful execution of the master Egret, Secretary of Education, DeSoto. While our code didn't specify that we rotate among the classes of Herons, common sense told us, when we first discussed these details, that we should. Julian felt that he was far more damaging to our cause as a propagandist than as a professor so, he was tagged as a Bittern. Although Alexander was only 32 years old, he had played an integral role in our nation's collapse. Unlike the others who did so over decades, Vay had accomplished so much more in a matter of years. He was training his successors, and this had to be stopped. I agreed and so began the stalking and planning for Alexander Vay's patriotic event.

The Plan

* * * *

Alexander was present at the Drip on the Monday where Julian and I had first planned DeSoto's execution, a minor detail that he failed to apprise me of. We sat in the back — he sat up front, across from DeSoto, yet they knew each other. Still there was no chance of his overhearing our conversation, it was coded, anyway. His beverage of choice, a non-fat, decaf, soy latte. He was a pale, skinny little bastard, a classic basement dweller befitting someone in his line of work.

While I had tagged the Rev as responsible for Cassis' death and DeSoto was himself a vicious rapist and killer, Vay's close association and recruitment activity with some of the worst domestic and foreign terrorist groups was part of what brought him to be next in line. Alexander Vay made videos — recruitment videos all while writing and posting pure BS stories through his social media channels and teaching his failed ideology to impressionable minds at Mason. Like DeSoto, he represented the circle of treason. Julian had yet to inform me which social media channel he administered — there were hundreds. But "He controlled the mother ships," was all Julian told me.

This was a test of my ability to follow orders and to stay

truthful to our code. Leading a double life constrains one's time, but I felt it necessary to expand my knowledge and what better way than to attend Professor Vay's class. Before the Collapse, graduate students would concentrate only on their intended degree, but after our downfall, they required us to take electives for a more rounded knowledge base. I dropped the useless Art History class and enrolled in "News-writing and Reporting 201," a lecture hall class with over 300 students, allowing me to blend in and disappear among the masses. It was an early morning class, so it didn't conflict with my others or my work at the restaurant. Julian approved of my enrolling in that class and complimented me on my initiative.

Propaganda 101

* * * *

Avoid 8:00am classes at all cost if your commute is twenty minutes or more. I got there ten-minutes before Vay's was to begin then waited outside while the other students strolled in and took their seats. I sat mid-hall on the far right to avoid any direct stares from Vay. He was ten minutes late, and I noted that in my mental notebook. "Not punctual."

"Good morning kiddies," he shouted as he entered the hall from the left door. I hated him — "kiddies?" We're college students not elementary heathens.

"Welcome to News Writing and Reporting. My name is

Professor Vay and I'll be your mentor for the next twelve weeks." What an ass! He stood behind a podium the entire hour and appeared to follow a written script throughout the lecture. He was short, even shorter when standing behind a tall podium which rose midway to his chest. I was witnessing a talking head, literally. Scripted lectures proved once again that college was a colossal rip-off. When the curriculum was nothing more than rehashed progressive liturgy, sending us the script would have saved us time and money, both of which were in short supply. I glanced around the hall to gauge the mood of my fellow students, three-quarters of whom weren't paying attention while the rest, the "front and center crowd," took notes and leaned forward to hear Vay who spoke in hushed tones. Even I knew that the traditional formula for a good opening paragraph to any news story should answer the five W's, who, what, why, when and where, and sometimes — how. Not anymore and Vay made that point clear as water when he began his lesson for our first day of class.

"When conveying your opinion, do so up front in the column you're writing. Keep the facts towards the end," he began. "Why?" asked a fat redhead in the front row who seemed enamored to question Vay.

"Because, most people will only read the first couple of paragraphs, if that. You won't be accused of bias." This confirmed what I already knew — journalism was dead. It had so completely transformed into something more sinister, fraudulent propaganda, that it was little wonder that no one read newspapers anymore. It begged the question why Journalism was still being taught in college.

The rest of the class focused on the importance of impactful, powerful titles, content, freedom of the press (to lie) and even a passing reference to Liar's Poker, although he termed it "smoking out the enemy," something he was a master at. The temptation to ask a question was unbearable, but I stuck to my agenda and sat patiently, shaking my head amazed that the state was offering this stuff up as legitimate higher education. This wasn't Journalism — it was a class hell-bent on teaching propaganda. I wished I had stuck with Art History as my elective.

Vay's final comment to the class was most revealing of his beliefs regarding the subject of journalism in 2024.

"Journalists have two objectives and that is to both report and to sway opinion against the enemy." Class dismissed. It was enlightening, even shocking, but not unexpected. History is far more interesting especially since I was making it.

I had a few hours to kill so stayed on campus but stuck my head into Julian's office to check in. He was in a good mood but unusually busy and seemed rushed.

"How's journalism?"

"Boring"

"Drip, 2:00. Let's discuss your exam." Our code words came more easily, and it sounded routine. That was it. I backed out of his office and he abruptly shut the door behind me.

The Drip

* * * *

I'd arrive for our coffee clutch, order a macchiato and scone then grab my usual seat in the back while waiting for Julian, who was always late. But knowing Vay also appreciated great coffee, albeit a sissified version, I stood inside the doorway and scanned the room to see if he was there. He was and, just as before, seated clear across the room from our section, all alone. He had no friends, just students who he thought were his friends. Students will befriend a professor just for the grade, so I'd guess, based upon the first class, that half hated him while the rest would become future propagandists. He was unlikable, but a danger to our society where free and open speech were bedrocks to our existence.

"Ignore him," Julian said, sneaking up from behind me with his hand pressing down on my shoulder.

For the next half-hour we spoke in code, which was essentially a history lesson on our subject whom we had named "The Propagandist." Julian had a lengthy dossier on him.

Vay lived in a ground-floor, two-bedroom apartment in Sector 2 where he had a bank of computer monitors and a professional green screen backdrop, which was perfect for creating and editing videos. He had several other graphic panels he could flip, depending on the message he'd be recording, including one featuring the ISIS flag. Not only did he record his own stuff, but he edited other's videos provided they fit his narrative, which was always anti-American. Julian knew this because he had been to his apartment before.

"You've socialized with this guy?" I asked.

"Not socialized, more of a technical visit. He asked if I'd help recover some data a few years ago. I did and then backed it up to my thumb drive which is how I know so much about him. He's tech ignorant, but dangerous." I found it odd that a young man whose lot in life was driven from a computer's keyboard could be so technically illiterate — even more odd that he'd call Julian, a history professor, for help.

Julian handed me his phone which showed a series of pictures he had taken in Vay's apartment. Even though we had sat in our usual spot, I checked again for cameras — habit.

"Cautious today, aren't we?" Julian said.

I glanced through the pictures, mostly shots of his office filled with banks of large monitors each with a different image on the screen. He had walls plastered with old Che and Mao posters and a hammer and sickle shadowboxed in a black frame adorned the wall in front of his monitors. Julian watched as I scanned through the pictures - I knew he wanted me to look more carefully, so I swiped through them again, but this time moved more consciously through the albums. Zooming in on one of them showed the sites he controlled. Occupy Democrats, Occupy Wall Street, 99%.com, The Democratic Underground — he controlled them all. But most interesting was a folder named "Exaction," which means bribery. The Exaction folder stood out among a sea of Windows yellow folders, red with a gold star.

"He's blackmailing people?" I asked.

"Not just anyone. Congressmen, Senators, judges, you name it — he's built closets for every branch." That was Julian's way of noting that these folks, who were conservatives, had "Skeletons in their closet." Calling them RINO (Republican in Name Only) was popular among conservatives and, with each passing day, seemed to grow in membership as more of our principled leaders on the right turned a blind eye to the positions they held which got them elected in the first place. The right was moving left but the left never shifted right, causing all sorts of conspiracy theories as to why this was happening, bribery being the most likely. I had always thought this, but now had confirmation.

The Drip was more crowded than usual, and others were invading our space, making it difficult to carry on a conversation about nefarious plans, even if coded. We agreed to regroup that evening at Julian's place. As we got up, Vay eyed Julian from across the room — and it wasn't a friendly stare. Julian waved, then headed out the door. There was a sense of unfamiliar hatred in his reaction. Very little was accomplished at that meeting.

Dinner with My Mentor

* * * *

Dinner at Julian's' was less formal than our previous meeting. We ordered Chinese and had it delivered. Our discussion focused on the content of Alexander's hard drive. He handed me the thumb drive — "It's a ledger," he said.

Hitler had Goebbels — the Herons had Alexander Vay, the man behind the screen who wrote most of the fake headlines and news stories responsible for whipping the enemy into a frenzy, altering several elections, and causing some damn destructive riots. A family affair with a mom on the front lines and the son digitally vomiting fake news out to the masses was a brilliant partnership, and very effective.

Part and parcel to most of the Herons was their propensity to lead secret, immoral lives beyond the traitorous ones that placed them on Julian's list. While I led a double life, I wasn't a sexual deviant, the keeper of kiddy porn or blackmailing a government or judiciary official. Chef and executioner — two words that described me.

Vay did them all. He had dozens of folders labeled after spice names — pepper, salt, oregano, cinnamon and nutmeg, each filled with images only the most demented could appreciate. He traded them among like-minded cohorts in much the same way I traded baseball cards as a kid. Instead of First Baseman or Catcher, his idols were blonde/skinny or pudgy/redhead. The deviant network was extensive, and everyone operated under pseudonyms to protect their otherwise fake moral identities. Several elitists and politicians hid among those ranks — even a few "conservatives." Those became easy prey for his blackmailing schemes. I always thought the Patriots played by the Marquis of Queensbury rules and the Herons looked upon politics as a blood sport. Perhaps I was too harsh. Blackmail added an extra sprinkle of politeness to the representatives we had sent to Congress. No wonder they never seemed to accomplish anything.

While his extracurricular activities were morally reprehensible and worthy of a trip through the Barka, blackmailing was more dangerous to the nation. Most blackmailers sell their silence for money, but Vay wanted votes from congressional leaders and rulings from the bench favorable to his cause. His target list was filled with familiar names, the ones my father grew tired of because they often voted opposite of the patriotic constitutional party they represented. Mystery solved. The Herons had hacked our party years ago. Filming our leaders in compromising positions, some of which were setups, others highly edited, did the trick and Alexander Vay was the producer who lorded over the casting couch. Videos and pictures leading to legislative extortion was something I had expected from the former Soviet Union or even modern-day Russia. I had to remind myself that we were living in an extension of the former Soviet Union and, this was part and parcel to their modus operandi. He was a busy, entrepreneurial little bastard. I completely understood Julian's obsessive desire to finish him off quickly. An important legislative bill would be coming to the House floor in the coming weeks and we couldn't risk increasing the herd of turncoats. The plan had three objectives. I was to execute Vay, retrieve his latest copy of the Exaction folder and then Julian would inform those noted in that folder that the coast was clear, and they should vote their moral conscious. But Vay's execution was to serve an additional purpose — to send a message to his mother, which would require me to photograph

Vay before he became compost for my garden. Julian had slipped the boundaries of our code and added a footnote to our most crucial edict. No body, no crime.

My concern, as always, was not so much with his execution in my pit, but more so the detailed planning necessary to get him there. Where did Vay spend most of his time? Did he frequent bars, or late-night clubs or was he content to just sit at home and fantasize all sorts of sick shit in front of a screen while perusing the spice cabinet? As always, my need to clarify that which became the final justification behind Vay's execution still stands. It was his traitorous acts against the United States of America, pure and simple. His leisure activities were of no concern but, like DeSoto, made me hate him even more. A pattern was emerging.

Nagging Questions

* * * *

A young man running an elaborate blackmailing scheme from his apartment who wants only to alter legislative votes made little sense. Experience told me that the most fervent socialists/communists sang from a different hymnal when it came time for compensation. That's when capitalism kicks in, but they'd never admit to it. Someone was paying him to alter the legislative landscape, and I wanted to know who that was. Perhaps another name on Julian's list? At that point, I had no idea.

Julian had combed through most of the documents and

emails on Vay's system and found exchanges noting that he'd meet a few of his students on a regular basis at a bar in Centerville, just fifteen minutes away from my place. Thursday was his usual night for those off-campus outings at a bar called The Cage, a well-known meat-factory for both young and old. After the Collapse, many of those joints took on new identities as underground barter houses and one item frequently bartered was sex. Sex for food, sex for housing, sex for drugs, sex for whatever a man or woman needed, it was always on the menu at The Cage. While Vay didn't have a permanent girlfriend, he probably had a temporary one.

The next two weeks had me shifting my work schedule around to shadow Vay and, hopefully, catch him at The Cage. Massimo was well qualified to take over at the helm and was more than happy to fill in when patriotic duty called, although he knew my excuse to be college exams, not lethal ones. My career, which required working at night, was impeding my ability to roam the corridors of hell after hours.

The first Thursday was a bust. The Cage was packed, but Alexander wasn't there. I hung around, grabbed a drink and a bite to eat. Scanning the bar to see if familiarity with any of the patrons might cause a problem, I sat for two hours sipping a martini while people watching. This was my old stomping ground, but its clientele had changed, and I recognized no one. I had given little thought to how'd I'd react should someone find the need to high-five Aiken McHale since I had long since put my true identity to rest. Although I had changed my appearance, one never knows when an old flame or high school buddy would pop in and see through the disguise. Socializing in my sector didn't seem like a particularly good idea, but it was necessary.

The following Thursday I hit pay dirt. Vay was hosting a group of the "front and center" crowd. I was witnessing what would eventually become a changing of the propaganda guard and noted which of my classmates to avoid. I had no patience for them. They sucked up to Vay at every opportunity and were obviously future Goebbels in training.

Reconnaissance is for gathering intelligence and that evening I had gathered enough to move the following Monday's meeting with Julian to stage two of our planning sessions — the grab. Normally Julian would have asked that I follow the subject for two weeks but with Vay, it wasn't necessary. He wasn't guarded.

Alexander Vay drinks bourbon — lots, eats fried okra and stuffs his mouth with cashews. He stayed until closing, which opened the opportunity to dose him while staggering to his car after the place had cleared out. He had that temporary girlfriend who was, at least for that evening, one of our Patriots. Sector 7 Representative Anne Hargrove was all over him with one hand on his shoulder and the other one stroking his skinny, flat ass. Anne wasn't attractive, so imagining them as a couple wasn't a huge stretch. She was, however, from our side of the aisle, so ideologically they couldn't be more different. The good professor was multi-tasking — teaching, slugging down bourbon, chomping on nuts and extorting, all while trying to impress his students with his celebrity friend. That thumb drive he handed her in an awkward attempt at a concealed handshake wasn't a lesson plan. It was evidence, real or contrived, that Ms. Hargrove had broken some of God's commandments. It was his solicitation to vote for something contrary to her beliefs. That's how bribery works.

What began as a simple snatch, execute and pulverize operation was taking on a more complicated structure. A stolen hard drive was as important as fresh fertilizer for my garden. This necessitated my entering his apartment, something that was counter to code, but which Julian had made another exception for. Was this all baked into Julian's logic for choosing Vay as my third subject, adding God's eighth Commandment to the list of those that I had shunned — Thou shalt not steal? Was I to break all ten of them?

I had seen enough for the night and headed home, but before leaving checked the parking lot to see where Vay parked his car. He drove a white Prius and parked away from other cars in the back behind a cigar shop that closed at 9:00pm. You'd a thought it was a Ferrari. A quick check for cameras and there were two, one pointing in the general direction of Vay's car and the other the opposite direction. I'd disable them when the time was right. I knew how and when to take him down. As for the hard drive — I'd take his keys and return to his apartment after chipping him which would be early in the morning before anyone woke up.

Goodbye Professor Vay

* * * *

Friday morning class and, while my preference would have been to skip, I bucked it up and attended. A formal introduction was in order, so I waited outside of the door that Vay entered through and introduced myself, not as the antagonist I was, but as an admirer of his teachings and ideology. One good fraud deserves another. I wanted him to feel comfortable when I approach him by his car the following Thursday night. Never antagonize a future subject as doing so makes them suspicious and less easy to snag. An unthreatening student with a dead battery wouldn't alarm him. It's amazing the minor details I considered when planning these events. My skills were sharpening at an exponential rate. The devil is in the details and I was feeling very much like that devil.

"Good morning Professor, Josh Hunter, love your class," extending my hand for a handshake that he never acknowledged.

"Glad you like it. I've seen you around campus, History, correct?"

My subject already knew me. Mutual stalkers? Potential cog in the wheel that might change things.

"Sit up front. I'd like to hear your perspective on history and how it relates to journalism — sort of the history of journalism." So much for being incognito in class. My answer, if asked, "True journalism died years ago."

"I would, but I have an appointment I need to get to, so I

wanted to let you know that I'd be missing class today." Taking a chance that he'd draw attention to me among a class of hundreds of students, many of whom worshiped him, had to be avoided. The class size and my ability to disappear among its masses was the reason I chose it in the first place. Expose me and I'm a potential suspect.

"No problem, perhaps next week," he said as he turned and entered the class.

"The Cage, Thursday?" I added. He didn't reply, but I knew he heard me and, to be honest, I wanted him to know that I knew as much about him as he knew of me. I couldn't skip class anymore.

Eliminating the 1st Amendment

* * * *

Two's company, three's a crowd. Julian and I sat at our usual spot and our subject sat up front, sipping that deaf soy latte, again, all by himself. Having a coded discussion about executing the guy across the room reminded me of high school antics when we'd gang up on the class loser sitting alone at the lunch table. I hated that shit, but maturity hadn't visited my friends yet, and they were all I had. Loneliness, I knew how it felt, but for Vay I didn't care.

"Ignore him," again Julian was guiding my eye contact, but this time I had reason not to listen.

"He knows me and my major."

"Class roster, don't sweat it," Julian replied in the most nonchalant manner to something I took seriously.

While I had left out a few mishaps in my DeSoto recap, I got that uneasy feeling that Julian wasn't being completely forthright with me either. Dismissing that our next subject knew both of us and was sipping just fifteen feet away wasn't sitting well with me. "Probable suspect," kept banging around in my head.

Julian was the cautious one and considered every nuance, that might affect our outcome, to be potential game-changers. But for Vay he became matter-of-fact and didn't seem to care as much. I played along, ignored Vay and listened as Julian listed the details that needed covering for this next event. We added two new code phrases to our vocabulary since data deletion and photographing the subject had entered the formula. I picked up on the new terms immediately. "Mugs," normal when speaking in a coffee shop. "Cleaning my car" was our reference to wiping the hard drive clean.

"There are some interesting mugs on that shelf. You should buy one before your exam." Julian wanted a mug shot of Vay before I finished him, bound, gagged and probably beat up, for effect. Ours was a nuanced criminal vocabulary and was starting to feel like another language. The message to his mother was that we had kidnapped her son and he was being held hostage for ransom — legislative ransom. Julian had done the congressional math and calculated that one more vote was needed to pass legislation to allow Sectors to secede from the statist union that was formerly the fifty United States. Vay's mother was to vote with our side of the aisle and allow for the secession of any Sector that could garner a 2/3 vote to leave. Although passage would require the signature of our esteemed dictator, which would never happen, clearing the House would send a strong message that the resistance was alive and well. Payback's a bitch, but I preferred the less subtle messages of "Look what I did to your son — you're next." Still, I was pleased that we finally sent a message instead of shredding bodies with no positive consequences for our side of the aisle, other than to feed my garden. A small step towards the manifesto I had always wanted was emerging.

The mission had morphed from a simple execution and body disposal into something more complicated. By adding political extortion, which is precisely what Vay had done for years, and destruction of property, there were many more areas to consider as each was wrought with potential evidence leading back to me. I would have thought that Vay's hard drive might have held valuable data for us and that stealing it would have been a better plan, but Julian insisted that I erase it and then leave it on his desk. It made little sense. Something on that drive wasn't meant for my eyes, but he was emphatic that leaving it would draw attention away from his apartment should I screw up and leave any evidence. I wasn't buying it. Finger prints, hair fibers, foot prints, DNA - each became a checkpoint as I'd now be entering the first place any investigator would scour — the subject's apartment.

One complicating factor, at least for me, was leaving Vay's abandoned car behind The Cage, which would draw attention to those who had played sexual barter or just showed up that night for a drink. Being a semi-regular made him a familiar face with the bartenders, waitresses and others. Offering up a bar full of potential suspects and witnesses concerned me. "Think ahead," Julian would say. I did, and I didn't like it.

DeSoto's car was left in a crime-ridden area and I had avoided entering the 3M that night which, unlike The Cage, was known for attracting all sorts of deviants, even violent ones. The list of potential suspects was long. Julian didn't share my concern but offered me a choice. "Don't go in if you're concerned about not acing your exam" he suggested.

"Good, I won't." then winked and asked that class be adjourned. I had my marching orders and, as with DeSoto, I was to stay clear of that "last place he was seen alive." I glanced towards the front of The Drip and Vay had already left. On my car windshield was a note — "Aiken, The Cage on Thursday?" He was stalking me, but why? Knowing my major was disturbing enough, but knowing my real identity was frightening. That note sealed his fate.

Vay's Final Report

✳ ✳ ✳ ✳

Emotions begin in the brain and then wash over our bodies to specific regions depending on the emotion you're experiencing. Love goes from head to toe. Danger and fear isolate in the chest area. Anger is the only emotion that triggers strong feelings through the arms. My chest and arms were pulsating with an uncomfortable feeling. Danger and fear — meet anger, a terrible combination.

Thursday couldn't come quick enough as I had already skipped Vay's Tuesday class, fearing that he'd call upon me, or worse, expose my true identity to three-hundred students. The ultimate battle — liar versus liar was taking shape. Leaving that note on my window had purpose. Would he tell the class when I wasn't there? Would he speak to my drone video they had already called fake news? When Wednesday rolled around my stomach joined in the emotional party that the rest of my body was experiencing. Danger, fear and anger — meet anxiety.

I texted Julian to see if he felt that I should skip Thursday's class to avoid an unexpected confrontation. I don't handle those well.

Vay's Permanent Sabbatical

* * * *

As much as I wanted to play hooky, I followed Julian's absolute order, attended class and sat up front — something I never did, not even in his class. Students sitting behind me would never see my face should I get called out, but I was still nervous about the hour that lie ahead. You associate academic nervousness with taking a test or giving a presentation you hadn't prepared for.

Sitting close to a professor you plan to kill that evening takes the cake on things that might cause academic trauma. The feeling was mutual as Vay avoided direct eye contact with me, something that gave me some small sense of relief that he had no intention of exposing me during that class. But that soon dissipated.

Sock-puppetry and the need to verify sources was that day's lecture, and he directed his initial comments at me. Would he stop mid-sentence and make an example of me as someone who wasn't who he claimed to be? It crossed my mind.

"Mr. Hunter, tell the class why verifying sources is so important?" Calling me Hunter and not McHale was a relief.

"A story is only as good as the source." I answered and then added, "If those sources communicate through social media while hiding behind digital walls, that's a cop-out." One good turn deserved another but, in retrospect, not smart since he could have countered by exposing me. My cockiness took hold, but I reigned it in.

"Great," he said and then focused on social media. It was he who was driving so much of that on-line conversation. Two frauds in the same lecture hall, both in name and occupation. Neither of us blinked. It was a cat-and-mouse moment, something I shouldn't have played. He ignored me for the rest of the hour and focused on the "front and center" crowd who awaited his next spout of brilliance.

"Josh, Cage night, correct?" he said as his class dismissed and we were shoulder to shoulder exiting through the same door.

"Sure, I'll be there later," I mimicked his whispered tone.

Mutual but weird admiration — I could see it in his eyes. The rest of the afternoon had me in Julian's European History class, and Middle Eastern History, taught by a Grad student. I was more participative than usual, raising my hand and asking serious questions attempting to show myself as normal and happy in case someone queried the behavior of Vay's students once he went missing.

Why Me?

* * * *

Before the Collapse I binge watched a Netflix program about serial killers and what went through their minds before committing their murders. Turns out, it was wrong, but they hadn't met me yet, so I cut em a break. It was a documentary and the killers they highlighted mostly had issues with their mother or were loners and bullied at a young age while some just had the genetic abnormality that caused them to seek pleasure in the mutilation of animals which progressed to humans. I was going through my checklist of items I needed to pack as if I were heading on a business trip to close an important deal. And then it occurred to me that I was, in fact, headed on a business trip, albeit just fifteen minutes up the road and, yes, I was closing a deal — ending a life. I loved my mother, had no genetic abnormalities, as far as I knew, and couldn't hurt a fly. What was it that made me so comfortable taking on the role of a serial executioner while also experiencing pleasure in doing so? Was this always a part of me, hidden within the fiber of my genetic code? Or, was this God's plan? When asked what made me do these things, I'll simply reply, Patriotism. That should befuddle them.

Time to Pack

* * * *.

Tazer, fully charged, the syringe filled with etomidate, my van filled with boxes of tomatoes, black mask, gloves, license plate cover, business cards, laser, nerves of steel and a small portable hard drive. I wanted those files before I deleted them. I was ready to roll. God cooperated again offering a cool, cloudy night with a steady rain. Cops avoided spot-checks on rainy nights. Why would anyone want to stand outside while getting rained upon, given the pittance they paid them after the collapse?

Having to wait is absolutely the most nerve-wracking of this entire process. You'd think pulling the trigger, or jabbing a long, serrated blade deep into someone's heart would cause more of the jeebies. Good lord, stuffing an intact human body into a shoot and then flipping a switch which ignites razor sharp stainless steel blades into a pulverizing, synchronized ballet would stop most people dead in their tracks. But nope — it's the anticipation leading up to the moment I close my van's door and head to my appointed location. Like a baseball player needing to get on first to drive the winning run home in the bottom of the 9th when the count is 0 and 2. But unlike that baseball player who's last at-bat takes up two minutes of his time, my anticipation was over twelve hours of sitting, imagining every possible scenario and then repeating it. Each time I'd rehearse my crime a new potential obstacle hits me square in the face causing me to rethink my plan. Adjustments always sit in the waiting room of my cerebral cortex as I drive to my appointed location. It's not fun.

11:00: "Headed to class," I texted Julian.

A thumb-up emoji, was his reply.

On my way to The Cage, I rehearsed what I'd say to Vay while waiting behind the cigar shop in cloud-covered darkness and pouring rain. Needing a battery jump? Apologizing for being so late? If he was, as Julian said, a creature of habit, then he'd park his car near the dumpster which seemed a more appropriate spot to plant myself. What bothered me was knowing that Vay knew who I was and why was he so eager to meet?

Just short of Centerville Road, a mile from The Cage, I pulled over covered my license plates with the black tinted screen that would render the digits unreadable on any traffic cameras I might pass. I donned my black cap and gloves and arrived around 11pm. My creature of habit had indeed parked where I wanted him, ten feet from the dumpster. It thrilled me to see his Prius, because the thought had crossed my mind that, my being so late would have caused him to leave early. I needed to disable two CCTV cameras. They were older models — the kind that focused in a narrow area, allowing me to avoid video capture while pointing my laser at the lens to disable the optics.

I grabbed the tazer and syringe, then sat down on the pavement along the only corner where I'd be invisible to anyone walking through that area. It was pitch dark and so was I. Black coat and hat silhouetting a black dumpster and asphalt pavement made me one with my surroundings. Night time camouflage.

More anticipation, more anxiety, I am not good at the "waiting game." The Cage closed at 1:00am, but the long wait as he slugged down bourbons while exerting his academic stature over some future propagandists, wasn't so bad, even in the rain. I was feeling more like a soldier and soldiers never complain on the battlefield and certainly not about the weather.

Around 11:35 a heated conversation turned the corner and headed my way. Once again — two's company, three's a crowd. One loud voice and one soft. I didn't recognize the loud voice but the soft one was Vay's. God, threw me another curve ball.

"I told you before, I can't help you now," said Vay.

"You promised that tape." The voices came close enough to hear their footsteps, one stepping in a puddle. Splash.

The two stood together by his car for a minute and continued to argue, even Vay was beginning to shout. I imagined him driving away as the other person kept shouting at him. Twelve hours of painful anticipation wasted.

"I did what you asked and now you renege on your promise? You're an ass," the loud one shouted. Although arguments in the back lot of some meat market wouldn't attract attention, I worried that this time it would.

"I'll see you in class tomorrow. Let's talk then." The other, a student, walked over towards the dumpster opposite the side I was on, opened the door, tossed something in and then walked away. It wasn't paper, it was glass. I waited a few seconds until he turned the corner and was out of view and earshot. Vay's car door opened, and I stepped out, holstering my tazer in my right pocket.

"Sorry I'm so late, still wanna catch a drink?" I asked just as he sat in his seat. Man has evolved to consider every approach from a stranger late at night to be a potential threat. Vay slammed his door shut and then sat there staring straight at me through the rain-spattered window. He cracked it, just enough to hear what I was saying. Like two cowboys at high-noon, each waiting for the other to make his move, he towards the button that would lower or raise the window and me towards my tazer, I kept gripped but gently pulled halfway out of my pocket. My syringe was tucked into my left. God help me if he reaches out to shake my hand as both were busy. It was dark and, for a moment, I could understand his reluctance to acknowledge me. That blank fearful stare continued for longer than I would have expected. He lowered the window and spoke.

"Geez, it's you. It's almost midnight. I thought you were coming earlier."

"Yeah, me too," and then reached through his window which was halfway down, and jammed my tazer directly into his bulging carotid artery. Tazers transmit electricity which takes control of the body's electrical impulses that cause normal muscle functions. But more important, it's painful as hell which also causes loud screams. Vay's teeth gritted together in a tight clench causing those hushed screams to turn into loud grunts. I reached around to the other side with my syringe and jammed it into his neck then emptied its contents. I counted and, at six he slumped over. He was out cold.

I removed his cell phone from his pocket, ejected the battery and bent the circuit board which I then broke in half, then opened his door and pushed him over to lay sideways across the driver's and passenger's seat in case anyone felt the need to respond to a man screaming, although not that loud.

Backing my van up, I opened the rear doors and slid Vay into the false bottom drawer, then slid the tomato shelf over top of him. "Mission accomplished."

The rain picked up in intensity, allowing me to breathe more easily knowing that the chances of hitting a check point were even less likely than when I had first left my home. It was pouring.

The trip back to my place was quiet, not a peep from the cargo, the roads were void of traffic. After removing Vay from the sliding drawer, he was still unconscious, I dragged him from under his arms across the muddy pebbled driveway and into the garage. Mud covered his pants and his left shoe fell off. While dragging him to the edge of the pit I remembered how cooperative DeSoto was when asked to shimmy down the stairs while his hands were tied, but he had already awakened. Vay was still out cold, and I had forgotten to tie his hands. In fact, I had left the rope on the floor in the pit. My packing list was incomplete, and I had made a small, but potentially lethal mistake. But Vay was meek, and I was armed. Advantage me.

It's not a bone breaking drop from the top to the bottom but it would hurt like hell, especially if I were to push him into the pit face down, which is what I did. Thump. He was still unconscious. Much smaller than DeSoto but injected with the same amount, I tied his hands together, placed him in the chair and then battened down the straps and buckled the seatbelt to secure him before he came to. Safety first!

Coming out of his drugged stupor, he glanced around, whipping his head left to right then back left again and with each turn of the head he let out a sigh of exhaustion as if he had just finished running a marathon. He glanced down at his strapped-in hands then kicked upward attempting to loosen the seat belt.

"Where am I?"

"It's my pit." I told him in a tone that was loud and clear.

"Sounds scary, should I be, (long pause) — scared?" he stuttered.

I'm dealing with a young man whose entire career was based upon lying and yet, I debated whether to play his game of falsities or to be truthful. I opted to lie.

"Not as long as you cooperate." Weak answer and he wasn't buying it. I could read his eyes which are truly the window to our soul. A deep pit, hands tied and then strapped into a chair with a seat belt tugged tight — never mind the American Flag hanging on the wall covering the Barca that was behind it.

"Kiddy porn and blackmail won't advance your career," I added.

"I know who you are, Aiken, and now you know me. I'd say we have the classic version of a stalemate or mutually assured destruction here."

"Yes, we do. But, let's start with me. What do you know beyond my name?"

"Bet you wish you had never asked your drone buddy, Queek, to join you on that trip," he smiled in a wry, taunting manner.

No matter how many times I asked where he was, he refused to answer except to say, "He's alive." He was a propagandist, so taking him at his word was naïve. It was he who alerted Homeland Security to my location which led to the raid that ended in my parents being taken away. He reminded me, as if I needed it, to trust no one in my circle of friends, which was odd since my circle was small and included only Julian and my coworkers at Il Portico. Justification reached a new pinnacle. I relished killing him.

"How did you know it was me that posted that video and where I lived?" I inquired.

"You'd never understand, probably over your head." Talk about a quandary. Julian assured me that Vay was technically ignorant and only wrote and posted garbage on the sites he administered. I tried again.

"Try me. I am tech savvy."

"A friend helped me," taunting me while emphasizing the word "friend." I asked six times who that friend was, and he never revealed him or her. Oh, how I wished for a waterboarding set-up, but all I had were items meant for immediate extermination — knives, guns, drugs and the Barka. Vay was surprisingly strong in his loyalty to someone. It was often said that "the punishment should fit the crime," so I edited that phrase to something more appropriate to address the need for torture. It should neutralize the crime, which meant that his fingers would be sacrificed should he refuse to answer that question. Kinda hard to type without those five little digits.

I pulled out a pair of Massimo's pruning sheers from his gardening shelf and worked its handles in and out to signal my intentions to my subject. You could hear that beautiful shhhh sound as they opened and closed. They were sharp.

"Need those fingers for typing don't you?"

"I don't know his name. We'd communicate by email only. I'm telling the truth." Liar, I thought.

Julian always told me to not over-think things. Carry out my missions with speed, precision and with no hesitation. Vay's hands were strapped to the arm of the chair, so the only decision to make was which finger would meet the intersection of the pruning sheer's blades. Easy — Index.

When I was young, our Christmas trees were always live, never fake. Dad would tell me which errant limbs or branches to cut with his pruning sheers to shape those beautiful trees into a perfect triangle. Except for blood spurting from the area that was severed and a blood-curdling scream from his mouth, cutting a finger off has a similar feel — soft at first and then, when approaching the bone, some small bit of resistance which is neutralized by applying more pressure. It ends with a soft squishy feeling and then, it's done. That simple torturous act put my subject at ease, thinking his finger would be the only victim of his time in my pit. He continued to insist that he didn't know his friend's name, and I had to believe him. He lost an important tool for his career and would have lost nine more, but still the answer would have been the same — he seriously didn't know. I wrapped his hand at the point of severing to stop the bleeding and showed some sense of compassion for what I had just put him through. A moment of weakness, but a necessary one.

We talked for an hour, much longer than normal. All the while he seemed at ease with his situation and not the least bit nervous. Either he had no idea that I would kill him, or perhaps had arrived at that moment of peace knowing that there was no escape. It impressed me. We'd often mock them as weak, but in reality they were strong willed and willing to die for their cause, as were we. Mutually assured destruction.

I've tried to put myself in those situations, tied up in a pit with someone who hated me, knowing that I'd not get out alive. Would I chat? Would I cry, or beg for my life? Or, would I take it like a man and ask my capturer to just get it over with, like my heros in the movies? I believe that, in moments of certainty, when a man realizes that he is no longer in control, a burst of emotional testosterone kicks in. I have verifiable data on that in case anyone is interested. The only issue might be the size of my sampling, but I'm still working on that.

And then, Vay did what came natural to him. He tried to barter with me. A man of the written word was now a man of the verbal kind. He continued to talk, question, mock and basically annoy me.

"Do you believe in mutual assured destruction?" he asked again.

"Your birth country did too."

"Birth country? Oh, you think I'm Russian?"

The Herons on Julian's list were all born in the former Soviet Union, shipped, like cargo, to the shores of America, and then adopted by parents willing to raise little traitors. What I didn't know, but should have, was that those Herons were, by order of their handlers, breeding and passing the baton to their offspring. The enemy was, not only within, but was expanding. Our attempt at minimizing future damage was feeble. They were slowly taking over.

"Your mother, your father. They were born in Russia?"

"Both, Moscow" he replied. The more Vay talked the more at ease he was with his past, his upbringing and his accomplishments for such a young traitor. He was smug with himself, proud and with no regrets.

"Who is your friend that helped you with your technical issues?" I felt I knew the answer but wanted to hear it from him. Kilgore.

"I'm done talking," he said and then tilted his head down, mimicking prayer, which was bull shit since they were all secularists. God was a joke to hem, thus his removal from our public square.

The moment of truth was upon me, but I was still unsure of how the hell was I going to finish Vay off. It's not like my options were many — gun, knife, drugs, but at that moment, I wanted to take a break and continue the conversation later, hoping that he'd offer up more once I showed some compassion, or maybe fed him something. He was already drunk so booz was out of the question.

My father's last words were instructions to never rescue him. That bothered me. Vay's were to "Trust no one" and that had the same effect, but begged for clarification. He sat and stared at me. I hated that smug stare — it was as if he was saying "I've gotten under your skin, haven't I?" I removed the flag which covered the opening to the Barka, hoping he'd offer me more while staring at those enormous, stainless steel blades which glistened in the light that was directed at them. His stone-cold, impassioned stare changed to a look of sheer terror. His already pale complexion became transparent. I could see his veins. What should have had a healthy pink glow was blue. It was that whiter shade of pale. I had seen this before with DeSoto. Te Barka is the great equalizer and will render even the strongest of men to a crying mess.

"You're kidding aren't you?" his voice quivering, his face gazing directly towards the chipper. "Don't over-think, Don't hesitate," I repeated to myself. Before introducing him to a rousing rendition of the National anthem, I snapped his picture. He was neatly wrapped in the rope like a Christmas present. The only thing missing was a bow — a bright red one atop his head. "Say cheese," I said, then placed the Beats headphones over his ears and cranked up the volume to a deafening level. I had lost my patience. All he could do was shake his head in all directions, squint his eyes and clench his teeth. I wondered if the blaring volume or the lyrics bothered him. I refilled the syringe with the etomidate and assured him that he would feel nothing. Unless he was a lip reader, he never heard my parting words of comfort —

"The rockets red glare" was reaching its crescendo. I proceeded to anesthetize Vay before performing surgery. No scalpel, no stitches, no oxygen mask, or comforting nurses to blot his forehead with a cold cloth, just the Barka, too much apple wood and six shovels of cow manure. He went peacefully. I had hoped the grinding noise didn't wake him up before it rendered him into that gooey pulp which would become one with the wood and manure. That would have been cruel and unusual punishment for sure. Yes, I shoved him in alive but sedated. Chelsea became his surgeon.

What I had forgotten to remove from Vay's possession before pulverizing him were the keys needed to enter his apartment and complete my mission. The devil is in the details and it would piss Julian off! That's two mistakes I had made that evening. "Get it together Joshua," I screamed at myself.

Like clockwork, Julian's standard message hit my phone, "Did you pass your exam?"

"Yes, but I forgot a KEY question." He knew what I meant and wasn't happy about it. Three mean emoji followed by a word I had never heard him say, "Fuck"

The physical area in my garden where the remains of my human compost end up is small, maybe ten square feet and only a foot high. The last section of the chute pointed downward close to the ground which encouraged a piling of the remains instead of scattering it all over the place. Figuring that the brass key was too small and hard to be ground up and that it would most likely be expelled intact from the blades, I grabbed my flashlight and a rake then headed out back for some mid-night gardening.

The smell was horrendous, very pungent. I hadn't raked DeSoto until a week after he was chipped and the cool weather and heavy rain had neutered his essence to a mild scent that smelled more like a bad cigar than what accosted me that evening. Vay was odorous beyond my comfort level which was already low. It didn't take long for the usual reactions that accompany a pungent smell to invade my entire being. The grimace of my face, the unsuccessful attempt to breathe shallow, then stepping away from the source just to breathe clean air. It ended with gagging, choking and projectile vomiting. I can't imagine a more horrible combination of elements to rake through and now it included the contents of my stomach. The site, smell and, for me, the mere mention of vomit is like a daisy chain — it causes more of it. The key was there, laying among, what appeared to be, brain matter and wrapped in strands of unpulverized hair. Other than some serious surface scratches and coagulated blood it was unharmed. I texted Julian "Found the answer. Going to clean my car."

Breaking God's Eighth Commandment

* * * *

Breaking God's Eighth commandment wasn't my thing even though the Sixth was more serious. It was two-fifteen in the morning when I arrived at Vay's place — not a soul in sight, but

I wore my black hat, ski mask and gloves just in case. Despite the scratches and dings, the key worked. You can tell a lot about a person by the furnishings and art they surround themselves with. I'm still not sure what to make of Vay's decorating choice except to say that his apartment was a total mess with clothes scattered on the floor, empty Chinese takeout boxes on the coffee table and posters from the bygone era of Che Guevara, Marx and Castro in their younger years adorning every square inch of wall space. It was as Julian had showed on his phone. It smelled of pot too. The walls and ceiling of his bedroom took on a different genre with heavy metal bands being that room's theme. Unlike the cannabis scent of the living room, his bedroom reeked of body odor — the man was a slob.

I transferred all of Vay's digital content, excluding the spice cabinet to my portable 1-Terabyte hard drive, then erased his drive twice. For good measure, I reformatted it making whatever bits of data that remained unretrievable. After reloading the spice cabinet back on to his system I left through the back door and walked three blocks to my van, returning home around 3am. I slept surprisingly well that night, which actually scared me. Who was I becoming and could I stop if needed?

Friday's Class

* * * *

Vay was always ten minutes late for his class, so my classmates stuck around for twenty, expecting him to show up with his usual 'kiddie" remark," but he never did. A substitute professor walked in at eight-thirty, but half of the class had already left.

"We've been trying to locate Professor Vay but haven't been able to, so I'll substitute today. Can someone tell me what you've been working on?"

I raised my hand and offered a good starting point for this new professor.

"Yes, we were discussing how to spread our stories over a wide network."

You see what I did there?

Bitterns

* * * *

On Christmas Day 1991, Soviet President Mikhail Gorbachev announced to a shocked world the dissolution of the Soviet Union and his resignation from its top post. 40 years of teetering on the brink of nuclear destruction built upon a Cold War between the Soviet Union and the United States had ended. What had been the world's largest communist state split into 15 independent republics, making America the sole global superpower. Members of the Soviet high command abdicated power without a shot being fired. This did not sit well with the Goliaths now standing outside the Kremlin. A new leader emerged who had been actively involved with the progression of D6. He saw an opportunity to navigate Khrushchev's bold plan to its ultimate conclusion — the collapse of the U.S. dollar. Key among his objectives was to instill a Heron soldier into the White House and this would require an army of propagandists to mold a message necessary to accomplish that. A tall order for sure, but they successfully pulled it off.

Step one — activate the full force of the embedded Bitterns, script their messaging and then train them in the art of Soviet propaganda. Begin with the local, small metropolitan papers then gradually promote them to the national rags. From there, groom their on-air personalities and skills. Finally, invite them on the major cable channels as "experts" which will eventually garner them job offers to be permanent TV media personalities. From that point, get control of book-review assignments, editorial writing, and policy-making positions.

Before the Great Collapse most already felt that our media was prejudiced against the Patriots, and it was. But this didn't stop them from their march forward to more thoroughly propagandize our citizens through the airwaves and printed pages they controlled. Clueless is not a word Americans apply to themselves as a country, a people, or a government, but this time it did. Our education system, guided by their own Egrets, had sufficiently dumbed us down to the point where we'd be receptive to a propagandist message which ultimately paved the path for this media takeover.

The United States was wide open for Maskirovka — deception. Unlike American organizations in Russia, we welcomed Russian public relations firms, put Russian programming on our cable television and distributed its message without censorship. Its diplomats were welcome to attend think-tank seminars in Washington, the entire system of American politics was an open book for them. The natural progression of that was an easy infiltration into our media. The New York Times, Washington Post, Chicago Tribune, ABC, NBC, CBS, MSNBC and CNN were ripe for the picking. The Goliath in Moscow fed them their story lines, helped to groom their on-air personalities and, before you knew it, American media was no longer American, it was a full blown Soviet propaganda arm of RT, Russia Today, with headquarters in New York, LA, Chicago, Washington, DC and most other major cities in America.

The dark side of Russia's political system with its corruption, selective use of law, and low tolerance for opposition, was gradually overtaking the American media. By exploiting misleading historical analogies, and ignoring areas that did not fit their narrative, journalism in America experienced a cataclysmic change. The message was always the same. Capitalism was bad, scrap the first and second amendments and our borders should be open for all who seek refuge in the world's last and only superpower. And paramount in those messages was the need to divide our citizens across every line imaginable. Repeat it enough and ultimately it takes hold. Their most valuable asset — Christopher T. Jenkins.

Subject #4

* * * *

We continued with our Monday morning routine of meeting at The Drip for our "event" recaps. Being consistent was important to Julian, and I was beginning to understand why. While most people dread that day, I didn't. It's the start of a new week and, as my successes piled up and confidence grew, those sessions were also mine to gloat about a job well done. We'd discuss the next subject but not before addressing any issues that might have popped up with a previous one. What could be better than an espresso, scones, our own coded language and murder?

Julian would open each session by recapping his notes from our previous meeting and would then ask if I had anything to add. I never did — subject executed, chipped and spread across the garden.

"Comments?"

"Not really."

What else could I say? Never mind I'd have to comment in coded language, which opened the distinct possibility that I'd blurt something out while struggling to find the correct codeword. He'd lectured me in his stern professorial manner, just as he did in his classroom, if perfection wasn't achieved. Something like; "You need to study more and make sure that you bring all your supplies to the test." He was anal, but I learned from my mistakes and never repeated them again. I was fast becoming a smart, efficient executioner but, in all honesty, I wasn't completely forthcoming with every minor mistake that might have happened — there was always something that didn't go as planned. Shit happens, and I'd just as soon avoid a coded tongue lashing. Silence really is golden.

It was Monday, September 11th, a sad day for many Americans, but most had long since swept those horrific memories under the rug. Like the falling dust particles that were once the essence of concrete floors from those twin towers - history dissipated.

Gazing through my kitchen window and admiring my well-tended antithetical garden of Eden, I couldn't help but think about the nearly three-thousand who had lost their lives and how it forever changed America — first for the good and then for pure evil. I wondered if the Herons had secretly initiated that event just as they had set into motion the foundation for the Great Collapse. I believe they did but have no concrete proof to base that on.

Thinking about my parents was a daily struggle, but I followed my father's edict to never attempt their rescue. Julian agreed and would run routine mood checks to ascertain that I remained focused on the mission at hand. "Idle minds screw up," he'd say. His version of "Idle minds are the devil's workshop," which seemed more appropriate, but I gave him a pass. He meant well but always messed up well-known American phrases.

Time for Fall Fertilizer

* * * *

Smells and sounds bring back memories for me, and that morning the crisp air and the orchestrated screech of cicadas had subdued to a calming white noise. It reminded me of the end of summer, a time to prepare for a new school year and new friends, most of whom I didn't like. I reflected on the seasonal changes and how the breeze kicks up from the north and things begin to die. Leaves change color, tomatoes wilt and no longer bare fruit except for a few dozen green ones that never ripened. Fried green tomatoes - a favorite at Il Portico!!

The zucchini was encroaching outside of the garden's normal boundary, the tomatoes had done well — plenty of sunshine, hot weather and prime fertilizer, and the mushrooms looked presentable. Just as the season was changing, so too would our menu. Cold summer gazpacho shifted to fall's warm Pappa al Pomodoro. Vegetable based sauces would change to a hearty Bolognese, but my organic fertilizer was running low, and I wasn't about to start an unpatriotic shift towards using chemicals for feeding my garden. I was certifiably organic and vowed to keep the chemicals for my subjects. Besides — I was on the cusp of perfecting the formula. My learning process was very much in the realm of Goldilocks and the Three Bears. My first attempt (DeSoto) was too wet and gooey, the second (Vay) had too much wood — too dry, but my third concoction should be perfect. One part body, a half a cord of wood, twelve large shovels of cow manure, chip the hell out it and spread across the garden. Wood and manure were in abundant supply, but I was one ingredient short — a human.

That dark region of my brain, the part allotted for "all things evil" shifted its attention from the seasonal changes that would put my garden into dormancy to a focus on — Herons. It was time to spin the wheel of misfortune or, as Julian would say, it's time to play Russian Roulette.

Spinning The Wheel

* * * *

Avoid patterns — confuse the profilers. We thought long and hard about our sequence of executions, not wanting to draw unwelcome attention by eliminating only Senators or Congressmen in succession. Doing so would entice unwanted notice to our battle plan, which was nothing more than a list of names in no specific order. Like the vegetables in my garden, we'd rotate them — a Bittern this week, an Egret or a Blue the next, although at that point we hadn't moved beyond Egrets and Bitterns. I was eager for a Blue and the challenge they'd present, since certifiably insane and well-armed subjects would tend to fight back. Sounds weird but I needed to kick it up a notch. I also understood the process and Julian's affection for targeting education and the media, so I didn't question him. Unguarded and less likely to fight back, he considered them to be adequate target practice — a training ground for his young protégé — me.

The roulette wheel that Julian had "acquired" in Macau became our wheel of misfortune (my term) when deciding which subject would be our next. It was a simple process. We'd assign multiple digits to each name, depending on the size of the group they belonged to. If a group had twelve names, we'd assign each of them three numbers. Think of a roulette wheel but black or red didn't matter — just the number. This was to determine that each number, one through thirty-six, would yield an execution order. We had no patience to spin endlessly like playing spin the bottle.

Still, we'd discuss the subject at some length and then agreed that he'd become our next approved target — rendering a sophomoric thumb-up to seal the deal. Julian had ultimate veto power and would go to great lengths to discuss their historical background, difficulty in extracting and could pardon any subject, but only temporarily. Like a police file, Julian had pages upon pages of information on each subject. Of course, my curiosity as to how he came upon that information peaked every time we discussed them but, like a child in Sunday School accepting what was taught as gospel, I never questioned Julian. He held back the most difficult ones until such a time as he felt confident enough in my abilities to not screw up. If their number came up, "Spin again."

The only thing not drawn from that wheel was the group we'd be targeting. That decision was entirely Julian's and was more strategic. Again — crop rotation.

Julian never appreciated my calling it the Wheel-of-Misfortune. "This is serious business," he'd remind me. Humor relieved the stress I went through since I was the one taking all the risks. My incessant need to remind him of this slighted dynamic was to no avail. His stone-cold face and that abbreviated chuckle one gave when signaling that what you're telling me is of no concern, was all I'd get back.

Like a kid at the carnival I'd watch the wheel spin round and round. He'd walk away, asking me to let him know which slot the ball landed on and who owned that number. Emotionless and detached with that part of the process, his energy level would kick into high gear once we discussed the details, the history and background of the chosen one. This is where he flourished.

A pattern was emerging because, once again, Julian returned to Bitterns. He obsessed over them. Goebbels would have been green with envy with their ability to share and make viral the false stories that would capture and hold the twenty-four-hour news cycle. Fake news was their curriculum. With Vay out of the picture it made sense to knock off a few more commentators.

He spun the wheel and the shiny steel ball bounced from slot to slot, going air-born at one point, then settled into slot #32. Christopher T. Jenkins, or as the world knew him, Chris T., the host of the low-rated "American Caucus" TV show was next in line for a spectacularly patriotic event complete with the standard fair of our national anthem blaring at deafening decibels through a pair of Beats headphones taped tightly to his fat head.

We were to meet that afternoon to discuss our next subject,

Subject #4. I hated that guy and was most eager to begin.

Things aren't always as they seem.

* * *

Several questions continued to confound me, yet I never dwelled upon. Some things were best left in the dark recesses of my mind, only to be yanked out at a later date when those recesses overflowed with all sorts of nasty things I had shoved in there. I'd take one out — then put another one in. House cleaning.

These questions I filed under the cerebral cortex region known as "curiosity." Did the Herons know of their birthright as orphans from other countries, adopted out to parents all too willing to raise them in, what most would consider, sinister means?

At what point did they begin their training?

Did they have handlers?

Was there an indoctrination process?

Who was the master?

Try as I did with DeSoto and Vay, I never got answers to these. Questions that needed answering, not because it would alter our mission or my feelings towards the subjects, but it would have been helpful to know what we were up against. It would have freed up mental space for even worse things yet to come. In a nutshell — were they willing participants in that traitorous game or just duped and abused as children? Three subjects into the list and I had never asked those questions of

Julian, but knew he'd have an answer. Why I never asked, I suppose, was due to the working relationship we had at that moment in time. I was still the young, dutiful apprentice and, therefore, more focused on "how" and "when" — "why" was of little consequence. Perhaps subject #4 would shed some light because, at that point, it bothered me. Morbid curiosity, I suppose.

Interrogating a subject was forbidden in the hastily assembled code that Julian insisted we follow. I ignored that commandment and just as hastily added interrogation as a footnote for my next mission. Stalk, incapacitate, transfer the body, interrogate until near dead, kill, chip, dispose. A small checklist for such a complicated and dangerous procedure.

A birth parent's right to privacy versus an adoptee's right to know was a debate as old as time. With Herons, their biological parents were prisoners in some decrepit prison oceans away or, more than likely, dead. But, just as my father had warned, things weren't always as they seemed. Cruel lies to these children were a critical component of the Heron's patient strategy. There were no "Parent of the Year" awards among the entire lot of adopters and, at some point, they became more interesting than the actual targets. Why weren't they on the list? After all, these parents were the Generals, yet Julian remained focused on the foot soldiers. Privacy rights of parents weren't the issue with D6, it was the secrecy of rogue administrations that had been occupying the White House for decades — not all, but enough to pull this thing off. How ironic that D6 was the only long-term plan that had ever worked for our communist enemies. Industrial, military, social and economic planning at the state level were all colossal failures. But with D6 - it worked better than expected.

Subject 4:
Christopher Jenkins - The Misogynist
* * * *

Christopher Jenkins was among the few who knew his birthright and I suspect that was due to his age when he was crammed onto shipment #43. He was four. His Russian name was Arkady Sokolov, but the story they told him was a complete fabrication, starting with the lie that his parents had both died in a car accident. Julian knew the truth and cars played no role in their death. Both were barbarous serial killers, a rather sick pair known for their propensity to kill slowly. They purposely prolonged their victim's suffering, earning them a nickname in Soviet media which translated to "Chinese Water Torture" in Russian. It gave them a high. I was thinking ahead. Like father like son, not in deeds but in the manner of dying. Only the weapons were different. His biological parents used knives and sledge hammers while he used his voice. Christopher should suffer a similar fate because his actions took years to take effect, so too should the manner in which he dies.

His father, Alexi, was a fan of dull, serrated knives while the mother preferred hammers - huge ones. Knives sharp enough to slice open the victim's skin but dulled enough to rip the flesh apart, inflicting maximum pain and a more expeditious flow of blood. As for her love of hammers — the bigger the better as she became orgasmic at the mere sight of exploding bone fragments. She'd scream at the top of her lungs with undertones of sadistic laughter while the victim was being pulverized. Legs, arms, hands, any bone that wouldn't kill them. They worked as a team. Cut, rip and then hammer the crap out of the victim until they died.

They executed Alexi by firing squad on November 12, 1960, while his mother, Elena, served the rest of her life at White Lake, Russia's version of Alcatraz. Alexi got the better end of that deal — quick and painless.

Isolated by the White Lake in Siberia and built to hold the most heinous criminals, the restricted life of living in cages with paper-thin walls and no washing facilities surrounded by freezing cold water and blinding snow left the prisoners psychologically devastated, physically deteriorated and eventually they'd die. One wonders if she experienced the same sick orgasmic reaction as she slowly withered away in the cold, Soviet tundra. There is no crueler way to die other than drowning or beheading, two of my biggest fears. Buried alive was my biggest.

Arkady was three when they committed his mother to that facility after which they took him to the Kruszschky Home for Children in Oneida Russia. How ironic that his last name, Sokolov meant "bird of prey" in Russian. Kruszschky was a virtual country club, by Soviet standards, for these young children, most of whom had lived in abject poverty. It was step one in the long-term process of implantation into the U.S. and indoctrination against us — treat them like kings in Russia, and like shit in America! They chose him to go there.

At four, well beyond the established age limit for transfer, Arkady boarded the Vsevolod, shipment #43 along with 442 other children. They noted none were older than two in the ship's log and entered Christopher Jenkins into the system as: 7947 — departing from Minsk. They had chosen the host parents in the United States before each child boarded the ship. At two years of age, memories of the Soviet Union would disappear. At four — that was risky but, never-the-less, they added him to the cargo at the last minute. It's likely they wanted nothing to do with a mature Sokolov, fearing that bad genes would render him a serial killer just as his parents were. What better way to inflict damage on your enemy then to send them a genetically inferior child — off he went, bound for Montauk.

Young Arkady, having serial killers as parents was tagged 7947, meaning he was to become a "Blue" — a murderous criminal himself and part of the sinister plot to change American public opinion over our right to bear arms — what was once our 2nd Amendment. A point of clarity though — I was never one who touted the 2nd Amendment as the justification for our right to bear arms. That right came to us from God himself, not our federal Government. As we'd constantly remind ourselves — the government giveth, and the government taketh away.

7947's mission, upon achieving maturity as a "Blue," was to carry out a mass execution using an assault rifle and then commit suicide to avoid being captured and questioned. They preferred young victims, even children, as it had a more dramatic and emotional effect on swaying public opinion towards their goal of disarming the American citizenry. It was effective.

Upon arrival off the shores of Montauk, New York they transferred him upstate to Brighton placing him in the Monroe County Founders Home, an orphanage for Russian children, which was just a halfway house to their final destination as traitors to America. Alvictus in Virginia was a safe house for defecting Russian KGB, the Monroe County Founders Home was a secret house for newly arriving Herons — step two before their final destination to their adoptive parents all over the United States. Unlike our government financed safe houses for defecting spies, the Sberbank of Russia funded that orphanage.

By all measures he was a well-behaved child, exhibiting none of the murderous psychotic tendencies of his parents. Somewhere along his path to personal destruction, Chris crossed into the world of politics as an advisor to a key U.S. Senator from Pennsylvania. His parents convinced their Soviet handlers that Chris was a masterful communicator and that they'd be much better served with him in the media. No parent wishes to see their child commit suicide or mass murder, no matter how much the masters paid for that lethal talent. They agreed, and he snagged the powerful position of Communications Director which led to his becoming the media sensation he was. It was at that point that a small tinge of psychosis reared its ugly head and exited his mouth in the form of nightly, virulent, anti-American commentaries. Words became his weapon, and he used them effectively, every damn night.

On September 24th, 2024, Julian handed me a small clipping from Izvestia, an old Soviet newspaper. A single two inch column with a black & white photo reporting the execution of Alexei Sokolov and the life sentence given to his wife Elana for the crime of murdering six innocent people by a dull machete and an enormous sledge hammer. Their only surviving child, Arkady, was noted as having been turned over to the state where he would remain until adopted by loving parents. His story ended there. No acknowledgement of his voyage to America.

"Hand this to him, give him a moment to digest and then smile before finishing him off," Julian insisted with a look of personal vindication I had not seen before from him. This wasn't revenge. This was personal. Our code was eroding, and we were just beginning our battle. Damn.

The Misogynist

* * * *

You can tell a lot about a person's character by how they treat the waitstaff or act when they're inebriated. There's a small kernel of truth in every outburst a drunk makes. Jenkins was an arrogant ass to the waitresses and even worse when he was drunk, which was often. Every sentence was littered with f-bombs and he'd loft obnoxious and derogatory remarks at my cute waitress, Caitlin. I'd describe him as a serial misogynist, but it was his ties to the motherland and incredible success at painting the Patriots as home-grown terrorists hellbent on blowing a school bus up or indiscriminately riddling a classroom with rounds from an AR-15 that earned him a spot on Julian's list. Bad social skills weren't enough to render a death sentence. Still, Julian was tempted to give him a momentary reprieve in favor of another on the list but, for the first time, I got the upper hand in settling his quandary. We were having such success with Bitterns why rock the boat? So much for the concept of rotation.

Christopher's suitable skill-set at arousing the low-informed among us into believing the Patriots were all out to get them and that collectivism was their only path to utopia was admirable. He was effective and, for that reason, I looked forward to eliminating him. That combination of ideological differences and his broadcast listing the Top-10 fake news stories of 2020 where mine, exposing Vega 7, came in at number three, added to my insatiable desire to plan his event. It thrilled me to see his name on the list.

As for his lust for collectivism, we all know how that turned out. After the crash, our economy resembled Venezuela where everything was in short supply. Main Street USA resembled many banana republics where the scarcity of toilet paper, food, medicine, you name it, created a thriving black market. The Herons, however, had their own commissaries, so shortages didn't exist in their world. The Great Collapse was also the great divider as devastation hit the masses while our leaders, many of whom planned for it, skated.

Jenkins' nightly material was straight out of some grocery store tabloid, the kind that featured headlines so absurd only uneducated morons would believe them. But instead of "Aliens Land in Downtown LA" or "Dog Receives Man's Head in Secret

Experimental Transplant," he'd commentate on stories of rape, murder, mayhem, lies and, his favorite, the Preppers holed up in some dark caves in the northwest preparing for their final battle to take back their country. We were always the instigators. He'd end his nightly shows with the usual "Utopia was just over the horizon," crap. To be fair, you could find gullibility on both sides of the aisle and we had our share of idiots. I looked forward to our final meeting — a feeling I didn't share with the others. Julian's unemotional, detached attitude changed with Jenkins. He also had a lethal affection for the man. But, as usual, his was more closely related to the subject and more personal in nature.

They had set the bar low for Bittern media ratings before the collapse but afterwards it was all state-run, so ratings didn't matter. His was near the bottom yet still aired nightly and for good reason. Jenkins was the supreme propagandist for the Neville regime. Be damned the ratings — it's the content they're interested in. Like clockwork, he'd end his nightly segment by calling us "traitors among our comrades." Pot meet kettle, you've just been called black.

Among his many despicable social traits was a propensity to overindulge in pricey liquor while obsessing about the opposite sex after having done the aforementioned. Dirty old man comes to mind, but that's being too kind to him and too harsh for dirty old men. His temptations were wrapped in silk, satin and lace then drizzled with heavy doses of Single Malt scotch and an inherent hatred towards America.

Chris was a regular at Il Portico, a huge fan of risotto fungi. Preferring it more wet than an aficionado, we'd add a six-second pour of Pinot Grigio before its final basil garnish. He was fanatical about mushrooms, especially the ones from my garden. If only he knew what fertilized them. He'd consume at least three tall scotch rocks, each with a single cube of ice and not one more. It was always expensive Macallan 12-Year-Old single malt. He enjoyed the slight chill but was careful to avoid dilution if those cubes melted. His speed of consumption was hurried; the cube was still intact even after sipping the last drop, so it really didn't matter.

An obnoxious drunk, he'd force our waitstaff to keep a careful eye on his glass, readying the next one once the scotch level approached two fingers. If we were late, his audible level would rise until his next round appeared. Our guests became uncomfortable during those outbursts until a new pour had rendered him silent. This bears repeating: Before you wince at the thought of my executing a man for poor taste in preparing risotto, bad manners, or the constant mistreatment of women, understand that he, like all of our subjects, was a Heron and was deeply involved in decades of planning which led to our nation's collapse. He was a traitor and, in my mind, the man who triggered the raid by HomeLand Security which sent my parents to incarceration. In fact, Jenkins might very well have been the person most responsible for turning me towards the dark side. Payback's a bitch.

Christopher Jenkins

* * * *

Arkady Sakalov: Born May 23rd, 1964: Orphaned Kruszschky Home for Children, Oneida Russia. American Identity: Christopher Jenkins. TV Commentator. Bittern

Securing top billing on a major network gave him unfettered access to the White House and Neville's inner sanctum. The administration's communication director approved and edited his nightly scripts before he'd go live. Unbiased journalism, my ass — this was pure, unmitigated PRAVDA propaganda and Chris was their go-to boy. His demographics were perfect — young, naïve and thoroughly dumbed-down. The underlying message each evening, to slyly positioning Communism as a worthy goal, yet he always avoided using the "C" word unless berating the old Soviet guard from the 60's. That was a popular ploy among them. Communism still had a terrible connotation even though our nation was blindly marching towards it. Liberals became Progressives and then, over time, morphed into Communists, yet they never openly identified with the devil. A nation that fought so many wars against the spread of Communism around the world, losing hundreds of thousands of young Patriots in the process was itself gradually becoming Communist. Still — the average American was oblivious to our conversion. Heck, they had no clue what the 1st or 2nd Amendments were and the importance they played in a free and civil society. The Constitution was an impediment to their movement which was shrouded in pleasant sounding names like "Progressive."

Income equality, fairness, community activism, social and economic justice pervaded his nightly broadcasts and were bucket-list items among the regime's adoring masses. God Bless America, thanking our military, police and veterans were never uttered. American exceptionalism was to be mocked. Personal responsibility was a foreign concept because blaming others for one's shortcomings became fashionable and rendered millions of Americans into victimhood status. He was relentless and predictably boring, but his audience lopped that shit up. The Reverend Atticus Phelps was a frequent guest until the unthinkable happened. I was relishing the thought of telling Jenkins that it was I who had sent Phelps to hell and that he'd soon be joining him. Anger was invading my sole.

Jenkins loathed our military and once held a contest to redesign the American flag, noting a requirement that the use of red, white or blue was not allowed. Seemed odd not to use the color red as that was an obvious choice for a spectacularly traitorous background. China, the Soviet Union, Cuba even Venezuela — you get my drift. I suppose his logic was an association with the former red states, which meant Patriots. Julian filled in the more salacious details — the kind they hid from the public, knowing this would damn the Heron. Christopher Jenkins was taking his orders from Moscow and was the epitome of a Soviet Agent.

Jenkins communicated frequently with Russia in his early 30's and spent summers vacationing at Batumi on the Black Sea, presumably to report on his progress while basking in the chilling beauty of their northern shores. He was as much a Russian as an American; a hybrid, but the scales tipped towards his birthplace as he aged and became disillusioned with the country they had dumped him in as a child. Imagine that, hatred towards America yet love of the former Soviet Union where his mother was left to die in the bitter cold tundra and his father was executed by firing squad.

It wasn't long before Martha's Vineyard became the new Batumi; Moscow in Massachusetts we'd call it. As with the others, Julian had a deep biography of his entire life but, much to my surprise, rated him only a 5 on justification scale, right smack in the middle. We could have gone either way, but it was I who tilted the scale in favor of his execution.

His closing remarks the evening he tagged my video as "Fake News" sealed the deal. "Someone needs to find that deplorable kid." And so they tried, the very next day. Tried but failed. My innocent parents were, to them, collateral damage. You can understand my blaming him for what happened to my family and, therefore, his deserving of a spot on that list. I'm not looking for your approval, just an acknowledgment that Christopher Jenkins was a justifiable target and deserved everything we gave him. While he couched safely in a comfortable studio broadcasting lies about me on national TV, I hunkered down in a 3-by-5-foot bunker inhaling fiberglass insulation, listening to my mother screaming while praying they'd not find my safe room. Thirty terrifying minutes wondering when they'd smash through the small door and capture me. I had broken no laws and needed vindication. His execution was justified.

Alas, Julian allowed my vote to carry more weight as he relinquished his veto power. After a less-than-careful consideration I mimicked the Emperor Caligula when deciding Jenkins's fate, offering an exaggerated thumbs down gesture to Julian once we had weighed all of our options. Judge, jury and executioner; For a moment, I felt like the God who I had disavowed for most of my life.

Stalking a Pig

* * * *

I am a patient guy but will admit to a disproportionate loathing of the tedious task of planning these executions. But, whiteboarding every detail of the mission, profiling, socialize with and then stalking our subjects was necessary. While I would have preferred going straight in for the kill without the pomp and circumstances, Julian would have never agreed to that.

In golf, avoiding water and sand traps requires a repeatable routine to hone your skills. Murder is no different except the water is you lying six-feet under and the sand traps are prison bars. That can influence the most skilled executioner and I was still a novice. Julian warned me — cockiness will be the death of you, Josh. Still, my confidence never overshadowed that constant fear of getting caught or killed. Julian shared my fear, but for a different reason. Socializing with the enemy was unbearable but less so since it took place at Il Portico where I'd go "extreme capitalist" on them by watering their drinks down or cutting their portions short. I know that's not exactly taking the high-road, but every once in the while, I needed to go low for my sanity. Forced to paint a happy face and then act thrilled to be in their presence, I'd smile, shake their hand then graciously welcome them to their table. Upon returning to the kitchen, I'd imagine which vegetable would benefit most with their essence scattered across my garden and then I'd suggest it as tonight's special. Jenkins was a fat guy, or in the politically correct vernacular, a man of size. Mushrooms, preferring moist soil, would benefit from his essence. Mushrooms — his favorite food — now that's poetic justice.

Chris was a creature of habit. He'd grace our establishment every Tuesday and Thursday night, then finish each evening inebriated enough by 10:00pm that Uber was always on call, even though he lived less than a mile away. His world was compact, extending from Sector 1, New Columbia to Sector 43, New York City. As best I could tell, he spent the bulk of his time in the studio, the Monocle, harassing young women, Il Portico or his townhouse. His routine was just that — routine. Stalking wasn't necessary, but I did anyway, per Julian's insistence. I needed to know what made him tick. What were his hobbies or, dare I say, what turned him on?

You'd think planning an execution for a notorious drunk would be easy. Stumbling, not paying attention to their surroundings, and an inability to fight back in a coordinated manner — all the things you'd think would simplify the process being neutered by their intoxication. But, those traits are problematic when disposal of the body is necessary. Drunks are not easily persuaded to meet you somewhere. They're suspicious, almost paranoid. They want to go home and sleep it off. They can be loud and obnoxious. I know this because mom frequently was.

Fish are attracted to shiny lures. Ducks will flock towards the sound of an authentic duck call. Traitors must be coaxed, especially drunk ones. In Chris' case, booze and broads would do the trick, two things he enjoyed, both in excess.

"Getting him drunk is easy, the woman part, not so much," I told Julian.

"Why a woman?" he asked. "He staggers home from The Monocle on Monday's. Follow him back to his place and then finish him off," he continued.

It shocked me to hear Julian suggest an execution be carried out at a subject's home. Even extractions were to be done at neutral sites that had been thoroughly vetted. This was counter to our code. Evidence left behind and removing a dead body without knowing where video surveillance cameras might be, was out of the question. When someone goes missing or is murdered, the first place investigators will go is back to their residence. No matter how hard you try, hair strands, fingerprints, shoe impressions, fibers of any kind, even blood splatter is never completely removed. Julian's favorite acronym — DNA meant DO NOT ATTEMPT. Our work was always to be finished back at my place and the body to be completely eradicated. It was sterile, like a well-devised operating room and I was just getting used to the process. Incapacitate, drive home, kill, chip, spread.

"Are you serious?" I asked.

"Yea why?" He shot back in a perturbed tone.

An unnecessary reminder of our code and he corrected himself, stating that he had other things on his mind at the moment. He wasn't himself. Something was bothering him. This too was becoming a pattern. I was always "in the moment," while Julian was three steps ahead.

"You're right. Keep it simple, don't get cocky." And then he walked away and disappeared for a few minutes. He had shown weakness in his conviction — something he shouldn't have done. Upon returning, the subject shifted to post mortem detail - body disposal, a subject I assumed we had already settled on since we had done it twice before.

"It's not humane," he said,

"And murdering is," I countered. Julian was growing queasy of my wood chipper even though he had never witnessed the thoroughness of the Barka. A few minor tweaks were still necessary to refine the consistency of the final output and I had planned for Subject #4 to be the test subject.

"It's sick, Joshua." He repeated three times and then walked away.

Murder, no matter how well planned, always came with the risk they'd find some trace of the victim's blood or the perpetrator's DNA. Body disposal was messy. Humans are filled with all sorts of nasty stuff and pulverizing it through a machine that wasn't meant for that product just increases the size of the area it lands on. "No body" meant just that — no discernible parts a stranger could remotely identify as being human or even animal remains. My formula was near perfect and I wasn't about to change my routine. This was the final solution — a few more pieces of wood, due to his largess, was all it should take to render a perfect batch for the veggies.

Julian obsessed about DNA and blood spatter. He was convinced that the chipper was wrought with both. What he didn't know, was that after each use, I'd flood its chambers with salt water and chlorine bleach. It was glistening clean and there were no traces of blood as far as I knew. But, as with most things criminal, assume nothing. Modern technology was my enemy in so many ways.

I wasn't a fan of burial because somehow, someday, some animal or child will accidentally dig up the remains and reopen old wounds, the kind I disposed of once the Barka had rendered the body into organic fertilizer. I could just as easily have reminded Julian that he was never there but, on that occasion, he was in no mood for piling on. I left that in those recesses of the back of my mind that were about to overflow again. Three dead traitors and, except for the Reverend, no bodies were ever found. It bothered me that the end game was not well defined and out of the blue, Julian was distraught with my disposal method.

We winged it with each successive execution yet were extraordinarily successful working that loose strategy. Still, it bothered me — that lack of an objective. What was our end game, our goal — just mass executions? Was ours to eliminate each traitor one by one or to send a message as a manifesto to the Herons that they too were being hunted and could be next?

Were we to strike utter fear in our enemy, a worthy objective if you asked me, or was it to please ourselves knowing that we had executed those we despised? I'd suggest that it was both and that messages can just as easily be conveyed through the back channels of social media or through snail mail as long as we remembered to never lick the envelopes. DNA. The Herons were like weeds — nasty, annoying weeds. Dig one up, or in our case, pulverize one, and another takes its place. Their bench was deep with backups and I was feeling like we were fighting a losing battle.

We agreed to disagree on body disposal that day, but Julian accepted that wood chipping was to be the approved method. Subject #4 was an experiment and that I should play doctor by adding drugs into our repertoire of weaponry. We were moving into an experimental phase - Christopher Jenkins was about to become our first lab rat. Death by lethal injection. I hated needles!

Decisions, Decisions

* * * *

Hard drinking, obesity and a rough lifestyle were easy markers for a heart attack and Jenkins exhibited all of them. A simple drug Julian had procured, which was completely undetectable once given to a subject, could easily start that cardiac event. We could chalk it up to medical research and use Jenkins as our guinea pig. At some point I was determined to carry out executions in broad daylight like those cool assassins did in the movies or real-life CIA and KBG agents from the Cold War — truly poetic justice. This was important to us as, at some point, we'd amend our code and leave bodies scattered across our battlefield, just to shake things up or when transport to the pit was too risky.

The easiest manner in which to kill someone and leave no trace of a crime having been committed would be to initiate a heart attack by using chemical substances that break down as naturally occurring compounds within the human body. Undetectable post mortem, assassins frequently used injectables for decades going back as far as the Cold War. Bump into your target on a crowded street, jab them with a needle and then walk away while the drug takes effect. It's simple and requires only a basic knowledge of anatomy for proper dosing and the best point of injection, something I had mastered through the internet. I Googled my way through an abbreviated version of medical school but was always careful to remove my search history.

My drug of choice was Potassium Chloride. Slow acting and allowed for enough time to get through the entire rendition of our national anthem before they croak. Potassium Chloride causes severe heart arrhythmias and mimics a heart attack. It's virtually undetectable as it breaks down into its individual components, potassium and chlorine, both of which are found naturally in the human body. The presence of either of these would not raise suspicion by the attending coroner unless needle marks were visible. Too much potassium in the body causes a wickedly rapid heartbeat, sometimes called tachycardia, which then can lead to cardiac arrest if heavily dosed. Your grandfather often experienced that feeling and always packed a vial of nitroglycerin wherever he went, in his car, at his office, he was neurotic about those tiny pills, but never had to pop one. I worried that he was now without them. Once injected, the heart spasms out of control and then stops functioning. The process takes only a few minutes, less if you use high doses.

Here's the beautiful part. The heart is one huge muscle and whenever muscle tissue is damaged; the body releases large amounts of potassium into the bloodstream. A medical examiner would most likely list the cause of death as a fatal heart attack. Knowing that I'd still have the pleasure of watching him suffer from the effect of the drug while forcing the subject to listen to our patriotic fight song pleased me. The sounds of bombs bursting in air and rockets red glare, all in perfect unison with his rapidly increasing heartbeat, until finally exploding at the precise moment of the final crescendo. Now that's art!

There was one nagging concern that bothered me and that was "trust." While Julian had procured enough Potassium Chloride to kill an elephant, there was always that fear that whoever gave him access to it would turn on him for any number of reasons. Procurement requires trust and will deplete existing inventory. It leaves a record and involves a third party. Air is free and abundant, doesn't require a third party and can yield a similar result with a direct injection of 60 ml into a syringe and then into any vein. This causes the chambers of the heart to fill with air, which leads to the massive heart attack. If a small enough gauge needle, such as a tuberculin one, were to be used, the mark would be barely noticeable.

I remember thinking to myself — "Decisions, decisions. Drugs or air?"

Still, I was more concerned with getting Jenkins to my execution chamber. How I'd finish him off was of no consequence other than for science — the science of planning for future public executions. Potassium Chloride won our affection. Christopher Jenkins was about to experience a lethal heart attack or, as my father called them, a "catastrophic event." All that was left to consider was devising a foolproof way to get our staggering drunk to my pit. Julian withdrew his brief consideration of sparing the body from the chipper thus neutralizing our concerns over using an undetectable drug and of worrying about needle marks and dosages. Ashes to ashes, dust to dust, drugs and needle marks to fertilizer.

In his mind Christopher Jenkins was donating his body to science as a test case allowing me to experiment with doses to determine the proper amount for various body sizes. I was to take notes. While Julian's underlying concerns over cruelty weighed on his mind, I didn't give a shit. There may come a time when leaving the body is necessary so induced heart attacks were always on the repertoire for future consideration.

It's late. More tomorrow.

A Fishing Expedition

✳ ✳ ✳ ✳

Our digital world was filled with a virtual buffet of apps for cheating men and women to connect, date, text, hookup, or just to FaceTime for the sheer pleasure of human contact — millions used them daily for their next conquest. There were categories for every penchant. Gay, straight, confused, transgender, married, single, fat, anorexic, you name it.

I struggled at asking a girl to my high school prom and still haven't accepted the reality that dating is no longer a process or courtship like my parents had, but instead a moment in time where two like-minded people hookup and then disappear in search of their next conquest. The social proclivities inherent with dating had all but disappeared after the collapse. Strangers connected without so much as having a cup of coffee or a beer before shacking up. It was more efficient I suppose, like ordering from a fast-food joint. It was primordial.

Chris was a well-known womanizer — a pathetic misogynist who prayed on those who might find him an attractive catch based entirely on his celebrity status. He wasn't attractive — kinda odd looking with endless bad hair days and, as noted — fat! Rich and famous, two good traits to have, even more so during times of national crisis or when the economy was in the tank worked to his advantage — it overshadowed his unattractiveness. He wasn't a good conversationalist either and had a habit of expelling spittle when speaking — not large amounts but enough to make you wonder what the hell was wrong with him. His conversational tone was that of an aggressive defense attorney brow beating a confession out of a criminal. He'd constantly interrupt. That tone followed him into the dating arena, making his relationships short term for obvious reasons. I witnessed his interrogating style frequently, and he'd always have someone new with him when he dined at Il Portico. It wasn't pleasant, but his dates stuck around and presumably went home with him, even though he had nothing going for him beyond his fame. Swiping left and right on Tinder, an app which utilized GPS location, Facebook images and whatever fake personal bio he posted, had swollen his fingers and calloused their tips. Hackers had breached Ashley Madison, an adult cheating site, long before the collapse, so Tinder became the new tool, even for dinosaurs like Chris. Not knowing that you had been told "No" by hundreds of users who swiped left when your picture appeared was perfect for the easily offended members of society that were a growing phenomenon.

For obvious reasons, I never had a real Facebook page, but had two bogus ones — one as a woman and the other a man. Estelle Wright and Joe Scarlatti, my alter egos allowed me to anonymously "friend" those whom I despised and digitally follow those who were targets. Both were residences of New Columbia so would certainly show up in his Tinder feed which was based on proximity to each other. Like real estate, hookup success was predicated on location, location, location. Gas was still too expensive to travel far for a brief interlude.

It was Thursday evening. I logged on as Estella — checked

my pictures and moved the most suitable ones that I knew would catch Chris's eyes to my Tinder account. He loved blondes and, based upon an eavesdropped conversation, had a penchant for the more vivacious, curvy ones. Model-thin need not apply. I recalled him arguing, one evening with a friend over a picture of a rail-thin young lady who was attractive, from what I could tell when I first glanced at his cell phone. Standing there while waiting to serve his risotto, he asked my opinion of that woman.

"Is she cute or not, I mean the whole package," he asked, slurring, from his third scotch, as he zoomed out to show the woman's full body.

"Well, I'm partial to blondes, so yea, she's hot," I replied.

"See, Chris, and that's from a young man who has stricter standards than you, my old friend," his colleague weighed in. How he knew about my standards was a mystery since I had none at that moment.

"Too damn skinny, like a patriot who'd been wandering the streets looking for food scraps," he quipped. That reference was deplorable. He scrolled across his screen swiping left on most but would pause on a few images and then swipe right noting his affection for the ones he liked. The common theme had little to do with their written profiles but focused only on their looks. And darn near every one of them was blond, middle aged and curvy. Bingo! I knew his type.

The beautiful thing about Tinder is that it allowed me to swipe left on everyone except Chris, assuring no digital trail from others who might show up as matches. I still used a burner phone, so no worries about tracking my movement or true identity. After I snagged the bastard, I'd delete my profile leaving no digital trail to his disappearance.

I launched the app, set Estelle up as a lonely teacher with a subtle socialist bent to her profile. I was careful not to seem desperate or slutty in my wording. Chris enjoyed the hunt and wouldn't attempt a rendezvous with someone so obviously looking for just a hookup. He was ego driven, and that was part of the fun. As a teacher, good grammar and spelling in the profile was important. I opted to be coy, and slightly philosophical in crafting my profile and my messaging.

"Hi, I'm new to Tinder and looking for a mature gentleman 50-60 yrs who is passionate about social justice. Nothing serious — I live for the moment. Convince me that you're worthy of having coffee with and I promise to get back to you quickly." Then I added the usual pictures, five maximum, each airbrushed to pass the zoom test from guys like Chris checking for wrinkles, and skin color — he hated pasty white and preferred a healthy tanned glow. Since I had 223 more characters available for my profile, I finished with an infamous quote from one of Chris's favorite idéologues, Vladimir Lenin. "Freedom in capitalist society always remains about the same as it was in ancient Greek republics: Freedom for slave owners." What a crock! That was Julian's idea. How did he know? The profile was epic, perfect for drawing Chris in, thinking he'd get laid by a comrade and that afterwards they'd blissfully lie in bed, sipping cocktails and smoking cigarettes while discussing the ongoing revolution. Comrades in the sack.

To start the ball rolling, I needed to begin my Tinder

session close enough to Chris's studio or townhouse which were only a mile apart from each other. I was never sure if our Stasis could isolate exact GPS locations for someone who was Tindering, so stayed careful to post from a remote park bench on Capitol Hill in an area that I knew to be void of cameras. Yes, I was that neurotic, and it was "that" park bench. Once again — the murderer returning to the scene of his crime and that gave me a moments pause. But, based upon continued news coverage noting that no cameras had videotape the Rev's execution, I knew this to be a secure spot to play my Tinder ploy.

Technology complicates everything when planning the perfect crime. His cell phone was my enemy, although I'd chip it along with him - No cell, no body, no crime. But when someone disappears the first place authorities will check, along with his residence, are cell phone records, locations, GPS tracking, each of which could lead them to me or at least to where I began the executional process. Even a completely destroyed phone has a digital footprint of where it had been, and they'd keep those records at his service provider. Nothing was fool proof, but I took the necessary precautions before proceeding. I was still using a burner. I'd need, at most, a day or two of enticing messaging with Chris before inviting him to meet. Again — not wanting to seem desperate, I understood the importance of patience. Like a tiger, he enjoyed the hunt, so let the hunt begin.

Time to Tinder

* * * *

Launch Tinder. Estelle's image pulsated as the program searched for suitable matches within my designated radius and age requirement, 2 miles and 45+ years. Five-seconds later and page upon page of potential matches that I could anonymously swipe my feelings upon, left if not interested or right if I liked. Left, left, left. It was a busy evening in the Tinder world, lots of Herons and Patriots looking to hookup. I scrolled through dozens of images expecting to see Chris' at some point. Nothing! I had hit the end of that night's lonely heart's club but no pay dirt. The pulsating image appears again noting that it is searching for more prospects but it found none. Membership has its benefits, but I wasn't a premium member which would allow me to hit the recycle icon — giving me a second look at those who I had dismissed. For every technical problem, there's always a work-around and with Tinder that meant deleting my account and then re-starting. But this time I'd be less hasty with my swipes and pay more attention to the images that popped up. This was work. A few swipes in and an interesting profile picture caught my eye. Not the best image when fishing for hookups, probably why I had passed over it. The image — an out of focus young blond man, maybe mid 30's, and a hammer and sickle flag adorning a building in the background. The name on his profile was noted only as CJ. Christopher Jenkins? Tapping his bio I could view the other images he had posted. Various scenic pictures of the DC monuments prior their destruction and a small town, clearly not in America, as the architecture wasn't what you'd expect on this side of the pond. His last image, the fifth, showed the Kremlin with the caption "Beautiful architecture, I've broadcast from there," written below it. What a relief when my best laid plans seemed to be heading south. I'd found my target. Swiping right I hoped for a mutual connection. He had no profile beyond noting that he was a "lover of the news."

Chris played it smart by avoiding his professional headshot and instead posted a picture of his favorite place in the world, not New Columbia but Russia. That coy fat bastard, I remember thinking. The man was a celebrity and, like so many others, preferred to keep his anonymity.

Payday — the words "Match" popped up on my screen. "Let the game begin," I mumbled. Typically, a woman would wait for the gentleman to initiate a conversation, but waiting for that bastard to drop me a note wasn't something I had the patience for. He had tried my patience already with his fake profile and certainly he had other suitors. Gold diggers and celebrity chasers were everywhere, and I needed to get on his calendar. Chivalry died years ago and women were more likely to make the first gesture, so I did.

"I'm sure you must have tons of matches from beautiful women," I began with the requisite compliment. Egotistical guys relish compliments, especially from a beautiful young women like Estella.

"My father was born in the Ukraine? You?" Familiarity and

establishing common ground always helps, and I wasn't sure where it was taken. I wasn't 100% sure it was even Chris. My match responded a minute later with a simple reply,

"Odessa. What brings you to Tinder and New Columbia?" Inquiring as to why they were on Tinder was his standard reply. He'd brag about his textual prowess and ability to ensnare a woman by sounding normal, unthreatening, someone genuinely looking for a relationship and not a hookup. "It dropped their guard and thinned the herd," he'd say.

Not wanting to come across as a desperate whore in search of attention or money, I decided to play the lonely woman in search of someone to share a common cause with, like social justice or economic equality. Identity politics - something I detested, but just the approach that he'd go for.

"Been alone for a long time now, looking for the company of a gentleman, someone with shared beliefs."

"Same here." Short, sweet and nothing else, followed by his standard: "Tell me more about yourself," and then his standard BS about everyone being illiterate.

"Let's meet for coffee or a drink." Followed that one. He was a creature of habit and those replies were his standard fare. Pretty sure he had saved them somewhere in a text file and just copied and pasted it into the threads of Tinder matches — it came too quickly. He didn't care one whit about intelligence. I tossed him the usual comment about spelling geniuses who didn't know the difference between "Your," "you're" "their," "there," "they're." That was another one of his favorite posts and was also saved in a text file for later use. I left the last spelling annoyance off to see if he'd bite.

"Yep and to, too and two" That sealed the deal as intellectually compatible kindred, elitist spirits."My name is Estelle, what's yours CJ?"

"Chris." Good enough for me. This was definitely Christopher Jenkins.

Still, I reviewed his texts and profile one last time just to be sure. First name, last initial, pictures from his past and reference to his Bittern career — he'd taken the grammatical bait — Target verified! The next step — reel him in.

"I love to cook. Don't typically do this, would you like to join me some night this week? I'm a great chef." Honest and bold, for sure but I had to plant a seed lest his calendar fill up with other needy prospects. He was on this week's docket and Julian was anxious to get it over with.

"Sure, how about tonight? I'm leaving for NYC tomorrow." Curve ball and completely unexpected. Check in with Julian.

"He wants to take the test tonight — gone the rest of the week."

"You prepared to give it?" I paused for a long time to consider my answer. "??"

I hadn't run my usual pre-exam ritual the night before, which included moments of sheer panic, night sweats, dry heaves and all the mental and emotional baggage you'd want to get out of the way before taking on a mission. Just as well I thought — get it over with. I hated the jitters and night sweats but hated him more.

"Yep."

"Meet him in the class room." The abandoned townhouse on 3rd and M Street, or classroom, as we called it, was lit, my van was parked out back, syringe and ephadol were always in the glove compartment. I'd wing it and settle on his final solution while heading back to the pit. I still wasn't sure about lethal injection but that was what Julian expected.

"Sure. I live on Capital Hill. How about 7:00?" I texted him. I followed with the address and asked that he bring some Pinot Grigio, noting how much I loved to cook with it. I was pushing the envelope but enjoyed the little red flags I had tossed his way. Rushing me — something I didn't like.

3211 M Street NE, an abandoned old townhouse a stone's throw from the Capital dome. It was our designated rattrap for ensnaring subjects in the immediate vicinity before carting them away to the pit. Julian and I had combed the site weeks before and ran a pretty thorough stakeout for two weeks each evening to be sure it was completely abandoned and not a flop house for drug dealers or prostitutes. This was the first time I had used it. We also ran a check on the property records — abandoned.

The sun had set, lights were on and the sign I had hung on the back gate was visible from the hint of glow creeping out of the kitchen window. Estelle's Patio! Inviting, reassuring yet unnecessary, I hung it anyway. Small touch. By the time he'd enter my world he'd be toasted and would have no reason to be suspicious. A sense of calm relaxation came over me. I was building a "RUSH" routine, and it was working.

Dinner at 7 with the main course being our drug of choice. Time of death should be an hour or so later. 45 minutes to the house, another five to set him up, a short tongue-lashing and then a minute or so for the full, glorious rendition of our national anthem. I should have led with this, and I apologize if I have already said this, but don't bother looking for remnants of my handy work. The chipper has been sanitized through a thorough bleaching process and, for good measure, taken apart and tossed in the bay. The garden has been tilled over a hundred times and years of rain have washed all remnants into Goose Creek. It's no longer organic. Hell, it's no longer a garden. It's history.

Knowing that no one would enter a building with no lights on or visible signs of life, I always brought my small generator and two floor lamps when hunting. It's amazing how handy Dad's generator became. Like mosquitoes to blue light, it attracted my prey. Ambiance was important, so I lit her up that evening waiting for Chris to come calling. My last message gave him my cell phone number and instructions to text me when he was almost there.

A narrow crushed-stone driveway led to the townhouse's backyard cluttered with an old refrigerator, washing machine and some beat up mattresses. Abandoned properties were easy to find, even after five years. It backed up to another abandoned townhouse on N Street. A line of tall weeping willows separated the two properties, making it impossible to see beyond them. It was pitch dark and cloudy, but the skies were clearing and the moon would soon be full. No one would see me loading the van. I parked in the back, around the corner from the gate, left of the house. It opened inward forcing whoever entered to move right as the gate was tight and dragged the ground. It took some effort to get it moving. Their back would be to me. Perfect for a quick jab to the neck with Etomidate, neutralizing any resistance from him. I waited for his text alerting me that he was almost there. After what seemed like an eternity, his text came through but said, "At your front door, the bell isn't working." Exactly what I didn't want.

"Out back, come through the gate on the left." I replied. Burner phones weren't instantaneous at sending or receiving messages. Texts went through a series of services, each grabbing a small portion of revenue for every send and receive. I knew it would take a minute for him to receive my reply and by then another for me to get his. Two minutes is an eternity. He might get anxious or worse, suspicious. Not off to a good start, I thought. It was eerily quiet that night. I could have heard a pin drop and my heart was beating at that now familiar quickened pace; the kind where you hear the pulse rushing through your ears. He began knocking continuously on the front door — not a quiet knock but the hard banging you'd expect when Herodias were about to use the battering ram to bust through — a drunk knock, he seemed pissed. The sound of a ping noting my text was received, then footsteps walking down the front path, a pause and silence again. He was stopping, thinking, while I was bearing down to discern his movement, I heard him approach the gate, mumbling profanities while struggling to open it, he entered my space but turned left instead of right, as I had hoped he would. We came face to face. "Josh?" I was unprepared for that and surprised that he even recognized me in the darkness and while drunk.

It's at those moments when time stands still and you pray to God, even if you're angry with him, that your best laid plan had better proceed without a hitch. There are no lies big enough to explain the series of events that led to our coming face to face. The pulsating through my ears changed to a continuous flow of sweat dripping down my face and that shaking in my hands.

"Yep, welcome to America you fat bastard." and followed that with a swift knee to his groin while grabbing his shoulder. One knee, one incapacitated target; damn effective. He bent over writhing in pain while grabbing his groin and screaming, "fuck, fuck." I yanked the syringe out of my pocket and jammed it into his neck while holding his shoulder. One, two, three, four, five and he's out. Quicker than I had expected. Maybe God was looking over me, a huge cloud covered the moonlight as Chris fell to the ground. Shaded in total darkness, I dragged him twenty feet to the back of the van, reached in his pocket, took out his cell phone, turned it off and removed the battery. There would be no record of his whereabouts or of his trip to Sector 7.

With each lifeline God threw me I became more of a convert to the whole Christianity thing and believed he supported my mission. Still, I wasn't about to go to church on Sundays and confess my sins to some stranger behind a curtain or to the many hypocrites among the congregation. Why ask for forgiveness when they kept as many secrets but had probably disobeyed more commandments than I, which at that point was still two. Sunday morning Christians raising their hands like little antennas as if that brought them closer to God was something I wanted no part of. Once the service was over, many returned to their less than perfect lives, screaming at their wives, cheating on their taxes, drinking excessively and even Tindering for a new mistress or two. There's at least three commandments right there. My biggest worry was ahead of me, the ride back to my place. Once my human cargo was in place, I moved the old boxes of tomatoes and zucchini to the center of the floor. I had added some extra insulation around the walls to silence any screams of desperation should a subject awaken before arriving at the pit. My stack of business cards featuring my photo in full chef regalia were stuffed neatly in the center console. I covered all the bases. One must think of these things when running such a risky operation. Julian taught me well. Even though the back of my van had a false bottom, allowing me to place my conquests beneath the visible flooring, a K9 unit could easily pick up a human scent. I scanned the roads well in front of me and kept a careful eye on cars approaching from behind. I never sped or broke any traffic laws. The drive back to my place was quiet and, except for a few random gangs cruising for food, the roads were deserted.

Etomidate is effective for about an hour and then he'd wake up with a massive headache and confused. I hadn't taken into consideration the extra body fat and the likelihood that he'd awaken before getting to my house. Awakening in a dark hole while hearing an engine roaring down the highway would scare the shit out of anyone. Like being buried alive or wondering if the driver was planning to ditch the car in some lake, it was cruel too. Buried alive — another phobia of mine. It's interesting that, while transporting my subjects to the pit, my mind always wondered towards phobias — mine. Drowning, beheading, buried alive — I was afraid of death, or more specifically, dying alone. Sure as shit, my uncooperative passenger awoke, and he was not a happy camper. "Let me out! Let me out" he screamed over and over, each soliloquy separated by a series of kicks to the floor above him. Senseless, pathetic, but I had a pinch of empathy. I'd have done the same.

We were five-minutes out so I cranked my radio volume up expecting it to drown out his cries for help. It didn't, they got louder and more frequent the kicks got stronger. The tomatoes and zucchini boxes were heavy, and the lock was sturdy as hell. There'd be no chance of him breaking through the floor cover, crawling over the seat and strangling me while I was driving, although it did cross my mind.

"Shut up and relax. We'll be home in a few minutes."

"Where's that?

"My place — used to be Leesburg, sector 7 now, thanks to you." Better to converse then to scream. I turned the radio off, and he became quiet. He asked a few questions but the only one that really mattered, was what's going to happen to him. He kept asking that over and over again. I ignored it. The silence was deafening. Hard to admit because I couldn't stand listening to the bastard on TV or at Il Portico when he was drunk and belligerent. But, while holed up in the back of my van, I preferred some conversation so I knew what he was up to and still alive. The last words he said before pulling up the driveway, "I'm not talking till I get out of here."

"Suit yourself. We're here," I informed him. A 45-minute ride on the perfectly smooth asphalt and then heavy stones crumpling under the van as it drove over potholes was a change in venue and clearly we weren't in New Columbia anymore. You're in the country now, Chris. Patriots have stone driveways and they don't particularly like Herons.

"Chris. How you feeling?"

"Let me the hell out of here."

"Calm down. I'm opening the floor."

"Hurry, I'm claustrophobic."

He was remarkably lucid after the drug had worn off. I opened the lock, lifted the panel and stared at his eyes as he looked straight up, pupils dilated from the darkness and fixated on me.

"Shh, Shh Shh" I touched my lips like a mother quieting an unruly child. "Not another word."

He pulled himself out of the hole and slid to the edge of the van, sitting for a few seconds to catch his breath and scan the area.

"Joshua?"

I pointed my Glock at his forehead and motioned him out of the van and into the pit.

"You have a gun, why this?" He asked. Another good question, he was assessing the situation. I could see it in his eyes, they wandered everywhere. What he didn't realize was that I'd soon be dosing him with a lethal injection of potassium chloride and I couldn't risk his taking control when I am in direct contact with him. I estimated his weight to be around 220 pounds but asked him, anyway. A Glock is a remarkably effective tool at getting my subjects to answer my questions then to descend the ladder and take their rightful position in the chair, even strapping themselves in without threatening them beyond what is already a pretty serious threat.

"So, how much you weigh these days?"

"230, why?"

"Dosage."

I suppose there comes a time in everyone's life when they reach the conclusion, based upon the situation surrounding them, that death is near. That single word, "dosage" was Chris' moment. His facial expression went blank and his skin tone changed to the whitest shade of pale I had ever seen. The conversational dynamics changed at that very moment.

"You've done this before?" He quivered as he uttered those words and I actually felt sorry for him. Seeing a grown man in that state of pale panic. Knowing he's about to meet his maker, if he had faith, is an uncomfortable thing to witness.

"Yes, I have." No need to elaborate any further. Patriot versus traitor. I asked the questions, he provided answers.

"Actually I'm Aiken McHale. Remember me?" He looked stupefied. Either my birth name wasn't registering, or he was just playing stupid.

Adding that there was no chance for a reprieve, or escaping, and that I was fully committed to executing him would completely shut him up and Julian would have been pissed. An intelligence report was expected the Monday following any executions, although I was beginning to feel as though Julian knew more than he let on and those reports were for my knowledge only, not his. Each mission, except for the Reverend, had two objectives. The extraction of as much information as possible about the Herons, their network, where their orders came from and, of course, finishing them off. At first glance, not complicated, but when considering that I exposed my true identity every time, extracting information proved to be problematic. The smarter ones knew their fate and clammed up hoping for time to be on their side and that somehow they'd be rescued by some Heron superhero before I could finish them off.

"Yeah. Once or twice."

"So why me and what are you going to do?"

"Guess that depends on how cooperative you are. There's always hope."

My entire life was a lie, and I had already executed three of his comrades, so offering a sliver of hope came easy even though he should have known better. It's not like I was going to send him on his merry way to sing my praises to the police. He knew. Herons never considered themselves traitors but instead Patriots in their own right, fighting for their country against an enemy they didn't understand — us. In a sense, my pit was a battlefield, and I was about to chalk up another victory.

"Traitor!" I whispered in his ear.

"How so?" He asked with that incredulous expression you'd expect from someone who understood what I had just said, but would rather I explain it further. Although interrogation outside of Julian's approved questions was prohibited, I wanted three more questions answered before I finished him off. The first was to ascertain whether they knew their true birthright. The second; who gave them their orders or were they their own masters. Finally, I thought it helpful to ask who else they thought most deserving of the fate they were about to receive. The intent on that last one was twofold. To build our list beyond the original names and then identify the bosses, like a smalltime drug pusher, we wanted the kingpins. Highly unlikely he'd rat out an underling so whoever he gave up would have been above him in the pecking order and deserving of a patriotic event themselves. My interrogation began with his true birthright. Did he know? Like a typical journalist, Chris weaved a story worthy of a documentary. It was fascinating though mostly false, but he was well aware of his being born in Odessa and cooperated beyond my wildest imagination, filling in many of our open gaps and even some we had never considered. It seemed a shame to have to say goodbye as the evening came to an end for both us. His was permanent and mine, just temporary.

I can attest that at some point in the broad scheme of things, man mentally surrenders to his impending fate and begins to negotiate with himself on how he wants to depart this earth. Some will clam up and say nothing, others will take the scorched earth approach and sing like a song bird desperately hoping for a reprieve or just to screw those above them who abused them. Chris lived and died in the latter camp and sang like a song bird.

"Why the interest?" he asked. I didn't answer, just repeated the question.

"I was born in Odessa. My parents were killed in a car

accident when I was four."

He continued with his fabricated tale, but who could blame him since that was the story told to him by his adoptive parents. He recalled, in vivid detail, the seven months he spent at the Founder's Home and how cruel and abusive they were to him and the other children. Things were starting to fall into place for me. As a young child his first glimpse of life in America is at an orphanage where the children are all abused, a far cry from the royal treatment he had received in Odessa. This was planned. Adopted at the age of five by a young couple from Selinsgrove Pennsylvania, Amish country, Tom and Vickie Jenkins, raised Chris as their only child. Tom, dodged the draft during the Vietnam war while Vickie taught fifth grade, the perfect candidates for sowing the imperfections of America in the 60's. Beyond that, he said nothing more of his family life other than it was a happy one. I did ask when he first learned to speak English and whether his adoptive parents spoke any Russian. Oddly, he started learning English while in Russia and his adoptive parents didn't speak a lick of Russian. Part of knowing who you are is to know where you came from and what your lineage was. For Herons, that beginning started in another hemisphere before joining their adoptive family, and a child of five would certainly want to know more about that history. Chris was a journalist, so his inquisitive nature would have been ingrained in him, or at the very least, taught to him. It was at that point that Chris began speaking in Russian. I couldn't understand a damn thing he was saying, but I remember how pissed-off it made me. Since he had lived his first four years in the Soviet Union, it made sense, but he was speaking as an adult and his grasp of the language was not fluent, but pretty damn good. Speaking the language of our enemy didn't help his cause, so I reminded him that I neither spoke nor wished to learn it and he'd best refrain from doing so. My focus shifted to who gave them their orders. In the case of Chris, no one, but most of the younger ones had their own handlers who would visit regularly to check up on their progress or to initiate new objectives when necessary. The visits began as early as six years old, just about the time they'd be starting first grade and lasted well into college.

He sighed then leaned back. The chair would have tipped over had it not been bolted to the concrete floor.

"I'm a handler myself," he bragged.

"And a boss?"

Another sigh and he leaned back again, this time with tears rolling down his cheek. He knew the end was near.

Anything worth dying for must be important enough to pursue. I pulled out Julian's Izvestia clipping and shoved it under his chin, stabbing my finger several times at the names of the two criminals it was about — his biological parents. He glanced at the paper, shrugged his shoulder looked away and said nothing. There's two kinds of looks one gives when presented with evidence, "shock" and "so what?" His was the latter and so the mystery deepened. Chris stopped talking.

A remarkable thing occurs when one is preparing to take a human life. No matter the hatred towards the victim, humanity is the result of God's will, his creation, good, bad, or downright evil. While I take solace in each execution, I gained no pleasure

— it still bothers me. It's my job, my patriotic duty and I've tried to convince myself that it was God's will. Still, I wasn't ready to let go of Chris just yet, so I continued the conversation, hoping he'd start talking again. Role reversal or just plain stalling on my part, getting to know them actually helped ease my anxiety at breaking God's 6th commandment. The more we spoke, the more I hated them. I had three questions to which I got only one answer; I had dozens more.

"Birth certificates?"

"I believe you call us the deep state. We're everywhere and I'm done talking."

Knowing how deeply embedded into the fabric of American society they were was all I needed to know even though Julian had already confirmed that picture. Martin Brody famously said, "We're going to need a bigger boat," as he stalked that Great White shark. All I could think of was that we'd eventually need a bigger pit and a much larger army. The two of us certainly had our work cut out for us.

"Well Chris, it's time."

Much to my surprise he didn't break down, wince or plead with me. He took it like a man. I explained what would happen and how he'd feel, making it seem more like death by lethal injection where he'd simply drift off to sleep. Sounding very much like an anesthesiologist right before putting you under for minor surgery — I was remarkably compassionate. Of course I lied and knew that he'd feel excruciating pain, and it would last for two very long minutes. He lied — I lied. Placing my noise-cancelling headphones on him, I cranked up the volume. Sixty-seconds of patriotism, the real stuff. "Oh say can you see…." I wondered which was more painful, the drugs or those words.

"Left or right arm?" I asked.

"Left," no surprise, but I moved to his right side and inserted my syringe into his right arm, just below the inner portion of his elbow. I didn't immediately push the plunger, but watched his expression as the needle went in. Some people look away when giving blood or having a shot, others stare at the needle and point of injection watching every single drop of liquid entering their veins. Chris watched, took deep breaths and then closed his eyes as if sleeping. At first, a peaceful glow surrounded his face as his breathing became more shallow. Then, the drug took effect and that peaceful glow changed to shear terror. He shook violently, clenched his teeth in agony and started moving his head left and right until it ended. His stare was dark and blank. The tendency when experiencing a heart attach would be to grasp ones' chest or left arm as this is where the pain is most noticeable. The straps prevented that, which I suppose would cause the violent head movements. Like being jolted by a few thousand volts of electricity, he convulsed. Saliva, resembling activated hydrogen peroxide, oozed from his mouth, something one would expect after being gassed. The timing was perfect and his head slumped down just as the "O'er the land of the free and the home of the brave" blared through the headphones. A fitting end for someone who so despised freedom yet he bravely handled his execution. I learned much from him and was ready to report back to Julian that this mission was accomplished. I left him secured to the chair for fifteen minutes to ascertain that he was dead, then dragged his body to the Barka, slid it in, closed the door and pushed the button to start the chipping blades. The proper amount of wood and manure had already been loaded into the chamber. Everything went as planned, nothing out of the norm.

My tomatoes were at the end of their season and the squash was doing just fine. I fertilized my mushrooms in tribute to Chris. He would have appreciated that.

Subject #5

* * * *

The act of killing is both physically and emotionally exhausting. My emotions during those down-times between subjects was reminiscent of how dad must have felt as he awaited that next self-employed paycheck to arrive from a client. The constant worrying about bills, bank balances and, most concerning, my mother who'd lambast him for their dismal financial situation wore him down. He'd stare into space with that blank look on his face that telegraphed what was going through his mind. Fear, helplessness, a letter in the mail announcing that electric, cable or gas might soon be shut off manifested themselves as wrinkles, and dark circles under his eyes. I was convinced that he'd hang himself or overdose on heart meds.

I felt the same after each event, but never considered suicide. It wasn't the mailbox that bumped my anxiety; it was the

TV while I binge-watched the cable networks for updates to the crimes I had committed. My fears were that the Herons were on my trail and that my perfect crimes weren't so perfect after all. Instead of taking the easy way out, I'd devise improvements in my strategies. I was in this for the long haul.

Decent night's sleep were intermittent. Four hours became my norm. My circadian rhythms were totally out of whack so, at the ripe old age of twenty-eight, I showed serious signs of wrinkles, and dark circles under my eyes. I wasn't aging well and ulcers were a distinct possibility. But the issues that engulfed my mind with fear didn't end there as a new one, a joyous one, arrived on October 3rd in a mailbox I never checked. Your mother informed me that she was pregnant with you! Yes, there was an initial shock, but that quickly faded to pure joy which was a welcome emotion considering my current state of mind.

When a young man discovers he's about to become a father, it's a surreal feeling — something I can't quite describe. Say goodbye to your social life; get plenty of sleep now; your life will never be the same; — I'd heard them all. But for me, you were to be born six-thousand miles away; I had no social life; sleep had already evaded me and my life was a total mess. I was a serial killer — add to that, a new father.

A Moment of Pause

* * * *

Always obey the law, follow the golden rules and honor your code as though God himself had written it. It's never a good idea, though, to throw caution to the wind. Wisdom imparted upon me by my father. But as I look back, in the heat of battle, we broke laws, abandoned rules, refined our code and that whole cautious crap took a back seat as our next subject was a rush job — we got sloppy.

Six months and twelve days had passed since I had put Jenkins down and, for the first time we agreed to ignore all of that. Time was not on our side and my dispassionate attitude towards what I was doing caused me to question my sanity. A bad combination when living under a false identity while avoiding the authorities consumed my every thought. Obsessive fear, sleepless nights and lack of moral clarity were the extent of my days.

I can't imagine what's going through your mind as I casually wax poetic about executing human beings. God's Sixth Commandment held no spot in the morality part of my brain, but I knew its importance — just didn't care. To be honest, I missed the thrill of the kill. Like my mother when she hadn't had vodka in what seemed like an eternity, her urge for that shot, became mine for our next subject. Fomenting for that unsettling expression as their hearts took one last beat became an unwanted obsession of mine. I'd whisper to myself "what's wrong with you," wondering why the hell such disturbing images would invade my thoughts, but in a pleasant way. It's hard to shake, and I wondered if I had crossed the line into serious psychosis and, if I had, could I ever return to normalcy — whatever that was.

What permeated a good portion of my thoughts had strangled my ability to concentrate on things other than killing. My grades suffered, and it ingrained my every waking moments as our subjects drifted from consciousness into the realm of no return. Visuals of humans being fed into a tube, only to emerge seconds later as a pile of goo that fed my vegetables, increased my breathing and heart rate in the middle of the night. Was that good or bad? Dreams and nightmares occupied the same space, and it was impossible to distinguish the difference between them. Was I insane? There's mitigating circumstances for that but it must be temporary. Mine continued for seven long years. I'm thinking that won't work as a legal defense, although others in my situation had used it to avoid the ultimate punishment. Call it God's work or just a soldier doing his job, but remorse never entered my mind. I didn't give a shit about them or their mourning families. This was war, they were the enemy, and I was a Patriot.

Those six months seemed like a well-deserved vacation. But precision, in no way, described those first four events. They weren't perfect but, like my golf swing, with practice, they'd soon be. I was hooked, but hadn't earned that time off yet. It was time to head back into the battlefield.

My personality had changed and I knew it had. Julian, however, was more interested in scanning the landscape in the aftermath of those momentous executions while also following the emerging secession movement in Sector 1010, Utah. Planning for our fifth was off the radar. It bothered him thinking I might have left evidence.

We continued to meet at The Drip, Tuesdays and Thursdays but our discussions centered more on school, Sector 1010 and what Neville and Congress were up to than on the war we had just begun. Julian was in "pause" mode. Roundups of armed Patriots continued, but their tactics grew more violent than when they visited us two years prior. Nazi Germany in the twenty-first century landed squarely onto America, but this time, the Jews were Patriots and Sector 1 was Berlin.

Newton once noted that life was an echo. What you send out comes back, what you sow you reap, what you see in others exists in you. Our government was more than an echo, it was an echo chamber. We were sending them signals, just the wrong ones. Julian's disconnect added to my frustration with not sending the proper messages into that chamber. No body, no crime was getting us nowhere and my obsession with the instilling of fear in the enemy had taken complete control of me. Once again, manifestos kept swirling through my mind.

Thankfully, working five nights a week at the restaurant and the struggles associated with keeping my grades up made time fly and, in some small way, distracted me from becoming a full-blown psychotic human being. Branching out with a small catering business which used the resources of Il Portico, and my days all ran together. To be honest, it seemed like only yesterday that I had fertilized the tomatoes and mushrooms with Jenkins and yes, they were doing splendidly.

It's your pick Julian

* * * *

I understood Julian's need to have the Secretary DeSoto, Alexander Vay and Chris Jenkins eliminated in that order and convinced myself that he was being more strategic about choosing our fifth target. The common theme among the first three, was perversion, even though they had accomplished so much destruction through their actions and careers as anointed Herons with a singular mission to destroy America from within. It occurred to me that those were test subjects meant to hone and assess my skills as an assassin. We used their weaknesses against them which played a crucial role in capturing them without being caught.

The 3M, Tinder and a popular bartering bar allowed me the safety of drawing my subjects into my web of death with little resistance. I was still a neophyte but looked forward to getting my next assignment who would have some serious deep state history as a spy. I had my own ideas, but it was his turn at the wheel, so I let it ride.

People who play the lottery would wait up all night to see which numbers made millionaires out of some random guy who'd blow through his entire winnings in a year, ending up flat broke and right back where he came from, living in a trailer home. My lottery was Julian's list and, on May 23rd, 2025 he broached the subject and was most eager to put this next character in the completed column. Time was of the essence and an upcoming election was our drop dead date, pun intended. Subject #5 was a rush job. His name was Barry Levinson and he was both perverted and a spy. He was about to become Governor of Sector 43 and that simply couldn't happen.

Subject #5:
Barry Levinson: The Pervert
* * * *

Barry was the kind of guy your mother would call "a despicable little pervert" and warn you against ever becoming friends with. A New Yorker forced to resign his congressional seat due to a propensity to post lewd pictures of his genitalia for an adoring horde of young, high-school-aged ladies, maybe a few men too. Add to that, his membership in the Heron society and he held a special place in our hearts — not a warm, fuzzy one, just a special place. Eddy Haskel came to mind every time I saw him on TV. I despised the man, but finding him on Julian's list surprised me.

All of that lewd behavior shit was before the collapse. Like a waning moon, our morality gradually disappeared, morphing us into a modern day Gomorrah. He fit in well among the cast of Gomorrahites that held high positions within our government.

Amoral values, the destruction of the nuclear family, a government and media no one trusted, but who was I to talk? I was a serial executioner, and apparently on the verge of insanity.

Criminal behavior or failure at one's job had no serious consequences as political mulligans were doled out liberally on the left. It was musical chairs, and they played it often. Shamed Herons moved easily from one career to the next. From political office to the media or the other way around, it didn't matter. Screw up here and we'll move you over there. It was hard to keep track of them. Levinson's shaming in the public sector for his criminally lewd behavior had no consequences other than shifting him to academia. Preferring the under-aged earned him a tenured professorship at NYU. Political Science. Ironic, huh? Our plan was to prevent him from ever returning to elected office, but there was more to his background than being a sexual deviant. He also traded in documents, the classified kind.

I continued to wonder if ours was a war against sexual perversion or was it truly a patriotic one whose targets were traitors to our constitutional republic. Word on the street and through our back-channels, was that Levinson had pedophilia tendencies and, although they were just rumors, I was inclined to believe them. Sexual predators know no boundaries and young children were often their first victims. It was his pedophilia that got him caught up in the fine art of trading classified documents with our enemies — bribery was constantly at his doorstep. Apparently Levinson had graduated to sixteen-year-old girls, assuming that they would be more acceptable among the bribing class. They weren't and so he continued to pass the most secret, highly classified documents to every damn enemy we had, the Russians, Iranians, Chinese — he was an equal opportunity traitor.

Although D6 was designed to defeat us from within, Levinson dealt in backup plans. As a ranking member of our Foreign Intelligence Committee he traded in the secrets of our most sophisticated weaponry — more specifically, our Guardian Anti-Ballistic Missile system. He left America vulnerable to an attack from outside. All bases were covered in his world — defeat from within or from outside, it didn't matter.

Since the early days of the Cold War and continuing long after it had ended, secrets were traded among spies who dined regularly at a quaint little restaurant on Wisconsin Avenue in the center of Georgetown - Au Pied de Cochon. Conveniently located close to the Russian embassy, it was a favorite spot for late night meals after long hours of boozing it up at the slew of international nightclubs that dotted that part of the city. Old men with young ladies in tow, always in desperately short skirts and high heels, would move from the bar scene of colored martinis and Cosmopolitans to the bistro atmosphere for a slice of quiche and a cup of Café au lait. Barry was a regular. Ever alone on Wednesday nights, he ate quiche Lorraine and sipped an espresso for hours. His cordovan colored leather briefcase which was tucked under the table he occupied was filled with our most highly guarded secrets. Dining alone gave him ample opportunity to continue with his bad habit of forgetting that briefcase, which was always safely returned to him the next time he dined there. It was a Wednesday/Thursday routine. Plausible deniability came from his weak bladder necessitating constant visits to the men's room. He never once handed over documents to the enemy, yet the treasure trove of information he allowed them to steal and then scan contained details of some of our nation's most secret projects. Barry Levinson was nicknamed "The Drop Boy" among his Soviet counterparts. He was one of our most prolific traitors in military intelligence, yet no one ever suspected him of being one. They were focused on his dick, not his documents.

How ironic that his humiliation came from trading lewd pictures of himself to underage woman rather than detailed schematics of the Guardian Anti-Ballistic Missile program to our enemies. After his banishment from public office, you'd have thought he'd escape our final solution. Unfortunately, the bastard reinserted himself back into the political domain as the recidivist pervert I knew him to be. We agreed that the man must not regain office as his new ventures would open him to more serious bribery. Julian had no choice but to throw his name back into the till and to add "rush-job" as a footnote due to the high office he was about to take - Governor of New York City, Sector 43. The standards Patriots were held to by the opposition and our own party's purists were unattainable. Like tigers, we ate our own. The media would pound us daily until political surrender was at hand. Many of our moral, decent candidates were either forced to drop out or just got clobbered in the polls. Damn they were good!

Defeat at the hands of perfection

* * * *

Every four years the Patriots would hoist a squeaky clean candidate onto the public stage, thinking he or she was our next great hope. But those damn Herons would harken back into the candidate's history, going as far back as elementary school, to find some unwitting participant who'd say the darnedest things about them. Kicking them in the nuts, pulling their hair or calling them a name, each were considered capital offenses in the political world where no statute of limitations existed for Patriots. To the Herons, our squeaky clean candidates with perfectly normal teenage antics in their background were unworthy of holding public office. The media would drip with utter contempt for them and, in the end, they'd never get elected. Theirs, on the other hand, even those who were traitors in state secrets or sexual deviants, were to be applauded as pillars of the community and fighters for the common man, most notably, the middle class.

Amazingly, there was enormous empathy for Barry's revival as he masterfully duped his former constituents into believing he was a changed man and would now seek an even higher public office than the one he was forced to resign from two years prior. With six days remaining before the election, Barry had a firm lead, and this time the polls were correct. America's most public pervert, traitor and open Marxist was well on his way to becoming the esteemed Governor of Gotham, all five boroughs.

The consequences for monetary transactions were enormous as Wall Street was now in the hands of our Federal Government and bribery was rampant between sectors. Had he set his sights lower by running for city council member or even Governor of a smaller, less critical sector, he would never have gained Julian's attention. He wasn't interested in low hanging fruit.

Barry, the teacher

* * * *

Barry was most effective at orally annihilating our side during televised debates on his favored, supportive networks, which were most of them. Patriots, on the other hand, were never effective at passionately promoting our values and, those who the networks chose to be his foil weren't from our starting lineup. Dad screamed at our digital devices hoping someone inside would hear him and repeat his searing replies to the lame questions being asked. This was our biggest weakness, no one effectively debated the statists even though we had accumulated decades of knowledge from which to build our repertoire of responding zingers. We had their playbook — just never did anything with it. Again — blackmail is a powerful weapon and with Vay out of the picture maybe we could go on the offensive, for once.

Those who painted socialism, even communism as vastly superior to capitalism made my skin crawl. Barry Levinson was the lead cheerleader for team "S." But who could blame my generation for believing that crap? We were never taught the history of socialist nations or of the dictators who ruled them. Castro was to be admired and Mao was a favored "Leader." Total economic decimation, vast poverty and killings by the millions never struck a chord with my fellow students. They were clueless, yet they voted! We'd call them low-informed voters, but in reality, they were absolutely overflowing with information, just the wrong kind. You can begin to see the beauty in D6 and of the effectiveness at controlling education as the foundation for its success. Dumb us down — they did!

Barry Levinson became subject #5. We didn't even spin the wheel.

Our First Complications

* * * *

The complicating factor beyond urgency, which prevented adequate planning, was that Levinson lived three-hundred miles due north in Sector 43 and was rarely seen in New Columbia. My pit was looking less likely as a venue for his final farewell, but we still weren't ready to take our show on the road.

Like real estate, the perfect murder is predicated upon location, location, location and Barry's caused a temporary change to our code, and it was a big one. Leaving Sector 7 to venture deep within enemy territory to assassinate a subject was a game changer for me. Translation, it scared the living shit out of me. Depending upon Julian's comfort level, the pit might not play a role in Subject #5's final solution, but could be used for final disposal. Not that it mattered, but transporting a dead body across Sector boundaries seemed more risky than running an unconscious one thirty-minutes up the road along back roads I was familiar with. "Careful what you wish for," started to make sense.

When adopting an appropriate stalking plan and method of execution for Barry, we considered the litany of issues that accompany a patriotic event outside of the pit. It forced us to consider things we hadn't worried about before and this opened a line of discussion that was more divisive than any I had previously experienced with Julian. Our opinions were polar opposite and, while Julian showed a level of confidence in the successful completion of this mission, I didn't share that feeling. The pit was my comfort zone, but now I'd have to worry about evidence left behind, blood splatter, DNA, unfamiliarity with the territory, unknown cameras and witnesses. Julian rattled them off as his evidence that I should be less cocky and more contrite when accepting this mission. It was his pick, and he had put the tight time-line on it. Cockiness wasn't anywhere near my domain when discussing Subject #5. I was the one harboring elevated levels of fear, not Julian.

Agreeing to our next subject with all the requisite complications, not the least of which would be a long-haul transport of his odorous, decomposing body back to my place, was akin to tossing me into the cold Atlantic Ocean as a child and then saying, "swim." Cigarette smells linger in the cars of those who smoke. Road trips are great for drunken college kids with a designated sober driver but the thought of three-hundred-fifty-seven miles with a rotting corpse in the back of the van, made my weak gag reflexes activate. Body bags came to mind and I knew what kind to get and where to secure one.

Julian had his reasons for the baptismal strategy and those revolved around building my confidence quickly while testing our enemy's response to the missing subjects. I was feeling like his guinea pig. How committed were they to finding them or the truth to their disappearance? There was no body and no crime. For Levinson, however, Julian was willing to return to his roulette wheel for another spin, leading to a less risky subject's name being pulled. He sensed the drop in my confidence level and told me so. It was all too confusing since executing Levinson was Julian's idea. Once again, my partner's illogical mood was surfacing.

Almost immediately following DeSoto's execution, the media began a daily speculation about his whereabouts across all their networks and through their well-controlled social media outlets. As a cabinet official, many alarms would have gone off just hours after he went missing and, with him, they did. Their stories changed daily.

A first attempt at explaining his disappearance was to build a heartwarming story around his personal missionary trip to some remote village in Central America where the children had no books or school supplies. When he still didn't show up, they followed that by reporting his extended, well deserved vacation which ended in him missing at sea while on his thirty-two-foot yacht. He had sailed thousands of miles to that village and, upon returning, hit nasty weather and was never seen again. Fake news now hit their obituaries as it was difficult for them to grasp what was actually happening. We were having an impact, a small one, yet in each case their attempts to find us hit a dead-end. The "perfect crime" was begining to feel like a reality. I obliterated the bodies and they obliterated the truth.

Like DeSoto's yacht, we were off their radar. The irony was dripping from that story, but I liked the narrative because it mentioned neither me nor Julian. Still, we were careful to not get cocky, figuring we had gotten away with the perfect crime. During the Cold War, the Soviets would make up fantastical stories about missing spies all the while building a war chest of evidence while finding the perp. Today — they leveraged social media and those fake stories drew the criminal out — hoping they'd brag about getting away with something.

Pretty much the same for Jenkins, but with a different twist involving an extended medical leave overseas, which was comical since our single-payer healthcare was to be the envy of the world. It wasn't. The murder of the Reverend was tagged on another Patriot who made the stupid mistake of taking credit for our work. He was executed the following week. I took pride in my work as did Julian but, while imitation is the highest form of flattery, taking credit for an act you never committed was the lowest form of plagiarism. Serves him right.

A visit to Il Portico by the local Stasi two weeks after Jerkins' execution threw me into a panic until I realized that they had no clue as to the whereabouts of their comrade. Questions centering on his recent visits to our restaurant just days before he had gone missing and if we had noticed anything unusual in his behavior was the totality of their investigation with me. My answers — "Nope, he was his usual jolly self and we have missed not having him here as our dinner guest but shall keep his Macallan Scotch in our vault should he resurface."

Administration policy was to keep high profile crimes out of the public domain lest the enemy gain confidence and assassinate more of them. Ruining their idyllic utopian society was to be avoided. Violent crime was down in their narrative, but reality told a different story — it was at an all-time high and Patriots weren't the ones committing them. While I continued to push my "manifesto" narrative to Julian, I thanked him for adhering to his no body, no crime code for the first four of our subjects. We were lucky, very lucky.

Like most of our reasoned thoughts, there was logic behind our decision to never carry out executions on days where the subject had dined at Il Portico. This removed us and our establishment from the subject's daily schedule or an investigator's timeline. Late night kills gave us adequate time to clean up any missteps or messes before daybreak.

There was an inverse relationship between the degree of difficulty for a mission and the actual time spent planning it. DeSoto and Jenkins were straight forward yet we had discussed each for weeks before carrying them out. Barry Levinson's was more complicated, but our planning lasted only two days. After a hurried discussion about how to eliminate him, we settled on something out of the norm, but fitting for his farewell. Anything would have been ok with Julian. He was beyond eager to check this one off the list.

The Solution

* * * *

Our solution, complicated as it was, required no weapons, would leave no blood splatter and minimal direct contact with my victim. Mr. Levinson was about to take his own life upon learning of new public allegations, revealing that his lurid behavior continued in spite of his admission that he was a changed man. His latest victim was indeed a young boy. Yes, we were planning his well-deserved suicide with an assist from none other than me.

Method of execution: hanging. Location: the Levinson barn, South Hampton, Sector 43.

Given the severity of those allegations, Barry might have carried out his own suicide. But since Herons never ratted each other out, those stories would have never surfaced, especially in light of the fact that the election was six days away. He was safe. Information gleaned through Julian's back channels described in disgusting detail Barry's latest illicit exploits. But, as expected, his sycophant accomplices in the media held off on releasing those stories. The fix was in, at least until after he had won his election. After taking office he'd be a prime target for controlled blackmail, meaning Barry was about to become a figurehead, a mere puppet with someone far worse than him controlling his strings. Morality preached that his pedophilia behavior should have been the only justification for his execution, but morality played no role in that decision. His transfer of sensitive, top-secret American military documents to Alexi Yubrov was the sole reason for his lethal sentence. Julian constantly lectured me on separating morality from patriotism.

The evening before I was to begin my journey north towards Long Island, multiple personalities banged around my head. Alternating between Professor Moriarty and Sherlock Holmes, I'd visualize how I'd accomplish this mission, one step at a time. It perfectly combined that diabolical villain and the crafty detective who spent his entire life trying to catch him. Moriarty occupied the frontal lobe of my brain while Holmes took up residence in the back, the logic area. Contrary to what experts have said about the frontal lobes being smaller on psychopaths, mine was not but, then again, I wasn't a psychopath.

I presented a simple solution. He'd hang himself from those wonderfully placed rafters with his own rope. All the tools were there and belonged to the victim even a sharp serrated knife from the kitchen that I had used a year before for carving up his Labor Day pig. Ironic, huh? I was already envisioning a spectacular addition to what should have been a straight forward hanging and, yes, it involved blood splatter and a pig, the human kind.

If it's true that idle hands are the devil's workshop than idle minds are his assistant. I had gained some unusual habits after beginning this war, and one of them was to visualize the wildly exaggerated, completely false stories the media would hoist upon the public once our subject had gone missing. Not once was I correct in my imaginative skills. Missing at sea, extended medical leave, missionary trips, even the obvious vacations, I never got it right. This time, however, our subject would not go missing. He'd be hanging, sans penis, in plain site for everyone to see. No body, no crime was ditched for subject #5.

In Barry's case the macabre came through and I gave it another try, so I scribbled the following on a notepad: "They found Barry Levinson hanging from the rafters at his barn in South Hampton. His penis lay below him along with the knife he severed it with." Keep in mind that severing his penis was never approved by our committee of two. It oozed such irony based upon our subject's history of posting selfies of that appendage that I couldn't let it go. I loved it and, after counting the characters plus five cringe-worthy emojis, decided that it would make an ideal Tweet from some reporter at the New York Times to Barry's adoring minions. Taking it one step further, "Severing my ties to my addiction and am officially hanging up my career in politics forever," was a Twitter worthy suicide note to send from Barry's cell phone. He was a Twitter addict and had several hundred thousand followers, so going viral was a certainty. I knew exactly how this would all play out, right down to the final suicide note his cold, dead fingers would tap into his Blackberry.

I was actually having too much fun and that can be dangerous when the subject is not fun.

I knew Barry well.

Like most, Barry frequented my restaurant and had once asked if I'd chef for a small, casual dinner party at his Capital Hill Townhouse. This necessitated the exchange of private cell phone numbers for which I was grateful. I'm also grateful to him for spawning my small catering business which allowed me to socialize with so many disreputable Herons that my head exploded just thinking about the enormous task ahead of us. Had it not been for my own sensibilities I could have just as quickly poisoned them all during that dinner party. It was overflowing with traitors, communists, a virtual nest of Herons.

The party was standard fare for a Capital Hill gathering, light h'ordeuvres and heavy on the booze, but Barry bragged all night about his family's beautiful estate and rustic old barn in South Hampton. Inherited wealth, typical.

"I can't thank you enough for helping to make this evening such a success," he fist-bumped me as the party was wrapping up and the final guest was leaving. And then offered to help extend my culinary reach to a market beyond New Columbia by working his annual Labor Day hoopla in the Hamptons. I hated that place, even with its immaculate, white sand beaches, enormous estates and kitschy restaurants. Strictly upperclass but adding "the" before Hamptons made it even more pretentious than it already was. The Hamptons.

Patriots weren't welcome in the Hamptons, at least not openly. It was enemy territory from one of end of the island to the other. East Hampton, however was less snooty, but the restaurants were crappy. Ironic that just two miles off shore was their first landing place. Montauk — the Plymouth Rock for infiltrators.

That summer, with the help of Barry and his cohorts I expanded my market's reach one-hundred-twenty miles out Sunset Parkway and into the Hamptons for one huge Labor Day BBQ. Many in attendance were on Julian's list, but their party invitations for a future event would be more accurately themed as their last suppers. Praise the Lord!

The barn was decorated for the holiday, with streamers and balloons in red, white and blue placed everywhere. Flying the old stars and stripes was traditional on holidays before the collapse, but afterwards, no one had the guts to do so, lest they be tagged as a Patriot. My father didn't care and placed them, for all to see, on every corner of our house, front, back, side and always on our mailbox. He loved to tempt the enemy.

Barry was proud of that place and couldn't wait to show me around. I took careful notes of every nook and cranny and, although I wasn't in the murderous mindset at that moment, I scanned everywhere for video cameras and alarms. What I found most interesting during that tour wasn't so much the house, but instead, the barn and an area in the back corner next to a picnic table with two rafters, each hanging low to the ground. A heavy gauge rope with a bucket of water attached to one end made for all sorts of possibilities. A decorative touch from the wife or a necessity for some barn chores, I didn't care. My mind wondered to those rafters, the attached rope and lack of a security system. It's amazing how the mind changes focus when execution becomes a career choice.

The election was six days away, the clock was ticking and I needed his schedule, something that would have taken a week to lock down. His wife had left him, so she wasn't an issue, but the possibility of unwanted house guests loomed. A sexual deviant wouldn't likely be spending much time alone. Twitter and texting were his preferred methods of communicating, so maybe that's where I needed to focus. It's funny how things work out. Purchasing three non-traceable burner phones from the local 7-11 months before my return to the Hampton's allowed me to contact him using a local area code. Burner phones were my friend.

Julian and I met one final time to discuss the plan and agreed that it was too risky to reach out to his team for schedule details even though Julian had the means to do so. Julian had the means to do almost anything and that was beginning to concern me. How? Not only was this to be a road trip, but it turned out to be an extended one, requiring an overnight stay. The complicating factors kept piling up. Long drive, unfamiliar territory, hotels, restaurants and my addition of penile blood splatter, what the hell were we thinking? What could be more risky than a stake-out in South Hampton while sitting in an old navy blue van that stood out like a sore thumb among a sea of Ferraris, Mercedes and BMWs? Julian's collection of state license plates came in handy. He handed me a brown paper bag containing two from the former state of New York. Sector license plates were last on the list of changes the driving populous was required to make. They still allowed state plates, but their deadline was looming.

A Deviant's Rendezvous

* * * *

Equipment check: Glock, drugs, syringe, body bag, a woman's wig, sunglasses, rubber gloves, ski mask, burner phones, rope, duck tape, boom box and steady nerves.   My Glock wasn't necessary, but I packed it out of habit.   I added the rope as a backup in case Barry had redecorated the barn and removed his. Bringing a body bag was precautionary in case our assisted suicide turned out to look like murder, in which case I'd have to tote his rotting corpse 300 miles back to the pit. Barry loved fried zucchini, which was in season. My tools-of-the-trade remained hidden in the body compartment and under containers of tomatoes and herbs. Our plan was to arrange a blatantly flirtatious meeting with Barry. Deviants weren't selective so that part was easy. Text him as I did Christopher Jenkins with the promise of good company, a few drinks and then ending with some lurid sex.   Perverts had no boundaries and couldn't care less where or from whom they got their fix. While his sexual exploits were his personal business, trading in secrets concerning our military technology was a deal-breaker for any last-minute reprieve. Barry played many roles as a Heron. Congressman, professor and throughout it all, he was passing documents he received while serving on the Foreign Intelligence committee. No one ever knew of the document drops. Julian knew though.

Road Trip

* * * *

Avoiding the major highways, like I-95, I headed north from Sector 7, taking the back roads through Maryland, Pennsylvania and across New Jersey all the way to the end of Long Island. Two-hundred-sixty-two miles of open roads, no tolls, police or traffic, but it rained cats and dogs the entire way, making the trip longer than it should have been. Six hours became eight. That required an overnight stay.

Despite the devastation that followed the collapse, America was a resilient place, not so much in the inner cities which were still war zones, but in those small towns off the beaten path. People cared about their homes, property, their neighbors, guns and religion. You could see patriotism behind those drawn curtains and smell it in the backyards. Flags and burgers. I'm glad I took that route. Even in the pouring rain, it gave me some sense of hope that Main Street USA would eventually return.

I arrived around dinner time and ate in East Hampton. Less snooty, cheaper and more to my liking, the town felt homey, as if it didn't belong on that long stretch of the island which was inundated with elitists who despised the Patriots. Avoiding South Hampton was necessary, as a stranger from somewhere else was quickly noted as exactly that — a stranger from somewhere else. My dented old blue van would have drawn attention among the Ferraris, Mercedes and BMWs lining the streets and filling the parking lots.

A little joint called Nick and Toni's seemed the perfect place to grab a bite. Just north off of Sunrise Highway and housed in an old stone building that had seen better days, it was Italian and the food was just as authentic as Il Portico. There was a family history behind those crumbling old walls and it made me curious to find out what it was. It reminded me of your mother.

Always check for cameras where ever you go. Restaurants were notorious for having several as food theft was a popular crime when the price for a loaf of bread surpassed $12.00. I saw none but noticed an interesting old ceramic dinner plate hung on the back wall, a proud reminder of their Sicilian heritage. I could sense camaraderie the moment I walked in as they watched me through the open kitchen before acknowledging my presence. Patriots were suspicious by nature, and the armed ones even more so. I'm sure they were armed.

Like so many secret societies, we also had our secret signs, not a hand shake, but a piece of paper we'd inconspicuously flash when in the presence of strangers to see if they'd return the gesture. It was our private calling card allowing us to speak openly with those we didn't know well enough to trust. Reagan's "Trust but verify," changed from concerns about enemies abroad to concerns about enemies within. We'd take an old Land' O Lakes butter package, flatten it and then with an X-Acto knife make strategic cuts and folds which, when done properly, would add boobs to the Indian woman on the front of the package. I took mine out and laid it next to my fork, hoping that Nick or Toni would oblige. It stayed on the table through the entire meal. Being a total stranger put a cautionary pause on any extended camaraderie but, when Nick brought the check with the words "complimentary dessert and espresso" written across the top, he dropped his on the table, right next to mine.

I looked up and smiled, then gave him twice what the cost of those freebies plus a healthy tip. Cash, of course. He smiled back. As I was leaving, I asked for his recommendation for a decent motel to spend the night. He recommended the Island Inn which was a mile down the road and in the general direction I needed to go. Before heading there, I drove to the end of the island, parked the van about a half mile from Barry's place, then walked the rest of the way to see if he was even there. The place was dark except for lights in the back southeast corner. That was his bedroom, which was also part of that tour. Relieved that he hadn't spent the night in the city, I prayed that he'd still be there the following night when our plan would unfold. It's funny the things I prayed for beyond God's standard forgiveness which was looking less likely.

Just hanging around

* * * *

There's something calming about waking up to the sounds and smells of a sunny morning at the beach. Soft waves teasing the shore and the scent of the salty breeze are relaxing, especially when my day entailed nothing more than sitting in a musty old motel room going through the motions of what lie ahead — murder. It was rehearsal time. Planning my text messages, anticipating a pervert's reply and then banging out a suitable response to keep things moving was necessary to engage that subject who had a short attention span. I'd imagine the conversation, type my response and then save each to my phone's notepad. A coy approach worked with Jenkins but with Barry, I had to kick it up a notch. He was ten-years younger than Jenkins who was just a pig, not a pervert.

By noon, I was beyond bored and opted to walk the beach towards the Levinson estate. Pretty much everything on that end of the island was an estate. Small and cozy, enormous and ostentatious, it didn't matter, they were all estates. Thirteen miles separated the middle class East end of the Hamptons from the bourgeois of the South. A suitable distance to keep the "help" far enough away from the "helped." I drove twelve, one mile short of his place, and parked in an area with direct access to the beach. Beach patrol, Gilgo Beach, Tower 14, lots of dunes and tall grass and no lights, perfect for an evening ambush. Satisfied with the area of extraction, I returned to the motel and waited

— and waited.

Tick Tock, tick tock. I watched the clock for the next several hours. Text message initiation would begin just after sundown, which was around 7:30, but I jumped the gun and sent my first volley at 3pm. I needed to keep him on that island, so I decided on sending a little tease, something that would guarantee he'd stick around and not bolt into Manhattan for more enticing pleasures.

Short and sweet. "You around tonight? I'm coming to SH!" What followed was thirty minutes of pacing in my motel room, waiting for a reply. The room was small, the circumference was tight, so it was circular, like a dog honing in on the perfect spot to pee. Burner phones didn't acknowledge when your text had been read or received, and Net Neutrality turned everything we once controlled into a crap shoot with a cabal of nations monitoring everything. They'd leave you wondering if they ever received it or was it floating around cyberspace due to an unexpected spike in traffic. You're used to that, but it was once much better.

It occurred to me that the onslaught of allegations surrounding Levinson might have caused him to change his number. The digital scent of celebrity miscreants always goes viral and, before you know it, that private cell phone number is now public. I texted Julian my concern, but before I hit send, someone replied. Disaster averted.

"Who's this?"

I don't recall the exact name of the fictitious women, maybe it was Olivia, but adding that she was lonely and needed company did the trick. He wasn't going anywhere that night and, in fact, shared similar sentiments. That damn picture he sent me was not what I had expected, but not surprising when considering the source.

DELETE!

I replied, but didn't include a picture, even though he had asked for one. Knowing that the successful completion of this mission required a full-body shot, I began Googling pictures that the little prick would find suitable to hookup with. Brunettes with dark skin, Hispanic, not skinny, not fat, not too cutesy or model-like. Average looking, the cute, but not hot girl next door. It's amazing what guys will talk about with their wife within earshot. Just as I had scanned his place for cameras and alarms, I also eavesdropped on several conversations where the topic was females and the type he preferred. Latinos, the kind who'd work the McDonald's drive-thru window — it was a power trip for him. I made sure not to pick an image from the first few pages of Google's results, but instead captured one that was fifty-two pages into my search. A man scorned as often as he was would have been suspicious of unknown suitors. "You'll have to wait but I'm worth it." Levinson was easy prey and he enjoyed the hunt, the tease.

Those damn motel clocks are annoying enough when the previous guest sets their alarm for 2:00am, but whoever stayed in room 115 before me had set theirs for 4:30 PM, just an hour into my desperately needed a nap. It was still three hours from launch time and I couldn't get back to sleep. I circled the floor, and thought.

"Beautiful day. Wanna walk the beach this evening? I'll be in SH around 730," I texted him.

I posed as a former student of his and built her bio as the shy one who always sat up front in his lecture hall. One of her friends had given her his cell phone number because she was too shy to approach, let alone ask such a personal question. Seemed perfect but, just in case, I deconstructed it to see if there were any obstacles that Barry might throw my way, tripping me up and ruining the evening's ploy. I tried to imagine every possible query he'd send me and then constructed the perfect reply. Prior planning comes in handy especially with murder.

"Who was the friend?" Answer: "I promised her that I wouldn't tell you because you had asked her to never give out his number."

"What class was I in and what year?" That was easy: "Political Science, Spring semester, 2024 in Manor Hall from 3 to 4 on Wednesdays and Fridays. The room was freezing."

"Had we ever met outside of class?"

"Nope, I was too shy and I worked all the time. McDonald's."

"What was my name?"

Damn! That one could cause problems as he most likely had a list of his students, past and current. I pondered that one, but didn't want to use a real student's name. Code: Protect the innocent and never, ever bring anyone else into our executioner's world. It was Julian and me, period. What worried me most, though, was the potential shift from text to voice. Those who hide behind digital screens posting all sorts of lurid and bold remarks that they'd never say to someone's face, do so for one simple reason, they're anonymous. Social media made us more rude, and weaker as a society, but also more honest and deceptive at the same time. It enabled guys like Barry to imagine themselves as internet Chippendales. Fake identities attached to fake pictures can carry you only so far, but when a voice or actual face-to-face communication is required to seal the deal, many don't have the nerve to see their ruse to its natural conclusion. Real human contact has stabbed many a digital dating fraud in the heart. What if Barry wanted to speak with me? I must have stared at that damn phone for fifteen minutes before sending that text. All I could think of was, "my phone was broken and I can only text." Or, "I'm out with friends and it's too noisy to talk." Not my best excuse but I've had both happen before, so they're plausible.

Driving over three hundred miles in the pouring rain, then pacing the floor of an old motel room that you'd never stay in if you had taken the time to plan the mission, minimizes minor details that might put the kibbutz on the whole mission. That's when you throw caution to the wind and pray to God that the unlikely never happens.

I hit send!

It was said that he saved lewd texts from his admirers as images so he could re-read them for some sort of sexual gratification. Strange, because men are more visual yet Barry, like a woman, held emotional attachments to words. That proved to play in my favor as he never asked for me to call him. Had he called my number, I wasn't sure what I'd do, but fortunately that never happened. He must have screen captured every lurid text I sent him. Note to self: make sure you delete them once in possession of that phone.

His reply came through quickly. Four words in typical millennial brevity.

"where r u now?" he shot back.

"Walking the beach near Gilgo Tower 14. Just left a party in East Hampton and Uber'd to South."

"Sorry, not interested!!!"

Of all the times for him to gain a conscience, this was not that time. His suspicion arose and he wasn't interested in a meeting. When panic sets in, most people breathe harder, in and out, in and out, gasping with each breath. I handled panic differently and, while my breathing pattern seemed strained, my rapid response mechanism kicked in, causing me to imagine a series of suitable followups to turn him around. Time to close the sale or that trip would have been a complete bust and Julian would have been pissed.

Blackmail!

"I have video!"

"BS, you have nothing. blocking u" he shot back.

It's a text message that oozes with confidence and made me wonder if I had pushed the wrong button. It occurred to me that blackmailing a man everyone already knew to be a colossal asshole was pointless. Mistake #1.

Sure, it was a hasty text and, to be honest, I hadn't thought it through as Julian would have insisted. But Barry's fervent ego might have caused him to question his memory, so I took the shot.

"How's class this evening? Getting your homework done?" Julian wanted an update.

I hated confrontation, which was odd, since my career path wasn't pointing me towards the priesthood but instead guided me towards the ultimate confrontation with my subjects, killing them. This was the first time a major glitch had entered my lethal world. No surprise, rush jobs are wrought with them. I shuttered to see Julian's response. What began as a simple ploy for an amorous meeting on Gilgo beach, then ending at his barn, changed with one simple text. What would stop Barry from calling the local police who were likely in his corner, and sending them to wherever I had asked him to meet me? Damn how I hated the annoyances that came with committing acts of war. Thankfully, ours had no rules of engagement.

"Where do we meet? When?" he texted back. Levinson had pondered my threat. He either recalled having video'd one of his exploits or couldn't remember and was playing it safe in case he had. The other scenario was that he was sick and tired of getting caught and was setting me up for the fall. Either way, the game was on but I had to change the venue. The path to least resistance and the fewest surprises was at the subject's house, or in that case, his barn. I'm not one to ponder what I say before blurting out something, but at that moment I started to. Getting him out of his house and into an area where I could dose him was all I cared about. Throwing caution to the wind, I decided on a simple ambush, but on his turf. Our well devised, cautionary assassin's code was obliterated. I was going rogue.

Sometimes it helps to play role reversal and imagine yourself as the one being hunted. Had a stranger asked me to meet in my barn in thirty-minutes, I'd immediately go there, then position myself to be able to jump my stalker should they prove to be a threat. I drove a mile up the road and down the narrow, sandy Beach Patrol path to Tower 16, parking my van in an area with no lights but plenty of tall grass to hide. It was his beach property.

"Your barn in thirty minutes?"

I knew the property well and headed towards the barn. Stopping to view through his back window which ran from the floor to the top of his twenty-five foot palatial ceilings, I saw Barry who had moved from the bedroom to his living room. His was a spectacular view of the ocean, but on that night, for me, an unforgettable window into the mind of a man on the cusp of his own grandioseness, yet also on the verge of a personal vendetta. Sitting in his brown leather high-back chair, he stared motionless out that window with a cell phone in hand. "Dilemma" was written all over his face. Viewing the face of the condemned had assaulted my mind for months and the look was always the same; fear, finality and an intense attempt at holding back tears, kinda boring. Viewing the face of the blackmailed was far more interesting. It's that worried, pensive look, gazing up and around as if the answer to their quandary would somehow magically drop into their lap. They'd pace the floor and then sit down again. Caged animals came to mind as he took those strides and had that look. What interested me most was that cell phone and whether he'd dial the authorities. I hit send, then watched as he received my text. His reply showed a lack of patience with his secret blackmailer but also frustration, anger and some small sense of excitement. "I might get laid," was embroidered across his pursed lips. Reading faces is a handy skill and Barry was clearly conflicted.

"K" He pounded into the phone and then put it back into his pocket. No call to the authorities. Course correction locked in. I let out a sigh of relief so loud that it might have carried right into that living room. Although my equipment regimen included a women's wig and sunglasses, the change in plans negated my bringing them, it was dark anyway. Pointing my Glock at his forehead as he exited his house would do the trick, but exposing my identity risked shutting him down, leaving me with nothing to learn. Floating the possibility of a reprieve for good behavior made my interrogations so much easier, but the wig and shades were back in the van. The latex mask would have to do.

My phone vibrated again. That time it was Julian with his standard, "I'm checking in" text. When a mission was still in process, our agreed upon reply was to text "6". That's code for all's good but can't talk now. "9" or no reply was an alert that something had gone wrong. That night was a solid "7" somewhere in the middle. We had no code 7 though, it's just how I was feeling. "6," I replied.

As expected, Levinson took that head start to the barn and

walked right out the back door where I was standing, off to the side. Always find the dark corners with strong lights behind you. Doing so makes it impossible to identify the person facing you. Just as you'd hear in the movies, as the thug accosts his victim, I said exactly the same thing. "Don't turn around, throw your cell on the ground, take off your shoes, then kneel with your hands behind your back," The order might have been different, but not turning around came first.

Shoes are removed to eliminate footprints on evenings where they'd show up after rain showers or snow. It's also a sure-fire way of slowing down a fleeing subject should he try to escape. Brand identifiers on the soles show up in mud or sand, so I opted to remove that element from potential evidence of something going awry and blowing a hole in the suicide scenario.

Over-thinking? Maybe, but one can't be too cautious. I had sanded my soles down, on Julian's order, but still took them off. Footprints are always something they'd focus on and two different sets would raise concerns.

"Relax, do as I say, don't turn around and you'll live."

"OK, OK, Don't shoot."

Getting Barry to the barn without him briefly glimpsing my face would be damn near impossible, so I pulled out my syringe, put a choke hold on him and then injected the drug into his neck. He offered no struggle which surprised me because he was a gym rat. The old myth that muscle weighed more than fat is true. He was heavy, but then again dead weight always seems that way, even when alive.

Into the Barn

* * * *

The barn was just as I had remembered from a year prior, but this time the ground was soft with a heavy layer of hay, maybe three inches, strewn across the floor. Not sure why, because he had no horses to feed and no stalls to board them in, but it covered the entire floor. A welcome mat for me that looked as though it had just been spread or maybe it was a decorative touch from his former wife. No footprints in that stuff but dragging him across those blades made a mess and required me to put it back in place. Finding a needle in a haystack came to mind. Any careless evidence left behind would be that needle and his haystack was enormous.

The rope was no longer hung from the rafter but was rolled up in the corner by the picnic table. All in all, little had changed. I glanced around one last time, scanning the ceilings and walls to determine that there were no hidden cameras or an alarm system placed within the rafters. It was clean. I stepped back, took one last deep breath thinking to myself, it's showtime. Let the hanging begin.

Barry was still out cold and stretched across the hay strewn floor. Thirty-minutes was all I had before he'd come to.

The "rush" part was finally over and my subject was in position awaiting his final act, suicide. Hoisting him onto the chair and then tying the noose tightly around his neck was all I needed to do. Then, with one swift kick backwards, he'd be swaying in the wind. Even though he was my fourth, it didn't get any easier. I was still breaking God's sixth Commandment. Those deep breaths I'd take went hand-in-hand with equally deep thinking, forcing me to meander through the motions of what was about to happen. I'd ask myself, was it justified and would my conscience join me while driving back to Sector 7? Going through those mental gyrations tells me that I still had one.

I unraveled the rope, tossed it over the rafter, tied a hangman's noose, then placed the chair directly under it. Something wasn't right. Google was a wonderful thing. It taught me the eight easy steps to master that lethal knot which was known as the Jack Ketch knot. I could determine the ideal drop height for a pain-free hanging of a man who weighed 185 pounds and was six feet tall. I measured the end of the rope, making sure that the noose was only six and a half feet from the ground leaving six inches from the bottom of Barry's shoes to the barn's floor. Who knew that math was so important when hanging someone. But, the chair wasn't high enough.

There are two kinds of hanging; the execution type which is a drop hanging and the suicide kind which is more akin to strangulation. The first, which severs the spinal cord, is quicker and less painful while the second, is excruciatingly painful and takes longer to finish. For a man of Levinson's size and weight, I estimated that a drop of five-feet-two-inches would sever his spinal cord while avoiding decapitation, but would require more than the chair I had to achieve that height. You can see my dilemma. On the one hand this was an execution but on the other, it was meant to look like a suicide.   More thinking was needed!

Barry Levinson was a perverted pedophilia and a traitor to our nation who had traded classified defense documents to the Russians. Why I even cared about his level of pain or the time he'd be dangling, bothered me. Was I going soft? It was at that moment that I shook those concerns over impending psychosis and was thrilled that I even cared about his level of pain. To top it off, I doubt that his strangulating pain would come anywhere near the intense sting he'd feel as I cut his dick off with the serrated knife from his kitchen. Now that's gotta hurt when you're still alive and, yes, he'd have to be alive in order for this suicide ruse to work.

It all sounds easy, but hanging someone while making it look like suicide is no easy task. It's wrought with small problems that can turn a simple suicide into a complicated murder. Severing a part of his body added to the complication. I cringed at the thought of touching it, let alone slicing it off.

The first problem was having a chair tall enough to position Barry so that, when noosed, he couldn't simply step off of the chair and touch the ground. This required a chair whose seat-height was slightly more than Barry's length from waist to ground. That chair was too damn short. The second is avoiding any confrontation with the subject that might show up as exactly that, confrontation. Suicide victims must be clean of any unusual external marks that might raise the ire of investigators leading them to question the suicide. Julian drilled that into my head even though it was painfully obvious. Finally, there's the issue of his hands. Tying them tight with ropes would leave ligature marks. Perhaps Julian's approval of Levinson's assisted suicide was his coy way of driving home the beauty of "no body, no crime."

Clearly the easiest way to fix those issues was to first, find a chair that was tall enough to eliminate the possibility of his simply stepping off and to use soft cotton or silk to avoid ligature marks. As for the genital severing, perhaps I'd be able to convince him to do it himself. Threatening him with a swift kick to the chair or a shot to the head if he tried anything would eliminate any possibility of him throwing punches towards me. It's nearly impossible to untie a knot once the body is swinging in a hangman's noose. If properly tied, it's designed to tighten with every swing. He'd only make matters worse and that was fine with me.

Barstool chairs! Thirty inches high and I remembered he had six in the kitchen surrounding the center island where his friends drank while watching me cook. They were sturdy. I walked to the house and entered through the back door, the same one Barry came out of. Grabbing one, I returned to the barn just in time to see Barry wiggling on the floor, still groggy but the drug was wearing off. No more deep breathing exercises and no more thinking, I donned my latex mask, grabbed Levinson, dragged him to the chair, propped him up, put the noose around his neck and waited. His feet were six inches off of the ground. Perfect.

Latex masks are wonderful. They're tight fitting, more like a second skin that follows your facial contours but completely changes your appearance. They're also hot, extremely hot, leaving little room for the skin to breath. I kept a black knit hat on my head — very thuggish looking. Now this is where it got weird if you can suspend belief that everything until that point wasn't weird enough. I had convinced myself that cutting his dick off was a great idea and that the suicide tweet I had concocted was beyond perfect, it was downright poetic. Self congratulatory behavior was inappropriate though. Focus on the mission and always, keep it simple. There comes a time in every man's life when sacrifices are made, sometimes for love, sometimes for country. I couldn't bring myself to do it. The question I faced was, did Barry love that appendage more than life itself and would he be willing to make his own sacrifice for love or country.

Homer once said, in the Iliad, "Better to flee from death than feel its grip." Grip it, cut it off and you'll survive seemed like a reasonable request to make.

My Subject Awakens.

* * * *

If you've ever awoken in the middle of the night from a terrifying nightmare, the tendency is to sit up quickly, shake your head out of the daze and then take a deep breath and exhale. I know this because it became my nightly routine. Coming out of a drug induced sleep causes a different reaction, you leap forward. Compound that with having a noose tied around your neck and some masked stranger standing in front of you pointing a gun at your head and that reaction becomes violent and potentially lethal. It's not good when slipping off of the chair you're seated in will cause strangulation to begin because you're six inches too short to touch God's safety zone. What followed was a brief, slurred coprolalia spewing of profanity laden sentences. And, by brief I mean as long as it took before he slipped and the rope choked him, which was less than five-seconds. Talk about a quandary. There I was, on the verge of a perfect execution and I'm put in the position of having to save his life, if only for a few minutes, because my work wasn't done. There were questions I needed answers to. I shoved him back onto the chair and demanded that he calm down or that our meeting would be brief and not end well for him. I gave him that tiny sliver of hope that he'd escape with his life, although not his dick, if he'd cooperate. He did. The tease was in.

He was a quick learner. His panicked expression conveyed a man who well knew what was about to happen. Ropes around your neck tied in a hangman's knot are effective at conveying dire consequences. There were no lingering affects from the drug other than a slight uncoordinated swaying as he tried desperately to maintain his balance, knowing that one slip would cut off his life. I steadied the chair until he composed himself. The soft cotton cloth I had tied his hands with, left no noticeable ligature marks.

"Who the fuck are you and why are you doing this?" The Herons frequently used the "f-bomb" — they were an unsavory bunch.

My standard reply, "I'll ask the questions."

I gave my usual speech; family history, peppered with Patriotic talking points, sister killed in riots, parents in Vega 7, Constitution, freedom, blah, blah, blah. I was getting bored with repeating those lines. I needed new material but the National Anthem would go on and, for him, I'd crank the volume up to its maximum level when considering the changed acoustics from a large open barn. No headphones for him.

Just as the others did, Barry paused for a moment, longer than you'd expect, before answering a simple question. But unlike Vay, Jenkins and DeSoto, his answers were brief, one or two words and no details. Eye movement reveals much about what a person is thinking or remembering, truth or lies, and his eyes darted all over the place. Looking down and to the left meant that he was talking internally to himself. Looking up in that same direction and he's visually recalling images of things remembered. Looking up and to the right, he's constructing visuals or responses, most likely lies. I watched carefully with each movement he made and then determined truth or bull shit. Bull shit necessitated a followup question and a solid punch to his groin — just for the hell of it.

Lessons learned from Barry

* * * *

There were three questions I asked each subject before carrying out their execution, and they were always the same; Who, what, and where. I might have already mentioned this but, in case you forgot, I'll repeat.

Who they reported to was always first and, with DeSoto and Jenkins the answer was, no one. Barry, however, was not at the top of their food chain. Having arrived on shipment #64, he was relatively young for a Heron to have gained so much power, and in my world, damn near a child to be facing execution. Knowing his master was critically important as Julian and I planned our next phase. The second was to determine their marching orders as they grew up and once they had obtained their designated position within our society. "Forward" was critical to their ideological mission and became the tag line for their entire movement. "Forward to what?" was my concern and the answer was always "progress." But progress, like D6, was never to occur quickly, and this allowed them to string their naïve minions along for decades, since what they promised was always several generations into the future. As an example, "If we don't address global warming today, we'll all be dead thirty years from now." This removed all accountability from whatever they had promised. The third question focused on their parents. Were they indoctrinated at an early age by them or did that occur later in life as a revelation from an outside handler? In other words, were the parents party to their infiltration and, if so, how. If not, who was? Before answering, he asked that I remove my mask so he could see who I was.

I understand that whole "needing to know your accuser," and would have obliged, but continuing with the ruse that, remaining disguised to avoid his identifying me once I let him go, was critically important. Stress makes the shoulders rise and the back arch forward in a slumping motion. Relief has the opposite effect with the shoulders and head arching backwards and an audible sigh of relief being expelled from the mouth. He was relaxed and probably believed that I'd let him go. Damn near fell off the chair. It's sad when you think about it. I can't imagine a worse type of lie than the ones I dangled in front of my subjects just to get answers to three simple questions.

"Thanks for being so cooperative and now I bid you farewell, permanently." That's cruel.

Although he was uncooperative during my initial interrogation, I gleaned some intelligence for our cause but mostly relief from my agitated mindset. One-word answers aren't helpful when having to report back to Julian so I'd fill in the blanks to make it more colorful, but always remained truthful. I couldn't shake that nagging feeling that he already knew the answers and those questions were meant as teaching moments to guide me towards that sense of justification that continued to haunt me, all the while paving my path to hell. I felt the unbearable pain of cruelty that evening as I forced Levinson to do something so horrible to himself while promising a freedom I knew I couldn't abide by — severing his manhood.

The penis differs from arms or legs in that the arteries surrounding it dilate and contract more than those found in other appendages. As a result, bleeding from a severed one can be extreme and very messy.

It pains me to recall in such vivid detail how I persuaded a man to cut off his member and then exactly how he did it. Consider the facts surrounding the situation that night. Barry was standing high on his chair with a perfectly tied hangman's noose tight around his neck and a stranger wearing a silicone mask pointing one badass looking Glock at the center of his forehead. That lethal combination, I dare say, would make most men do almost anything. "The first cut is always the hardest," I reminded him, as though I had done it myself, while touching the tip of my Glock to the back of his head and then uttering one word "click." I upped the ante by reminding him that I'd either kick the chair out from under him or blow his brains out if he didn't cut it off himself. But before he did, he answered in great detail how he was raised, who his handler was and, unsolicited, also provided a remarkable recollection about the two years he spent at The Founders Home in Rochester, New York before being adopted at the age of six. This place, I was not aware of, but recorded his detailed description of life in that institution on my cellphone. The Holy Grail, I thought and wondered why Julian had never mentioned it. Unlike the others, Barry was not preadopted when he arrived off the coast of Montauk. Like Chris, he was a late stow-away.

Again, "Click." He grudgingly obliged. The perfect combination of negative and positive reinforcement nicely wrapped up in rope and stainless steel. He cried with every back-and-forth swipe of the knife and in such deafening levels that, had I not cranked up the volume of our national anthem, the entire enclave of South Hampton would have heard it. Barry's penis remained dilated, bled profusely all over the floor and continued to do so for almost five minutes. What a mess!

It's true what they say. God gave man a brain and a penis, but only enough blood to run one at a time.

The Wisdom of Aristotle

* * * *

Aristotle once said that "youth is easily deceived because it is quick to hope." He was right. Barry was young, easily deceived and quick to hope that I'd let him go. I learned much from him, much more than from the others. Young, naïve and hopeful, it's an executioner's dream. Man is the cruelest creature on this planet and, if there is a God, he must be hiding, ashamed of his creation and the cruelty they inflicted on each other in his name. I felt no shame and the thought of cruelty never entered my mind. The cruelest thing I could have done to a genius would be to render him a vegetable, incapable of speaking or thinking and then letting him live, but he was no genius. For a sexual pervert, pedophile and traitor, like Barry, it would be to ask that he sever his own penis, rendering him incapable of doing what he most enjoyed and then letting him live. I did the former but drew the line at the latter. Thus my earning a free-pass from the cruelty-to-humans brigade. While death by hanging might seem the ultimate act of cruelty, he was far more manly while dangling from the rope than he was while using that serrated blade that was only meant to cut pork or chicken, not human flesh. Perhaps death was his final release from a lifetime of pain and the humiliation he received as a child and that I had forced him to inflict upon himself.

Ready, Set, Kick

* * * *

I had expected one final encore of pleading from him, but he simply said "no," repeatedly" shaking his head left and right with each "no." A calming sense overcame him as he quietly surrendered to the fate that awaited him. His time was up and he damn sure wasn't moving to Gracie mansion. Heaven wasn't on his trip manifest either, so I wondered what the conversion in hell would be like as, one by one, the Herons were sent there for all eternity. Barry was still oblivious as to who this masked man was, so I removed the silicone and my hat, then greeted him properly. The bastard didn't even remember me!

"Josh Hunter. Il Portico. I did your dinner party on Capital Hill and your Labor Day barbecue right here," I said, raising my tone as if to say, "come on, don't you remember me?" I'm uncertain which one clicked with him but, Barbecue might have been the trigger, my name meant nothing. And with that he did that arching shoulder thing, but this time it was forward with no audible sigh of approaching doom coming from his mouth. He knew who I was and that it sealed his fate.

No matter how dire the circumstances, man will always find it within themselves a small sliver of hope that something will change, and that the inevitability they face will, as well. Like shifting winds that bring forth the bright sunshine in the wake of an approaching storm, Barry's was not to be. There were no winds, only calm. He with the inevitability of his death and me with another notch on Julian's list. Mission accomplished. That faint queasiness revisited me and I recall gagging, expecting to vomit over the rapid flow of blood that spurted onto the ground like water from a garden hose. Hold it in, DNA, DNA, I reminded myself, then shoved a wad of gum into my mouth to ease the nausea. With that, I cued the music one more time and then pulled his left foot back allowing him to kick the chair over, as it would have happened had he actually committed suicide. I moved towards his front and watched as his face filled with the rush of blood from a slow strangulation. Low rafters, a short rope, long, painful death. I wanted him to thoroughly absorb the satisfaction I was getting from watching him swing from his own rafters and to hear the entire rendition of our national anthem twice. He choked, gurgled several times and then, there was silence. I removed the cloth from his hands and watched as he continued to sway in the breeze, kicking his feet like a child just learning to ride a bicycle while grasping the exposed area where his penis was once attached. It was quick, and remarkably similar to the way they always depicted it in the movies. His face changed from red, to blue and finally to ashen gray and then pale white. Most unsettling, but patriotic when you think about it.

As the final act of what I had hoped would be another perfect crime, I grabbed his cold, rigid index finger and tapped the send button on his Blackberry announcing to his thousands of followers that he was summarily dropping out of the race. The tweet read:

> *"Severing my ties to my addiction and am officially hanging up my career in politics forever!"*

What an awesome way to cleverly disguise the execution of one of life's little pricks, all in less than 160 characters. I had a long walk back to my car and a 5-hour drive back to Sector 7. Here's what I learned from Barry?

That mission began with my knowing only of Barry Levinson's political background, his public shaming, document passing and the ship number he arrived on forty years prior. It finished knowing the dark secrets of his past, and of his mentors. The inhumanity dished out to young children at a place called the Founder's Home in upstate NY affected me, and could have played some role in his developing the persona he had. A constant need to expose himself, to impress others and to assume a dominant role was learned behavior. Barry was abused and neglected for three years at that home, but learned that there are many ways to draw attention to yourself, some good, some bad. Kids grow up, they learn the difference between good and evil, patriots and traitors. Barry learned none of that and so I refused to be swayed by the victimization story he told me. He knew all too well what he was doing and, in fact, proudly admitted that.

They packed Shipment #64 with fifty more infants than normal, the most ever noted on a manifesto. They took those extra children to the Founder's Home which was already overcrowded with children not yet adopted from the previous shipment. Barry slept in a room with twelve other kids and unknown to him, was last to get fed and only then when there were leftovers to give him. The training began almost at infancy and, like dogs, they trained them to trade toys for food.

Aristotle once said, "Tolerance is the last virtue of a dying society." Although I believe I have justified these extreme measures as necessary for God and my former country, I continue to harbor serious doubts about what others might think of my method for altering the left/right paradigm that leans farther left with each passing day. There are millions of Patriots who share my views but, for now, I accept my duty to remain an anonymous hero. I have seen too much dying on our side and not enough on theirs. Consider this my personal fairness doctrine, my belief that, yes, everyone should pay their fair share in life. I am no longer a tolerant Patriot. Confirmation from the enemy that our war was justified was sweeter than anything I could have imagined experiencing that night. Those moments of doubt, questioning my sanity and lack of moral compass were all vindicated in a matter of minutes and disappeared the moment Barry took his last breath. He sighed and so did I. But Barry left me with as many questions as I had answers. Who was Julian

Kilgore? Why did the words of my father still haunt me and what happened at the Founder's Home?

The Orphanage

* * * *

Curiosity got the cat. It's an old saying that bit me in the ass a few times as a kid, and on three occasions as an adult. The first while trying to prove a conspiracy surrounding detention facilities for innocent Americans and killing fields for those who resisted our tyrannical leaders, resulting in my parent's detention at Vega 7 and my having to change my identity. The second as I stood over the Reverend's lifeless body longer than I should have which, thank the God I didn't believe in, amounted to nothing, and the third when I thought it a brilliant idea to road-trip to upstate New York to visit the Monroe County Founders Home. I couldn't get Levinson's final words out of my mind, even though he was gagging for air as he sputtered them out while bleeding to death all over his barn. Visiting the Founders Home was another story and one that brought more questions than gave me answers.

It was early October, but in Rochester it felt more like December. The leaves were absent from the trees and the piles under the huge maples were waist deep, something kids loved to frolic in. There was an old man with long, scraggly silver hair, dressed in dark green overalls at the back of the property feverishly raking them up, but the stiff lake-effect breeze from the west was quicker at scattering them back to where nature had first dropped them. It was an exercise in futility.

As I entered the rusted iron gates that once centered a majestic stone columned entrance, I thought to myself, "So this is where it all began." That déjà vu feeling washed over me, but I wasn't sure why. Isn't that the way it always is? Dark clouds and a strong lake effect breeze elevated the creepiness of what I was staring at. That feeling of uneasiness that this was not a good place could not have been more strong.

The stone wall which must have originally stood twenty feet high was now piles of crushed rocks scattered around its original concrete base. It told a story of lives ruined — youthful evil. There was an analogy in those rocks - crushed, scattered, just as the infants who once occupied that orphanage. Time had performed irreversible damage on what was once a majestic old mansion. Some might say it belonged in a story book, but I'd counter it was more fitting of a horror flick. It was just plain scary, yet strangely familiar.

The groundskeeper didn't seem to mind my entering the abandoned property and kept raking as I walked towards the front door which was slightly ajar. They had broken the brass hinge which once held its heavy metal construction at the top. That door was a deep red color, and the stones were whitish grey, the kind you'd see on an Episcopal church or at a monastery. This wasn't a place of God — it was a bastion for the devil. Yes, it was an orphanage, but a secret one. Why would an orphanage be secret?

Reflections

* * * *

Describing the musty smell that wafted over me as I entered the foyer isn't necessary as a similar smell was most likely present when you entered my place. It happens when the residents leave in a hurry, as did I. But this smell was familiar, I had experienced it before.

Smells detonate memories in our minds while transporting us across a weed infested landscape that covers our entire life. The first day of school, which was always raining, little league and the smell of fresh cut grass, the hot pavement of the school yard while getting the crap beat out of you by a gang of thugs. There's always a trigger to those senses and standing in that house triggered one I hadn't experienced before. Things happened here and children were at the center of those events.

It's late and the guards are coming. Juda's gate will soon open and my food delivered through a door within a door. God how I miss real food, the fruits and vegetables that once filled my garden of antithetical Eden.

Vega 7. It exists.

More tomorrow.

50573048R00217

Made in the USA
Columbia, SC
08 February 2019